My first novel, *A Cuckoo in Candle Lane*, was published twenty years ago! I can't tell you how proud I felt. Since then, I've penned a further sixteen books. But several years ago, my health prevented me from writing. Thankfully, my daughter picked up the baton, and stepped in to write the Kitty Neale books. This was another proud moment for me!

Sam has since written the last nine stories. Her style is so like mine that I don't think many readers noticed there was a change in author.

Unfortunately, my health has deteriorated and I'm not sure that I will be here when this book is published. But it brings me great joy to know that my wonderful readers will continue to support my daughter's work and that the Kitty Neale name will live on!

Thank you so much to all who have picked up one of my books and taken the time to read it. I hope you've enjoyed my stories as much as I did when writing them.

Love and rainbows,

Kitty xxx

An Orphan's
Hope

Kitty
Neale

ORION

First published in Great Britain in 2024 by Orion Books,
an imprint of The Orion Publishing Group Ltd
Carmelite House, 50 Victoria Embankment
London EC4Y 0DZ

An Hachette UK Company

1 3 5 7 9 10 8 6 4 2

A CIP catalogue record for this book is
available from the British Library.

ISBN (Mass Market Paperback) 978 1 3987 1369 7
ISBN (eBook) 978 1 3987 1370 3

Typeset at The Spartan Press Ltd,
Lymington, Hants

Printed and bound in Great Britain by Clays Ltd,
Elcograf S.p.A.

www.orionbooks.co.uk

For my Mum, Brenda Warren
The bravest, strongest, kindest and most generous
woman I've known.
Your love made me who I am. You're my inspiration
and my hero.
The best mum and my best friend.
Love always xxx

I

Cautiously edging slowly forward and using a wall to feel her way through the thick smog, thirteen-year-old Grace Lockwood baulked when a stranger loomed out of the murk in front of her.

'Beg your pardon, miss,' the stranger muttered, stepping around her.

Grace hadn't seen the man coming towards her which was hardly surprising considering she couldn't see as far as her hand in front of her face!

Her eyes stung. The foul-smelling smog burned the back of her throat. Grace wanted to turn and run back home but it was imperative that she got to the post office. So, with one hand on the wall, and another holding a handkerchief over her mouth, Grace pushed forward. Her stomach growled with hunger. It was the only sound she could hear. The smog had muffled the noises of everything around her. Battersea had never been so silent. She didn't even hear the bus approaching and could barely see its dimmed headlights. The heavy smog blanketing London had blocked out the light from the weak, morning, winter sun. And Grace noticed that the fog, mixed with the smoke of a thousand chimneys, had a peculiar yellow tinge.

Eventually she reached her destination, grateful to be out of the suffocating atmosphere. Yet even inside the post office, the smog hung in the air. Approaching the counter, Grace saw that the postmaster had a scarf wrapped across his face, covering his mouth and nose.

'You caught me just in time,' he said. 'I was about to close. Early, I know, but I can't imagine that many folks will venture out in this today. Now, what can I do for you, young lady?'

Grace pulled out her grandmother's old-age pension book from her coat pocket and slipped it towards the postmaster. 'I need to collect my gran's pension,' she answered, her chin jutting forward.

The postmaster looked inside the book, shaking his head. 'You can't. Your grandmother will have to collect it herself or nominate an adult to collect it on her behalf.'

Dismayed, Grace insisted: 'But I have to get it! My gran can't come out in this peasouper, and she really needs her pension money!'

'Sorry, dear, thems the rules.'

'Please, mister. Can't you just cash her pension this once? I won't never ask again. *Please.*'

The postmaster shrugged. 'I can't. I mean, how do I know that you haven't stolen this pension book, eh?'

'I ain't a thief!' Grace blurted, indignantly.

'I'm not suggesting that you are, but the rules are in place for a reason. You see my point?'

'Please, can't you break them?' she implored.

The postmaster shook his head again and Grace knew that he wouldn't change his mind.

Deflated, she headed back towards home, a small two-up, two-down terraced house that she shared with Bertha, her grandmother. Grace had lived with the elderly woman for as far back as she could remember. Her mother had died giving birth to Grace, and her father had passed away a year later. She didn't know the cause of her father's death. The man had been Bertha's only child and the woman refused to talk about how he'd died. But, since Grace had been orphaned, Bertha had taken care of her, providing her with a comfortable home and nurturing her with love and affection. Now that the woman was poorly, it was Grace's turn to take care of her beloved grandmother.

'I'm back, Gran,' Grace called, quickly closing the front door behind her, hoping to keep the smog out. Traipsing up the creaky stairs to her gran's bedroom, she wasn't looking forward to explaining how the postmaster had refused to cash the pension.

As she walked into her gran's room, Grace's heart plummeted at the sight that met her. Bertha was on her side, hanging out of the bed, coughing as she gasped for breath.

'Oh, Gran, what are you doing?' Grace asked, dashing to the bed.

'Fags,' Bertha croaked weakly, lifting her thin arm to point towards the bedside cupboard and the packet of five cigarettes on it.

Helping her gran back into bed, Grace admonished, 'You can hardly breathe, Gran. I don't think you should be smoking.'

Bertha rested her head on her pillow and closed her eyes. Her thin, white hair lay in wisps around her wrinkled, pale face. 'No point giving up the fags now,' she wheezed, struggling to pull air into her damaged lungs. 'Did you get me money?'

Grace sighed as she slumped into a chair beside her gran's bed. 'He wouldn't give it to me,' she replied. 'But don't worry, Gran, I'll think of something.'

'Need coal,' Bertha said, and coughed again. 'Food and rent an' all.'

'I know, Gran, but I said *don't worry*. You just concentrate on getting better.'

Bertha reached out her gnarled hand which Grace quickly took in hers.

'I ain't gonna get better, Gracie. But you've got to promise me something…'

Gently squeezing her grandmother's bony hand, Grace choked back a sob that had caught in her throat. 'Don't say that, Gran. Of course you're gonna get better. It's this smog that's making you ill. It'll pass, it always does. And then you'll be as right as rain.'

'You've got to face facts, dear. I'm dying, and I'm worried sick about you. Promise me, Gracie, promise that you won't call the doctor or an ambulance. It don't matter how bad I get, promise you won't tell a soul.'

Grace's brow creased and her eyebrows knitted together. Yanking her hand from her grandmother's, she tucked a strand of her raven-black hair behind her ear. 'Don't talk like that, please, Gran.'

'I must. I'm worried sick about what will happen to you, Gracie. If anyone finds out how poorly I am, they'll take you from me. I can't stand the notion of you going into one of those children's homes. So, promise me, Gracie. Promise me that no one will find out about me.'

Grace gulped. She didn't like the idea of a children's home either, but worse, she couldn't face the thought of losing her dear grandmother.

'Promise me,' Bertha urged, her voice frail.

Grace nodded to appease her grandmother. 'I promise. But you ain't gonna die, Gran. You'll be all right. You'll see.'

2

Winnie Berry stood behind the bar of the Battersea Tavern. With her hands on her wide hips, she glanced around her pub, tutting.

'Tell me you're not thinking of opening up today, are you? This London particular is about the worse I've ever seen,' Carmen stated.

Winnie rolled her eyes. 'It doesn't seem worth it. Who in their right mind would come out for a drink in this smog? Look at it, Carmen, it's seeping in everywhere. Give me a hand to wet some towels. We'll put them under the door and around the windows to try and keep it out.'

'It's making a right bleedin' mess,' Carmen moaned, wiping her finger across the bar and holding it aloft to show Winnie. 'Everything is covered in a layer of greasy, black stuff. I've seen some peasoupers in my time, but never anything as bad as this!'

'Let's hope it passes soon,' Winnie sighed.

They heard a hammering on the door and exchanged a quizzical look.

'Who the flippin' 'eck could that be?' Winnie thought

aloud as she came from behind the bar and pulled back the locks on the pub door.

Piano Pete stood there, his flat cap pulled low, and his hands shoved into his trouser pockets. 'It's bloomin' freezin' out here,' he grumbled, a roll-up cigarette stuck on his bottom lip, as usual.

Winnie ushered him in. 'Come on, get inside, hurry up. Don't just stand there. You're letting all the smog in with you.'

Quickly closing the door behind him, Winnie waved her hand in front of her face in a miserable attempt to disperse the vile stench of the smog.

'Cor, Win, you oughta see it out there!' Pete exclaimed.

'No thanks, it's bad enough in here.'

'I've never seen nothing like it. And do you know what? Even the smoke out of the Battersea Power Station is blowing downwards. Fancy that, eh? It's blowing right down on all of us. No wonder the hospitals are full of dead people.'

'What are you on about?' Carmen demanded.

Pete looked past Winnie to Carmen, explaining, 'The hospitals. They're packed. They ain't got no spare beds and the mortuary is overflowing. There's dead bodies lined up in the corridors.'

A cold shiver crept down Winnie's spine. 'Are you sure? How do you know?'

'Me sister told me,' Pete answered, adamantly. 'She's a cleaner in the hospital.'

Winnie turned to Carmen. 'This don't sound good,' she said, gravely.

'There's even kids dying, Win,' Pete added with a note of sadness.

Winnie looked towards the ceiling. Her grandchildren were

upstairs. Twelve-year-old Martha and Benny, the same age, lived above the Battersea Tavern alongside Rachel, Carmen, Maureen and herself. The thought of anything dreadful happening to her grandchildren left Winnie's heart plummeting. 'We ain't opening today, Pete. Every time that door opens, more of that muck from outside blows in here. Carmen will get you a drink, but then you'll have to leave.'

'No, it's fine, thanks, Win. I didn't come in for a drink. I just popped by to make sure you're all all right?'

'Aw, thanks, Pete, that's kind of you. And yes, love, we're all fine.'

'Good, I'll get off then and hope that I can find me way home. It's worse than the blackouts during the Blitz, this is. I bumped into three people on the way here and nearly knocked an old dear to the ground.'

'Would you like a flashlight, Pete?'

'Nah, it's all right, thanks, Win. I ain't got far to go.'

Once Pete had left and the door secured behind him, Winnie and Carmen set to work with wet towels. They were a good team and Winnie often questioned how she'd manage the pub without Carmen, especially as she was getting on in her years and her bones were beginning to ache. Mind you, Carmen was no spring chicken either, both of them approaching sixty. Nonetheless, they worked well together, and Winnie had never had any regrets about bringing Carmen to live with her and work in her pub.

'That was nice of Pete,' Carmen smiled.

'Yeah, he's a good egg. What he said about the hospitals is worrying, though.'

'Push it out of your mind, Winnie. You're all right, I'm all right, Maureen's all right and Rachel and the kids are fine

8

too. None of us are strangers to smog and, just like all the others, this will blow over soon enough.'

'I suppose so. But like it or not, I'm gonna have to go out.'

'What on earth for?' Carmen questioned.

'My kitchen cupboards are like Old Mother Hubbard's. I've got to get some groceries in.'

'Oh, Winnie, I'm sure we can manage until Monday.'

'I doubt it, love. Benny is eating us out of house and home. There's nothing to feed the boy.'

Carmen smiled. 'That grandson of yours is a growing lad.'

'It's funny, that. He's not *really* my grandson, not by blood, though I'd never treat him any differently. From what Rachel tells me, Benny's mother was as skinny as a rake and his father was on the thin side too. I don't know where the boy gets his sizable frame from. And bless him, he's growing outwards instead of upwards,' Winnie giggled. Then patting her rotund belly, she added, 'I'm a fine one to talk! You're lucky you've still got a trim figure.'

'I'm the same size I was before I had my kids, many, many moons ago now. Not that it makes any difference. Slim or fat, I'm not interested in the fellas.'

'Well, love, at our age, I reckon we're past it. Contented widows, that's us. We've got each other for company, and we can look after each other in our dotage.'

Winnie always managed to put on a happy face, but in truth, she often caught herself longing for affection. Just a cuddle. A light kiss on the cheek. Someone to give her a compliment and to snuggle up to in bed and keep her warm on the cold, winter nights. During the war Tommy had offered her a new life with him in a quiet, country cottage, but Winnie had decided to stay put in the Battersea Tavern.

She sometimes daydreamed, imagining how her life would have been if she'd accepted Tommy's hand in marriage. She didn't regret turning down the ex-copper, but she doubted that she'd ever receive another marriage proposal. This was her lot, Carmen, Rachel, Maureen, the grandchildren and Hilda. Though only blood-related to her granddaughter Martha, Winnie thought of them all as family, and her *family* were enough for Winnie – most of the time.

'What are you thinking about?' Carmen asked, snapping Winnie from her thoughts.

'Eh? Oh, nothing much. Just thinking about what I need from the grocers. Not that there's ever much choice. I can't bloody wait for rationing to end. How long's it been since we won the war?'

'Too long,' Carmen replied. 'I thought Britain would have been back to normal by now. But it's been years and years of ration books and shortages. I'm sick to my back teeth of it.'

'Me an' all, love. Me an' all.'

'Are you sure you need to go out today?' Carmen checked.

'Afraid so.'

'I'll go, Winnie.'

'No, love, thanks. I'll be fine. I've got lungs like bellows. It'll take more than a bit of smog to knock me off my horse.'

Later that day, Winnie looped her empty shopping basket over her arm.

'Here,' Carmen called, hurrying to the back door, 'if you will insist on going out, then put this over your face,' she suggested, handing a silk scarf to Winnie.

'Thanks, love, but it'll get ruined.'

'I don't care. It'll help stop you breathing in that filth.'

Outside, Winnie was shocked at just how bad the smog was and her heart thudded in fear as she walked the familiar route to the grocery shop. But with such poor visibility, feeling disorientated, she couldn't be sure that she was going in the right direction. The kerbs were almost impossible to see. Winnie had tripped twice, both times stumbling but managing to save herself from falling flat on her face.

The short journey to the grocery shop took her twice as long as it normally would. By the time she arrived, her eyes were sore and streaming with tears.

'Good morning, Mrs Berry,' the grocer chirped.

'I think you'll find it's afternoon now. I'm surprised to find you open although I'm glad you are, I thought I might have been wasting my time.'

'You know me, Mrs Berry, I've never lost a day's trading, not even during the war. I don't often see you in here on a Saturday. Is the pub closed?'

'Yes, I've not opened today and I shan't tomorrow if it doesn't clear up.'

'I'm sure it'll blow away soon. What can I get you?'

Winnie fished in her pocket and pulled out a shopping list which she handed to the grocer. As he collected her goods from the shelves behind the counter, Winnie heard the bell above the door ring as it opened. She turned to see a young girl enter along with a mist of smog. The girl had her mouth covered with a grubby handkerchief and she looked around with big, dark eyes.

The grocer hummed a Perry Como tune which Winnie thought was quite modern for him ... As he busied himself preparing her shopping, she glanced over her shoulder again at the girl. To her disbelief, she saw the girl take two tins of

Spam from a wicker basket near the window and shove them in her coat pockets before scarpering out the door. Snapping her head back round to look at the grocer in disbelief, it was clear that he hadn't seen the theft.

'I'll be back in two ticks,' Winnie called as she dashed to the door and then out onto the street.

Looking left and right, it was impossible to see which way the girl had run. Instinctively, Winnie headed left, walking as fast as she could, hoping to catch the little thief. Then, through the murkiness, she saw a small figure and Winnie knew it was her, the girl she'd witnessed stealing from the shop! Picking up her pace, she caught up with the youngster and grabbed the girl's arm, yanking her around.

The girl stared back at Winnie with her big, dark eyes.

'I saw what you did,' Winnie accused, firmly.

The girl tried to wriggle her arm free, but Winnie had a tight grip.

'Get off me!' the girl protested.

'I've a good mind to march you down to the police station!' Winnie retorted.

The girl snarled. 'You can't prove nothing,' she spat.

'What's this then?' Winnie said, and reached for the girl's coat pocket.

The girl snatched her arm free and spun on her heel before running off into the dense smog.

Winnie stared after her, but she was soon out of sight. Turning back towards the shop, she hoped that being caught stealing had been lesson enough to stop the girl from doing it again. Though somehow she doubted it would be. But something about the girl's dark eyes had struck Winnie. She'd seen fear in them and sadness, too. It occurred to Winnie;

the girl hadn't been much older than Martha. Had she been stealing food out of desperation, and she'd had no choice? It was a sobering and heart-wrenching thought.

Grace ran as fast as her legs would carry her. She couldn't see clearly where she was heading and hoped she didn't bump into something or someone. Her heart felt as though it would pound out of her chest – the old bag who'd seen her pinch the Spam had threatened to take her to the police station!

Rounding a corner, Grace stopped and bent over, resting her hands on her legs just above her knees as she tried to catch her breath. Looking behind, she felt confident that the woman hadn't followed her. Thank Gawd, she'd gotten away with two tins of Spam – dinner for tonight for her and her gran and breakfast in the morning too. They would have full bellies, but they'd be freezing cold unless she could get some coal. And the rent that was due … Grace pushed her woes from her mind – she wouldn't think about the rent money now.

Back at home, she dashed up the stairs to her gran's room and quietly tiptoed across the floorboards before peering down at the woman. Even in sleep, Bertha's breathing was laboured, and Grace noticed her lips looked a blueish colour. *Oh, Gran,* she thought, wishing that Bertha would allow her to call for a doctor. Gently stroking her gran's wispy hair off her forehead, Grace could feel the woman's clammy skin and knew that she had a fever. 'Please don't die,' she whispered, tears welling in her eyes. 'Please don't leave me, Gran.'

Pulling herself away, Grace padded softly down the stairs and placed the tins of Spam in the almost bare larder. She took the last two rooted potatoes, but then she put one back on the shelf to save for tomorrow. Standing over the kitchen sink that only had a cold tap, she peeled the skin from the spud. And though she was ravenously hungry, Grace decided that her gran should have the chips with the Spam. Grace would go without chips, and she hoped that a good meal would give her precious gran the strength to get well again.

3

Rachel stamped into the kitchen and pulled out a chair at the table, flicking her blonde hair over her shoulder.

'What's given you the 'ump?' Maureen asked.

'This flippin' weather,' Rachel replied, more huffily than she'd liked to have sounded. 'I'm losing business. I can't open my stall in this smog.'

'Don't worry, love,' Winnie soothed. 'It'll be gone soon and you're not exactly short of a bob or two, are you?'

'No, I'm doing all right, but that's not the point. What's causing it? Why is it so bad?'

'Gawd knows,' Carmen answered. 'But Piano Pete said that the hospitals are full, and people are dying. So, I shouldn't worry about losing a day or two trading. After all, there's worse things that could happen.'

Rachel swallowed hard. Carmen's words had made her feel selfish. Londoners were losing their lives and she'd been moaning because she couldn't set up her shellfish stall outside the pub.

Winnie poured a cup of tea and pushed it across the table

towards her. 'We're all safe indoors so long as we can keep the smog out. I hope you're not planning on seeing Roy tonight?'

Rachel shrugged. 'I was supposed to, though I probably won't now.'

'Good. I had to go out earlier to get some shopping, but I don't want any doors or windows being opened unless it's absolutely necessary.'

Maureen looked sheepish. 'Sorry, Winnie, I was going to do the shopping yesterday, but I got caught up in an order for a christening gown that I'm making for Mrs Firth.'

'Don't worry, love, we've all been busy, and it's done now. I must say, I had quite an adventure on my travels. It was rather challenging navigating my way to the shop and then I caught a little imp stealing a couple tins of Spam.'

'What did you do?' Maureen asked.

'I chased after her, but she got away. Then I thought to meself, how desperate must she be to be stealing Spam, eh? *Spam* … yuk! The poor love was only about Martha's age. I can't imagine Martha having to steal to eat. If I'm honest, well, the thought of it broke my heart.'

'I've been there,' Carmen said, 'when Harry died. Not a pot to piss in. My useless husband left me penniless. We do what we must do, sometimes.'

'Indeed,' Winnie sighed. 'I wish I'd given her a shilling or two instead of threatening her with the coppers.'

'You're too soft, Win,' Rachel smiled. 'But that's why we love you.'

Maureen reached across the table for Rachel's hand. 'Let's have another look at your engagement ring,' she asked, her eyes twinkling.

Rachel proudly showed off the gold band with a small but

sparkling diamond. Maureen was still married to Brancher Fanning who was locked up behind bars and had been for years. The man had ruled over Maureen and made her life such a misery. Life for Maureen had been so awful that she'd thought it would be a better option to throw herself off a bridge into the River Thames. Thankfully, she'd been stopped, and then Winnie had shown her usual compassion and had taken Maureen in. Years later, the old Maureen had gone, replaced by a confident, bubbly woman. And though Maureen said she didn't want romance in her life, Rachel suspected that she craved the love of a good fella.

'I still can't believe you're getting married,' Maureen lamented. 'And it's a smashing ring,' she cooed.

'And Roy is a smashing fella too,' Winnie added.

'He is,' Rachel beamed, bursting with pride. 'Rachel Russel ... what do you think? Mrs Rachel Russel. I quite like the name.'

'You could have been Mrs Rachel Garwood if you'd married my brother,' Maureen smiled, cheekily. 'But Rachel Russel has a nice ring to it.'

'Yeah, well, it never really got going with me and Stephen and then Roy came along and swept me off my feet.'

'I would have loved for you to have been my sister-in-law, but it wasn't meant to be. Anyway, Stephen seems happy enough. And you couldn't ask for a nicer bloke than Roy. You landed on your feet with him.'

'How are your wedding plans coming on?' Carmen asked.

'I thought I'd get Christmas out of the way and then book the registry office. I don't want a big do, just us lot and my mum.'

'And Roy's family,' Winnie interjected.

'Unfortunately, yes, Roy's family too. To be honest, I wish we didn't have to invite his brother and his dad. I can't stand the way they talk to Roy.'

Winnie nodded. 'I know what you mean, love. They ain't got any manners and only half a brain between them, but they're the only family Roy has. We're lucky. We ain't real kin but we're a real family. And soon Roy will be a part of our family too. Mind you, I shall miss you and the kids when you move out.'

'You're not moving out, Rachel, are you?' Maureen asked, looking upset.

'Of course she is,' Winnie replied. 'She'll be a married woman and will want to set up her own home, ain't that right, love?'

'Yes, but I won't be moving far from here. And I'll still be outside every day, on my stall, selling my cockles and winkles.'

Maureen looked surprised. 'Is Roy going to allow you to carry on working once you're married?' she asked.

'It's not up to Roy, it's my decision.'

'Good for you,' Carmen encouraged. 'All the women around this table have had husbands who've treated them badly. Take my advice, Rachel, you make sure you stand up for yourself from the start. Don't let Roy get his ring on your finger and take control of you.'

'I doubt there'll be much chance of Roy controlling Rachel,' Winnie guffawed. 'She never does as she's told, and never will. Rachel is her own boss.'

'Did you hear that?' Carmen asked, shaking her thumb towards the passageway. 'Someone is knocking on the back door.'

Winnie blew out a long breath. 'For Christ's sake,' she

moaned, 'I wanted to keep the doors closed. Go down and check, Rachel – it might be your mum.'

'I doubt it,' Carmen said, 'Hilda wouldn't be daft enough to come out in this smog.'

Rachel scraped back her seat and hurried down the stairs. When she opened the back door, she was delighted to see Roy standing there.

'Quick, get in. Winnie ain't pleased about the door being opened.'

Roy stepped inside and unravelled the knitted football Chelsea supporter's scarf from around his head. 'Sorry, I couldn't stay away. I had to make sure that you and the kids are all right.'

'Oh, you silly sausage. You didn't have to worry about us. You know we're fine here.'

Pulling Rachel into his arms, he gazed down into her eyes. 'I know you're all fine here, but the truth was, I couldn't stay away from you, and I just wanted to see you,' he said huskily.

Rachel looked lovingly back at him, staring into his brown eyes, but then she frowned when she noticed a red mark above his eyebrow. 'What happened there?' she asked, concerned, gently touching the bruise.

'Nothing.'

Rachel felt his body tense and his expression hardened. She assumed either his older and much larger brother, Alan, or his bullying father, Douglas, had given Roy a thump. Her heart broke for the love of her life. Roy was a gentle man, not a thug like his brother and father. He tried to act tough and be like them, but Rachel knew that Roy wasn't a fighter. She didn't push the matter of the mark above his eyebrow any further. Experience had shown her that Roy would clam up rather than talk about it.

Cleverly changing the subject, she smiled. 'I've been looking for houses to rent and with your wage as a clerk and my earnings from the stall, we'll be able to afford a nice place when we're married.'

'I can't wait,' Roy enthused, and kissed her forehead.

An excited voice from the top of the stairs called down. 'Is that Roy?'

Rachel chuckled. 'Your biggest fan has rumbled that you're here.'

'Yes, it's me,' Roy called back up the stairs. 'I'm coming, Martha.'

Following Roy up, Rachel whispered under her breath, 'Martha gets more attention from you than I do.'

Roy looked over his shoulder. 'Are you jealous?' he grinned.

'No. I'm happy that my kids love you as much as I do, and you love them back.'

'Roy!' Martha squealed, 'Me and Benny are playing cards. Do you want to play too?'

Without waiting for an answer, Martha took Roy's hand and led him into their bedroom.

'I'll bring you a cuppa,' Rachel called.

In the kitchen, Winnie, her lips pursed, asked, 'I take it that was Roy at the door?'

'Yes, sorry, Win. The door was only open for a second.'

Now smiling, Winnie mused, 'And I suppose Martha has collared him already?'

'Yep. They're playing cards.'

'The man's a fool to come out to see you in this weather, but love makes fools of all of us. How is he?'

Rachel lowered her voice. 'I reckon Alan or Doug has given him a thump again.'

Winnie sucked in a long breath. 'The sooner you two are married, the better. He needs to get out of that house and away from them bastards. 'Scuse my language, but the thought of Alan and Doug picking on Roy makes my blood boil.'

'I know, Winnie, me too. His mother and his twin sister would be turning in their graves.'

'Huh, I doubt it,' Winnie scoffed. 'Well, his sister, maybe, but not his mother. From what I remember of her, she was a lovely woman, really kind but she was a little mouse. Mrs Russel would never have stood up to her husband. I reckon your Roy takes after her.'

'Well, I'm glad he doesn't take after his father like Alan does. Hopefully, once we're married, Roy won't have to see much of them.'

'I hope so, love, for both your sakes.'

4

Grace placed a steaming plate of Spam and chips on Bertha's bedside table. Gently shaking her, she coaxed, 'Wake up, Gran. I've cooked you a nice meal. Come on, Gran, wake up!'

Bertha groaned but didn't stir.

'Gran, come on, it's time to eat.'

Nothing.

Grace shook the woman a little harder. 'Please, Gran, wake up now and eat your dinner before it goes cold.'

Bertha's eyes remained closed.

Worry knotted in the pit of Grace's stomach, and so did hunger. 'All right, Gran, I'll leave you to rest for now, but you'll have to wake up later for some food.'

Picking up the plate, Grace trudged back down to the kitchen. Rather than waste the food, she sat at the small table and ate hungrily. As she rinsed her plate under the tap, a tear slipped from her eye. What if her gran never woke up? She couldn't face the thought of losing her and quickly pushed the upsetting thought from her mind. *Gran will be fine*, she tried to convince herself. The woman was thin but as strong as an ox. Though deep down, Grace feared that the

Grim Reaper was hovering just around the corner, ready and waiting for Bertha's soul.

Filling a glass of water, Grace took it upstairs to her gran. Thankfully, she found the woman awake, dozy but awake.

'I'll get you something to eat,' Grace smiled.

Bertha slowly shook her head. 'No food.'

'You must eat, Gran. When I've been ill, you've always told me I had to eat something to keep my strength up.'

'Can't face food,' Bertha said, faintly.

'All right, but drink this water, please.'

'Leave it there.'

'No, Gran, please, let me see you drink some.'

'Later,' Bertha wheezed, her eyes closing.

'Gran … Gran!'

Bertha appeared to be asleep again. Her breathing had become shallower, and every breath sounded like an effort. Grace was in two minds about calling for the doctor, but she remembered her promise to her gran. She'd sworn she wouldn't tell a soul how poorly Bertha was. But what if her gran died? Grace could feel her heart racing. What would she do? Who would she call? And would she be sent to live in an orphanage?

Tears welled in her eyes again. 'Oh, Gran,' she whispered, tenderly, 'I love you.'

5

The next day, when Roy woke, he opened his eyes to see a yellowy haze above his bed. Quietly throwing back his bed covers, he pulled back a chink in the curtains to look outside and was disappointed to see that the street was still shrouded in a fog of dirty, polluted air. It seemed to have worsened since yesterday and he couldn't see across the street to the terraced houses opposite.

Plonking himself down onto the edge of his bed, Roy looked over to his brother. Alan was still sound asleep, snoring. Roy knew that in the room next door, his dad would be sleeping too. And as his dad had swigged down a belly full of beer last night, Roy didn't expect his father would wake until midday.

Rising to his feet, he looked in a small mirror that was hanging on a nail beside the wardrobe. Studying his reflection, he didn't like the man who stared back at him. Granted, his features were nice enough. A square chin, strong cheekbones and deep, brown eyes framed by long, dark lashes. But Roy hated himself. And he knew that if anyone discovered his sordid secret, they would hate him too.

He drew in a long breath, feeling compelled to indulge his private pastime. It was a need, something he couldn't deny himself. But was it worth the risk to act on his impulses now? He didn't think so. After all, Alan or his dad could wake at any moment, and if they discovered him in the shed *getting up to no good,* they'd be disgusted with him. And he doubted they would keep his secret. Roy didn't want anyone to know what he did in the shed, least of all Rachel. She'd never understand. No one would. Only his twin sister had accepted him for who he was, but lovely Lillian had been killed during the war when a bomb had blown up the factory where she'd worked. He'd been in Europe, fighting back the Germans, and when news of Lillian's death had reached him, Roy had wanted to die too. Half of him was missing. The better half. Life had never been the same for him again.

Alan stirred. Roy glared at his brother; his heart full of resentment. *It should have been you who died, not Lillian,* he thought, coldly. Alan looked just like him. Both six-foot tall, broad, dark hair and brooding eyes. Everyone said they were two peas in a pod, both taking after their dad, but they were only alike in looks. Their characters couldn't have been further apart, though Roy had tried to be like his brother. He'd wanted to be confident and tough. He'd fought his way through school and acted like a strong man, but it had all been a lie. A façade to hide the *real* person. Roy cringed, ashamed of who he was. Repulsed with himself.

Please, God, don't let Rachel ever find out the truth, he thought, guiltily. If she did, Roy knew his future with her would be ruined.

★

25

Winnie pulled open her bedroom curtains with gusto, her heart sinking when she saw the smog was still lying heavily outside.

In the kitchen, Carmen was pouring a cup of tea. 'It's bad outside, much worse, in fact.'

'Yeah, I know. I don't suppose there's any point in opening the pub,' Winnie sighed.

'No, I don't suppose there is. It's eerie, Win. Everything is so quiet. I doubt we'll even hear the church bells ringing this gloomy morning.'

'The kids are gonna be bored stiff. Rachel normally takes them to the park on Sundays but it ain't safe for them to go out today. And if this bleedin' smog don't clear soon, I'll have to insist that they stay off school tomorrow an' all.'

'Roy might call in again. The kids think the world of him and he's ever so good with them.'

Winnie smiled. 'Martha has got him right where she wants him. She's a little madam, that one.'

Maureen came into the kitchen, looking bright eyed and cheerful, her mousy brown hair tucked behind her ears. 'Morning,' she beamed. 'Do you mind if I get a cuppa and take it to my room? I've nearly finished that christening gown.'

'Do whatever you want, love, but wouldn't you like some breakfast?'

'I'll have a bite to eat later.'

As Maureen carried a cup of tea out with her, Rachel passed her in the doorway and came in.

'I'm taking a cuppa back to bed. Martha and Benny are in with me. We're writing a Christmas play.'

'Cor blimey, it's like Clapham Junction railway station in my kitchen this morning,' Winnie chuckled to Carmen.

'Did you hear that?' Carmen asked.

'Hear what?'

'It sounded like the dustbin lid clanging.'

'Probably that stray cat. I warned you about leaving food out for it.'

'Maybe, but I'm going to check.'

'It's all right, I'll go. You finish your tea,' Winnie offered.

Traipsing down the stairs, she pulled a handkerchief out of her dressing-gown pocket and covered her mouth before opening the back door.

'Who's there?' she called into the dimness.

Winnie was met by silence, but she had a strange feeling that someone was watching her. 'I know you're there,' she said, stepping out further and pulling the door almost closed behind her.

Squinting her eyes through the smog, she saw the round, metal dustbin had been knocked over and the rubbish had fallen onto the ground around it.

'For Gawd's sake,' she moaned, as she tried to pick up the dustbin with one hand whilst keeping her mouth and nose covered. 'That bloomin' cat!'

As she bent over to collect the rubbish, something caught her eye – a small figure crouched behind an old, disused beer barrel. Winnie stood upright. 'I've seen you! I don't know what you think you're playing at, but out you come,' she demanded, firmly.

Slowly, a young girl emerged from behind the barrel. Winnie stepped closer and instantly recognised those wide, dark eyes.

'Oh, it's you! The little urchin from the grocery shop who pinched a couple of tins of Spam. What are you doing behind my barrel?'

The girl, looking defiant, placed her hands on her small hips. 'It ain't none of your business,' she snapped.

'You're outside *my* back door, hiding behind *my* barrel, and you've made a right bleedin' mess here! So, missy, yes, it *is* my business.'

'I ain't done no harm.'

'The contents of my dustbin are strewn all over the ground. That was your doing, weren't it?'

The girl nodded. 'I didn't mean to; it was an accident.'

'I should hope it was! So, are you going to explain to me what you're up to or do I need to call the police and you can explain it to them?'

The girl, looking terrified, went to sidestep Winnie, but Winnie skilfully blocked her path.

'Not so fast, young lady. You got away from me once before, but you won't again. Now, listen to me, I won't call the police. I simply want an explanation.'

The girl hung her head and her shoulders slumped.

'Let's start with your name, shall we?'

'Grace,' she mumbled, keeping her eyes lowered.

'Hello, Grace. I'm Mrs Berry. How old are you, Grace?'

'Thirteen.'

'I thought as much. So, would you like to tell me why you are here?'

Grace shook her head.

'It's early and flippin' cold out here. This smog won't be doing either of us any good and I expect you're hungry. I've got some thick bread upstairs waiting to be toasted and plenty

28

of butter. A cup of hot, sweet tea will wash it down nicely. Would you care to join me for breakfast?'

Grace's eyes shot up to look at Winnie, and they narrowed with suspicion as she questioned, 'You ain't gonna call the coppers on me, are you?'

'No, love, don't be daft. Come on, let's get some breakfast, eh?'

Grace shrugged but Winnie was pleased when she followed her inside and up the stairs to the kitchen.

'You're not a stray cat, so who have we got here then?' Carmen asked, looking surprised.

'This is Grace — she's joining us for breakfast.'

'Nice to meet you, Grace. Come and sit down, I don't bite.'

'She does,' Winnie laughed, 'but not on Sundays.'

As Winnie toasted the bread, she covertly watched Grace and thought the girl looked nervous. She could also tell that something was deeply troubling her, and she'd have to tread carefully in order to win Grace's trust.

'There you go, love, get stuck in. And don't be shy with the butter. I know it's still rationed but we've got plenty.'

As Grace buttered her toast, Winnie gestured to Carmen and silently mouthed, '*That's the girl I caught stealing yesterday.*'

'Do you live round here?' Carmen asked.

Grace nodded as she bit into her toast.

'With your mum and dad?' Winnie quizzed.

Grace shook her head, and when she'd finished chewing, replied, 'No, with my gran.'

'I see. And does your gran know that you're out this early in the morning?'

'I dunno. I reckon she probably does.'

'I get the feeling that all isn't well at home. I promise

you're not in any trouble, Grace. Do you want to tell me what's going on?'

Grace placed her toast back on the plate and jumped to her feet. 'I have to go,' she blurted.

'It's fine, Grace,' Winnie placated. 'Please, sit down and finish your breakfast. Like I said, you're not in any trouble. I just want to make sure you and your gran are all right.'

'We're managing,' Grace answered, surly.

'Good. I'm glad to hear it. Please, sit back down.'

Grace looked from Winnie to Carmen and then back at Winnie before sitting.

'But I would like to know what you were doing with my dustbin.'

'I–I didn't mean to knock it over, honest. I, er, I was trying to move the barrel,' Grace admitted.

'The barrel? Why?'

Grace audibly gulped. 'I, erm, I thought it was rubbish and that's why it was there next to the bin. I didn't think anyone wanted it.'

'Well, I don't particularly, but why do you want it?'

'To burn for the fire.'

Now Winnie felt she was getting somewhere. 'Are you low on coal at home?'

Grace nodded.

'And the Spam … were you hungry, love?'

Again, Grace nodded, and Winnie could see the girl was fighting from crying.

'It's all right, don't upset yourself. And thank you for being honest. Tell you what, how about this. You finish your break-fast and then you can take me home with you. I can have a word with your gran and lend her a few bob for some food and coal. What do you reckon, eh?'

Grace shook her head, fervently. 'No. No, you can't come home with me.'

'It's all right, love, I won't tell your gran about the Spam. Or the barrel.'

'No, you can't come home with me – my gran wouldn't like it.'

'Well, we can't have you going hungry and no coal at home to warm the house. I'm sure your gran won't mind me calling in,' Winnie gently urged.

'She would mind! You can't come home with me. Thanks for the toast, but I've got to go.'

'Wait!' Winnie protested, but Grace had dashed out of the kitchen door.

Carmen sprang to her feet. 'I'll follow her, Win. Something is very much amiss in that young girl's home.'

'Hurry,' Winnie urged. 'Don't lose her.'

Grace ran out onto the street, and was immediately struck by the thick, suffocating smog. She glanced behind her, pleased to see that Mrs Berry hadn't chased after her. The woman seemed kind, but she was a nosy busybody. And though Grace felt Mrs Berry meant well, she'd made her gran a promise, and she intended on keeping it. *Gawd,* she thought. Mrs Berry would have been shocked if she'd come home with her and seen the state of her gran's health. Mrs Berry's money would have been welcomed, but Grace couldn't allow anyone to see how poorly her gran was.

Picking up her pace and passing an old bomb site, Grace

was only a few hundred yards along the street when she almost stumbled over someone laying on the ground.

'Crikey, are you all right?' she asked, crouching down to the person. That's when Grace saw that it was an elderly chap who was struggling to breathe.

'Help …' the man croaked, feebly.

Grace looked around in panic. Even if there was anyone around, she'd never see them through the smog. She called out, 'Help! Someone help us, please!' But could tell her voice was muffled, and no one would hear her plea.

The man's head slumped to one side and Grace could no longer hear his rattling breaths. 'Hold on, Granddad, hold on! I'm gonna run and fetch help.'

Grace darted back to the Battersea Tavern and frantically knocked on the back door. She was relieved when Mrs Berry opened it.

'Come quick! There's an old boy on the street and I think he's dying!'

Mrs Berry turned and shouted up the stairs. 'Carmen? Carmen, run to the telephone box and call for an ambulance. There's a fella up the road who needs help.'

Then, turning back to Grace, she grabbed a coat from a peg behind the door and ordered, 'Take me to him.'

By the time they reached the elderly man, Grace was sure that they were too late. 'Is – is he dead?' she asked, anxiously.

'Yes, love, I'm afraid so.'

Grace stared down at the old man's face. She'd never seen a dead person before. His eyes were open and fixed, staring, blank, and his mouth was hanging wide. Thoughts of her gran rushed through her mind, and she could feel her body trembling 'What do we do now?' she asked, meekly.

'The ambulance will take him to the mortuary.'

Carmen, breathless, came to stand beside Mrs Berry. 'You found her again. I lost sight of her the second she was out the door.'

'He's dead,' Mrs Berry said quietly, flicking her head to the old man on the ground.

'It's gonna be a while before the ambulance arrives. It'll struggle to get through the smog. The poor bloke. What an awful way to go. All alone and on the street.'

'I reckon this awful smog finished him off, God rest his soul.'

Grace couldn't pull her eyes away from the man's face. She felt Mrs Berry's hand on her shoulder.

'You're shaking. You should go home, love. Carmen will wait for the ambulance.'

Grace nodded, still transfixed.

'I think you're in shock,' Mrs Berry said, gently. 'Show me where you live, and I'll walk you home.'

Without thinking, Grace nodded and began to lead Mrs Berry towards home. As they rounded a corner onto her street, she suddenly came to her senses. 'I'm all right now, thank you, Mrs Berry.'

'I'll be the judge of that. Is this the street you live on?'

Grace didn't answer.

Mrs Berry suddenly stood in front of her and grabbed her squarely by the shoulders.

'Listen, love. I know something isn't right. You're well turned out and dressed decently, so I don't understand why you need to steal food to eat and wood for the fire. I'd like to speak to your gran, and I won't take *no* for an answer.'

Grace hung her head to hide her tears. 'But I promised my gran...'

'What did you promise her?'

'I'm not allowed to say.'

'You can trust me, Grace. What did you promise your gran?'

'If – if I tell you, they'll take me away and I'll never see my gran again,' Grace sobbed.

'Who? Who will take you away?'

'The children's home... they'll cart my gran off to hospital and I'll have to live in an orphanage.'

'Is your gran poorly, love?'

Grace nodded as tears streamed down her cheeks. She'd betrayed her gran, but it was a relief to share her burden with someone.

'It's all right,' Mrs Berry soothed. 'We'll sort this all out. Now, which house do you live in?'

'What's your gran's name?' Winnie asked as she stepped over the threshold of the neat, terraced house.

'Bertha. And she ain't gonna be happy about seeing you here.'

'Don't worry, Grace, you leave your gran to me,' Winnie smiled, trying to ease the girl's worries.

Winnie would have taken her coat off and thrown it over the newel post, but the house felt as cold inside as it was outside. As she walked up the stairs, she could see her own breath misting in front of her face.

'She's in here,' Grace said, and pushed open a bedroom door. 'It's me, Gran. I've brought someone to see you.'

34

Winnie stepped into the room and stifled a gasp, horrified at what she saw. Poor Bertha was clearly close to death. The woman's lips were blue, and her raspy breathing was sporadic.

Grace rushed to her gran's side and held her hand. 'Wake up, Gran. Someone is here to see you.'

Winnie stood behind Grace and rested her hands on the girl's shoulders. 'I'm sorry, love, but I don't think your gran is going to wake up.'

Grace's head snapped round, tears spilling from her eyes. 'Please, Mrs Berry, don't let her die ... she's all I've got in the world. Please, do something. Make her wake up.'

'I can call the doctor or an ambulance, but to be honest, I think she'd be more comfortable here in her own bed.'

Seeing a chair, Winnie pulled it closer. 'Sit down, love. Keep hold of your gran's hand and tell her how much you love her. Tell her what a smashing gran she's been to you.'

'Are – are you telling me to say goodbye?'

'Yes, Grace, I'm sorry.'

Grace sprang to her feet and threw herself over her gran's frail body. She held the woman close and cried into her chest. 'I love you, Gran. I wish you didn't have to go,' she wept.

Winnie stood back in silence. She recognised the sound of those last few desperate gasps for air that would be Bertha's final breaths.

Gently easing Grace away, Winnie whispered, 'She's gone, love. Your gran is at peace now.'

Grace spun around and wrapped her arms around Winnie, wailing for the loss of her gran. Winnie tenderly stroked the girl's hair and fought back her own tears as she mutely cursed the smog for claiming yet another life. Bertha may have survived a few more years, but she'd been taken prematurely and Winnie didn't like to think about how many more lives had been lost. She guessed that anyone with lung problems would be the first to succumb to the stinking air.

As Grace's sobs subsided, she pulled away from Winnie. 'What do I do now? And what will happen to me?'

Winnie sighed heavily. She'd wanted to help a young girl with an empty belly, but now it appeared she'd lumbered herself. She couldn't bear to see Grace get carted off to an orphanage. No, that wouldn't do. Winnie felt she had only one option. It would be a tight squeeze, but Grace would come to live at the Battersea Tavern.

6

The smog didn't clear for another two days. And when the wind carried it away, it went as quickly as it had arrived. London had been at a standstill. Transport had ceased and boats on the River Thames were stuck in the docks. The smog had choked the city. But on Wednesday morning, London finally began to get moving again. And Winnie opened the Battersea Tavern. Her regulars were delighted to be back in the pub, but Winnie heard tale after tale about death and failing health. Thousands of Londoners had lost their lives due to the London particular, yet the government were playing it down.

'It's good to be back,' Piano Pete gushed.

'And it's good to have you back, Pete. Maureen worked like a dog to get the place cleaned up. Gawd, that black, grimy stuff was awful. It covered everything!'

'Yeah, the streets were slippery with it. Old Maunders from the café on Battersea Bridge Road went flying and broke his leg. Mrs Tilbury fell over a kerb and knocked three teeth out. The poor woman and her husband have only got one tooth between them now.'

'What caused the smog to be so bad? Does anyone know?'

'I couldn't say, Win. I've heard talk about it being the nutty slack we're all burning on our fires.'

'Eh?'

'It doesn't burn clean, Winnie. Just about every house round here is burning it, all day and all night. They say smoke from it mixed with the fog and then it poisoned thousands of people.'

'That can't be right, Pete, surely not? Churchill has been encouraging us to buy nutty slack. It's cheaper than coal and it ain't rationed.'

'Yeah, but why's it cheaper? It's poison, Winnie, I'm telling ya. My sister said they're still struggling for beds at the hospital. The smog has blown away over the North Sea, but folk are still dying from it.'

'Terrible, Pete, bloody terrible. I hear there's been a lot of crime too.'

'You can say that again. Looting, robberies, even murder!'

Winnie shuddered. 'Worse than the blackouts during the war.'

She enjoyed a chat with Piano Pete. The fella was a mine of information, and he always knew what was going on in Battersea.

The door opened and Hilda rushed in.

'Hello, love, are you all right?' Winnie asked, thinking that Hilda looked deathly pale.

'Oh, Win, I've been so worried about everyone. My neighbour got taken into hospital and passed away, so did a bloke at the end of my street. I wanted to come round sooner, but I was too scared to leave my house. I don't mind admitting that if I'd had a bottle of booze to hand, I would have knocked it back. My nerves have been in tatters.'

'Stop panicking, everyone here is fine and dandy. The kids are back at school, Rachel is at the wholesalers, Maureen has gone to see a client about a christening gown and Carmen is upstairs keeping Grace company.'

'Thank Christ for that! Grace? Who's Grace?'

'Long story.'

'I ain't in a rush,' Hilda smiled.

'Well, to cut a long story short, Grace is an orphan and her gran died yesterday. She had nowhere to go so now she's living here with us.'

Hilda rolled her eyes. 'You've taken in another waif and stray?'

'Yeah, something like that. But what else could I do, eh? Pack her off to a kid's home?'

'Erm, yes! That's what most people would have done.'

'Well, I ain't most people.'

Winnie noticed Hilda's eyes roaming along the bottles of spirits sitting on the back shelf. 'Forget it,' she warned. 'I won't serve you alcohol, Hilda.'

'I know, and I'm grateful, Win. But I think I'd better get out of here; the temptation is too much today. I thought I was all right but I'm really struggling. Give Rachel and the kids my love. I'll see her tomorrow. Oh, and I'll look forward to meeting Grace.'

'All right, love, but give me your word that you'll stay off the booze.'

'I will.'

'Good. You've not touched a drop in years, Hilda. I'd hate

to see you fall off the wagon. You're a bloomin' monster when you're drunk!'

'Don't worry. I've no intention of letting meself get in that sorry state ever again. I've got too much to live for: a beautiful daughter and two smashing grandchildren. I won't let Rachel and the kids down. See ya.'

Winnie bit on her bottom lip as she watched Hilda rush away. The woman would never be completely free of the demon drink. Hilda only had to get a sniff of the lid of a whisky bottle, and she'd be wanting to throw the contents down her neck. But apart from the occasional relapse, Hilda had stayed sober. Unlike drunk Hilda, Winnie loved sober Hilda and thought her to be a smashing woman. It had always baffled Winnie how the consumption of alcohol could change a person's personality.

Maureen returned, beaming as she walked through the door.

'You look very pleased with yourself,' Winnie smiled.

'They were over the moon with the christening gown.'

'I should think so an' all! You put a lot of work into it. That gown will be passed down the generations. You should be proud of yourself, love. You made a family heirloom.'

'Thanks, Winnie. How's Grace?'

'As you'd expect. Sad, scared, alone. The poor girl doesn't know if she's coming or going. I don't think I need to worry about informing the authorities that she's with me. They won't give two hoots about the girl. But I will let her school know. Anyway, Carmen is with her at the moment. She's going to arrange for Bertha's funeral and clearing the house.'

'Carmen is great at organising, she's the best person for

the job. I said I'd go round to the house today to collect the rest of Grace's things.'

'Thanks, love. We all need to muck in and show Grace that she isn't alone. I should imagine that she's feeling quite overwhelmed with us lot.'

'You took me in, Winnie, and helped me to turn my life around. I feel like part of the family now. Grace will be fine.'

'Perhaps you could take Grace under your wing, Maureen? I mean, you lost your mum and dad early in life and was raised by your grandparents. You've got a lot in common with Grace.'

Maureen nodded, a sad look in her eyes. She was obviously thinking about Len and Renee, her grandparents who'd perished in a house fire several years ago. Winnie glanced towards the end of the bar where Len used to sit. She still missed the whinging old man and his craggy face. Now, Mr Ainsworth sat there. A strangely quiet man who would call in as regular as clockwork, smartly dressed, always polite, Winnie had heard gossip that he had lived with his overbearing mother who had recently passed away. He seemed lonely, and Winnie saw a deep sadness behind his eyes. His quiet, daily drink seemed to be the only respite the man had from his miserable life.

The rest of the morning passed quietly. Winnie busied herself with serving customers and throwing a bit of banter over the bar, though something didn't feel right. She couldn't put her finger on what was wrong and a sense of foreboding kept niggling her. She tried to brush it aside, and carried on smiling, but Winnie had the feeling that a big bout of rotten luck was coming her way.

*

Roy kept one eye on the paperwork spread over his desk and another on the clock on the wall. It would be lunchtime soon and he could slip out of the office and dash home. Alan and his father would be at work, laying tarmac for the repair and construction of London's roads. The house would be empty which meant that Roy would have all the privacy he needed. And he felt the need for privacy more than ever now! Because for the past few days, apart from the few hours he'd enjoyed in Rachel's company, the smog had left Roy cooped up indoors with his family.

Being stuck at home had been miserable. Alan had teased him relentlessly, saying he had girl's hands because he worked in an office. And his father had joined in too, reminding Roy of what a disappointment he was. *You've let the side down with your nancy job,* his dad had sneered. *You ain't a real man.* Roy wished he had thicker skin and tried not to let their bullying words get to him, but they did. Always did. *Call yourself a man? You couldn't punch your way out of a paper bag.* They were right, he couldn't. But there were many times when he wished he could. He'd relish whacking Alan and blacking his eye. And his father? Cor, Roy would have loved to have had the strength to knock the man to his arse. Indeed, if Roy didn't get to spend a precious half an hour in the shed today, he thought he might go insane!

Using her shoulder to push open the door of the Battersea Tavern, Rachel lumbered in, laden with shopping bags.

'What have you got there?' Winnie asked. 'I thought you were at the wholesalers.'

'I was, but I came home via Clapham Junction and bought the kids some Christmas presents.'

'Blimey, Rachel, did you buy all of Arding and Hobbs?'

'No, just a few bits from there. Most of what I bought is from Woolworths. I took the liberty of getting Grace a few bits for Christmas too.'

'That was thoughtful of you, love. Christmas without her gran is gonna be hard for her. By the way, your mum popped in earlier. She said she'll see you tomorrow.'

'Lovely. I'm just gonna hide this lot in my room and then I'm going to get my stall cleaned up, ready to open again tomorrow.'

'Maureen will give you a hand if you ask her nicely.'

'It's fine, I can manage, but it's looking filthy. I'll have it shipshape in a couple of hours.'

Twenty minutes later, Rachel carried a bucket of soapy water outside to the front of the pub and surveyed her shellfish stall. It was her pride and joy though she thought it could do with a lick of paint to freshen it up.

Hot, soapy water dripped down her arm as she rubbed away the greasy, black muck the smog had left behind. Her thoughts drifted to Christmas. It would probably be her last one in the Battersea Tavern. Next year she'd be a married woman, living in a cosy, little house with Roy. She pictured them sitting around the Christmas tree and the children opening their Christmas gifts as a tasty bird roasted in the oven. A proper family morning. Perfect. Though she'd miss the big Christmas party that Winnie would be throwing in the pub. But next Christmas was going to be very special, and she couldn't wait to spend it with just Roy, Martha and Benny.

As she plunged the sponge into the bucket again, Rachel felt the hairs on the back of her neck stand on end. An uneasy sensation washed over her, and she had the feeling that someone was watching her.

Looking around, the street appeared empty. Her eyes roamed the windows of the houses nearby. She couldn't see any curtains twitching. Yet she felt sure that she was being watched.

'How are you getting on?' Winnie asked, poking her head through the pub door.

'I'm nearly done.'

'Good. I'll be closing in a tick.'

'Just finishing up. I've got a strange feeling though, Win, like someone's been watching me. I don't know what it is, but I don't like it.'

'Funnily enough, I felt a bit peculiar earlier. It's probably just having Grace here. The poor girl is so full of sadness it's bound to rub off somewhere.'

'Maybe,' Rachel answered, though she wasn't convinced that Grace was the cause for them both having an uncomfortable feeling. 'I might go and see Leena and get her to lay her cards for me.'

'Oh, Rachel, I wish you'd stay away from that woman and her crystal ball.'

'She doesn't have a crystal ball, Win. She uses tarot cards to tell the future.'

'If you ask me, it's all a load of rubbish and just a way to swindle money out of you.'

'It's not, Win, she's really good. Come with me and you can see for yourself,' Rachel suggested.

'No thanks. Bloomin' hocus pocus rip-off, that's what it is!'

Rachel chuckled to herself, but she had every faith in Leena's abilities. The dark-haired, mysterious woman had

Romany gypsy roots and had foretold that Rachel would meet a man and fall in love. Rachel had pooh-poohed the idea, but two weeks later she'd met Roy and now they were engaged to be married. No matter what Winnie thought of Leena, Rachel believed in the woman's abilities to predict the future and nothing that Winnie said would change Rachel's mind.

David Berry kept out of sight as he slyly watched Rachel from an upstairs room of a house on the other side of the street. It had been at least eight or nine years since he'd last seen her, but he didn't think she'd changed much. Her long, blonde hair still flowed, and she had retained her shapely figure. Rachel was a looker, all right, but David wasn't back in Battersea for her. He had a different target in his scope. Bigger fish to fry! And the big fish was called Martha – his daughter. She was just as pretty as her mother and the good looks the girl possessed were going to clear his debts. A shudder crept through him as he thought of the danger his life was in with his debtor, Mr Ratcliffe, breathing down his neck. The man had threatened to kneecap him and sink him in the canals of Manchester but David had managed to appease the gangster, for now, and had no qualms about sacrificing his daughter to save his own skin.

Stepping away from the window, David smiled wryly. The unforeseen smog of the past four days had delayed his plans, but now it was time to put them into action. Throwing on his camel hair coat, David combed back his thick, brown hair before stealthily slipping out of the back door.

Waiting under a tree near the school gates, David hoped he wouldn't be recognised, especially by any Old Bill, though he doubted that the coppers were looking for him now. Years had passed since he'd been in Battersea so his crimes were surely forgotten.

Soon enough, the sound of children's laughter and chatter filled the air as pupils filed out of the school. David craned his neck and spotted Martha. His daughter was the image of her mother and bore little, if any, resemblance to him. He'd been watching Martha's movements for over a week and noticed that she always had a young lad with her who lived in the Battersea Tavern too. David assumed he must be Martha's brother, but he knew he wasn't the boy's father and wondered who was.

As they came closer, he stepped in front of Martha, almost startling the girl.

'Hello, Martha,' he smiled.

Martha looked back at him, confused.

'You won't remember me. I'm David ... your father.'

The girl's blue eyes stretched wide, and her mouth opened but no words came out.

'I know me turning up out of the blue must be a shock for you, but it's so good to see you. I've missed you, darling.'

Martha stared, speechless.

'I haven't seen you since you were a toddler. You've grown into a beautiful young lady, just like your mother. It's because of your mum that I've stayed away. She didn't want me in your life, so I had to respect her wishes. But there hasn't been a day gone by when I haven't thought about you and wondered how you were getting on.'

'You're really my dad?' Martha asked, stunned.

'Yes, darling, I am. And seeing you today is the best day of my life. Can we go for a milkshake or something? There's so much to catch up on.'

Martha threw a worried look at the boy.

'You can come too,' David told the lad, 'What's your name, son?'

'Benny,' he frowned, glaring at David with distrustful eyes. 'I'm her brother.'

'How about it then, do you want to come with us?' David asked.

'We can't. We've got to go straight home,' Benny said, gruffly.

'Look, if you're worried about your mum, you can tell her a little fib and say you both had to stay in school for detention. I won't keep you out long, I promise. I'd just like half an hour with my girl, that's all.'

'I'm not sure about this,' Benny muttered to Martha.

'Come on, Benny, just half an hour. Mum won't even notice that we're a bit late home.'

Benny sighed heavily. 'All right, half an hour, that's all,' he answered, begrudgingly.

Sitting in a small café, David wished he could get rid of Benny, but for now, he'd have to tolerate the boy. When Benny excused himself to use the toilet, David plastered on a huge smile and pushed a guinea coin across the table. 'For you, darling. It's not much but treat yourself to something nice.'

'A guinea! I've never had a guinea. Thanks, erm, Dad.'

'I expect it feels a bit odd to call me dad but it's a word I've longed to hear from your lips. The thing is, Martha, your mum wouldn't like it if she had any idea that I've seen you. Do you think you can keep it a secret from her?'

'I, erm, I dunno.'

'I'd love to see you again, darling, but I can't if your mum finds out. I've got years and years of birthday and Christmas presents to make up for and I really want to spoil you rotten, but that can only happen if we keep it a secret. What do you think?'

'As long as I'm not lying to Mum, then I suppose it would be all right.'

'Good girl. And Benny, do you reckon you could persuade him to keep his mouth shut an' all?'

'Yeah. Benny does whatever I tell him to do,' Martha grinned.

'So, who is Benny's dad?' he asked, curiously.

'Benny's mum and dad died during the war, so Mum adopted him.'

'I see,' David smiled. He was pleased with himself. Step one of his plans had worked. He'd charmed Martha and now he had gained her trust too. It wouldn't be too much longer and he'd be whisking the girl back to Manchester with him.

7

It had been a week since Bertha's funeral. There hadn't been many people in the church, but Winnie, Carmen, Rachel, Hilda and Maureen had attended, which meant a great deal to Grace, especially as the women hadn't know her gran. And Winnie had held a small wake in the pub. Everyone had raised a glass to Bertha, which Grace had thought cruelly ironic, as her grandmother had been an advocate for teetotalism.

Grace had settled into the routines of life above the Battersea Tavern, and she liked being there. But she missed having her own space. The flat was crammed and she had to share a small room with Maureen. Everyone had been kind to her, but the lack of privacy had stopped Grace from shedding her tears. Thoughts of her gran were never far from her mind – losing the woman hurt more than she'd ever imagined.

Packing her satchel for school, Grace glanced at Maureen's dressing table and her heart began to race. Sneaking over, she grabbed a lipstick and quickly shoved it into her pocket. Her heart hammered and her blood felt as though it was pumping at twice the rate through her veins. For a moment, Grace felt giddy. Her pulse throbbing fast, she threw her bag over her shoulder and made for the stairs. 'I'm going to school,' she called towards the kitchen.

'Hang on, love,' Winnie said, standing in the frame of the kitchen doorway. 'You haven't had any breakfast.'

'I'm not hungry. See you later.'

Grace sprinted down the stairs before Winnie could stop her. She was sure the woman would see a look of guilt on her face and then she'd be found out as a thief. They'd throw her out. She'd be forced to live in the orphanage.

Meandering towards Battersea County, the local secondary school, her mind turned. She didn't need the lipstick and didn't even really want it. Why had she stolen it? The women of the Battersea Tavern had been exceptionally good to her, and Grace felt horrid about the way she was repaying them.

Passing the school gates, she wandered aimlessly, her thoughts in turmoil. She missed her gran and dashed away a tear that had fallen down her cold cheek. It was freezing. She could be sitting in the warmth of a classroom. Instead, Grace found herself ambling around Battersea Park, chilled to the bone, her heart breaking. Thrusting her hands into her pockets, she fingered the stolen lipstick tube. Then, standing beside a bin, she pulled the lipstick from her pocket and gazed at it before throwing it away. Stealing the lipstick had given her a thrill and filled her with a peculiar excitement. And during those few moments, all the grief and sad thoughts of her gran had disappeared.

'Penny for them,' Maureen said across the kitchen table to Rachel.

'She's probably worrying about what that Leena told her,' Winnie huffed. 'It's all nonsense, Rachel. Take no notice.'

Rachel pushed her uneaten bowl of porridge away and bit on her bottom lip. 'What if it's not nonsense, Winnie? Leena's always been pretty accurate before.'

'Tell you what,' Winnie snapped, 'Get me a pack of those tarot cards and I bet I can read the future just as well as Leena! In fact,' she said, pushing her chair back, and walking to a kitchen drawer, 'watch this.'

Winnie rummaged for a pack of playing cards and marched back to the table. Spreading several in front of her, she gazed at the cards before saying, 'Rachel, love surrounds you. A tall, handsome man is in your life and brings you much happiness. I can see you wearing white. Are you planning on marrying soon?'

'Don't be daft, Winnie,' Rachel scoffed. 'You know what's going on in my life, but Leena doesn't know me, and she predicted the wedding – as well as the death.'

Carmen bristled. 'People die all the time. It's part of life. Of course someone around you is going to die in the future. It's hardly a surprise, is it?'

'I know what you mean, Carmen, but Leena was adamant that there's danger lurking. She said the death would be violent and I can't help thinking that something bad is going to happen to Roy.'

'Didn't she also say she saw you moving home, making a fresh start?' Maureen asked.

'Yes.'

'Surely that suggests that nothing bad is going to happen to Roy? You're going to get married and find a new home together.'

'All right, so if it's not Roy, who else could it be? I can't stand the thought of a violent death happening to anyone I love.'

'That's enough!' Winnie barked. 'I've a good mind to go and give that Leena a right bloomin' mouthful. Filling your head with nonsense and having you worried sick. It ain't on. And to think you paid good money to listen to all that rubbish. More fool you, Rachel. I thought you were more sensible than that!'

Silence fell around the table.

Winnie rarely lost her temper but witnessing Rachel needlessly anxious had riled her ... 'Well, I'm sorry, Rachel, but I don't like seeing you upset. The woman is a charlatan, and I don't want to hear another word about it. Shit happens, that's life. There's no point in getting yourself all in a state and worrying about what's coming. Deal with it when it happens. I don't want to hear another word about Leena and her predictions of danger and death. Is that clear?'

Rachel gulped. 'As crystal.'

'Good. Now, who wants another cuppa?'

'Good morning, Martha,' David grinned as he collared the girl near the school gates.

'Oh, hello,' she answered, awkwardly.

'Can I have a word?' he asked. 'In private.'

Martha turned to Benny who was scowling at David. 'You go in,' she said, flicking her head towards the school, 'and I'll catch you up.'

Benny gave David a foul look before stamping away. The boy had made it clear that he didn't like him. David wasn't bothered. So long as Benny kept his mouth shut, he couldn't care less if the boy was enamoured with him or not.

'What do you want?' Martha asked.

'I thought it would be nice if we spent the day together,' David replied with a cheeky grin.

'But what about school?'

'You can skip a day. Only, I've got to leave soon and go back to Manchester so it'd be nice to have some time with you.'

'Oh, I'm not sure...'

'Go on, Martha, just one day. I've only seen you a few times this week, just snatched moments here and there. I really would treasure a day with you.'

Martha chewed her thumbnail as she thought. 'All right, but I hope Mum doesn't find out!'

'That's my girl! Come on, we can hop on a bus out of Battersea. No one need be any the wiser.'

During the journey to Tooting, David kept Martha enthralled with tales from his childhood. Everyone had always said that he could charm the birds down from the trees and his jolly chatter seemed to be working with Martha. The girl seemed content, hung on his every word.

'Put this in your pocket,' he said, and pushed a couple of shillings into her hand. 'There could be plenty more where that came from,' he said, and winked.

'What do you mean?'

'In Manchester... If you wanted to come with me.'

'Oh, I couldn't. Mum would never allow it.'

'Your mum wouldn't need to know,' David whispered.

'I don't see how.'

'A few small white lies. You could say that you're staying with a friend.'

'She'd want to know which friend and she'd check with my friend's mother.'

'But do you like the idea of coming to Manchester with me?'

'Yeah, I do.'

'Leave it with me, darling. I'll put me thinking cap on and I'll come up with a plan.'

David already had a plan, but he wasn't prepared to reveal it to Martha just yet. And no matter what, the girl would be leaving for Manchester. No one, not even Martha, would stop it from happening.

8

It was Friday and Grace had skipped school again. Cold and shivering, she couldn't wait to get indoors. Passing Rachel's shellfish stall, she saw the woman stamping her feet and blowing into her hands.

'You're back early,' Rachel said. 'The school bell must have only just rung.'

'I ran,' Grace fibbed. The truth was, she'd idled the day away wandering around the shops at Clapham Junction. At least it had been warm inside them.

Walking around to the back door, Grace was pleased to find the flat upstairs empty. Her heart began to race as she sneaked into Winnie's and Carmen's shared bedroom. Excitement, fear and worry snaked through her veins as her eyes darted around the room. Two neatly made single beds, a wardrobe, a photograph of a woman in a nurse's uniform hanging on the wall ... And then her eyes fell on the dressing table.

Grace, her mouth dry with nerves, crept towards the dressing table. Her heart skipped a beat when a floorboard underfoot creaked loudly. Breathing rapidly, her eyes scanned across the dark, wooden top. In a small, shell-shaped ceramic pot, she saw a pair of small gold earrings, each set with a delicate pearl. Glancing quickly behind her, Grace reached out and picked up the earrings, squirrelling them away in her pocket. She thought her heart was going to punch out of her chest, it was beating so hard!

Dashing out of the room, she ran to hers and Maureen's bedroom, closing the door behind her. Leaning against it, Grace held out her hands in front of her and saw that they were shaking. She closed her eyes and rested the back of her head against the door, drawing in a long, steadying breath and slowing blowing it out. The act of stealing had been a thrill! It hadn't felt the same when she'd pinched the tins of Spam. That had been out of desperation and she'd needed the food. Before that, Grace had never stolen anything. But daringly taking the lipstick and now the earrings, she'd felt exhilarated. And her harrowing anguish and all-consuming melancholy thoughts of her grandmother had left her mind for a few peaceful minutes.

'Thank goodness it's Friday,' Rachel said as she washed her hands at the kitchen sink. 'I'm desperate for a bath and can't wait to get the smell of shellfish out of my hair.'

'Having that water heater installed was the best thing I ever did. I used to hate dragging out the old tin bath,' Winnie reminisced.

Drying her hands, Rachel looked concerned, and asked, 'Have you noticed Martha and Benny acting differently?'

'How do you mean?'

'I'm not sure. They seem, I don't know, distant. I've heard

them bickering too, but they argue in whispers. Do you think they might be up to something?'

'If you're worried, then why don't you ask them?' Winnie suggested.

'Huh, they're not likely to admit any wrongdoing to me. Can you keep an eye on them, Win, and let me know if you hear or see anything out of sorts?'

'Will do. And don't worry. They're good kids with sensible heads on their young shoulders. I'm sure everything is fine.'

'Thanks. I'm going for my bath and then I'm getting my glad rags on. Roy is taking me dancing tonight.'

'Oh, smashing. I hope you'll both have a drink downstairs an' all. I'd like to have a chat with Roy.'

'What about?'

'You'll see soon enough,' Winnie smiled.

Rachel ambled off and Winnie sipped her tea. She wasn't concerned about Martha and Benny, but she was worried about Grace. The mourning youngster kept herself to herself, rarely joining them around the kitchen table. And there'd been little conversation either. Pushing herself up from the seat, Winnie padded along the passageway and lightly tapped on Maureen's bedroom door.

'Are you in there, Grace?' she called, pushing her ear to the door.

Grace pulled open the door, her face glum.

Winnie plastered on a welcoming smile. 'I'm having a cuppa and I was thinking about getting my good biscuits out. Would you care to join me?'

'No, thanks,' Grace answered.

She went to push the door closed, so Winnie quickly said,

'Well, love, whether you'd like a posh biscuit or not, you *will* be joining me in the kitchen. And that's an order.'

Grace huffed.

'And we'll have less of the stroppiness,' Winnie commanded, wagging her finger at the girl.

Trudging behind Winnie, Grace slunk into a chair and folded her arms across her chest.

'I hope you know that when I brought you here to live with us, it meant you became part of our family. I know we don't feel like family to you yet, love, but in time we will. We'd all like to get to know you better, and I'm sure that if you got to know us, you'd quite like us, though we're a bit of an odd bunch. Also, I don't think it's healthy for you to sit in that tiny bedroom every evening. I realise that you probably don't feel like it, but I shall expect to see you out here with us more often.'

Grace nodded but with obvious reluctance.

Carmen came into the kitchen looking flummoxed.

'Are you all right?' Winnie asked.

'Have you seen my earrings? The gold ones with the pearls.'

'Aren't they in your pot on the dressing table?'

'No. I could have sworn that's where I left them. Oh well, I'm sure they'll turn up. Maybe Rachel's borrowed them.'

'She's gone for a bath. Roy's taking her dancing tonight.'

'That's nice,' Carmen smiled. 'I bet she's taken my earrings to wear tonight.'

'I expect so, love.'

'May I be excused now?' Grace asked.

Winnie pursed her lips. 'I suppose so. But remember what I

said. I want you back in here in an hour to have your dinner with us.'

It appeared that Grace couldn't get out of the kitchen quickly enough.

'I'm worried about her,' Winnie whispered.

'She'll come round, Win. It's been a lot for her to take on board.'

'I hope so. I hope I did the right thing in bringing her here to live with us.'

'Of course you did! She's better off with us. She just needs some time.'

Winnie wanted Carmen to be right. She worried that she'd made a mistake by taking Grace on and couldn't help thinking that the people at the children's home would be more experienced in dealing with grieving children. Though none of them living above the Battersea Tavern were strangers to grief, least of all Winnie. Thoughts of Jan swamped her mind and she choked back a sob. Winnie had unofficially adopted Jan, but the young woman had died prematurely from cancer, breaking Winnie's heart.

'Do you think I've offered Grace a home to try and replace the hole in my heart that losing Jan has left me with? Or am I still searching for my daughter who was taken away from me at birth?' Winnie asked, dashing away a tear.

Carmen sat at the table and took Winnie's hand in her own. 'No, Win. I believe you offered Grace a home because your broken heart is a *good* heart. You know you'll never replace Jan or your long, lost daughter. But you'll never turn away anyone who needs a home. It's just who you are. Your intentions are always true.'

Winnie sniffed. 'No, I'll never replace Jan or my baby girl.

59

But Jan is here, Carmen. She often visits. I feel her. She gives me signs too.'

'I'm sure of that, Win. Jan loved you like you were her mother. And one day, Grace will love you too.'

David hunched his shoulders around him in the telephone box and pulled his trilby hat low. After the operator connected him to a number in Manchester, he drew in a long breath and tried to keep his voice steady. After all, he didn't want Mr Ratcliffe to know that he feared him. It wouldn't do to show the violent man any weakness.

'Mr Ratcliffe? Yeah, it's me, David. David Berry.'

Mr Ratcliffe answered in a low growl: 'Have you got her for me yet?'

'Almost. I will, soon. I just need a few more days and then I'll be back in Manchester.'

'You'd better be, Berry. Because if you're not back here by Wednesday with the girl you promised me, I'll send my men to Battersea, and they'll hunt you down. And when they find you, they'll cut off your balls and shove them down your throat. And that will just be for starters. Are you understanding me, Berry?'

'Yes, sir, Mr Ratcliffe, loud and clear. I won't let you down, Mr Ratcliffe. Me and the girl will be with you by Wednesday, I swear... but it's just photos, right? Nothing more.'

'You owe me, Berry.'

The line went dead.

David gulped as he replaced the telephone receiver. 'Bastard git!' he whispered, hating Mr Ratcliffe with every sinew in his body. But it had been his own stupidity that had landed him in serious debt with the gangster. And David knew that if he didn't deliver Martha to the vile man, his life would be over, finished off in a torturous way.

With his jaw tense, David pulled back his elbow and punched the telephone box wall. He heard his knuckles crack as an agonising pain shot through his hand and up his arm. 'You promised it would only be some risqué photographs,' he mumbled, now fearing that Mr Ratcliffe wanted more than just a few saucy snaps of Martha. David knew about men like Mr Ratcliffe. Sick men, perverts, who liked their women to be young girls. He didn't want to hand Martha over to Mr Ratcliffe's evil clutches, but what choice did he have? If he didn't, the man's gang would come for him.

David closed his eyes and shook his head. 'I'm sorry, Martha,' he sighed. Then justifying his actions, he quietly added, 'But you're almost a woman. It won't be too bad for you, and you'll be saving your father's life.'

9

In the kitchen on Saturday morning, Grace sat at the table with Maureen to one side of her and Rachel on the other. Winnie was busy frying something that smelled delicious as Carmen poured cups of tea.

'Thanks so much for yesterday, Win,' Rachel beamed.

'What do you mean?' Winnie asked, her back to the table as she turned something in the frying pan.

'Thanks for talking to Roy about our wedding reception.'

'Oh, that. Well, I'm glad he agreed to hold it here in the Battersea Tavern and I'm delighted to be treating you to it. You'll have the finest wedding cake that Battersea has ever seen.'

'I was always going to insist that we had our reception here, but I never expected you to pay for it, Win. Thanks again.'

Benny smiled awkwardly across the table at Grace, and Martha cocked her head to one side as she studied her fingernails.

'Before you ask, no, you can't paint your nails,' Rachel firmly told Martha.

'Please, Mum, I'll take the colour off before I go back to school on Monday.'

'No, Martha. And you'll be sorry if I find out that it was you who has my missing pink nail colour.'

'I haven't touched it, Mum, I swear.'

Grace watched as Martha pouted sulkily. The girl seemed spoiled, but Grace wasn't surprised as Martha had five women fussing over her. Grace looked from one to the other. She liked Winnie. The woman was strict but always jolly. Carmen was nice too. She was just as firm as Winnie but didn't smile as much. Rachel seemed a bit stand-offish, but had been kind to Grace, even buying her a new skirt and blouse. Maureen was quiet, and plain-looking. She wasn't as glamorous as Rachel and seemed more homely but Grace could tell that Maureen had a kind heart. Hilda hadn't joined them for breakfast and Grace had only met her once, though she'd instantly warmed to the woman. But Hilda appeared to be more highly strung than the other women and a bit on edge.

Guilt washed over Grace. The women of the Battersea Tavern had opened their home to her, going out of their way to make her feel welcome. Yet, apart from Hilda who lived around the corner, Grace had robbed something from each one of them. She'd stuffed her stolen treasure into a sock and hidden it under her mattress – Carmen's earrings, Winnie's brooch, Rachel's pink nail polish and Maureen's shiny, new buttons that she'd bought for a child's coat she was making. She'd thought about returning the items, sneaking them back to where she'd taken them from. But that would involve more risk than stealing them in the first place. Gawd, she wished she'd never pinched them, yet it had felt gratifying at the time. Now, she was full of regret and prayed she wouldn't be found out. *Never again,* she thought. *I'll never steal from these good people ever again.* Apart from feeling rotten, she knew that if she was caught, they'd throw her out and she'd have to live in the orphanage.

Breakfast over and cleaned away, Winnie gathered the washing whilst Carmen opened the pub. Laundry day was her least favourite day of the week, but at least they all mucked in and took it in turns. Today, it was Winnie's turn. And unlike most folk in Battersea, Winnie did her washing on a Saturday and not on a Monday. As she collected the laundry, Winnie dreamed of buying a twin-tub machine to help with the back-breaking work. Such luxuries were unheard of along her street, but now with another person in the household, perhaps she could justify the investment. Winnie chuckled to herself. She could imagine Benny's face if a twin-tub washing machine turned up at home instead of a television set. The boy kept asking for one and had been repeatedly told *no.* Television sets were expensive. And so was a twin-tub machine. But at least a twin-tub was useful. The only purpose Winnie could see for a television set was to sit and idle away the day. Even the prospect of witnessing the new Queen Elizabeth's coronation next year hadn't been enough to persuade Winnie that a television set was needed. The wireless would do.

The scullery backed on to the downstairs kitchen, and just lugging the laundry down the stairs was hard work. Winnie puffed and panted as she dropped the large load to the floor and turned on the copper to heat. Sorting the whites from the colours, and the cleanest from the dirtiest, she heard something jingling in a pocket of Martha's dress. Pushing her hand inside, Winnie pulled out three shillings. Frowning, she stared at the coins, wondering where her granddaughter had obtained the money from. She wiped her forearm across her brow before trudging through the pub and outside.

The cold, winter air cut through Winnie's thin dress. Pulling her cardigan tightly around herself, she hurried over to Rachel's shellfish stall.

'All right, Winnie?' Rachel asked, cupping a hot cup of tea.

'I was sorting the laundry and I found three shillings in Martha's pocket. Do you know where she got the money from?'

'No, I don't. Are you sure it was in Martha's pocket?'

'Yes. Three shillings is a lot of money for her to have.'

'It is. I can't think where it could have come from.'

'We need to ask her. I'll get Piano Pete to come out and keep an eye on your stall for a minute.'

'Thanks, Win,' Rachel said, looking worried. 'You don't think that it's Martha who's been pinching things, do you?'

'What do you mean?' Winnie asked. It hadn't crossed her mind that her granddaughter might be a thief.

'Carmen's earrings ... my nail colour ... Maureen has lost some new buttons, and didn't you say that your brooch has gone missing?'

'Yes, but, Martha wouldn't steal from us,' Winnie answered, defensively.

'No, I don't think she would, but she's been acting strangely. She's been very secretive, like she's hiding something.'

'I can't imagine for one minute that Martha has stolen the money or anything of ours. But we need to talk to her and get to the bottom of this.'

Upstairs, Rachel summoned Martha from her bedroom and into the kitchen. Benny followed, looking sheepish.

'Sit down' Rachel instructed.

'Have I done something wrong?' Martha asked, worriedly.

'I don't know, Martha, have you?'

'No,' she replied, curtly.

Winnie cleared her throat and interrupted. 'No one is accusing you of anything, love. We just want to know where you got three shillings from.'

Martha's cheeks flamed red.

'You're not in any trouble. Just tell us the truth,' Winnie urged.

'I found them.'

Winnie didn't believe Martha. She could always tell when her granddaughter was fibbing.

'I suppose you *found* Carmen's earrings and my nail colour too, did you?' Rachel snapped.

Martha shook her head. 'No, I don't know where they are, but I found the money.'

'I'm sorry, Martha, but I don't believe you. Tell me the truth,' Rachel demanded. 'Where did you steal the three shillings from? And where are the other things you stole?'

Martha's bottom lip began to quiver. 'I-I didn't steal anything!' she cried.

'It's all right, love, don't get upset,' Winnie soothed.

'No, Win, it's not all right! I want to know where the stolen things are and why she's stealing.' Turning back to Martha, she warned, 'You're not too old to feel my hand across the back of your legs! Tell me the truth, Martha.'

Benny suddenly leaped to his feet. 'She didn't steal anything!' he shouted. 'Her dad gave her the money.'

Rachel staggered and grabbed the table to steady herself before slumping onto a kitchen chair. Winnie felt the room spinning.

'Your dad?' Rachel uttered in disbelief. 'Your *dad*? When? When have you seen him?'

Bile burned the back of Winnie's throat as Martha began to sob.

Benny explained, 'He's been meeting her after school and the other day Martha got a bus with him instead of coming to class.'

'David – you've been meeting David?' Rachel quizzed, glaring at Martha.

Martha nodded. 'He said I had to keep it a secret because you wouldn't like it.'

'He's right, I don't! You have no idea of what that man is capable of! You're to stay away from him. Do you understand me, Martha? You're never to see him again. Is that clear?'

'Why? Why can't I see my dad? He's really nice and he's missed me.'

'That man doesn't have a nice bone in his body,' Rachel seethed. 'He's fooling you, Martha. I don't know what he wants, but he'll be after something.'

Benny spoke again. 'He wants Martha to go to Manchester with him.'

'Over my dead body!' Winnie boomed, finding her voice. 'Listen, love, don't get upset. This isn't your fault. But your mum is right. David isn't a good man, Martha. He'll hurt you. He hurts everyone he touches.'

'You've got it wrong!' Martha screeched, jumping up. 'He's my dad and he loves me! You can't stop me from seeing him.'

Winnie looked over to Rachel. The colour had drained from her face and her blue eyes were bulging with anger.

'Right, let's all calm down, eh?' Winnie suggested. 'Your mum is upset, and rightly so, Martha. Now, listen to me, love. You've not done anything wrong, though you should have told us about seeing your dad. Have you arranged to meet him again?'

Martha wiped her runny nose on the back of her sleeve but said nothing.

It was Benny who answered. 'She's meeting him today in Battersea Park.'

Speaking softly, Winnie asked the boy, 'What time and where?'

'In half an hour, at the big dipper in the funfair.'

'Right, leave this to me,' Winnie told Rachel. 'Martha, Benny, you're to stay indoors.'

'But my dad...'

'You heard your gran,' Rachel said. 'Neither of you are going anywhere. Go to your room. We'll talk about this later.'

Martha threw Benny a foul look as they sloped off. The boy had shared her secret, and it was clear that he was out of favour with his sister. But that was the least of Winnie's worries.

'What do we do?' Rachel asked, quietly.

'Like I said, leave it to me. You stay here and keep an eye on Martha. I'm going to meet David and find out what he's up to.'

'I'm worried for you, Winnie. Can't you take my mum with you?'

'There's no time – I don't know where Hilda is. But don't worry. David doesn't scare me, Rachel.'

'I hate to admit it, but he scares me.'

'And with good reason, love. What he did to you was disgusting and unforgivable. But he can't hurt you now.'

'I blame myself, Win. I should never have got that drunk. If I'd been sober, he wouldn't have been able to creep into my bed.'

'It wasn't your fault; you mustn't blame yourself. But Martha can't ever find out how she was conceived.'

'God forbid!'

'There's no time for this now. Just keep an eye on the kids. I've got to go.'

'Take care, Win. Please be careful. As far as we know, David is a murderer!'

'Yeah, well, we might never know if he killed that poor girl at the railway station, but I wouldn't be surprised if he did. David is evil through and through. I thought my husband was bad, but David is ten times worse. And I'll do whatever it takes to keep him away from Martha.'

10

The cold wind blew against David's face, making his cheeks numb. He wished he'd arranged to meet Martha inside, somewhere warm instead of beside the fairground attraction. The funfair had been erected as part of the Festival of Britain celebrations the year before and had been left in place with the big dipper proven to be the most popular ride of the fair. As the train trundled around the twisting track, David could hear the squeals from the passengers above, screaming at the exhilaration of the thrilling journey as it plummeted steeply down and raced through a reservoir of water. He thought the fairgoers must be mad to be here today in the inclement weather, and he hoped that Martha would turn up soon.

Stamping his feet to get some feelings back into his toes, David saw the silhouette of his slightly overweight mother marching towards him. He threw his half-smoked cigarette to the ground and angrily blew out smoke. So, he'd been rumbled, and Martha must have spilled the beans about him. Looking at his mother's thunderous face, David smirked. Granted, a lot of water had passed under the bridge and he'd robbed the woman more than once, but he hadn't seen her for a very long time and hoped to charm his way back into her stupid heart. His mother had always been a soft touch. Firstly, with his dad who had walked all over her, punching her to keep her in line. And David had grown up pampered by the woman, keeping her wrapped around his little finger. He felt sure he could worm his way back into her affections.

'Mum, it's lovely to see you,' he smiled, opening his arms wide.

His mother remained tight-lipped and stone-faced.

'You look wonderful, a real sight for sore eyes. Christ, Mum, I've missed you.'

'Don't try that with me, David. I'm here for one reason only: tell me what you want with Martha?'

'I just wanted to see my daughter. Is that a crime?'

'Bullshit. What are you up to?'

'Nothing, Mum, honest. I only want to get to know Martha with − with what little time I have left.'

'Going down for something, are you? You deserve to be put in gaol and have the key thrown away.'

David hung his head and forced tears to well in his eyes. Looking back up at his mother, he choked, 'I'm dying, Mum. I don't know how long I've got left. A month, maybe two. I just wanted to see my girl and make amends b-before it's too late.'

His mother's face didn't soften, and David was disappointed to see her eyes narrow.

'You lying, wicked git,' she ground out through gritted teeth. 'There's nothing wrong with you! What you need is a good dose of prison! What do you really want with Martha? I know you, David. Money is your God. Is that what you want, eh, money?'

David smiled wryly. His mother wasn't as much as a push-over as she'd once been.

'I knew it!' Winnie snapped. 'It's money you're after. What was you going to do? Kidnap her? Demand money for Martha's return?'

'No, Mum, of course I wasn't.'

'Then how was you planning to milk money from your daughter?'

'That wasn't my intention.'

'I don't believe a word that comes out of your mouth, David. If it's money you're after, I'll pay you to disappear and never come back to Battersea again.'

David scuffed the floor with his shiny shoe. 'Well, as it happens, I do owe some rather nasty men a bit of money. Quite a lot, in fact.'

'How much? How much will it cost me to keep you away from Martha?'

'Why should I stay out of her life? I'm her father. I'm entitled to see my girl.'

'No, David, you're not her father. You got Rachel pregnant against her will. But that doesn't make you Martha's father. You're entitled to nothing,' she spat.

'Rachel didn't say no.'

'She couldn't, she was unconscious!'

'It's my word against hers. But that aside, Martha is a beautiful girl, just like her mother.'

'Yes, she is, no thanks to you. I'll ask you one last time. How much will it cost to get rid of you?'

'Probably more than you can afford, Mum.'

'We'll see about that. Give me an hour. Meet me at the back door. I'll pay you all I have. It'll be worth it to protect

Martha from you. You're bad down to the core, David, and you taint everything around you. I won't allow you to ruin Martha. One hour. You'll get what you came here for. You'll have money. But then I never want to see you again.'

David nodded. 'You'd better make it worth my while, Mum... or I'll have Martha eating out of my hand.'

'One hour,' his mother barked before spinning on her low heel and stamping away.

David looked on as his mother faded out of sight. This hadn't been the plan, but taking his mother's money was a lot easier than dragging Martha up to Manchester. And it left his conscious clear. Offering his daughter up for nude photographs hadn't sat comfortably with David, and he was sure Mr Ratcliffe had desires to use Martha for his own entertainment. But if his mother paid him enough, David could return to Manchester and pay off his debts, and Mr Ratcliffe would be satisfied... he hoped.

Winnie paced the kitchen floor as Maureen sat at the table, her face pale as she nervously twiddled her thumbs.

Carmen stared out of the window. 'You can't pay him, Win, it's not right and it's not fair. Why should he be allowed to waltz back into Battersea and flounce back out with all your hard-earned cash.'

'I realise it's not right or fair, but what choice do I have, eh?'

'Call the police. David is still a wanted man.'

'The police wouldn't be bothered about him, not after all these years.'

'I bet they would!' Carmen argued.

'There's no time. He'll be here in twenty minutes. If I

73

don't give him what he wants, what then, eh? I can't risk him interfering in Martha's life. He's done enough damage already. The girl is already asking questions that none of us want to answer.'

'I feel sick,' Maureen mumbled.

'You don't need to be here, love,' Winnie said. 'Go. Run round to Hilda's with Rachel and the kids. You'll be safe there with them.'

'Are – are you sure you don't need me to be here?'.

'I'm sure. Thanks, love, but go.'

As Maureen made a hasty retreat, Carmen reiterated her plea. 'Please, Win, let me call the police instead of this. I don't think you've thought it through.'

'What do you mean?' Winnie asked.

'Well, what if he takes your money and then he decides to come back for more? Are you going to continue paying him forever?'

'No … oh, I don't know. Maybe I'm not thinking straight, but I wouldn't care if it cost me every penny I've got to keep him out of Martha's life.'

'Fair enough, but I still think you'd be better off calling the police.'

Winnie sighed heavily. 'I wish I could believe that the police would arrest him and whisk him away, but it's too late and even if there was time, the Old Bill wouldn't care.'

'There's still fifteen minutes.'

'I ain't scared of him but I'm scared of what he's capable of. Even so, for all his wicked ways, I couldn't call the police on my own son. No, paying him off will guarantee to get him out of Martha's life. There's nothing more important to David than money. And if he comes back for more, then I'll deal with it. For now, I just want him to go back to whatever rock he crawled out from under. Gawd, I'm shaking, Carmen.'

'It'll be all right, Win.'

'I hope so. I hope he takes the money and buggers off, never to be seen again.'

David sauntered up to the back door of the Battersea Tavern, keen to lay his hands on his mother's money. Nothing much had changed although the black door had paint peeling off and could do with a fresh coat. And on the street, he'd noticed the gaping holes where houses had stood before the war, now reduced to unloved bomb sites. He'd seen the prefabricated homes too. White, temporary bungalows that housed homeless families whose lives had been destroyed by Hitler's bombs. *Poor buggers,* he'd thought, without feeling any empathy. David only cared about himself. And he believed he was entitled to a share of his mother's wealth. Taking her money didn't leave him with any guilt.

Dark clouds covered the sky and heavy raindrops began to fall. As he lifted his arm to knock on the door, Winnie pulled it open and glared angrily at him.

'Nice to see you again, Mum,' David grinned, pleased when he noticed a cloth bag in her hand that he knew would be stuffed with cash. His mother had never believed in banks and had always kept her money hidden at home. *Lucky for him*, he thought.

'This is all I have. The week's takings and all my savings. Give me your word that you'll never come back to Battersea again.'

'You have my word,' David promised, though he was already planning another visit soon to fleece her for more.

'I mean it, David. You won't get another bean out of me. This is it. A one-off, a final payment to buy your assurance that you'll stay out of Martha's life.'

'I understand, Mum. And thank you. I don't want to take your money but it's getting me out of a bit of a scrape. I appreciate it.'

'I don't want your thanks, David. I just want you to promise to stay away – forever. Don't ever darken my doorstep again.'

'I promise,' David smiled, as sincerely as he could muster.

As his mother reached out her arm, and David went to take the stuffed bag, her eyes misted with unshed tears and she said flatly, 'You're dead to me.'

Just then, he heard a voice from behind.

'That's him,' a woman yelled, 'That's David Berry.'

David spun around to see a skinny woman with her white hair piled high on her head. Two coppers holding their truncheons aloft flanked the woman who was pointing accusingly at him. He knew the woman was Carmen. *Interfering bitch,* he raged.

'Hold it where you are,' one of the coppers warned. 'We've been looking for you for a very long time, Berry.'

David glanced at his mother. She looked as shocked as he felt. Pushing past her, he ran into the pub.

The policeman's voice followed him. 'We've got the place surrounded. There's no escape.'

Seeing uniformed figures through the windows at the front of the pub, David ran for the stairs and flew up them two at a time. The coppers who'd been at the back began to give chase, their heavy boots thudding up the stairs behind him.

David raced through to the kitchen, panic coursing through his veins. If the Old Bill arrested him, he feared he'd be going down for many years, and prison was something he knew he couldn't face. Grabbing a large knife beside the sink, he realised that he'd have to fight his way out.

The two policemen entered the kitchen. David waved the knife in front of him and edged backwards towards the window.

'Give yourself up quietly. Put the knife down. You're coming with us down the nick.'

David's mouth felt dry with nerves. His heart thudded hard, leaving him feeling light-headed. Panic coursed through his body. 'No,' he uttered, 'stay back,' he added, thrusting the knife forwards in a threatening manner.

The policemen parted, coming towards him slowly from each side. Another appeared in the doorway and David saw his mother standing behind the copper, her eyes stretched wide.

'Please, son, give yourself up,' she pleaded. 'It ain't worth it.'

David, feeling like a caged animal, glanced behind him. The window was his only escape. 'Don't come near me,' he warned, jabbing the knife menacingly. Then quickly lifting the sash window, he turned back towards the police who were about to jump him. 'Back off!' he shouted, slashing the knife through the air.

The policemen stepped back, out of harm's way, still holding their truncheons high.

David eased himself slowly out of the window, backwards, with his eyes fixed firmly on the coppers. He knew that just to the left, there was a drainpipe he could shimmy down, something he'd done once as a child when his father had been giving his mother a good hiding. As he felt around for the drainpipe, rain began pelting down and loud thunder roared above.

'David, please,' his mother called. 'Stop! Don't be a fool!'

He felt the wet and cold drainpipe in his hand. His knuckles were still sore from punching the telephone box, but he managed to get a firm hold of the drainpipe. In one swift move, David dropped the knife and, throwing himself out of the window, grabbed the drainpipe with both hands. Gripping the pipe with all his might he tried to hold on with his knees too. But his hands slipped on the wet cast iron and he could feel himself lurching backwards. Lightening streaked across the sky as he peered upwards, falling through the air, his arms flailing.

Thud! And blackness.

Winnie was breathless from running down the stairs and out onto the street. Peering down at her son lying lifeless on the wet ground, she gasped. Blood pooled under his head until the rainwater diluted the thick, red liquid and spread it further across the paving slabs.

A policeman held her arm and tried to gently pull her away. 'Please, Mrs Berry, come inside.'

Winnie yanked her arm free of the policeman's grip. 'Get off me!' she barked. 'That's my son!'

Dropping to her knees, Winnie's hands hovered over David's very still body, unsure if she should touch him or where she could touch.

He coughed, lightly, rolling his head as he groaned in pain. 'David … David, I'm here. Y-you'll be all right.'

His eyes flickered open. He looked confused. Scared.

Winnie grabbed his hand. 'You'll be all right, son,' she soothed. 'You've had a fall. An ambulance is coming.'

Again, David coughed, though it sounded more of a splutter, and Winnie saw blood in his mouth.

'Sorry,' he whispered, his voice gargling.

'Shush, save your strength.'

'Mum ... oh God ... so sorry ...'

'It's all right, David.'

'Forgive me ... please ... forgive me, Mum.'

Winnie peered into David's eyes. He was crying. Real, genuine tears rolled from his eyes and down his temples then into his thick, brown hair.

'Please ... forgive me, Mum ... I–I need your ...'

As she stared lovingly at David through her tears, she watched his life ebb away.

'No! Please, David, don't die ... David ... David! My boy!' she screamed.

'He's gone, Win,' Carmen said, holding her trembling shoulders. 'He's gone.'

II

'I can't believe it's been a week since David's funeral,' Winnie sniffed, holding a handkerchief to her nose. 'Look at the state of me. Still crying at the drop of a hat and I need to be thinking about Christmas. There's so much to do.'

Carmen pushed a cup of tea across the kitchen table towards her. 'Don't worry about Christmas. I've got it all under control. But if you want to cancel the big party, given the circumstances, I'm sure everyone will understand.'

'No, no, I wouldn't hear of it. The party will go ahead just as it does every year. And by God, I'll have a bloody good time. I just wish I could stop crying!'

'Stop being so hard on yourself, Win. You've lost your son, you're allowed to cry.'

'I know, but I was paying him to leave Battersea forever. I hoped I'd never see him again. I told him he was dead to me. Huh, be careful what you wish for, eh?'

'You never wished him dead, Win. You didn't really mean it.'

'No, of course I didn't. I couldn't stand him, but I never stopped loving him. You don't, do you? No matter what they do wrong, you never stop loving them. Gawd, the times I would have happily throttled him. I hated the things he did. But there wasn't a day that passed when I didn't think about him and worry about him. But now ... well, I'm never going to set eyes on him again.'

'I think about my Errol too, every day. I don't know if he's alive or dead and I doubt I'll ever see him. But like you say, you never stop loving your kids.'

'The doctor reckons that the back of David's head was caved in and that he died instantly. But he didn't, Carmen. He spoke to me. He begged for my forgiveness. I heard him. I looked into his eyes and saw him crying. I saw genuine remorse. The copper, the one that was there, he says David was dead as soon as he hit the ground, but he wasn't. I *know* he wasn't. I swear, he spoke to me.'

'You've got to try to stop reliving those last moments, Win.'

'I know. I keep replaying it over and over in my head. I don't understand why everyone is telling me that David couldn't possibly have spoken to me. I heard him. You were there – did you see him speaking to me?'

Carmen sighed. 'I wish I could tell you I did, but I'm sorry, Winnie, I never saw or heard him speaking.'

'Christ, am I going mad? Did I imagine it?'

'Maybe his soul was speaking to you, Win. David's body was dead, but perhaps his spirit was asking for your forgiveness.'

A lump of raw emotion caught in Winnie's throat, and she drew in a long, juddering breath. 'Yes, I think maybe you're right. I know that Jan's soul is often here so I must have seen David's soul, that's what it was. He wasn't always a good person, but his soul was better than him. That's it, Carmen, you're right – I heard David's spirit speaking to me. Thank you. You have no idea what a comfort that is.'

In Roy's front room, he pulled Rachel closer as she sobbed into his chest. Thankfully, his brother and his father were working overtime this Saturday morning and he had the house to himself.

'It's all right, my darling, it's all over now,' he soothed.

'I know. But I've been bottling up my feelings since David died.'

'You've been brave, for Winnie and for Martha.'

'I don't know what to tell Martha. She keeps asking me questions that I don't know how to answer.'

'The truth,' Roy suggested. 'Tell her the truth.'

'No, never! I can't tell her what David did to me. I know she's heard gossip. Everyone is talking about him and about how he's suspected of throwing Lucy under a train. She doesn't want to believe her dad was a murderer but I think he was, Roy. The man was evil, yet Winnie is broken-hearted. I don't understand.'

'You're a mother, Rachel. You must understand how it would feel to lose a child.'

'I can't begin to imagine the pain, but I thought Winnie hated David. It makes no sense. And do you know the worst of it? He died just feet away from where I set up my stall every day. I can't stand the thought of standing there, day in and day out, and seeing the place where David fell to his death.'

'Time is the best healer, Rachel.'

'I don't believe I'll ever be free of that man. But I'm glad he's dead. Does that make me a bad person?'

Roy placed his finger under Rachel's chin and tilted her head towards him. 'No, my darling, you're not a bad person. You are the loveliest woman I know.'

'Thank you. I don't know what I'd do without you. And thanks for letting me sob on you. I'm sorry, my tears have made your shirt wet.'

Roy peered down into Rachel's soft, blue eyes. He wished he could take away her pain and make everything perfect for her. 'I love you,' he said, huskily, feeling his groin stir. He couldn't wait for their wedding night when he could finally make love to her. They'd come close on several occasions, but Roy had always pulled back. It seemed to him that Rachel had never been respected by a man, and by abstaining until they were married, he hoped it would prove how much he cherished her.

Rachel pulled away and straightened her skirt. 'I should go. Martha and Benny will be home soon. Mum took them to the park, but I doubt they'll stay out long in this weather.'

'I'll walk you home,' Roy offered, wanting to spend every minute with Rachel that he could.

It was a ten-minute stroll to the Battersea Tavern. Roy noticed several people pointing fingers and tittering in whispers, no doubt about David's untimely death. Rachel didn't seem to be aware of the gossiping around her, or if she was, she ignored it. He admired her strength.

A bobby on a bicycle passed them, nodding his head to Rachel.

'He was there on the night David died,' Rachel said, her tone matter of fact. 'Carmen had run to the telephone box and called Tommy Bradbury. The fella retired from the police force several years ago, but when Carmen told him that David was at the pub, he immediately got onto his colleagues at the police station.'

'Once a copper, always a copper,' Roy mused.

'Sergeant Bradbury has always had a soft spot for Winnie. He proposed to her once.'

'Mrs Berry is a marvellous woman.'

'She is. And I feel sorry for her. I just hope she doesn't know that I'm not sorry about her son dying.'

Outside the back door, Roy lightly kissed Rachel's cheek. 'Can I see you tomorrow?' he asked, hopeful.

'Yes, I'd like that. I don't think it's appropriate for us to go out dancing tonight, but I don't want to be stuck in there all day tomorrow,' she answered, flicking her head towards the pub.

'You know where I am if you need me. I'll see you tomorrow.'

Wandering back home, Roy rounded a corner and glanced at his watch. If he hurried, he could spend some much-needed time in the shed. Alan and his father would be finishing work about lunchtime, but Roy knew they would head straight for the pub. He would have at least a couple of hours to himself. It was wrong, he knew it was, but after seeing Rachel so upset, Roy felt the need to be himself for a while.

Glancing over his shoulder, he pulled open the shed door. Sneaking inside he closed the door behind him and lit a gas lamp. Fear of being caught made his pulse race, but as soon as he opened his hidden box a sense of calm washed over him.

Pulling out a pretty, pink and white floral dress, Roy held it up in front of him, admiring the dainty print. The dress had belonged to his sister, Lillian, and had been the perfect size for her small frame. But Roy had carefully taken the stitching apart and added delicate lace panels before sewing it back together to make it the right fit for his muscular body. Quickly removing his boots, jacket, shirt and trousers, Roy slipped the dress over his head. Smoothing it down, he enjoyed the feel of the silky material against his skin. Then, taking a pair of stockings from the box, he pushed his feet inside, slowly pulling the stockings up to his thighs. Gently spinning around, Roy smiled with pleasure as the skirt of the dress swished around his knees. The dark-haired wig needed brushing, so Roy ran his fingers through the hair, thoroughly combing every strand, before expertly positioning it on his head. He glanced at his reflection in a large tin of oil, pleased with what he saw. Then he swept a bright red colour of lipstick over his lips. Finished. Roy's look was complete. 'I'll never be as pretty as you, my Lilly,' he whispered, tenderly. 'I miss you,' he said, as a tear fell from his eye.

Sitting on an upturned crate and crossing one leg over the other in a feminine fashion, Roy looked at his reflection again. 'Rachel's been having a hard time,' he sighed. 'I'm trying to comfort her, but I don't know what to say. It's hard being a man. I want to sort it out for her, to do something to make everything all right. But I don't know what. I wish you were here. You'd know what to do. That David must have been a nasty piece of work. He sounds as bad as Alan.'

Roy closed his eyes as memories of his twin sister flooded his mind. Lillian had always tried to protect him from their brother's cruel tongue and heavy fists. Alan had shoved her out of the way on many occasions to get to him. And Lillian had cried with him when their father had whacked him, offering comfort and nursing his wounds. No one understood him in the way that Lillian had. 'Alan thought it would be funny to challenge me to a game of slaps which I declined,' he admitted to the thought of Lillian. 'Me saying no kicked it all off again. Him and Dad started, the pair of them calling me names. Christ, Lilly, I hate him. I hate them both!'

After ten minutes, Roy had finished getting his woes off his chest. He felt lighter, as if a huge heavy weight had lifted from his broad shoulders. Satisfied, he went to stand up and relish in the feeling that wearing a dress gave him, but he was startled when the shed door flung wide open. He stood, horrified, mouth gaping at the sight of Alan.

Alan stared back, breathing fast. 'Roy? What the *fuck*? What are you doing?'

Roy gulped. His worst fears had been realised. His unbearable brother had found out his sordid secret. 'It's not what you think,' he blurted.

'You're sick,' Alan yelled. 'A fucking pervert!' he screeched, before stomping away.

Roy felt ill. His stomach twisted. Quickly whipping off the wig and yanking the dress over his head, he pulled on his shirt and wiped his lips on the back of his hand as he ran from the shed and chased after his brother into the house.

'Wait! Alan ... let me explain!'

But Alan charged up the stairs and slammed the bedroom door shut.

Roy burst in, his heart hammering. Alan was sitting on the edge of his bed holding his head in his hands. 'Please, Alan, you don't understand!'

'Too fucking right, I don't. What are you? Some sort of

poofter? Bloody hell, Roy, I thought our Lillian had come back from the dead. You scared the shit out of me!'

'I'm sorry – but I'm not a poof. It's not like that.'

'Just get out of my sight. I can't stand to look at you, you sick bastard.'

'Alan, please—'

'FUCK OFF! And you needn't think you're sleeping in that bed tonight. I ain't having a queer kipping in the same room as me!'

'Alan, I'm your brother! And I ain't queer.'

Alan jumped to his feet and pounded towards Roy, grabbing him by the throat and holding him against the wall. His face was so close to Roy's that Roy could feel his brother's breath on his cheek.

'You ain't no brother of mine,' Alan spat. 'You ain't right in the head.'

Roy struggled for breath. 'You're choking me …' he creaked.

'I'd like to wring the bloody life out of you,' Alan snarled, finally releasing his grip. 'Get out. Get out of my sight!'

Roy stood, rubbing his neck, his legs feeling weak. 'You won't tell anyone, will you?'

Alan looked down his nose, his eyes full of disgust making Roy feel even more ashamed than he already did.

'Please, Alan, I'm begging you. Please don't tell anyone.'

'Don't worry, your revolting, filthy, dirty, sick secret is safe. How can I tell anyone? I'd be a laughing-stock. *My* brother, me own flesh and blood is a bleedin' poofter! I ain't having the finger pointing at me too. Now fuck off before I kick the living daylights out of you.'

Roy scarpered, hurrying back to the shed. Stuffing his outfit away in the box, he quickly dressed, his heart heavy.

He couldn't trust that Alan would keep his secret. He felt sure that his brother would tell their dad who had been known to attack homosexuals and Roy feared he'd soon be at the end of his father's fists. He could picture the scene, his father screaming that he'd rearrange Roy's face. The blood. The pain.

Roy's jaw clenched and his stomach flipped. Maybe he could buy Alan's silence? He'd leave his brother be for a while and let him calm down. Then he'd try to speak to him again. Whatever it took, Roy had to convince Alan to keep quiet.

12

It was Christmas Day. Grace sat at the kitchen table feeling lonely and overwhelmed as everyone rushed around her. She was used to spending a quiet day with her gran, the pair of them exchanging gifts, enjoying a nice meal and then listening to the King's speech on the wireless. Though with King George passing away earlier in the year, Grace wondered if the new, young Elizabeth would be making the Christmas Day speech instead.

Grace sighed as life hurried on around her. She wasn't used to the hustle and bustle of Christmas morning in the Battersea Tavern. Everyone seemed to have a roll – even Benny was busy decorating Christmas gingerbread.

'You look lost there, are you all right?' Maureen asked, as she rushed past the table with a bowl of peeled potatoes in her hands.

Grace tried to smile and nodded.

Martha came into the kitchen carrying a pen and paper. 'I've done a seating plan,' she announced, proudly.

'Good girl. Have you remembered to leave some blank spaces?' Winnie asked.

'Yes. I know what Christmas is like here, Gran. There are always extras who turn up.'

'If I remember rightly, we had seven unexpected guests turn up last year, on top of the twenty-eight who'd been invited,' Carmen chuckled.

Winnie wiped her hands on her apron. 'You know me,' she grinned, 'I always have an open-door policy for Christmas lunch.'

'I hope we've got enough veg,' Rachel pondered.

'We'll manage. We always do. No one ever leaves hungry. Right, take these parsnips and carrots downstairs. We'll cook all the veg in the pub kitchen. What's the time? Terry should be here soon to move the tables and chairs. And where on earth is Hilda?'

'Oh, Mum popped in earlier and said she'd be late cos she's helping with the Sally army. She's gone to round up the homeless to make sure they get a good meal inside them.'

'Blimey, trust Hilda,' Winnie laughed, tutting. 'Just so long as she doesn't bring them here. We've got enough to feed as it is. I could have done with Hilda's help today. All hands on deck and now we're one short.'

Grace sighed, wondering if she was invisible. She could help, but she didn't know what to do. Sloping out of the kitchen, she wandered down the stairs and into the pub. Everything was gleaming. Maureen had polished the brass last night. Martha and Benny had made colourful paper chains that Terry had hung from corner to corner across the ceiling. A large tree filled the corner, decorated with pretty handmade ornaments that had been collected over the years.

The sound of a joyous tune reached her ears, and Grace saw Piano Pete seated at the old piano, expertly tinkling the ivories. She meandered across and stood beside the piano, looking at Pete. The roll-up that was always stuck to his bottom lip never seemed to be alight. And he always wore a flat cap, even indoors. A short fella with a red, bulbous nose, Pete's rosy cheeks were deeply lined, and when he smiled, his eyes crinkled too.

'Any special requests, Grace?' Pete asked and winked.

'Do you know "Gloomy Sunday" by Billie Holiday?'

'Yeah, but it's Christmas, duckie. Can't you think of a cheerier song?'

'No, not really. I don't see what's so great about Christmas.'

'Blimey, you're in the doldrums. What are you so miserable about?'

Grace shrugged. 'Nothing.'

'You missing your gran?'

'A bit.'

'Your gran wouldn't want you moping around on Christmas Day. She'd want you to have fun.'

'There ain't nothing fun about me,' Grace sulked.

'Now why would you say something like that?'

'I'm jinxed. Bad luck follows me.'

'You're just being daft now.'

'No, no I ain't,' Grace argued, adamantly. 'People die when I'm around! My gran died, and before that I found an old man in the street, and *he* died. Martha's dad died and even me own mother died giving birth to me.'

'Duckie, none of that was because of you. Your gran and the old man were killed by the smog. And David's death had nothing to do with you. Your mum – well, that's ever so sad, but it wasn't your fault. People die every day all over the world. So, cheer up, eh? It's Jesus's birthday. Pick another song, a happier tune. I guarantee a jolly tune will make you feel better.'

Grace shrugged again. She doubted that whatever tune Pete banged out on the piano would lift her dark mood. *Oh, Gran,* she thought, *I wish you was still here with me.*

Rachel bounded up to Roy, throwing her arms around his neck and kissing him on the cheek. 'Merry Christmas,' she smiled. But her smile soon diminished when she saw Alan and Doug walk in behind him.

'Sorry,' Roy mouthed silently to her, looking tense.

'Hello, treacle,' Doug grinned. 'Room for two more?'

Rachel glanced behind and caught Winnie's eye, who hurried over.

'Good afternoon, Mr Russel, Alan,' Winnie said, politely.

'Please, Winnie, drop the formalities. Call me Doug. After all, we're almost family.'

'Hmm, not quite,' Winnie replied, sourly. 'Take a seat, over there. I'm sure we can squeeze in two more.'

'Thank you, Winnie. Me and me boy ain't half looking forward to a good Christmas lunch. It's been many years since we've had anything decent. My Lillian was a good cook, she took after her mother, God bless their souls.'

'Well, I can't promise ample meat or spuds but there'll be plenty of veg and gravy. Go and make yourselves comfy and Rachel will bring you drinks.'

Doug nudged his oldest son hard in the ribs.

'Thanks, Mrs Berry,' Alan said, as what seemed like an afterthought.

As Doug and Alan made their way to their table, Roy

leaned into Rachel. 'I didn't want them to come but I couldn't say no.'

'Don't worry. I've saved you a seat next to me. Martha will be excited to see you.'

'How is she?'

'Better. She's got thick skin, like me. The gossiping about her father doesn't seem to bother her. Anyway, the old crones will soon be bored of talking about David and they'll find some other poor bugger to chinwag about.'

Rachel took Roy's hand and led him to a table on the other side of the pub from his dad and his brother. Martha rushed over, clearly delighted to see him. Benny followed, also beaming. Rachel's heart warmed as she watched her little family exchanging Christmas greetings. Roy was going to be a smashing stepfather and judging by the look on his face, the sooner they were married and away from Alan and Doug, the better.

'Are you all right?' she asked quietly in his ear, 'only you appear to be a bit on edge.'

'I'm fine, darling.'

'You don't seem yourself. Your smile isn't reaching your eyes.'

'I'm just worried that my brother and my dad will ruin Christmas Day and show me up. They don't know how to behave when they've had a drink.'

'Don't worry, Roy. Winnie and Carmen are used to dealing with drunken men playing up. They'll keep your brother and your dad in line.'

Roy smiled at her, but she thought he still looked concerned.

'Relax and enjoy yourself. I'll take them some drinks, but I'll make sure they're only served small ones.'

The hours flew by as over thirty people enjoyed Christmas lunch in the Battersea Tavern. The sherry ran out and they were low on port, but jugs of beer were plentiful and flowing freely.

'I wonder where my mum is?' Rachel asked Winnie.

'She'll be here, love. Your mum wouldn't miss seeing the kids on Christmas Day.'

'Talk of the devil,' Rachel smiled affectionately, as Hilda almost fell through the door, her arms laden with gifts.

'Merry Christmas,' she called, 'I see you've started without me,' she said, laughing.

Rachel rushed over and took some of the load from her mum. 'Flippin' 'ell, Mum, have you bought the whole shop?' she asked.

'If I can't spoil my grandchildren at Christmas, then when can I spoil them?'

'Let's take it all upstairs. They can open them after dinner. I've saved you a plate, it's in the oven.'

'Thanks, sweetheart. I'm knackered and bleedin' starving.'

'You're so late, I thought you might have decided to have lunch with the Salvation Army and the homeless people.'

'Cor, I was tempted. My stomach was growling something rotten as I dished up the lunches. But I couldn't have taken a meal and deprived someone in need.'

'You deserve a sainthood, Mum. I'm so proud of you.'

Upstairs, Rachel and Hilda arranged the Christmas presents on the kitchen table.

'I got a little something for Grace too,' Hilda said.

'That's nice. She's been ever so quiet.'

'It's early days for her. She'll be all right. Anyway, what have I missed? Has Mrs Dobbins managed to keep her teeth in? And Mr Everett, has he done any of his magic tricks yet?'

'Yes, Mrs Dobbins has kept her teeth in, sort of. She did take them out for a short while and went to drop them in Maureen's glass, but Winnie gave her a telling off. And yes, Mr Everett has been pulling pennies from behind the kids' ears.'

'I see that Roy's brother and father are here. You weren't expecting them, was you?'

'No, Mum, I wasn't! And Roy ain't happy about it. To be honest, neither am I. Alan keeps staring at me. He's giving me the creeps. And he's knocking back the beer. I reckon he's already drunk.'

'Just ignore him, sweetheart. Don't let him ruin your day. Right, take me to the food. Honestly, Rachel, I could eat an 'orse.'

Back downstairs, Maureen was handing around the puddings. Trifle or Christmas pudding.

'This is bloody handsome,' Terence Card shouted as he tucked into his Christmas pudding.

'Thanks,' Maureen answered, coyly. 'I made it just like my gran used to.'

'Renee would be very pleased with this, Maureen,' Winnie assured.

Rachel could feel Alan's eyes boring into her and tried to ignore him. He was making her feel uncomfortable, but she didn't want to be rude to him.

'Rachel! Rachel, over here, treacle,' he called.

'Flippin' 'eck, what does he want now,' she mumbled under her breath.

'Stay where you are, I'll see to him,' Hilda offered.

'No, it's all right, Mum. You eat your lunch.'

Ambling over, Rachel squirmed under Alan's scrutinizing long stare. She could tell he was having inappropriate thoughts about her.

'Any chance of another jug of beer?' he asked, and ran his large, calloused hand up the outside of her thigh.

Rachel gasped and stepped back. 'Keep your hands to yourself!' she admonished.

Alan sneered. 'You know what you need, Rachel – you need – a *real* man.'

'What, like you?' she scoffed. 'No thanks. I wouldn't touch you if you were the last man on this planet.'

'Yeah, you would. And I'd make you very happy,' Alan said, licking his lips.

Rachel's stomach lurched. 'You're a pig,' she hissed.

'She's a feisty one,' Doug said, looking as though he was chewing a wasp. 'You can see who'll be wearing the trousers in her and Roy's marriage.'

Rachel marched away, feeling sick. She'd seen something in Alan's eyes that had unnerved her. A smug look, and it had felt like a smack in the face.

'Are you all right?' Hilda quietly asked.

'Yeah, yeah, I'm fine,' Rachel fibbed. 'Shall I get you a cuppa?'

'Just a glass of water, thanks, sweetheart.'

Rachel gave Roy's shoulders a gentle squeeze as she passed his chair. Behind the bar, she found a tall glass which she rinsed before pouring her mum a glass of water from the tap. When she turned around, she was alarmed to find Alan blocking her way.

'Excuse me,' she said, trying to edge around him.

Alan pushed his body against her, pinning her to the small sink behind the bar. She could smell the beer on his breath and could see he'd drunk too much.

'Get out of my way,' she demanded, quietly, not wanting to cause a scene in front of everyone, especially her children.

Alan's face came closer, and he whispered in her ear, 'Don't make out you're the Virgin Mary. How about me and you slip down to the cellar, and I'll put a bloody big smile on that pretty face of yours? I know what you want, Rachel.'

Rachel instinctively lifted her knee, bringing it up hard into Alan's groin. As he groaned and reached for his nether regions, she quickly side-stepped him.

'Stay away from me!' she hissed, her heart pounding with fear.

Alan looked furious. 'You stuck up cow,' he growled. 'What's the matter with you?' he barked, his voice becoming louder.

'Shut up!' Rachel spat, aware that the pub had fallen silent.

'Are you frigid?' Alan snarled, 'Is that why you're marrying a poofter?'

Alan hadn't seemed to notice that everyone's eyes were on them, and people were listening to his every word. Rachel looked around and saw that Roy appeared anxious as he leaped to his feet.

'You're not half the man your brother is,' she snapped. It was clear to her that Alan was spouting obscenities because she'd rebuked his drunken advances.

Alan's face twisted with anger and his eyes darkened with hatred. 'Don't tell me you don't know that my brother is a queer? Yeah, that's right. He's as bent as a nine-bob note. He likes to dress up in women's frocks an' wear lipstick an' all.'

Rachel heard a chair scrape back and crash to the floor. She glanced over her shoulder and saw that Doug was on his feet, waving his large fist in the air.

'That's enough, Al. Don't talk about your brother like that,' he warned.

Alan staggered along the bar, his words slurring. 'It's true, Dad. Tell him, Roy. Tell him about what you do in the shed. Tell him how I caught you dressed up like a tart. It's disgusting and you oughta be ashamed of yourself.' Then looking back at Rachel, he jeered, 'And the pervert offered to buy my silence! I wasn't gonna tell no one, but *that thing* there, he ain't no bruvver of mine!'

'Shut up!' Rachel screamed. 'Shut your filthy mouth! How dare you come in here and talk about Roy like that, and in front of my children!'

Winnie rose to her feet and puffed out her chest. Throwing her arm towards the door, she pointed, and bellowed, 'Get outta my pub! Go on, clear orf and don't ever set foot in here again!'

'Aw, look at Roy. He's got all the girls sticking up for him,' Alan mocked.

'I think you should leave right now,' Terry warned, stepping towards the bar with Piano Pete right behind him.

'I'm going. I don't want to be in the same pub as that poofter. You fellas wanna watch yourselves. You'll get tarnished with the same brush, and you could all end up in jail.'

'Out, now!' Terry growled.

Doug looked deflated as he peered across at Roy. 'It ain't true, is it, Son?' he asked.

Rachel gazed at Roy too. He didn't need to answer. She

could see from the mortified expression on his face that everything Alan had said had been the truth.

'How could you?' she uttered, tears pricking her eyes. 'You was going to marry me,' she said, shaking her head, before running to the stairs.

'Rachel!' Roy called.

But Rachel ran on up the stairs and into her bedroom where she threw herself onto her bed. Face down, muffling her sobs, she cried into her pillow as her heart was once again broken by a man.

13

The following day Grace sat at the kitchen table surrounded by the women of the Battersea Tavern, all but Rachel who was licking her wounds in her bedroom. Grace wondered if anyone had acknowledged that she was there. Did they see straight through her? Was she invisible. Wrapped in her own depressed thoughts, the chatter continued around her.

Hilda poured hot tea from her teacup and into her saucer. She blew on the liquid before putting the edge of the saucer to her lips and slurping the tea. 'Well, that was a fine Christmas Day,' she grumbled.

'You can say that again!' Winnie bristled, her back stiffening.

'Poor Rachel,' Maureen sighed.

'And poor Roy,' Carmen added.

'*Poor Roy,* my arse!' Hilda barked. 'That man almost had his ring on my girl's finger. What sort of life would she have had if she'd been married to a homosexual? I shudder to think.'

Maureen sighed again. 'I know, but life isn't going to be easy for Roy now. You know how gossip spreads in Battersea. He's likely to get beaten up or arrested.'

'I don't like to think of any harm coming to Roy. He's a

nice fella, but I won't forgive him for hurting my Rachel. He's lied to her. It's not on.'

'Let's not jump to conclusions, eh?' Winnie said. 'We only have Alan's word.'

'Roy didn't deny it,' Hilda spat. 'He had every chance to call his brother a liar, but he didn't. I'm sorry, Win, but I think Roy's silence speaks for itself.'

'There's no spuds left for any bubble and squeak,' Carmen remarked.

Hilda slurped more tea. 'I couldn't eat. My nerves are too jangled.'

'I can't say I've got much of an appetite either,' Maureen said, adding, 'And I don't suppose Rachel will be hungry either.'

Winnie pushed herself to her feet. 'Maybe not, but Benny will want something. I'll make him some sandwiches with pickles and I think Martha is just as upset as Rachel. It was an awful shock for everyone.'

Grace yawned. She hadn't slept well. The sound of Rachel crying from across the hallway had kept her up for most of the night. Her stomach growled. The thought of sandwiches with pickles appealed, but Winnie hadn't asked her if she wanted anything to eat and Grace didn't like to ask. Once again, she felt ignored. Unimportant. No one cared for her.

'Are you opening the pub today, Winnie?' Hilda asked.

'I should think so. Boxing Day is normally a busy day for me. I'm sure my customers will have plenty to say about Roy and I feel I should defend him but how can I after he's broken Rachel's heart? Cor blimey, what a bleedin' mess.'

As Winnie buttered bread, Maureen got up and walked to the door, quietly pushing it shut. Then turning back to the table, she asked, 'What do we do if Roy comes here and asks to speak to Rachel?'

'He'd better not have the nerve to show his face,' Hilda answered brusquely.

'I think it's Rachel's decision to make, not ours,' Carmen added.

Grace's eyelids felt heavy, but she was too hungry to sleep. She was pleasantly surprised when Winnie shoved a plate of food in front of her.

'There you go, love. Get that down you and then perhaps you'd like to have a late morning nap. You look shattered. It must have been a lot for you to take in yesterday. Honestly, if it's not one thing, it's another in this pub. But you'll get used to us and all our dramas,' Winnie chuckled.

'Oh, thank you,' Grace said, grateful that they hadn't forgotten her after all.

Hilda grabbed Winnie's hand. 'It's good to see you smiling again.'

'I don't always feel like smiling, but I refuse to shed any more tears over David. It'll always leave a pain in my heart, but as harsh as it sounds, at least he can't hurt Martha now.'

'Something good has to come out of something bad.'

'Yes, Hilda, it does. Though I'm struggling to see how anything good can come out of this dreadful situation with Rachel and Roy.'

Grace bit into the chicken and pickle sandwich, closing her eyes as she savoured the taste. Life had been simple with her gran. Sometimes boring, but simple. She yearned for some of that peace and quiet now. The constant chatter between the women, the drone of customers' voices drifting up from the pub below, the doors banging – the incessant noise filled

Grace's head, hardly leaving any room for her to think clearly. But maybe that wasn't a bad thing. Because when Grace was alone in her head, her thoughts were dark.

'Do you want a nap after your sandwich?' Winnie asked.

Grace shook her head. 'No, I don't think I would. Do you mind if I sit in here with all of you?'

'This is your home, love. You don't need to ask.'

Benny bounded in, moaning, 'I'm hungry.'

'Good, I've got a sandwich here for you,' Winnie grinned.

Carmen stirred her cup of coffee, then tapped the metal spoon on the edge of the cup. Maureen ran water in the sink to rinse out her teacup. Winnie threw the butter knife into the sink. Hilda slurped again. Benny thudded across the kitchen and scraped back a seat at the table.

Noise. Lots of noise. Grace listened. She was grateful for the continual sounds around her that pushed away the gloomy and often scary thoughts that gnawed at her mind.

Roy threw the thin blanket off and leaped from the bed. He was sure that bed bugs had been biting him throughout the night. But he realised, even though the lodgings were filthy, he'd been lucky to find a bed on Christmas Day. It had been better than sleeping rough on the streets – though a park bench or a shop doorway might have been more comfortable than sharing his bed with an infestation of bugs. But he knew he wouldn't have survived the cold. He dared not go home, sure that his father would beat him to a pulp. And no doubt Alan would join in too. He'd seen the look of disgust in his dad's eyes. And sadly, in Rachel's too.

Rachel, oh Rachel, he thought. Since Alan had discovered him in the shed dressed as a woman, Roy had lived in fear, suspecting that his secret might be revealed at any time. But he could never have envisaged that it would have come out in such a spectacular and public way. Everyone in the borough would know by now. They'd be laughing at him. And some would hate him. Yet no one could hate him as much as he detested himself.

A small sink was in the room with a cold tap over it. Roy splashed the icy water on his face. He had to see Rachel. She deserved an explanation.

Bracing the stormy weather outside, Roy kept his head down as he made his way to the Battersea Tavern, hoping that no one would recognise him and confront him. The pub wouldn't be open yet. He didn't feel brave enough to breeze in and face the contempt of Winnie's customers. But he wasn't looking forward to knocking on the back door either. The women of the Battersea Tavern were a fierce bunch and protective of one another. He dreaded to think of the wrath that might be coming his way from Winnie, Carmen, Hilda or even timid Maureen.

Gritting his teeth, Roy knocked on the door, his heart hammering. *Please let it be Rachel who opens it,* he thought, hopefully. He was disappointed when he saw Carmen standing there, eyeing him disdainfully.

'You've got some nerve,' she said, sourly.

'I need to speak to Rachel.'

'I can't think what you can have to say that will make Rachel feel better. But I suppose you can't make her feel any worse than she already does. Wait there. I'll see if she wants to speak to you.'

The door slammed closed. Minutes later, it opened again and Winnie was stood there with her hands on her hips.

'I had a feeling you'd turn up today. What do you want to say to Rachel? It's a bit late for any confessions, young man. We all know what you are. I'm not judging you, each to his own, I say. But I'm furious with you, Roy. You almost led Rachel into a right merry dance. You wouldn't be the first queer fella to marry a woman. I know blokes who've done the same, lived a lie to cover their true natures, and I get it. But to use Rachel to hide your homosexuality is unforgivable, Roy.'

Roy swallowed hard. He wanted to explain to Rachel, not to Winnie. But his words fell out. 'I'm not a poofter. I don't fancy men. I've never been queer and never could be. I admit, I have an illness. Ssomething ain't right with me. But what I do in my own time is my own business. I don't hurt anyone. I just dress up and … and I find comfort in it. That's all.'

Winnie folded her arms across her ample chest. 'That's all? You like to prance about dressed as a woman? That's *all*? Can you hear yourself, Roy? It ain't normal.'

'Don't you think I know that better than anyone,' he spat, instantly regretting his outburst. 'Sorry, I didn't mean to sound so angry. I know what I do ain't normal. It's a sickness. I can't help it. I've tried to stop, but I can't.'

'So, let me get this straight. You're telling me that you ain't a homosexual, but you feel compelled to wear women's clothes?'

Roy hung his head and nodded. Then looking into Winnie's eyes, he said, 'I've tried to be a normal man. But when my mum passed away, I dealt with it by pretending to be a woman. I came out of my own head and went into someone else's. I knew it was wrong, but it helped me to cope. Lillian knew. She understood. And then, when she was killed, my sickness got worse.'

Winnie looked confused. 'What do you do when you're in women's clothes?' she asked, her face a little softer.

Roy shrugged. 'Talk to myself mostly. Sometimes I talk to Lillian. Don't get me wrong, Winnie, I know my sister is dead and she's not really there. But talking to her about how I feel makes me feel better. I'm always moaning about Alan and my dad. I can't tell anyone else how Alan puts a pillow over my head at night when I'm sleeping and pretends he's going to kill me. Or about my dad throwing his dinner at my head and punching me in the stomach cos he thinks I'm not tough enough. I'm too ashamed to admit to anyone that Alan and my dad take it in turns to hit me to toughen me up. And the names they call me ... but I tell Lillian everything.'

There was a lengthy, silent pause, and then Winnie drew in a long breath. 'You honestly don't fancy the fellas?' she asked.

Roy shook his head vehemently. 'No, Winnie. I'm a red-blooded man and I only have eyes for Rachel.'

'Well, I can't say that I understand what you do, but it's up to Rachel to make up her own mind. I don't think she's ready to see you just yet.'

'Please, Winnie, let me talk to her, just for five minutes,' Roy pleaded.

'I can't force her to talk to you, Roy.'

'I know, but she listens to you. Please, ask her to meet me. I'd never hurt her, Winnie, I just need the chance to tell her what I've told you. I'm not going to beg her to forgive me. I know she couldn't love me anymore. But the least she deserves is an explanation.'

After a long sigh, Winnie said, 'All right. I can't promise

anything. But if Rachel is willing to see you, then she'll meet you outside the church by the river at noon today.'

'Thanks, Winnie! Thanks very much.'

Roy wasn't convinced that Rachel would meet him, but he held on to hope. Even if she wouldn't forgive him, at least he might get the opportunity to apologise to her. He loathed his brother for ruining his relationship with Rachel, yet deep down, Roy knew he could only blame himself.

Rachel was sitting on the stairs, anxiously chewing her fingernails.

Winnie closed the back door and turned to her. 'I suppose you heard all of that?' she asked.

Rachel nodded, her stomach in knots. Part of her had wanted to run into Roy's arms but the other part of her felt repulsed at what she'd listened to.

'Are you going to meet him?' Winnie asked.

'I don't think so. I love him, Win, with all my heart, but – but I don't know, it's weird. I don't understand him.'

'I know, love. I'm not sure what to make of it either, but I know a couple of fellas who might be able to shed some light on the situation.'

'What do you mean?' Rachel asked.

'Teddy and Stan.'

'The old boys that live above the haberdashery shop?'

'Yes.'

Rachel's eyebrows raised. 'Rumour has it that they're, you know, more than just friends who live together.'

'Yes, love, they *are* more than friends. They've been together since long before I moved into the Battersea Tavern.

They're a proper pair of sweeties, smashing blokes. I reckon they'd be willing to offer some advice.'

Rachel was in two minds about meeting Roy. Some clarification on the matter would be helpful and very welcome. 'When are you going?' she asked.

'There's no time like the present. I'll take them a plate of mince pies. I'll be back in time for you to decide what to do about meeting Roy.'

Winnie rapped hard on the door, hoping that Ted and Stan would hear her knocking from upstairs. Tapping her foot, she waited a short while and then banged again.

Ted pulled open the door, squinting his eyes at Winnie. 'Winnie Berry, is that you?'

'Yes, love, it's me, Winnie. I've brought you and Stan some mince pies.'

'Oh, how thoughtful of you. Come in, come in. Stan has just put the kettle on so your timing is impeccable.'

'Thank you. I hope you don't mind me calling round without an invite,' Winnie said, as she trudged up the steep flight of stairs that led to the flat above the shop.

'You should know *you* never need an invite,' Ted assured, showing her into the lounge with a gesture of his hand.

Winnie gazed around the bright room. The place was spic and span. In fact, it was so clean, Winnie would have been happy to eat her dinner off the floor. 'You have a smashing home,' she smiled, admiring the blend of colourful yet tasteful materials that hung from the large sash window and covered the plump settee and armchairs. 'You certainly have an eye for décor.'

'That's Stan; he's very talented and quite particular. If it was down to me, we'd be living in chocolate brown colours. Please, Winnie, take a seat.'

'Thank you,' she said, handing the covered plate of mince pies to the elderly gentleman.

Stan came in, his rheumy eyes twinkling when he saw Winnie. 'Oh, my dear, it's such a pleasure to see you,' he grinned.

'And you, Stan. You're both looking very well.'

'We can't complain, Winnie. The bones ache more than they used to, but life has been kind to us. Now, tell me, what brings you here on this fresh and crisp morning?'

Winnie looked from one old man to the other. 'I need advice.'

Ted and Stan exchanged a worried glance. 'Is everything all right, Winnie?' Ted asked.

'Yes, I'm fine. Everyone at home is fine. It's just, well, it's a bit of a delicate matter.'

'I like nothing better than a delicate matter. Stan will fetch us tea and we'll enjoy a mince pie. You know you can talk freely with us.'

Winnie had felt awkward but now she was really glad she'd come. Ted and Stan were wise old men, and if they couldn't provide answers about Roy's peculiar behaviour, then no one could.

'Where do I start?' Winnie asked with a heavy sigh.

'At the beginning,' Ted urged.

'Right. Well, here goes. Rachel has fallen in love with a smashing fella called Roy and they're engaged to be married. He absolutely adores Rachel and we're all over the moon for her. But yesterday it came out that Roy sometimes dresses up as a woman. Now, as you can imagine, Rachel is devastated.

But Roy told me today that he isn't homosexual. I don't understand, and I was hoping that you could enlighten me.' Winnie gulped and shifted uncomfortably. It wasn't an easy subject to discuss.

She watched as Ted and Stan again exchanged a glance.

'You know, Winnie, men have been dressing as women for centuries past. And more recently, during the war, it wasn't uncommon for a soldier to entertain the troops adorned in woman's attire.'

'Yes, I know men often dress up for entertainment purposes. But Roy isn't on the stage.'

'And he insists he isn't *in our club*?' Stan asked, smiling cheekily.

'He says he's not.'

'This is a practice he does in private?'

'Yes, and he's mortified that everyone now knows. He said he first started doing it when his mother died and then it got worse when his sister was killed. He told me that he talks to himself or to his sister about how he feels.'

'You're concerned that by marrying Rachel, he is using her to conceal his true sexual nature?'

'Yes, Stan, I am. It's not fair on Rachel.'

'From what you've said, I've no reason to believe that Roy is homosexual.'

'Really? Then why does he pretend to be a woman?'

'You know, Winnie,' Ted smiled, 'Stan is very clever and extremely well read.' Then turning his neck to look at Stan, he asked, 'Do you remember that study you told me about by that German chap. It was years ago, before the Great War of 1914. If my memory serves me correctly, we were in Paris at the time.'

Stan clicked his finger. 'Yes, Teddy, indeed, I remember it well. Magnus Hirschfeld, a German Sexologist coined the term *transvestite*. I was fascinated with his work. I would discuss his studies with you for hours and days at a time. Bless you, I must have driven you mad, but you were so patient with me.'

Winnie was touched by the doting look that she saw pass between Ted and Stan. No one had ever gazed at her with that much affection.

'That's the chap,' Ted confirmed. 'And to prove that I was listening to you all those years ago, please, allow me to explain to dear Winnie.'

'Go ahead,' Stan smiled, sweeping his hand in front of him.

Winnie sat on the edge of the chair, keen to hear what Ted would say.

'The German chap whose work Stan was so engrossed with, he categorised *Transvestites*. A word he used derived from Latin to describe men who dress as women. A section of the men he studied were indeed in *our club*. Others were entertainers. Some believed they were women and wished to live as such. And many gleaned a certain arousal from the act. But there were men who were perfectly content with their masculinity and were what we would call *straight*.'

Winnie thought for a moment. 'I'm none the clearer,' she admitted.

'There are men who are men who dress as women driven by a deep-rooted anxiety or simply because they want to explore the feminine side of their characters. One must remember, Winnie, that men are known to repress their feelings and emotions. *Big boys don't cry.* As a woman, a man may feel enabled to express himself.'

It was beginning to make sense to Winnie, but she still didn't fully understand. 'So, you're saying that Roy is a normal bloke?'

'Yes, Winnie, I am, though I wouldn't refer to myself as *not normal*.'

'Sorry, Ted, I didn't mean to offend you.'

'You haven't, my dear, I know what you mean. But yes, I believe Roy is *normal*. You say he loves Rachel. Well, as pretty as Rachel is, she isn't my *sort,* if you know what I mean?'

'Yes, I think I do.'

'Good. More tea?'

'I'd love to stay, but I must get back and speak to Rachel.' She had a lot to discuss with the young woman, and she hoped that Rachel would give Roy another chance. Winnie thought a lot of Roy and she wasn't sure that Rachel would ever find a nicer bloke to settle down with.

14

Roy stood outside the church and craned his neck to look for Rachel although deep down, he didn't believe she'd meet him. And he wouldn't blame her. But, to his shock and delight, he saw her coming towards him, blonde hair shining in the weak, winter sun. His heart seemed to miss a beat and his stomach knotted. He couldn't read her face, but she didn't look happy.

'I didn't think you'd come,' he said, lost for words.

'I wasn't going to, but Winnie convinced me.'

'What – what did she say?'

'Lots of stuff. My head is still spinning.'

'I'm sorry,' Roy said, feeling guilt-ridden and embarrassed. 'I can see by your eyes that you've been crying, and I know it's my fault.'

Rachel shrugged. 'I wish I knew what to think. Yesterday morning, I was engaged to be married. And then my world came crashing down and I was alone again. Now ... I don't know, Roy.'

'Does that mean there's still a chance for us?'

'I want there to be. I love you, Roy. But I'm not sure that you really love me.'

'I *do*, Rachel. I love you more than I could ever put into words.' He wanted to embrace her. To hold her close and never let her go.

'Do you? Do you really?' she asked, gazing up at him and searching his eyes.

'Yes! I'm not a poof. I don't expect you to understand, but please believe me, I want you to be my wife because I love you and want to spend the rest of my life with you.'

'Winnie reckons you're not the only fella in the world who wears women's clothes and you do it because it makes you feel better.'

'It does. But if you want me to stop, I will, Rachel. I'll never wear a frock again. I'll do whatever it takes to be with you.'

'I don't want you to be unhappy, Roy, but I'm not comfortable with the notion of you wearing a dress and make-up.'

'Then I'll stop doing it – and I won't be unhappy with you as my wife.'

'Are you sure?'

'Yes, Rachel, I'm more than sure,' he lied, hoping that he could fulfil his promise but not convinced that he would.

'If you can promise to stop doing what you do, then I suppose I'd better keep this engagement ring on my finger.'

Roy's eyes widened. 'You mean it? You still want to marry me?'

'Yes, Roy, I still want to marry you.'

Roy gathered her in his arms, lifting her feet from the ground as he spun her around. 'I love you,' he grinned.

'Put me back down, you silly sod,' Rachel laughed.

Though ecstatic, something else troubled Roy. 'I'm not as strong as you,' he said, his tone serious. 'And I'm not sure that I can live with everyone knowing about what I've been doing.'

Rachel shrugged. 'Just ignore what anyone says. It doesn't matter what they think, so long as we're happy. Who cares?'

'I care, Rachel. I'm not thick-skinned and I don't think I can hold my head high in Battersea.'

'What are you saying? That we should move away?'

'Yes,' Roy answered, gravely.

Rachel frowned. 'B–but ... Martha and Benny, their school and their friends?'

'They could go to a new school and make new friends.'

'A–and Winnie? My mum, my business? It's a lot to leave.'

'I know, but we'd be making a new life where no one knows us, Rachel. A fresh start. And you'd still visit your mum and Winnie, and they could visit us.'

'I'm – I'm just not sure, Roy. I always imagined our lives together, in Battersea.'

'I can't stay here. But I won't be happy unless you and the kids come with me. Think about it, Rachel. We could move to the seaside, Margate is smashing. The kids would love living near the beach.'

She smiled at that. 'Ha, yes, they would. I suppose it could be lovely. And I can understand why you'd want to get away from here.'

'What do you say, Rachel? A new life in Margate? I know we'd be happy together.'

Rachel bit on her bottom lip, her mind clearly turning. 'I want to be your wife, so if that means moving to Margate, then so be it.'

'Are you sure?'

'As sure as I'll ever be. I'll miss my life in Battersea, but leaving will be good for us. There are too many bad memories here. It's time to start afresh. But I'm already dreading telling my mum and Winnie!'

15

Grace sat on the bedroom floor, leaning her back against the bed, her knees tucked up to her chest. Sucking on the cuff of her grey, woollen jumper, her heart pounded with distress. She thought of fleeing, running as far as she could from the Battersea Tavern. But fear rendered her to the spot. She tried to block out the loud voices drifting from the kitchen.

Hilda shouted, 'Well bloody done, Winnie! Thanks to your interfering, Rachel is moving miles away and taking my grandchildren with her!'

Winnie yelled back: 'Don't blame me! I'm as upset about it as you, but so long as Rachel is happy, then I'll be happy for her.'

'She ain't your flesh and blood. She's all I've got and if you'd kept your beak out, she'd be staying here in Battersea!'

'If I'd kept me beak out, Rachel would have been miserable and alone. Is that what you want, eh? Christ, Hilda, you're a lot of things but I never had you down as so selfish.'

'Selfish? Me? I want what's best for Rachel and the kids. Do you *really* believe that she'll be happy stuck in blinkin' Margate with *him*? She's giving up everything for that pervert.

Her business, her family – and for what? I'll tell you for what? For a man who ain't really a man!'

'Don't talk rubbish, Hilda. Roy is every bit a man and he makes Rachel happy. He loves the bones of her and worships the ground she walks on. Let's be honest, you're upset because she's moving away, and you'll miss her. This is about how *you* feel.'

'Yes! Yes, it's about how *I* feel! Of course I'm gonna bloody miss her. And the kids. I don't want them to go, Win.'

'Oh, Hilda, I know it's not easy, but you've got to let them go with your blessing. It's not as if you're never going to see them again. Think about the nice holidays we'll all have in Margate.'

Maureen's voice reached Grace's ears and she tensed, panic pumping through her veins. This was it. Everyone was going to discover the truth. They were all going to hate her and Winnie would probably throw her out. Grace shrank down as she pictured their scathing faces. Why, oh why hadn't she got rid of that damn sock with the stolen things hidden inside? She'd had every intention of throwing it away weeks ago. Now it was too late. Maureen had found it, and Grace would be revealed as an ungrateful thief.

'Erm, sorry to interrupt,' Maureen said, nervously, 'but this is important.'

'What is?' Winnie asked.

'I found this under Grace's bed.'

There was a stunned silence. Grace couldn't see what was happening in the kitchen, but she guessed that Maureen had handed Winnie the sock.

'Carmen's earrings? And—'

Heavy footsteps thudded along the hallway, coming closer.

Any second now the bedroom door would fly open and Winnie would barge in.

Grace thumped the side of her head. *You idiot,* she hissed in her mind. *You stupid idiot. You've ruined everything!* Her knuckles hurt as she thumped her head again and again, telling herself how foolish she'd been.

'Care to explain yourself, young lady?' Winnie asked, holding the sock towards her.

Grace glimpsed up through squinted eyes. She sucked desperately on the wool of her cuff before hitting herself hard on the side of the head again.

Maureen pushed past Winnie and dashed towards Grace. Crouching down, she threw her arms around the girl. 'What are you doing, Grace? Please don't do that to yourself,' she soothed, gently rocking her back and forth.

Tears streaked down Grace's face and she struggled to breathe through her snotty nose. 'I'm so sorry I-I'm an idiot,' she sobbed.

'No, Grace, you're not an idiot. Shush, now, calm down, it'll be all right.'

'It won't be all right though, will it? Winnie is going to throw me out.'

'No one mentioned throwing you out, Grace,' Winnie assured. 'Here, take my hanky and blow your nose.'

Grace looked up at Winnie and saw that she didn't appear to be as angry as she'd first looked. 'I'm really, really sorry,' she sniffed, accepting the handkerchief.

'Dry your eyes, love, and then you can tell us what this is all about.'

Grace swallowed hard. How could she explain that she hadn't stolen the things because she'd wanted them. She'd taken them because it had made her feel better and had given her a thrill for a few moments.

'You could have had my buttons if you'd asked. I would have given them to you,' Maureen said softly, and gave her a gentle squeeze.

Grace had already felt guilty; now she felt twice as bad.

Winnie thrust the sock forward. 'Here, take it,' she ordered. 'You're to return all the items and apologise to everyone, starting with Maureen.'

'I really am very sorry,' Grace sniffed.

'Apology accepted. And next time, if you want something, just ask.'

'Is that it? Aren't you going to chuck me out?'

Winnie sighed. 'No, love. You've not really had a chance to settle in and we've all been so wrapped up with this, that and the other, that we haven't really made much of an effort to help you feel at home. Everyone gets a second chance, you included. But I shall be very disappointed, Grace, if I catch you pinching anything from us again.'

'I won't, I promise.'

'Good. You've probably heard that Rachel, Martha and Benny are moving out. That means you'll have your own room soon. Like it or not, Grace, this is your home, and in the Battersea Tavern we treat each other with trust, honesty and respect. I shall expect the same courtesy from you from now on.'

Grace nodded, feeling deeply ashamed of her behaviour.

'Onwards and upwards, Grace,' Maureen smiled.

'Yes, onwards and upwards,' she parroted, grateful for Winnie's kind heart.

★

Later that day Maureen sat at a table in the pub with her brother, Stephen, and sipped on a glass of lemonade. 'She's not a bad kid,' Maureen explained, 'we all make mistakes. I just think she needs more attention.'

'We know what it's like to lose grandparents who raised us. But at least we had each other. Poor Grace doesn't have anyone else. She's lucky to have all of you.'

'I still miss gran and granddad. I can't walk down the road where their house was.'

'You wouldn't recognise the house now. It's been repaired since the fire and I've heard a family from India are living in it now.'

'Wow, that's very exotic. I hope they'll be as happy in the house as we were.'

Stephen glanced at his watch.

'Am I keeping you from something important?' Maureen asked.

'No. I, erm, I said I'd meet Vic in here.'

Maureen's eyes stretched wide, and she spluttered on her lemonade. 'Vic? Your best mate from school?'

'Yes.'

'He's coming here?'

'Yeah. He was really keen to meet in here when I told him you live and work in the pub.'

'Blimey, I haven't seen Vic since we were at school and I had a bit of a crush on him then.'

'I reckon he had one on you too. His eyes lit up when I mentioned your name.'

'Don't be daft! I was always just your little sister. I doubt that Vic even realised that I existed.'

'Hmm, I think you might be surprised.'

'Oh, Gawd, *really*?' Maureen asked, feeling her cheeks flaming red.

'Here he is,' Stephen said, nodding his head towards the door.

Maureen gawped at the tall, slender man walking confidently towards their table. Vic had hardly changed. His copper-coloured hair was greased back, making it look darker than Maureen remembered. As he stood in front of them, Vic's dark green eyes held hers.

'Hello, mate. You remember my little sis, Maureen?'

'How could I forget,' Vic smiled.

His soft, low voice and the way he held her gaze left Maureen tingling all over. She quickly averted her eyes, hoping that Vic hadn't noticed how she felt.

'What are you drinking, mate?' Stephen asked, rising to his feet.

'I'll get them in,' Vic insisted.

'Great, mine's half a bitter,' Stephen said.

'And for the pretty lady?'

'Oh, erm, just a lemonade for me, thanks,' Maureen answered. Butterflies fluttered in her stomach and her heart rate had doubled. Vic was just as good-looking as he had been all those years ago. She remembered how Brancher, her violent husband still behind bars, had been unkind about Vic. Looking back, Maureen could see now that Brancher had been jealous of Vic. And with good reason. Vic had left Battersea for a promising career as an engineer in America. She wondered what had brought him back to his hometown – and if he was married.

With Vic at the bar, Maureen leaned closer to her brother. 'How come he's in Battersea?' she asked.

'He came back for his mother's funeral. And then the company he was working for in America set up a manufacturing plant in Croydon, so Vic was asked to stay in England and run the Croydon branch.'

'Blimey, he's done all right for himself. Is he living in Battersea?'

'No, he's living closer to work. But he's talked about how much he's missed the place and mentioned that he might look for something in the area.'

'One half a bitter and a lemonade,' Vic said, placing the drinks on the table. 'It's great to see you, Maureen. I couldn't believe it when I ran into Stephen, and he told me you were living here.'

Maureen noticed that he'd picked up a bit of an American accent. She thought it suited him and made him sound quite sophisticated. 'Stephen said you're considering moving back to Battersea?'

'I am, and all the more so now I know that you're here.'

Maureen knew she was blushing. She glanced at her brother who looked as though he was trying not to laugh.

'Shall I leave you two to it?' Stephen teased.

'Sorry, pal,' Vic said. 'But would it be all right with you if I was to ask your beautiful sister to go out with me for dinner?'

'Fill your boots,' Stephen answered.

Maureen was pleased to have her brother's approval, but she wished she could stop herself from flushing red.

'Would you join me for dinner tonight, Maureen? Please, say you will.'

She didn't hesitate and nodded her head.

'Great. I know a nice place in Clapham. Do you like French cuisine?'

'I dunno. I like pie, mash and liquor or rock and chips. Do the French eat fish and chips?'

'They eat snails,' Stephen chuckled.

'Yuk, I ain't eating snails!' Maureen exclaimed, wrinkling her nose.

'Frog's legs?' Stephen mocked.

'Definitely not! Are you kidding me? No wonder the French surrendered to Hitler. They probably thought they'd get to eat better food under German rule.'

Vic laughed. 'If the lady likes fish and chips, then that's what we shall have,' he announced, holding his glass aloft. 'Cheers,' he said, and waited for Maureen to lift her glass before clinking it.

'Cheers,' she repeated, discreetly pinching her thigh under the table to make sure she wasn't dreaming. Dinner with Victor Stewart tonight. It felt too good to be true!

'Who's that bloke?' Winnie discreetly asked Maureen.

'My brother's friend from school. He's taking me out later. Oh, Win, I'm in such a tizzy. I don't know what to wear, and I can't ask Rachel because she's too busy packing.'

'Don't worry, you'll look smashing in anything you wear. What's his name?'

'Victor Stewart. He's been living in America, but he might be moving back to Battersea.'

'I can see by the soppy smile on your face that you're quite taken with him. It's about time you got out and found yourself a nice fella.'

'I do like him, Winnie, but I'm a nervous wreck.'

'You'll be fine, love. Just try to relax and enjoy the moment.'

Carmen came to stand beside Winnie. 'Have I missed something?' she asked.

'Winnie will fill you in,' Maureen grinned as she headed back to the table.

'Well?' Carmen asked.

'That bloke over there with Stephen is taking Maureen out to dinner tonight,' Winnie explained.

'Oh, is he. And what do we know about him?'

Winnie rolled her eyes. 'It's all right, we don't need to give him the once over. Victor is an old mate of Stephen's.'

Hilda came down the stairs, puffing and panting. 'I've been helping Rachel with the packing. Do you know, she's just informed me that her and Roy aren't getting married before they leave.'

'Eh?' Winnie said, frowning.

'She said they want to leave Battersea as soon as possible and will tie the knot in Margate.'

'They're going to live in sin?' Carmen asked, sounding astonished.

Hilda's lips pursed. 'Apparently so. I've told her that it's not a good idea to start a new life on the wrong foot. I've no doubt that tongues will wag in Margate just as much as they do here. But she's adamant, and you know how stubborn she can be.'

'For Christ's sake, you'll have to talk to her, Winnie,' Carmen said, sharply.

Winnie shook her head. 'If Rachel won't listen to her mother, then she won't take no notice of anything I say. At the end of the day, she's a sensible girl and if she's happy, what does it really matter?'

'You approve of her living with Roy before they're married?' Hilda asked.

Winnie shrugged. 'It's only a matter of a bit of paperwork and a wedding ring. I don't see what the problem is.'

Carmen tutted, and then said in a disapproving tone, 'I'm surprised at you, Winnie.'

'Leave off, the pair of you. You're both overreacting. They'll be married soon enough and then everything will be above board. 'Ere, fancy that, eh? A wedding in Margate. We shall have to buy new hats, ladies.'

'I've got to go,' Hilda announced with urgency. 'This is all too much for me to take in and if I stay here a minute longer I'll be begging you for a drink. Sorry about losing my rag earlier, Win. I'll see you tomorrow.'

Winnie worried about Hilda. The woman still didn't have complete control of her drinking. Granted, she's stayed sober for years, mostly, but with Rachel and the kids moving away, Winnie feared that Hilda might not have the motivation to stay off the booze. And the last thing that Winnie needed was drunken Hilda rearing her ugly head.

16

'Happy New Year to my future husband,' Rachel cooed, smiling lovingly at Roy.

'Here's to our new life,' Roy said, and gently pressed his lips on hers. 'It sounds like they're having a good time downstairs. Wouldn't you rather be joining in the celebrations?'

'No,' Rachel replied. 'I've seen enough parties at the Battersea Tavern to last me a lifetime. I'd much rather be up here with you.' She could imagine what would be said in the pub if Roy showed his face. It wouldn't be comfortable for either of them. In the kitchen, away from the local customers, she could protect Roy from their spitefulness. 'Mum helped me pack earlier although she's none too happy about us living together before we're married. Anyway, I'm just about all done now. I don't see the point in hanging around, Roy, we might as well leave as soon as possible.'

'The sooner, the better for me. My lodgings are awful, I can't wait to get out of there.'

'What's stopping us from leaving in a couple of days then?'

'Housing, Rachel. We need somewhere to live.'

'I've got a few bob saved and I know you have too. We

could find a hotel for a few nights whilst we look for a house to rent,' she suggested. 'It would be like a bit of a holiday.'

'Cor, you really are eager to get away,' he chortled.

'I just want us to be together.'

'No regrets?'

'None,' Rachel smiled. 'I've already made a deal with Terry for my shellfish stall. He's paying me a fair price for the business.'

'Terence Card? He's taking on your stall?'

'Yes. Terry has a bullet lodged in his spine. An injury from the war. The doctor said it would be dangerous to operate and if the bullet moves, he could be left paralysed. It's heavy work at the bakery, so when I mentioned selling up my business, he snapped my hand off for it.'

'That's great!'

'Yep, it really is. I feel like I'm keeping the business in the family. I know Terry isn't related to me, but he was Jan's husband and Jan was like a sister to me, so in my books, that makes him family.'

'But Jan wasn't Winnie's daughter, was she?'

'No, not by blood. But Winnie believed that Jan was the baby she'd had taken from her at birth. When it turned out that Jan wasn't, she still took her on as her own. They needed each other. Winnie saved Jan from a terrible life with her real mum. And the bond they had was so strong until the cancer killed Jan.'

'Tragic.'

'It was, Roy. It was so sad. Terry was in France, fighting the Jerries, and Jan didn't want Terry to know that she was dying, but once she'd passed away, Winnie wrote to him and told him. He was a broken man for a long time. It took him ages to get back on his feet. So it's smashing that he's taking over my business, and it's more money in the coffers for us. You see, we'll be all right. So why delay moving away? Let's go.'

'All right then, Margate here we come!'

'Just one thing, Roy – Mum was right about people disapproving of us living together. So, when we get to Margate, I'm going to call myself Mrs Russel. But I'll need a wedding ring.'

'I'll buy you a ring, Mrs Russel, and I'll be honoured to put it on your finger.'

Rachel knew she was doing the right thing, but she still felt uneasy, though she wouldn't admit it to Roy. Leaving her home, her family and her business was a big move. She was following her heart, refusing to listen to the worries in her head. *Everything will be fine,* she told herself. *This is exciting! You and the kids will be happy. A new year and a new life.* Memories of David Berry would never haunt her again.

Carmen had hurried down to the cellar to change a barrel, leaving Winnie rushed off her feet serving customers and collecting empty glasses. She'd normally be closing the doors at ten o'clock, but tonight she was staying open to see in 1953. She took a deep breath and a moment to look around her smoke-filled, packed pub. It was approaching midnight and spirits were high. Maureen was sitting at a corner table, clearly enjoying Vic's company. Piano Pete had paused on the piano, preparing himself to play 'Auld Lang Syne'. Laughter and merriment abounded. For one evening, Winnie's customers had left their woes at the door and were enjoying the festivities. It was a sharp contrast to the struggles of everyday life. Some were mourning the loss of their loved ones during the war. Families had been ripped apart and many were homeless too. The war had taken a terrible toll and the country had been left on its knees and in great debt. Rationing and queues for food and coal were getting everyone down. And there were those who were still fighting for their lives and dying from the after-effects of the recent heavy smog. Yet tonight, even Winnie had put on a brave face and had lifted her skirts to a knees-up around the piano. But behind her jolly smile, Winnie's heart was breaking.

'You all right?' Carmen asked.

'Yes, tickety-boo,' Winnie fibbed.

'No, you're not, are you?'

'I'm fine.'

'You can't kid a kidder,' Carmen said, and rubbed her hand up Winnie's arm. 'It's Rachel and the kids, isn't it?'

Winnie felt a suffocating lump in her throat and tried to swallow it down. She nodded at Carmen but couldn't speak for fear of tears erupting.

'I knew it. I knew you weren't happy about them leaving. Try not to worry, Win, I'm sure they'll be fine.'

Again, Winnie nodded. She had no doubt that they would be *fine*. She was sure that Rachel, Martha and Benny would enjoy their new lives. It would be a wonderful adventure for the kids, and Winnie had never seen Rachel looking happier. Nonetheless, Winnie's heart was breaking because she knew how much she was going to miss them.

As if reading Winnie's mind, Carmen reassured, 'We'll get the train to Margate at least once a month. And the kids can come and stay here during the school holidays. It's going to be different, but it won't be the end of the world.'

Winnie sniffed and jutted her chin forward. She would

not cry. She refused to allow any tears in public. She couldn't even cry into her pillow because Carmen slept in a bed next to hers. The only place that Winnie could cry in private was on the loo. But she hadn't yet. She'd fought hard to keep her emotions in check. But holding back the tears hadn't stopped the pain.

Winnie felt a rush of cold air as the pub door opened again, snapping her from her thoughts. Looking around, she didn't think she could fit many more customers into her pub, and she was struggling to keep up with the demand for clean glasses.

'Oh no!' Carmen moaned.

'What?' Winnie asked.

Her eyes followed Carmen's hard stare and her heart dropped when she saw Alan had walked in. 'What's he doing here? He's taking diabolical liberties!'

'I'll deal with him,' Carmen ground out.

Winnie placed a staying hand on Carmen's arm. 'No. I'll deal with him. If it's a fight he wants, then he'll bloody well get one from me!'

Marching from behind the bar, Winnie had to push past the revellers who were all keen to wish her a happy new year. Her lips set in a grim line; she rolled up the sleeves of her tightly fitting dress that stretched across her stomach.

Looking up at Alan with her hands on her hips, she barked, 'You ain't welcome here. Get out!'

'I've heard my brother's here.'

'So what if he is? You ain't seeing him and he don't want to see you.'

'Ha, you're still protecting the fairy. Is he hiding behind your skirt?'

'Sling your hook, Alan, or else!'

'*Or else* what? What you gonna do, grandma?'

Winnie hadn't noticed that Terry had come to stand behind her. He gently eased her to one side and stepped closer to Alan.

'You heard, Mrs Berry – piss off.'

Winnie saw Alan's fists clench at his side. If he dared to punch Terry, he could dislodge the bullet in the man's spine. Panic made her react. She shoved Alan hard, pushing him back. 'I won't tell you again,' she growled. 'Get out of my pub!'

Alan smirked. 'All right, old girl, hold your horses. I only came to tell Roy that our dad is in the hospital. If it was down to me, I'd have nothing to do with the poofter, but me dad is asking for him.'

Winnie's heart was pumping fast. She didn't know whether she should believe Alan. But giving him the benefit of the doubt, she asked, 'Is Doug all right?'

'No, he ain't. Roy needs to see him tomorrow, before it's too late.'

Winnie nodded. 'All right, I'll tell him.'

'He's in the Bolingbroke. Let Roy know that he's to meet me outside at twelve and I'll take him to our dad.'

'I will, and I'm sorry about Doug, Alan.'

'Yeah, me an' all,' Alan said glumly, before turning and leaving the pub.

As Winnie made her way back to the bar, someone grabbed her arm. Spinning around, she saw Hilda, looking furious.

'Was that Alan I saw walking out of here?' Hilda demanded to know.

'Yes.'

'Gawd, I wish I'd given him a piece of my mind! It's all his bleedin' fault that Rachel is leaving. If Alan had kept his trap shut, my girl wouldn't be running off with a bloke who wears frocks!'

'Pack it in, Hilda. You've got to stop talking about Roy like that. It's bad enough hearing my customers being unkind about him, without it coming from you an' all.'

'I'm only speaking as I find. We both know that Roy ain't good enough for Rachel.'

'No, Hilda, you're wrong. What Roy did doesn't make him a bad person. Christ, when did you become so flippin' bitter, eh?'

'I'm not bitter, Win, I just want more for my girl than her shacking up with a ... a whatever he is! Anyway, what did Alan want?'

'Doug's in hospital and it sounds like he might be dying. He's asked to see Roy.'

'Oh,' Hilda said, finally silenced.

'Happy New Year,' Winnie added with a hint of sarcasm.

'Yeah – and you.'

Back behind the bar, Winnie updated Carmen on what Alan had said. 'I should pop upstairs and tell Roy.'

'I wouldn't,' Carmen advised. 'They won't let him in the hospital tonight to see his dad. I'd wait until tomorrow to tell him.'

'Do you really think so?'

'Yes. There's nothing he can do now. I'll come with you first thing in the morning, and we can tell him together.'

'Thanks, love,' Winnie said, raising her voice over the sound of her customers counting down the seconds until the clock struck midnight.

Four, three, two, one ... The pub burst into rapturous wishes of *Happy New Year* and, right on cue, Piano Pete began playing 'Auld Lang Syne' with everyone joining in and singing along. As Winnie belted out the words, she plastered on a smile. Then, as she glanced along the bar, her heart plummeted even further down when she saw Hilda sneakily place an empty glass on the counter. Winnie couldn't be sure, but she thought Hilda had necked a double whisky. That meant only one thing – trouble!

17

Grace hadn't felt like celebrating the new year and the joyous sounds from downstairs had been a cruel reminder of how much she missed her gran. She'd been awake but pretending to be asleep when she'd heard Maureen tiptoe into bed in the early hours of the morning. And now, as Maureen pulled open the curtains to allow the morning light to flood the small room, Grace kept her eyes squeezed tightly closed.

'Happy New Year,' Maureen chirped, cheerily. 'It's the first day of 1953. Let's hope it's going to be better than 1952. Come on, sleepyhead. Wake up, or you'll miss breakfast.'

'I'm not hungry,' Grace groaned, and pulled the blankets up and under her chin.

'You can't lay in bed all day. Winnie will expect us all to muck in and clean up the pub from last night.'

Grace ignored Maureen and rolled over with her back to the woman. Why should she help to clean up? She hadn't been invited to the party. *You're too young,* Carmen had said. Not that Grace had wanted to be downstairs. She found the smoke from everyone's cigarettes choking. And she didn't like the smell of stale beer. The musty odour often drifted up the stairs, turning Grace's stomach.

Maureen huffed and slipped out of the bedroom, closing the door behind her. Grace wanted to go back to sleep, but her mind was turning with grim thoughts. She wondered who would miss her if she died. No one, she decided. In fact, everyone would likely be pleased if she passed away. It would be one less burden for them all to bear. *That's what I am. I'm a burden,* she thought.

A knock on the door startled her and when it opened, she heard Winnie's voice.

'I need you up and dressed,' the woman ordered. 'There's much to do and many hands make light work.'

Grace kept her eyes closed.

'I know you're awake. Come on, up you get.'

She lay still.

'Right, I'm not having this!' Winnie exclaimed.

Grace heard Winnie's steps coming closer and then she felt the blankets being whipped off her.

'Up! Now!'

Opening her eyes, she saw Winnie glaring down at her.

'You're not skiving out of doing some work. Everyone's got jobs to do today, including you.'

'All right,' Grace whined.

'Good. Five minutes and then I want to see you in the kitchen. You can't work on an empty stomach.'

Winnie wasn't a woman to argue with, so Grace nodded and when she'd wearily pushed herself out of bed, Winnie left her to get dressed in peace. But instead of going to the kitchen, Grace pulled on her coat and crept down the stairs, quietly slipping out of the back door.

The streets were quieter than usual. Grace tucked her hands into her coat pocket and headed towards her old house that she'd shared with her gran. Reaching the front door she stood staring at the brass knocker that had lost its shine and the step that hadn't been swept. Her gran would be disappointed. And weeds had grown through the cracks of the pavement outside. Bertha had only been dead a few weeks, but already the house looked unloved. And that's how Grace felt too – unloved. Happy memories of home flooded her mind. As tears fell down Grace's cheeks she reminisced about how life had been behind the front door, she noticed the front room curtain twitch. Wiping away her tears, Grace found herself looking into the curious eyes of a young lad with strawberry-blond hair. The boy smiled and waved through the window. Grace tried to smile back but she resented seeing the lad in *her* home. It should have been her looking through the window from the inside, with her gran in the kitchen boiling the kettle and baking something nice.

The front door opened and a young woman stood there with a baby in her arms.

'Can I help you?' the woman asked.

A surge of rage rose in Grace. Bending down, she picked up a small stone and threw it with force at the window. Standing wide-eyed, she watched a crack spread through the pane of glass. The little boy on the other side looked scared and began crying.

'What are you doing?' the woman asked, alarmed, as she stepped towards Grace.

Grace spun around and ran. She ran to the end of the street and around the corner, and she kept running until she was out of breath and felt sick. Gasping to pull air into her lungs and wet with sweat, Grace flopped onto the steps that led down to the muddy banks of the Thames. There she sat, hiding, hoping that the police weren't after her. She wasn't sure what had come over her. Why had she felt so angry? Why had she deliberately set out to smash the window? Grace didn't know the answers. She only knew that she wanted life to go back to how it was. To how it had been before her beloved gran had died.

'Where has that girl got to?' Winnie asked.

'Her coat has gone,' Maureen answered.

'Well, I'm sure she'll come home when she's hungry enough. In the meantime, there's plenty to do.'

'I'll go and see Roy now,' Rachel said, grimly. 'I can't say I'm looking forward to telling him about his dad. We were going to set off to Margate tomorrow, but I doubt that Roy will want to leave while his dad is in hospital.'

'Tomorrow?' Winnie spat, incredulously.

'Yes. I know it's a bit sudden, but I think it'll be for the best.'

'Have you told your mum?' Carmen asked.

'I'll pop into hers on the way back from Roy's.'

'I-I wasn't expecting you to be leaving so soon,' Winnie said, pulling out a seat at the table.

Rachel could see that Winnie appeared devastated and guilt jabbed at her heart. Winnie had been like a mum to Rachel, and she knew she was breaking the woman's heart by taking Martha so far away, especially right on top of David's death. 'I'm sorry, Win, but Roy can't stay in Battersea, and he said the lodging he's in are absolutely awful, but he can't find anything else available at this time of year.'

'I know, love, you don't need to explain. It's just a bit of a shock to find out you're going this quickly. I don't know why, but I assumed you'd be here for at least a few more weeks. Make sure you let your mum know before she finds out from anyone else.'

'I will,' Rachel promised. 'I'll go straight there after I've seen Roy.'

Trotting down the stairs, Rachel guessed that Winnie was fighting from crying. She'd seen the unshed tears in the woman's eyes. She didn't like to see Winnie upset, so as soon as she and Roy were settled in Margate, she'd send an invite to her. *It would be nice for Winnie to stay for at least a few days with me in Margate. The woman could do with a holiday,* she reasoned. But with Doug's ill-health looming over them, her departure might not be as imminent as they'd planned.

Rachel stood on the steps outside of Roy's lodgings. He wasn't permitted to invite guests inside. Rachel had said she was grateful as she didn't fancy stepping foot into the rundown building, and Roy couldn't blame her.

'What's wrong with him?' Roy asked on hearing the news about his dad.

'I don't know. Alan only said that he's in the hospital.'

'He must have had an accident at work or something. I'm surprised my dad wants to see me, though. The way he looked at me on Christmas Day, I thought he hated me.'

'Would you like me to come with you?' Rachel offered.

'No, thanks. I don't know what my dad wants to say to me and knowing him it won't be decent for a lady to hear.'

'I'm going to see my mum. Winnie said I need to let her know that we'll be leaving soon.'

'Tomorrow, *Mrs Russel,* we'll be leaving tomorrow.'

'But what about your dad? Don't you want to stay until he's out of hospital?'

'No. I'll listen to what he has to say for himself and then I couldn't care less if I never see him or my brother again.'

'All right. In that case, I'll see you later. Will you call in on your way home from the hospital? You could have your dinner with us tonight. I reckon Winnie will want to make a fuss, our last evening all together.'

'That will be great, so long as I'm welcome.'

'Of course you are, especially with Martha. Good luck with your dad. See you soon.'

Roy watched as Rachel walked away. He admired the slight wiggle of her hips and the way her shining blonde hair bounced up and down with each step she took. *I'm a lucky fella,* he thought, proudly. But then his mind wandered to his father. He wasn't looking forward to seeing the man, or his brother, and his stomach knotted with nerves.

Roy tapped a cigarette out of his packet and checked the time on his watch. If he left now and took a slow meander to the hospital, he'd be there just before twelve. As he made his way towards the hospital, he tried to push all thoughts of Alan and his dad from his mind, instead pondering how life would be in Margate with Rachel and the kids. She'd made it clear that she didn't want any more children and Roy was fine with that. He had a ready-made family and he'd grown very fond of Martha and Benny. They were good kids, and he was looking forward to being their father, though he hoped he'd be up to the job. He reasoned that he couldn't be any worse a father than his own dad had been. In fact, Roy thought adamantly he'd be a much better dad than

Doug Russel. The man was vile … and Roy didn't even like to call him *dad*.

Reaching the hospital, Roy looked around for his brother. 'Oi, over here!'

He turned around and saw Alan gesturing to him. Walking to his brother, he could feel his body tensing. Just the sight of Alan made Roy feel uneasy.

'How's Dad?' Roy asked.

'This way,' Alan instructed, and walked ahead.

Roy followed, wondering why his brother was leading him around the back of the hospital instead of through the main entrance. 'Where are we going?' he asked, his hackles rising.

'A shortcut,' Alan answered without a glance back.

A tattered sign read *Laundry* and then Alan led Roy past a whitewashed building and a rubbish collection area. Something didn't feel right.

'Down here,' Alan instructed, opening a tall gate that went to a narrow alley between two high buildings.

'Are you sure about this?' Roy asked.

Alan stopped walking and turned to face him, an intimidating, twisted smile on his face. 'Yeah, I'm sure,' he derided.

Roy was confused. 'What are we doing here? Where's Dad?'

'I'm right behind you,' Doug's voice sneered.

Roy looked over his shoulder and saw his dad standing there. It quickly dawned on him that he'd been tricked, and he knew what their intentions were. He wanted to run, but there was no escaping the alley. Alan was in front and his father had blocked his path behind him.

'Please,' Roy said, holding his hands in front of him, 'please don't do this.'

'You ain't got them old nags in the pub looking after you now,' Alan scorned.

Roy turned to his father. 'Please, Dad, I'm begging you.'

Doug glared with disdain. 'Get down on your knees then. Let me see you beg properly.'

Roy dropped to his knees. 'Don't hurt me, please, Dad,' he implored, his heart racing with fear.

'I never want to hear you call me dad again. You ain't no son of mine.'

Alan leaned over Roy. 'You make us feel sick, you fucking poofter.'

Roy hunkered down, holding his hands over his head. 'I ain't a poof, I swear I ain't.'

'You're a fucking liar and a nancy boy,' Alan retorted, and spat on Roy's head.

Doug sniggered. 'Go on, son, hit him. Fucking hit him!'

Roy tried to stand on his feet, but he felt an agonising blow to his face and heard his nose crack. Blood poured from his nostrils and his eyes watered. His brother punched him again, leaving Roy feeling dazed.

'Get up and fight me,' Alan insisted. 'Come on, fight me, nancy boy!'

Roy, leaning on all fours, looked at his brother through bleary eyes.

'I said, fight me, you spineless fucker!' Alan roared, kicking his booted foot hard into Roy's stomach.

The force of the kick winded Roy, and he rolled over onto his back, coughing as he stared up at the grey sky.

'Get up!' Alan shouted. 'Get up and fucking fight!'

Roy groaned, a metallic taste in his mouth which he knew

was his own blood. 'I won't fight you,' he whimpered, pain ripping through his body.

His refusal to fight didn't stop Alan from kicking him again, this time viciously in the ribs. Then, standing over Roy, Alan grabbed the front of his bloodied shirt and pulled Roy up towards him. Roy saw hatred in his brother's eyes as Alan's fist came towards his face.

The savageness of Alan's chin punch snapped Roy's head back. Again and again, Alan thumped him until he could feel himself losing consciousness.

The last thing he heard was his dad's wicked laughter and then him saying, 'That'll teach him, the filthy bastard.'

18

Winnie answered a knock at the back door, irked at being disturbed. Whilst Maureen was at Hilda's baking a 'good luck' cake, Winnie had been busy with Carmen, preparing a special evening meal to say a proper goodbye to Rachel and the grandchildren. She pulled open the door to find a young woman standing on her step with a pram in front of her and a lad holding her hand.

'Mrs Berry?' the woman asked.

'Yeah, that's me.'

'I believe that Grace Lockwood is in your charge.'

'Yeah, what of it?'

'She was at my house today and she smashed a window.'

'I beg your pardon? And who are you?'

'I'm Mrs Westbrooke and you heard me. Grace threw a stone at my window and smashed it. What are you gonna do about it?'

'Nothing, not until I know all the facts,' Winnie answered indignantly.

'The facts speak for themselves. I live in the house where Grace used to live. A neighbour spotted her standing outside and saw Grace throw the stone. I saw it with my own eyes too.'

'Really? You're sure it was Grace?'

'Yes, the neighbour recognised her.'

'Well, I must apologise for Grace's behaviour. Her gran passed away just a few weeks ago. She's been having a tough time coming to terms with it.'

'I'm sure she has but your apology doesn't fix my broken window,' the woman said, brusquely.

'I'll pay for any damage done by Grace, and believe you me, the girl will be punished for what she's done. Wait there a moment, I'll get me purse.'

Winnie hurried up the stairs.

Rachel was standing at the top. 'Is that Roy?' she asked, looking down the stairs past Winnie.

'No.'

'He should have been here ages ago. I wonder what's keeping him.'

Winnie found her handbag on the end of her bed and pulled out her purse. Rushing back down the stairs, she thrust several coins into Mrs Westbrooke's hand, saying, 'That should more than cover the cost of the window.'

'She scared the life out of my boy,' the woman said, pointing at the lad beside her.

'Like I said, I'm sorry for Grace's behaviour and I'll see to it that she doesn't bother you again.'

'What about my boy? He's terrified and is too scared to go back home.'

'I'm sure a few sweets will make him feel better,' Winnie replied, offering Mrs Westbrooke some extra coins.

'And the inconvenience it's caused me? It's taken my precious time to come round here.'

'If you're after more money out of me, then you can get on your bike, woman. Can you see *fool* written across my head? No, you can't, so bugger orf!'

'How dare you speak to me like that! I could have had the coppers on to Grace and this is the thanks I get?'

'I'll have the coppers on to you if you don't clear orf,' Winnie warned. 'Good day to you, Mrs Westbrooke,' she said, calmly, then slammed the door shut in the woman's face.

Drawing in a deep breath, Winnie wondered where Grace was and how she should approach the girl about her unacceptable behaviour.

Trudging back up the stairs, she found Rachel in the kitchen, peering out of the window. 'I'm getting worried about Roy. Do you think something could have happened to him?' she asked.

'I wouldn't have thought so, love. He's probably just spending some time with his dad. We don't know what's wrong with Doug. Maybe the man is dying and Roy is sitting with him.'

'I've got a bad feeling, Win ...'

'You know you can be a bit of a worrier, Rachel. I'm sure everything is fine.'

'No, Winnie, I don't think it is. Remember I had this feeling before and then what Leena said she saw in the tarot cards? I'm sorry to say it, but Leena was right about the violent death. And what if my feeling is right again?'

'Stop it, Rachel. You'll worry yourself into an early grave. Go and get in the bath like you said you was going to do. Relax. Dinner will be ready soon.'

'Who was at the door?' Carmen asked as she whipped batter.

'A woman asking for money to repair a window that Grace smashed.'

'*What*?'

'Grace went round to her old home and threw a stone at the window.'

'Oh dear.'

'I'll be having words with her when she bothers to come home.'

Maureen popped her head around the door. 'Is it all clear in here?' she asked.

'Yes, Rachel's in the bath,' Winnie answered. 'Have you got the cake ready?'

'Yep, and it looks smashing.'

'How was Hilda?' Winnie asked, suspiciously.

'She wasn't herself, but that's understandable because she's upset about Rachel leaving.'

Winnie wanted to ask Maureen if she'd witnessed Hilda drinking or if there was any evidence laying around the flat of the woman boozing. But she hoped that what she'd seen the night before had been a one-off. And if Hilda had been drunk today, Winnie believed that Maureen wouldn't be stupid enough to keep that sort of information to herself.

'For Gawd's sake, who now?' Winnie moaned when she heard another knock on the back door.

'I'll see to it,' Maureen offered, carefully putting the cake in the larder, before almost skipping towards the door.

'You've got a spring in your step, Maureen,' Winnie smiled.

'Yeah, I suppose I have. It's Vic. He's made me so happy.'

'Aw, it's lovely to see you like this.'

'I'm in love, Winnie. Head over flippin' heels in love!'

Minutes later, Maureen returned to the kitchen looking pale.

'What's wrong?' Carmen asked.

Maureen swallowed hard. 'That was Piano Pete ... he said Roy is in the hospital.'

'Yes, he is. He went to see Doug.'

'No, Winnie, Pete reckons Roy was attacked. He's in a bad way. How – how do I tell Rachel?'

Winnie felt a cold shiver run down her spine. Rachel had said she'd had a bad feeling. She'd dismissed the girl's worries, but Rachel had been right to be concerned. *Poor Roy*, she thought, silently hoping that he'd be all right. Fury simmered in the pit of her stomach. She knew full well who had attacked Roy. And for him to have ended up in the hospital, then Alan must have given his brother one hell of a beating.

19

Rachel sat beside Roy's hospital bed, willing him to open his swollen eyes. The doctors had warned her there might be permanent damage to his brain and that until Roy woke from the coma, they wouldn't know the extent of his injuries. *Internal bleeding, enlarged spleen, punctured lung...* Rachel had heard the doctor's list, but only the words *brain damage* had sunk in.

Tears welled in her eyes as she gazed at Roy, distraught. He was almost unrecognisable and heavily bandaged. 'Can you hear me, Roy?' she asked, holding his hand and hoping that he'd give hers a gentle squeeze. But there was no response.

A kindly nurse approached and checked Roy's pulse. 'You should leave now, Miss Robb. Mr Russel needs to rest.'

'He's unconscious. How much more rest can he have?' Rachel hissed.

'There's nothing you can do here. Mr Russel is stable and the doctor isn't expecting any immediate change in his condition. Go home and come back tomorrow.'

Rachel was reluctant to leave Roy's side, but she knew the nurse wouldn't allow her to stay any longer. As she pulled her coat on, she saw two policemen standing at the end of the small ward, talking to the doctor. A haze of cigarette smoke swirled around them. The doctor was shaking his head and the policemen looked disappointed.

'They're here to speak to Mr Russel when he wakes,' the nurse explained.

'Why?'

'To question him about the attack. The doctor has already told them that he'll call the station when Mr Russel is able to answer questions, but they're very persistent.'

'Roy only came to the hospital to visit his dad. I can't believe that he's ended up in here too. Does his dad know? And his brother, Alan, has he been informed?'

'I'm sorry, Miss Robb, but Mr Russel's father isn't in this hospital. The police have tried to locate him without success.'

'What do you mean? Roy had arranged to meet Alan outside at midday. Alan was going to bring Roy to see their father.'

'I, erm, I think you need to give the police officers this information.'

Rachel nodded, her eyes staring along the ward towards the policemen. Her mind whirled as the puzzle of who it was who'd attacked Roy began to fall in to place. But surely Alan hadn't inflicted this much damage on his own brother? Slowly walking towards the policemen, Rachel felt sick. Covering her mouth, she heaved.

'Hold on,' the nurse instructed, dashing away.

Rachel retched again, gagging on the vomit she'd swallowed down.

The nurse appeared, shoving a bowl into Rachel's hands. 'It's all right,' she soothed. 'There you go,' she said.

Rachel could feel the nurse gently rubbing her back as she violently vomited into the bowl.

'Sorry,' she croaked, as the nurse took the bowl from her hands.

'I'll fetch you a glass of water.'

Fishing in her handbag, Rachel found a handkerchief and dabbed her mouth. Then coughing to clear her throat, she approached the policemen. 'I have information about the men who attacked my fiancé, Roy Russel.'

The coppers looked at one another and then indicated to Rachel to go into a side room off the ward. She was invited to take a seat, but before sitting Rachel blurted everything she knew about Alan arranging to meet Roy.

One policeman took notes, the other asked questions. She could tell by the look on the copper's face that he suspected that Alan had attacked Roy, and he also thought that Doug might have been involved too.

'And you've no idea where Mr Russel's brother and father are?'

'No,' Rachel answered. 'Do you think they've gone on the run?'

'It's more than likely. The porter who found Mr Russel thought he was dead. I've no doubt that if it was his brother who attacked him, then he would have thought the same so he'll be wanting to avoid the law. Murder is punishable with the death penalty, after all.'

'I hope you catch 'em,' Rachel raged, 'And when you do, I hope they both hang for what they've done!'

20

Nearly a week had passed. Winnie had tried her best to keep Rachel positive, but the poor girl was distraught and the mood above the Battersea Tavern was low. They were losing hope. Nobody believed that Roy would ever wake up, and though they kept their thoughts to themselves, Winnie knew what they were thinking. If she was honest, she thought the same.

Rachel had left early to go to the hospital again. Winnie worried about her and wished she could do more to help. She'd tried to encourage Rachel to eat, but the young woman couldn't face food, and Winnie could see that she hadn't been sleeping. The dark circles that ringed her eyes were a giveaway.

Winnie sat at the kitchen table with Carmen, Maureen and Hilda, all of them sombre, and as she chewed on a bit of toast, she searched for something to say, something that might cheer everyone up. But her mind was blank.

Hearing a knock on the back door, Winnie heaved her body up, saying, 'I'll go.'

'If it's hawkers again, tell them to bugger off,' Carmen moaned.

It felt cold downstairs, and even colder when Winnie pulled open the back door.

'Morning, Pete,' she greeted, trying to make herself smile. 'What brings you here so early?'

The man beamed an almost toothless smile at Winnie.

'Spit it out then,' Winnie encouraged. 'You're looking bloomin' happy about something, and we could do with a bit of joy being spread around here.'

'It's Roy, Winnie. Me sister was on his ward this morning, and she said he's awake!'

'Are you sure?'

'Yeah. She said there was a right commotion around his bed, doctors and nurses all fussing. At first she'd thought that Roy had pegged it. But no, Winnie, the complete opposite. He's awake!'

'Oh, Pete, that's bloody brilliant! Thanks so much for letting me know. I can't wait to tell the others. Do you want to come in?'

'No, thanks, Winnie. I've got to see a man about a dog. I'll be back later.'

Winnie couldn't wipe the grin from her face as she rushed up the stairs and into the kitchen.

'Ladies, I've got some good news,' she exclaimed. 'Piano Pete popped by to let us know that Roy has woken up!'

'That's smashing, Win. Rachel will be so relieved,' Maureen smiled.

'Well, let's not get too excited just yet, eh. He's probably got a long road of recovery ahead, and the doctors won't know if he's been left with any permanent damage yet, I shouldn't think.'

Carmen spoke. 'Rachel will know more when she gets back from the hospital later.'

'I can't believe he's been asleep for six days,' Maureen said, shaking her head. 'Let's hope his brain has healed itself whilst he's been sleeping.'

'Has anyone heard anything about Alan and Doug?' Hilda asked.

'No, not a dickie bird. They seemed to have vanished off the face of the earth,' Winnie answered. 'It ain't fair that they're gonna get away with what they did to Roy.'

'We don't *know* that Alan and Doug *are* guilty,' Hilda reminded them.

Winnie bristled. 'Come off it, love, they're as guilty as sin. Why else would they have done a runner, eh? It was them, all right, you mark my words.'

'Well, as far as I'm concerned, you're innocent until proven guilty. Having said that, if I set eyes on either of them, I'd skin 'em alive, the evil bastards. I've never seen my girl in such a state. She's hardly slept or eaten. This business with Roy is making her ill.'

'Her mind might be more rested now that he's regained consciousness,' Winnie soothed. 'And she might have her appetite back. In fact, I think I'll pop up the high street and buy her some sausages and cook her favourite dinner – sausage, mash and peas with lashings of gravy.'

'She'll like that, Winnie,' Maureen agreed.

The winter weather had taken a turn for the worse. Heavy snow had fallen, making the streets hazardous. Housewives had cleared outside their front doors, shovelling and sweeping the snow and ice away, some sprinkling salt too, but passing the bombsites was treacherous, the snow almost ankle deep in places. Winnie trod carefully.

'Oi, watch it!' she yelled at two lads throwing snowballs at each other, one flying past her head.

'Sorry, missus,' one of the lads chortled.

Apart from a few kids enjoying their games, the streets were quiet. Hardly any traffic passed by Winnie. Her nose felt numb with cold, her toes too, yet Winnie found pleasure in the white scene around her. Battersea looked magical, clean and fresh. But it was quiet too. Like the smog, the snow muffled the sounds of London.

Winnie came out of the butchers with a dozen fat sausages in her shopping basket. Unlike some meats, sausages hadn't been on ration since 1944, but Winnie doubted the quality of her purchase. Meat was still scarce, and sausages were often filled with bread. Still, she wasn't bothered about that today. Roy was awake and that's all that mattered.

Heading home, and looking forward to being inside in the warm, she smiled at a large snowman with a carrot for a nose and an old khaki army scarf around his neck. 'Good morning, sir,' she said, chuckling to herself. Then rounding the corner of her street, she saw a familiar figure racing towards her.

'Why ain't you in school?' she asked Grace.

'Never mind about that!' Grace answered, panting to catch her breath. 'I've just seen Roy's brother and dad!'

'Where?'

'Working at the Hostel of God near Clapham Common.'

'Do what?'

'There's a new wing being built on the hostel. I saw them, Winnie, working on the building site!'

'Are you sure it was them?'

'Yes!'

'Right, come with me. We need to go straight to the police with this information. You'd better not be fibbing, Grace.'

'I'm not, I swear.'

As they carefully strode through the snow to the police station, Winnie warned, 'And when we get home, we will be having words about you truanting off school, madam.'

Today was a good day! Rachel filled her stomach with the sausages and mashed potatoes that Winnie had lovingly prepared. It was the first time in almost a week that she'd sat down to a good meal. And tonight, when she laid her head down to rest, Rachel knew that she'd finally get a good night's sleep.

'What a day, eh?' Winnie beamed. 'Roy is awake, and Alan and Doug have been arrested.'

'And the doctors are sure that Roy is going to pull through without any lasting damage?' Carmen asked.

'They think so,' Rachel confirmed. 'His speech is a bit slurred, and he can't remember anything from leaving me to go to meet Alan, but his doctor reckons that his speech will improve and his memory might return. To be honest, though, I think it's a good thing that he doesn't remember the beating he got.'

'Yes, I agree. It's probably for the best,' Winnie said.

'The police are confident that they have enough evidence for Alan and Doug to go down for a long time. They've found a witness who can identify them going into the alley with Roy and they've found the clothing they were wearing on the day. Alan's trousers were covered in blood.'

Winnie banged the flat of her hand down hard on the table. 'Good! The pair of them should swing for what they did. Prison is too good for them.'

'I'm just glad they've been caught,' Rachel sighed.

'Me an' all, love,' Winnie agreed.

'Yeah, and me,' Carmen added. 'I didn't feel safe with those pair of thugs on the loose. I can't believe they were only up the road all this time. You'd have thought that they would have run off a long way from here. They're obviously bloomin' stupid as well as thugs.'

Winnie pushed the gravy boat towards Rachel. 'Have some more,' she encouraged. 'I was talking to Piano Pete earlier. He said he heard that the police were none to gentle with Alan and Doug. He reckons they both got a good hiding and I bloody well hope so.'

'It's no more than they deserve,' Rachel said, pouring the thick, beefy gravy over her meal.

'Pete reckons that they tried to get away, and it took nearly a dozen coppers to bring them in. I reckon the Old Bill did well,' Winnie went on.

Carmen folded her arms. 'I don't always trust the police, but in this case, they couldn't have done a better job.'

'It was me!' Grace yelled, leaping to her feet. 'It was thanks to me that the police arrested Alan and Doug! But no one cares, do they? No one has said, *well done, Grace. You did a good job, Grace.* I might as well be invisible!'

Grace strode out of the kitchen, her arms swinging, with Winnie's voice following her. 'You'll not get a pat on the back from me for skipping school!'

'That girl needs a good talking to,' Carmen whispered.

'I'm worried that she might be a bad influence on Martha,' Rachel admitted.

'How?' Winnie asked.

'She's been playing truant, smashing windows and she's been caught pinching from us. She's out of control, Winnie.'

'That's a bit harsh, love, especially after what the poor girl has been through. She's acting up because she doesn't know how to deal with her emotions. Grace is grieving, but I'm sure she'll settle down ... eventually.'

'I hope you're right, Winnie, but I think you may have taken on a very big problem.'

'No, she's just a troubled young lady. It'll all work itself out.'

Rachel shovelled the last forkful of potato into her mouth. As soon as Roy was well enough, they'd be moving to Margate so Grace wouldn't be a problem for her, but Rachel hoped she wasn't leaving Winnie with an angry wasp with a nasty sting in its tail.

Later that evening, Maureen sat beside Vic in the Super Palace Theatre on York Road. Decorated in ivory and gold, Maureen admired the old-fashioned décor though she could see it was looking tired and shabby. It wasn't the most elegant of places to be, but given the freezing weather outside, she was grateful for the warmth within the small, private box that Vic had paid for. The theatre had once been a music hall but now it mostly aired films of variety acts.

Vic reached across for Maureen's hand. 'I would have liked to have taken you to a West End show, but I don't think it would have been wise to have ventured up to London in the snow.'

'I'm happy here,' Maureen whispered, feeling relaxed.

'You're very special, Maureen.'

'Am I?' she asked, astounded.

'Yes. Most women expect fancy dinners and expensive gifts from me. You're different from other ladies I've dated.'

'Have you dated many?'

'No, not really. I spent too much time concentrating on my career. But that's going to change now. I intend on giving you my undivided attention.'

Maureen was glad that the lights had gone down and Vic couldn't see her cheeks reddening.

'Is it too soon to say that I think I'm falling in love with you?' he asked.

Maureen's head snapped round to look at Vic. 'Say that again?' she said, unsure if she'd heard him correctly.

'I'm falling in love with you, Maureen.'

'Gosh,' she uttered. 'You Americans are very forward.'

'I'm not American.'

'I know, but you've obviously picked up their ways.'

'Have I said too much too soon?'

Maureen shrugged. She wanted to tell Vic that she thought about him every second of every day. She wanted to declare her love for him too, but there was one thing holding her back – Brancher. She was still officially a married woman.

'I'm sorry, Maureen, I didn't mean to make you feel uncomfortable. I realise that we've only known each other a short time, but I've never felt like this before. Please forgive me?'

'There's nothing to forgive,' Maureen smiled, bravely adding, 'I feel the same, but there's something you should know ...'

'You don't need to tell me anything. Stephen has already

explained about your husband. It doesn't change how I feel about you.'

'Really? But I'm a married woman.'

'Then it's about time you divorced him.'

Maureen gulped. She'd thought about divorce many times but hadn't had the guts to go through with it. 'I should. I will.'

'Good. Then maybe one day, you'll be my wife.'

Maureen's eyes widened and she gasped. She couldn't believe that she was dating Vic, and now here he was, talking about her being his wife! The man was good-looking and very successful. She questioned what he saw in her. After all, she was plain, boring and quiet. Maureen imagined Vic wanting to be with someone more like Rachel, a woman who was successful in her own right, and pretty. Yet he was sitting with her and talking about marriage. Was it too good to be true?

'I've seen an apartment close to Battersea Park. It's in York Mansions. I'd like you to have a look, see what you think.'

'Me?'

'Yes, Maureen. I value your opinion.'

'All right,' Maureen agreed, flattered. She thought it was a bit posh over that part of Battersea, and wondered if Vic was showing off. 'It's very hoity-toity there,' she remarked, unimpressed.

A sharp voice from the seats in the auditorium below drifted up. 'Shush! Some of us are trying to watch the film.'

Vic and Maureen looked at each other and giggled.

'Shall we get out of here?' he asked.

'Yes, please. I'd like to go home and find out from Rachel how Roy is.'

'We can have a drink in the pub, if you like?'

Maureen nodded. She'd like that very much.

Roy opened the car door for her, and she climbed inside. As he started the engine, he turned to her. 'I don't think you like *hoity-toity,* do you?' he asked.

'No, not very much.'

'In that case, forget about York Mansions. I'll find somewhere that I think you will like too. A place where you'll be happy to live.'

'But—'

'No arguments,' Vic interrupted. 'Like I said, one day, you'll be my wife ... if you'll have me.'

There was no doubt in Maureen's mind. She dreamed of being Vic's wife one day. The feelings she had for him were almost overwhelming. But before she could commit to anything with Vic, she had to finalise getting Brancher out of her life – forever.

21

Friday, 30 January 1953

Roy folded the newspaper and placed it on his lap as he looked along the ward for Rachel. When he saw her come bounding in, a smile spread across his face.

'Good morning, my darling,' he said, pointing to his cheek and waiting for a kiss.

Rachel smiled, kissing his cheek as instructed. 'You're looking bright and breezy. I see you've been catching up on the news.'

'Yes, and it's a sorry state of affairs when young, innocent men are being executed. We lost too many in the war, yet cos of some stupid law, a bloke who never killed anyone has been hanged.'

'Piano Pete said there were protests outside Wandsworth Prison on Wednesday morning when Derek Bentley was executed. He was only nineteen, not much more than a kid. He must have been terrified. And like you say, he never murdered anyone. It was a strange atmosphere in the pub that day, very sad. Anyway, how are you feeling?'

'Great. A little sore but the doctor has confirmed that I can go home next week.'

Rachel's face fell and she said, sadly, 'That's terrific, but I've got some bad news, I'm afraid, the landlord has already rented out your dad's house.'

'What? He can't do that! What about all my belongings?'

'All of yours, Alan's and your dad's personal things are boxed up and in the landlord's garage.'

'And the furniture? Most of it belonged to us.'

'The landlord bought it. He paid me a fair price for it and I didn't think you'd mind. After all, we won't be needing it in Margate, and it wouldn't be any use to your brother and dad where they are now.'

'No, I suppose not, but now I've got nowhere to go home to, and I don't want to be stuck in here any longer,' Roy moaned.

'I've been thinking. I could get a train down to Margate and find us somewhere to live. If you're up to it, when you're discharged, we could move straight into our new home together.'

'Oh, Rachel, that's good of you, but I couldn't ask you to go to Margate by yourself.'

'You're not asking, I'm offering. Anyway, I wouldn't have to go alone. I could take Maureen with me.'

Roy thought for a moment. He didn't want to be in Battersea. As it was, one of the nurses had been giving him peculiar looks. He'd seen her whispering with a porter and pointing towards his bed. Roy knew they'd been talking about him, and outside of the hospital the gossip would be much worse. He believed he was fit enough to manage the journey, and even if he wasn't, Roy was determined. Anything to get him out of Battersea. 'Are you sure it won't be too much for you?'

'Don't be daft. Having a nose around houses and fish and chips by the sea? I think I'll cope,' she grinned.

'I don't want to put a damper on things, but housing is in demand. What if you can't find anything in Margate?'

'Don't worry, I will. I don't want to sound snobby, but we can afford a bit more than the average person. Terry has paid me for my stall and we've got the money from the landlord for your furniture, plus my savings and yours. I reckon I'll find us a palace.'

Roy loved Rachel's optimism and he enjoyed seeing her looking so happy. 'When are you going?' he asked.

'There's no time like the present,' she chirped. 'I'll dash home now, pack a small bag and make arrangements for Martha and Benny. I'm sure Winnie won't mind watching them whilst I'm away. If all goes well, I'll be back by to-morrow with a set of keys to our new home!'

Rachel returned from the hospital before the pub was open and went straight upstairs to find Winnie. But the flat was deserted. Rushing down the stairs, she found Maureen wiping tables.

'Hey, Maureen, where's Winnie and Carmen?' she asked.

Maureen arched her back as she straightened up. 'Winnie's gone to the brewery to sort out a bill. She's been overcharged by quite a lot. You should have seen her, she was furious. I thought steam was gonna come out of her ears! I said I'd open up the pub.'

'Oh, and Carmen?'

'She's gone to Balham to visit her daughter and will be back tomorrow. I think Cheryl needs some help with her kids. How's Roy?'

'He's being discharged from the hospital next week.'

'That's wonderful,' Maureen gushed.

'Yes, but he's got nowhere to go. I was planning on going to Margate today to find us a house and I was hoping that Winnie and Carmen would mind Martha and Benny.'

'I'm happy to keep an eye on them for you. Will you be back tonight?'

'No, I doubt it. I shouldn't think I'll be home until tomorrow.'

'That's fine. I'm not seeing Vic until tomorrow night.'

'Are you sure?' Rachel asked. 'I was going to ask if you wanted to come with me, but on second thoughts, I need you here to watch the kids.'

'It's not a problem and I can't say that I fancy Margate at this time of year.'

'Thanks, Maureen. I'll go and pack.' Then, as an afterthought, she added, 'Maybe we should keep this between ourselves. What do you think?'

'Why?'

'Because they'll only worry if they know I'm in Margate by myself. I'll be back before they even realise that I'm gone.'

Maureen looked uneasy. 'I don't know about that, Rachel. Winnie is bound to ask where you are. I don't want to lie to her.'

'It's only for one night.'

'What should I say if she asks?'

'Just say I'm staying late at the hospital. She'll be busy down here tonight and won't give it a second thought.'

'I still don't like the idea of telling her fibs.'

'What would you rather? See her pulling her hair out with worry? You know what Winnie's like, Maureen. She'll be imagining that all sorts of atrocities are happening to me in Margate.'

Maureen bit on her bottom lip and thought for a while. 'All right. Anything for a quiet life,' she smiled.

22

Rachel got off the train at Margate Station and waited for the steam and smoke from the engine to clear before she made her way along the platform and walked outside. She stood for a moment and drew in a long, fresh breath of salty sea air. Admiring her surroundings, she was struck by how much greener it looked than London, and there was so much space! *Yes,* she thought, *me and the kids are going to enjoy living here.* Away from the greyness and muck of Battersea, Martha and Benny wouldn't have to fill their lungs with the rotten smog that plagued the city.

She hadn't visited Margate in many years, but she didn't think it had changed a great deal. Dreamland amusement park had been the highlight of Rachel's last trip to Margate, especially the bumper cars. *There won't be any rides for me today,* she mused, determined to find a nice house to rent, but with little time to search. First she needed to ensure that she had somewhere to sleep for the night. Margate had once offered endless hotels, but many had closed during the war. A lot of the pubs had accommodation too. Rachel was no stranger to being in a pub environment, but seeing as she was alone, she thought it would be best to avoid the public houses.

She wandered along a side street off the main road which overlooked the sea, checking windows as she went. The first house she passed had a scruffy sign displayed saying *vacancies,* but Rachel didn't like the look of the place. Several houses later, she came to a small hotel with concrete pillars flanking each side of the entrance to the lobby. She craned her neck back to look up at the impressive, tall building but the windows didn't appear clean and the curtains were thin.

'Are you looking for somewhere to stay?' a voice called.

Rachel turned around and saw a middle-aged woman standing in the doorway of the house opposite. 'Yes, I am. Can you recommend anywhere? It's only for one night.'

'I'd stay clear of that dump,' the woman replied, indicating to the hotel. 'And I can recommend my place. You won't find cleaner or cheaper in Margate.'

Rachel crossed the street.

'I'm Mrs Gates. You'll get a comfortable bed in my house, use of your own private bathroom and a hearty breakfast to boot. All for the cost of less than a train ticket back to London.'

'How do you know I'm from London?' Rachel asked, curious.

'I can always tell. It's the pallid skin that gives you away. I'm convinced that you Londoners don't get any sunshine. Are you by yourself?'

Rachel nodded.

'Come in. You'll be my only guest tonight so you won't have anyone bothering you.'

Rachel stepped inside and was immediately greeted by

the welcoming aroma of a meaty stew or something similar. Her stomach growled with hunger, and she realised that she hadn't eaten today.

'This way,' Mrs Gates said, and led Rachel up a flight of stairs.

The house looked bigger inside than it had done from the street.

'You'll be on the first floor. This is your room, and the bathroom is just across the hallway. It's all yours. Settle yourself in, then come downstairs and find me in the kitchen. You look as though you could do with a hearty meal.'

Rachel was pleased with her room and liked the pretty pale yellow and white bedspread that matched the curtains. She liked Mrs Gates too. The woman reminded her of Winnie – warm, kind and forthright. But where Winnie was an attractive lady, though a little plump, in contrast Mrs Gates was stick thin, with long, pointed features and thinning grey hair.

In the kitchen, Mrs Gates spooned two ladles of stew into a large bowl. 'There's more in the pot if you want it,' she said, handing the bowl to Rachel. 'Sit down and make yourself at home. Do you mind if I join you?'

'No, not at all,' Rachel smiled, grateful for the company.

'I haven't had any guests staying for a while. It's the time of year. There aren't many people who come to Margate in January. It's nice to have someone to eat with. What brings you here?'

'I'm looking for somewhere to live for me, my, erm, husband and two kids. We've decided we want to relocate from London.'

'A wise choice. Margate is a lovely place to live, albeit a bit quiet during the winter months. I can't say it'll be easy for your husband to find work here, though. What does he do?'

'He's a clerk, but my husband's also a chef. He was with the army catering corps during the war.'

'In that case he'll find plenty of summer work. How's your stew?'

'It's smashing, Mrs Gates, thank you. I don't suppose you know of any houses available to rent, do you?'

'I do, as it happens, you're in luck. Mr and Mrs Mapleford own a beautiful cottage just outside the town. It has three bedrooms and a kitchen I'm rather envious of. The gardens are spectacular and would be perfect for your children. I know it's just become available, but the Maplefords are away until Sunday. If you can stay an extra night, I'd be happy to introduce you.'

Rachel thought the property sounded ideal, but she was unsure about staying for an extra night. Maureen was expecting her home tomorrow, and Rachel wasn't able to contact her to let Maureen know otherwise.

'It'll be a shame if you miss the opportunity of the cottage. It's very nice, probably the best in the area. I doubt that it will be available for long.'

'I really would like to see the cottage because I think it might be exactly what I'm looking for. But staying until Sunday could be a problem.'

'I've got a telephone in the front room if you need to call anyone. You're more than welcome to use it. Just pop a coin or two into the box on the table.'

Rachel's mind turned. She thought about ringing the brewery and asking them to pass a message to Winnie. The draymen were always obliging and never seemed to mind running messages to the Battersea Tavern. But she'd make the telephone call tomorrow. That way, Winnie would only be worrying about her for one night instead of two.

'Thank you, Mrs Gates. I'd appreciate the introduction to Mr and Mrs Mapleford. And can you book me in for another night, please?'

23

'I'm flippin' annoyed with Rachel,' Maureen complained to Vic. 'She was supposed to be back today, but then I got a message from Charlie, the drayman, that she won't be back until late on Sunday. What am I supposed to tell Winnie?'

'The truth,' Vic suggested.

'Charlie said that Rachel said it would be best to avoid mentioning anything to Winnie or Hilda. Luckily, Martha and Benny haven't asked about their mum. They're assuming she's at the hospital with Roy. It's bad enough that she's sneaking around behind everyone's back and roping me into it, but she might be moving to Margate next week and hasn't had the courtesy to mention that fact to anyone. It's gonna knock Hilda sideways and break Winnie's heart.'

'But they know she had planned on moving before Roy was injured.'

'Yeah, that's true, but the move was put on hold. I don't think they're expecting her to be going as soon as next week!'

'Rachel seems to be quite an impulsive woman.'

'I wouldn't have said that about her, but I think you're right.'

'Will you miss her?'

'Probably. She's a good friend. We aren't *that* close but I'm ever so fond of her. I think I'll miss the kids more.'

'Would you like children, Maureen?'

A searing pain like a red-hot poker sliced through Maureen's heart. She would have loved to have had children and remembered the unborn baby she'd lost. Brancher's words taunted her – *You barren cow.* He'd said it often, and though she hadn't heard her husband's voice for many years, the memory of it still hurt.

'I'm sorry, Maureen, are you all right?'

'I can't have children,' she uttered. 'At least, I don't think I can.'

Vic picked up his glass and sipped his drink. Maureen feared her admission had changed how he felt about her.

'I've never seen myself as a family man. I enjoy my freedom too much. Think about it, Maureen, exotic holidays and nights out. Children would change all that. We'd be much happier with just the two of us.'

'Exotic holidays,' Maureen repeated. 'I've never been any-where exotic. I got a passport last year because we were going to go for a trip to the Isle of Wight. But I chickened out of getting on the ferry, and then I found out that I didn't need a passport to visit the island.'

Vic grinned. 'Where would you like to go?' he asked.

'I dunno. My gran always said she'd like to have seen Ireland because her grandmother was from Cork.'

'Ireland, hmm, I was thinking of somewhere warmer than Ireland.'

'What, you mean proper abroad?'

'Yes. I had every intention of going to Hawaii when I was living in the States, but I never got around to it. I'd love to explore the island with you.'

'Hawaii? Are you kidding?'

'No. I've heard it's beautiful.'

'I'm sure it is, but you'd never get me travelling to some-where like that!' Maureen exclaimed, remembering how she'd refused to even consider going to British Honduras with Clinton. She'd met the dark-skinned lumberjack during the war and for a while she'd believed, wrongly, that she was in love with him. Clinton had remained a friend, though, and they'd kept in contact through letters. She'd been overjoyed for him when he wrote from British Honduras. After all he'd been through, he'd finally made it home.

'Europe, then? Wouldn't you like to see the South of France or Italy?' Vic asked.

'Not particularly. I'm quite happy here in Battersea,' she answered, rather abruptly.

Vic smiled and broke out into laughter.

'What's so funny?' she asked.

'Nothing, nothing at all. I've just never met anyone like you, Maureen.'

Maureen shifted uncomfortably, feeling that Vic was taking the micky out of her.

He must have seen the hurt expression on her face, because he took her hand, and said seriously, 'I think you're amazing, truly I do.'

'I still don't see what's so funny about me not wanting to go on *exotic* holidays,' she said, sulkily.

'Like I've said before, I've never met anyone like you. And I wasn't laughing at you. I'd never laugh at you, Maureen, and I'd punch anyone who did. I was going to wait for a more romantic moment than this... but Maureen, will you marry me?'

Winnie was standing behind the bar and had to do a double take. She couldn't believe what she was seeing! Vic had dropped to one knee and was holding a small box with an engagement ring towards Maureen.

Winnie held her breath, waiting to see how Maureen would respond. She couldn't hear their words, but she saw Maureen nod her head and then Vic pushed the ring onto her finger and threw his arms around her.

Scrambling to find a bottle of anything fizzy behind the counter, Winnie popped the cork, grabbed two glasses and bustled over to Maureen's table. It was smashing to see the young woman smiling so broadly. Winnie didn't know Vic well, but it was clear to see that he loved Maureen, and he seemed like a nice bloke. 'Congratulations,' she said, loudly, handing Maureen and Vic a glass.

'I'm engaged, Winnie,' Maureen announced, her eyes glazy with tears of happiness.

'I know, I saw. I'm really pleased for you both. And I hope you'll consider having your wedding reception here.'

'Hold your horses, Winnie, we won't be getting married for a while yet,' Maureen said, then lowering her eyes, she whispered, 'I've got to get a divorce first though it won't be easy, and it may take a while.'

'Don't worry, love. There won't be a court in London that wouldn't grant you a divorce from that cruel bastard,' Winnie assured, as she discreetly wiped the dust off the bottle of champagne. She had no idea where it had come from, and it had been sitting behind the bar for years. It wasn't a drink that her locals ever requested. As she filled Vic and Maureen's glasses, the pub door opened with gusto, and Grace came running in. The girl darted through the pub and behind the bar, disappearing out of sight as she ran for the stairs.

'What on earth?' Winnie gawped. 'Excuse me,' she said to the newly engaged couple. 'I'd better go and see why Grace has got the wind up her arse.'

As she hurried back to the bar, she called to Piano Pete. 'Keep an eye out, love. I've got to nip upstairs.'

Winnie found Grace huddled on her bed. The girl looked as white as a ghost and was holding her knees to her chest.

'You know you're not supposed to come through the pub. What's wrong, love?'

Grace stared wide-eyed at Winnie but didn't speak.

'You look terrified. Has someone scared you?'

Winnie heard Piano Pete's voice from downstairs calling her name.

'I'll be down in a minute,' she shouted over her shoulder.

'You need to come down now,' Pete yelled back. 'The police are here.'

Winnie saw Grace baulk. 'Have you done anything that you need to tell me about?' she asked.

Grace slowly nodded.

'Out with it,' Winnie demanded, her lips pursed.

'I-I knocked over a stall on the Northcote Road market and – and I pushed the costermonger over too.'

'Why?' Winnie asked, stunned.

'I didn't mean to … I don't know … he was selling my gran's lamps, and her cups and saucers. I know it was my gran's stuff because I recognised a chip on one of the saucers.'

'Love, you know we arranged for a house clearance to take Bertha's things away. The money we raised helped to cover the cost of her funeral. I'm sorry that you saw your gran's stuff for sale, but why did you knock over the stall and shove the fella?'

Piano Pete shouted up the stairs again. 'Winnie, the police want you to come down right now, or they're coming up!'

Winnie sighed. 'Stay here. Don't you dare dream of running off anywhere. I'll get this sorted with the Old Bill.'

Grace nodded, still looking afraid.

Winnie trudged down the stairs, thinking about how she could appease the police. 'Sorry to have kept you, officers,' she smiled. 'Come through to the back kitchen. Would you like a cup of tea?'

'A cuppa would be welcomed,' the older of the coppers replied.

The younger officer threw the older man a disapproving look. Winnie could tell that the young man took his position very seriously.

In the small kitchen, she placed a kettle of water on the stove to boil. 'Please, pull out a seat,' she offered, politely. 'Sergeant Tommy Bradbury used to often sit there at my table. He's a very good friend of mine.'

'Good ol' Tommy. I hear he's enjoying his retirement,' the older man said as he sat down, leaving the other officer standing.

'Very much so, though I reckon he misses his job.'

'He keeps in touch and still likes to keep us on our toes.' Then, his tone becoming grave, he said, 'I'm sorry to bring this to you, Mrs Berry, but there has been an incident on the

177

Northcote Road market. And our enquiries have led us to believe that Grace Lockwood is involved.'

Winnie sat opposite the copper. 'Yes, she's just told me what happened. The poor girl is terrified.'

'And rightly so. Vandalism and an assault are very serious,' the younger policeman confirmed.

'Please,' Winnie said, 'Let me explain.'

'Go ahead.'

'Grace's grandmother passed away recently. The smog we had back in the early part of December finished the old girl off. Poor Grace was left with no one to care for her, so I took her in. But the girl is struggling to settle down. We're strangers to her, and, well, a lot has happened here of late.'

'I understand, Mrs Berry,' the older man said, 'But the charges against Grace can't be overlooked.'

'The thing is, Grace saw some items for sale that had belonged to her grandmother. As you can imagine, she found it upsetting. I'm not excusing her behaviour, but please, can't the girl be shown some leniency?'

'The stallholder, Mr Charring, had a lot of his stock damaged, and he may have sustained a broken wrist when Grace shoved him to the ground.'

'Oh, my Gawd! I'm sure Grace never meant to hurt the man.'

'Regardless of her intentions, she has committed a grave crime.'

'I'll pay for the damage. And I'll drag Grace down the market, and she'll apologise to Mr Charring. And I'll cover any costs associated with his broken wrist.'

'I can put your offer to Mr Charring, but he may still want to press charges.'

'But if he doesn't, will that mean that Grace won't be in trouble with the law?'

'I think, Mrs Berry, that considering the circumstances, if Mr Charring is agreeable, then we can let this one go. But I'm worried that the girl is out of control. She needs strict discipline. I would suggest a few hours in a police cell. Give her a short, sharp shock and some time to think about her actions.'

'Christ, no!' Winnie exclaimed. 'The last thing that Grace needs is the fear of God putting in her and time alone. What she needs is a firm hand with loving guidance.'

'I hope you're right, because I wouldn't like to see Grace in trouble with us again.'

When the coppers left, Winnie hung her head in her hands, her mind turning. Caring for Grace was proving to be more challenging than Winnie had anticipated. But she wouldn't give up on the girl. After all, Grace was a part of the *family* now …

24

On Saturday morning, Rachel strolled along the seafront, watching the waves crashing on the golden sands. The weather was wet, windy and cold, but Rachel didn't mind. She pictured a summer's day, Martha and Benny paddling in the sea, the sun shining warmly on their heads, and Roy fetching them ice creams.

Pulling a piece of paper from her coat pocket, Rachel studied the address that Mrs Gates had scribbled down. Rachel wouldn't be able to see inside the cottage for rent, but she could look around the outside to gauge if it would be suitable. Finding a taxi, she gave the driver the address, and as the car set off, she was filled with excitement. This could be her new home!

The taxi pulled up outside a picturesque house with a white picket fence and rose bushes on each side of a pathway that led to a blue-painted door. It was so pretty and reminded Rachel of a picture she'd seen on a biscuit tin.

'Can you wait a few minutes?' she asked the driver.

Climbing out of the taxi, Rachel opened the garden gate and walked around the cottage. She peered in a window to see a decently furnished front room with a large, open fireplace. It looked so cosy and she could imagine cuddling with Roy on the plump-looking settee. From what she could see, the property appeared to be her ideal new home, and she'd already fallen in love with it.

Heading back to the town, she wondered about the cost of the rent. Mrs Gates hadn't known, but the woman had implied that it wouldn't be cheap. Rachel hoped they could afford the dream place. She felt sure that Roy would love the cottage as much as she did. Now she had to be patient and wait to meet the Maplefords. Tomorrow couldn't come soon enough!

After dinner with Mrs Gates, Rachel decided to take another walk along the seafront. It had fast become her favourite place to be. The wind had picked up, blowing fiercely now and whipping up the waves. Rachel was spellbound by the white horses, rolling in and crashing onto the beach. The sky turned an inky-blue and dark, ominous clouds were approaching from the horizon.

A fisherman passed Rachel; his weather-beaten, ruddy face held low against the howling gale. 'There's a storm coming,' he warned. 'The tide's too high. Get indoors, woman,' he warned.

Rachel didn't need telling twice. Sea spray blew into her face and sand scratched her eyes. She held onto her knitted cloche hat, fearing it would blow off, and leaned into the wind, pushing towards Mrs Gates's house. The strength of the gale almost knocked her off her feet. By the time she arrived back at her lodgings, she'd lost her breath and felt exhausted.

Mrs Gates opened the door, fighting to stop the wind

from snatching it out of her hands. 'I was about to send out a search party for you,' she said, pulling Rachel over the threshold.

'Sorry,' Rachel panted, 'It suddenly got really bad and caught me unawares.'

'It can do that. You'll learn and you'll soon get used to the weather here.'

'I don't think I've ever seen weather like this before.'

'We get a lot of wind off the sea, but not usually as bad as this. I'm worried the windows will blow in.'

'We should draw the curtains,' Rachel suggested.

As night approached, the storm grew stronger, and the wind howled along the street. Rachel could hear the windows rattling, and debris blowing around wildly outside. 'I think I'll get an early night,' she said to Mrs Gates. 'I doubt I'll get much sleep, the wind is so loud.'

'I think an early night is a good idea. If you need anything, you'll find me down here in the back room. Just knock. If I don't answer, come in and give me a shake.'

'Thank you, Mrs Gates. Goodnight.'

Rachel hunkered down under the blankets, trying to block out the noise of the wailing storm outside. She heard a dustbin clanging down the street and roof tiles crashing to the ground. Shoving her head under the pillow, Rachel closed her eyes and pictured the pretty cottage. She hoped it wasn't being damaged in the gales.

She must have drifted off to sleep but was suddenly awoken by a piercing scream.

'Mrs Gates!' Rachel said, jumping out of bed and running to the top of the stairs. She blinked hard, trying to adjust her eyes to the darkness. Her mind wouldn't believe what she was seeing. Water was gushing through the opening where the front door had been! It had been washed off its hinges and was floating along the passageway.

'Mrs Gates!' she called, her eyes searching for the woman.

Rachel rushed down the stairs, pausing momentarily before stepping into the icy water. It was thigh deep and took her breath away. 'Mrs Gates!' she called again, her teeth chattering as she waded along the passageway, moving the front door that floated on top of the gushing water out of her way.

The water was rising rapidly and was now almost up to Rachel's waist. 'Mrs Gates, where are you?' she yelled.

It was a huge relief when she heard the woman scream for help.

Rachel shouted back, 'It's all right, I'm coming,' but as she got the words out, the force of the water pouring in through the house slammed Rachel off her feet. She fell backwards, her arms swinging as she tried to regain her balance and keep her head above the freezing water. Struggling for breath, Rachel panicked when she went under, totally submerged. She felt around desperately in the pitch-black, fearing she would drown. Her nightdress felt heavy, swirling and twisting around her body in the torrent, dragging her down. *I'm going to die,* she panicked, thinking of her children. Then her hands touched something. A wall. Reaching upwards, grappling for the surface, she gulped in mouthfuls of the dirty, salty sea. Finally finding her feet, Rachel coughed and spluttered as she tried to pull air into her lungs. The water had risen and was now up to her chest. 'Mrs Gates,' she called, and coughed again, 'Mrs Gates!'

Rachel didn't hear the woman shout back and worried that she was dead. 'Hold on, Mrs Gates, I'm nearly there!'

She thought she was in the back room now, but it was difficult to tell in the darkness. She tripped on something under the water. Fortunately, she didn't fall under the surface again. What was it? A box, maybe a case. Battling on, she edged forward. Her legs hit something. Rachel placed her hands into the water and felt what she assumed was a bed. A tall cupboard had toppled over and was lying across the bed, the top of it just poking through the surface of the water. And then Rachel touched something soft. A body – and knew she'd found Mrs Gates. The woman was under the water, trapped in her bed by the fallen cupboard. Rachel heaved on it, trying to pull it back. It was heavy, and the weight of the incoming sea streaming in hindered her attempts.

'Please,' she cried, 'somebody help us!'

But she knew that nobody was coming to their aid. Finding strength from within, and with one final yank she finally managed to move the cupboard. Then, ducking under the water, she pulled Mrs Gates up. The woman's body was limp. Rachel cried as she tried to hold Mrs Gates's head above the water.

'Wake up, Mrs Gates,' she pleaded. 'Please, wake up.'

Dragging the woman out of the room and back along the passageway, she thought she should get up the stairs to safety. Mrs Gates was heavy for a skinny woman, but the water helped to keep her afloat.

Her energy almost depleted, she finally reached the bottom of the stairs but didn't think she'd have the strength to pull Mrs Gates out of the flood. *You must do this,* she told herself. *Come on, Rachel, you can do it.* Gritting her teeth, she placed her hands under Mrs Gates's armpits and, stepping backwards, she slowly dragged the woman from the water … Gasping for breath, Rachel rested on a step midway up. Peering down at Mrs Gates, Rachel wondered if she'd just risked her life to save a dead body. But to her relief, the woman stirred, coughing, then spewing liquid from her mouth.

'It's all right, Mrs Gates,' Rachel reassured, helping her to sit up. 'We're safe now.'

'Up … we need to go up …'

Rachel shoved her shoulder under the woman's arm and draped Mrs Gates's arm across her shoulders. Gripping her around the waist and using the banister to pull herself up, Rachel helped Mrs Gates to the top of the stairs and into the bedroom. Shivering, she eased the woman onto the single bed.

'Thank you,' Mrs Gates rasped. 'I thought I was dead.'

'So did I. You gave me such a fright. What's happened? Where's all the water come from?'

'The sea. We've flooded. In the cupboard over there …' Mrs Gates said, weakly, pointing to the corner of the room. 'Gas lights.'

Rachel found the lamps and listened to the sizzle of the gas light as it illuminated the room.

'You need to get out of those cold, wet clothes,' Mrs Gates advised, still puffing and coughing.

'And so do you.' Rachel helped Mrs Gates to undress and tucked her into the bed. 'Have you got any dry clothes up here?' she asked.

'Yes, in the wardrobe in the room at the front. But don't worry about that now. Get yourself changed first.'

Once in dry clothes, Rachel went in search of the wardrobe. Her teeth were still chattering and she didn't feel any warmer than when she'd been soaked through to her skin.

As she rummaged for something for Mrs Gates to wear, a light from outside caught her eye. Moving to the window she looked out onto the street. It was flooded for as far as she could see. She saw a man in a small boat rowing past the houses with a torch. It seemed surreal. Opening the window, Rachel called out over the noise of the wind which had thankfully dropped a little.

'Hey, down there!'

The man looked up. 'Is anyone injured? Do you need help?'

'No, we're fine and safe up here. But what do we do?'

'Sit tight. Wait for the water to subside before you try to come out. Have you got food and water?'

'No, it's downstairs.'

'Don't worry. Help will be here at first light. We'll bring supplies.'

'Thank you!'

Rachel gathered some warm clothes for Mrs Gates and hurried back to her room. 'I saw a man in a boat outside. He said we're to sit tight and help will be here in the morning.'

'Good. Then we should try and get some rest. There's nothing we can do for now.'

Rachel turned her back as Mrs Gates climbed out of the bed and dressed.

'I'll sleep in the room at the front. There's dry bedding in there too, you'll need it for this bed. And if you're worried about anything, come and get me.'

'Thank you, Mrs Gates.'

'No, Mrs Russel, it's me that needs to be thanking you. You saved my life.'

Rachel felt tears stinging her eyes as the trauma of what

had happened began to sink in. She'd nearly died and so had Mrs Gates. Feeling sick and still shivering, she made the bed with the dry sheets and huddled under the blankets. She didn't feel safe enough to sleep, every noise jangling her nerves. As she lay awake, Rachel knew that she couldn't bring her children to live in Margate. They couldn't stay in Battersea either. Her search for a new home would be far, far away from the coast and the dangers of drowning.

25

'What's going on?' Maureen asked when she came into the kitchen on Sunday morning. 'You both look upset.'

Winnie looked up with tears in her eyes. 'We're listening to the wireless, love. There's been a dreadful tragedy along the east coast and up the Thames estuary. Hundreds have lost their homes in a terrible storm. Floods, right up to Canning Town. And it sounds like there's been quite a few deaths too.'

'Oh no, that's awful!'

'The news fella on the wireless was choking back tears, you could hear it in his voice. He must have seen some horrible sights.'

Maureen pulled out a seat beside Winnie and sat quietly listening to the live reports as they came in. Essex had taken a battering.

'Thank Gawd it never came this far up the Thames,' Carmen lamented. 'And thank Gawd for the embankments which hold the water back.'

'Can you imagine sleeping in your bed, and then in the middle of the night, you get swamped by freezing cold water?' Maureen said, shuddering.

'It wouldn't have reached up here,' Winnie commented.

'I know, but there's loads of people who live in ground-floor flats and bungalows.'

'Yeah, like Hilda,' Carmen said.

Winnie leaned back. 'I feel we should do something to help.'

'Like what?' Carmen asked.

'I don't know, maybe we could have a collection in the pub.'

'That's not a bad idea,' Carmen agreed. 'Every little bit will help the poor buggers who've lost their homes. I'll make a couple of tins and shake them under the noses of all our customers. I hope they dig deep.'

Maureen's ears pricked. The news reporter was talking about the Margate lighthouse being lost to the sea. It had fallen in, and the town was flooded. 'N-no! No, that can't be right,' she stuttered.

'What is it, love?' Winnie asked, sounding concerned.

'Margate has been flooded too.'

'Yes, right along the coast on that side of the country has all been badly damaged.'

'A-and didn't you say that people have been killed?' Maureen asked.

'Yes, it's tragic.'

Maureen's pulse raced and she suddenly felt hot all over. 'Rachel is in Margate,' she said, flatly.

'Eh? No, I think you're confused, love. Rachel will be moving to Margate one day, though she might think twice about that after these floods.'

'No, Winnie, you don't understand. Rachel is in Margate now!'

'She's not. She's in bed. *You* told me yesterday that Rachel was knackered cos she's been staying late at the hospital with Roy.'

'I lied,' she admitted, feeling the blood draining from her face. 'Rachel's been in Margate since Friday. She asked me to keep quiet about it because she didn't want you worrying about her.'

Maureen saw Winnie wringing her hands. The woman looked at Carmen. 'Can you believe this? Rachel didn't want me worrying so she got Maureen to lie for her. I tell you, Carmen, if Rachel is still in one piece, I'll bleedin' well strangle her when I get my hands on her!'

'You shouldn't have covered for Rachel,' Carmen stated, glaring reproachfully at Maureen.

'I know, and I'm sorry, but I didn't know what to say to her.'

'It's all right,' Winnie said, her voice cracking with emotion. 'Don't tell Maureen off. None of that matters now, does it? What are we going to do? How can we find out if Rachel is safe?'

'Do you know where she was staying?' Carmen asked.

Maureen shook her head.

'I don't know what to do,' Winnie sniffed. 'The reporter on the wireless said communications are down in most places, and the power is out. Oh, good Lord, what if something has happened to her?'

Carmen patted the back of Winnie's hand. 'Try not to worry, Win. I'm sure Rachel will be fine, and she'll be home as soon as she can be here.'

'You don't know that! If the storm and the floods claimed

the lighthouse at Margate, what chance would Rachel have stood? And what the bleedin' hell am I going to tell Hilda?'

Maureen felt awful for fibbing to Winnie and Carmen, but that was the least of their worries now. Rachel could be injured, or worse. *Please God,* she prayed in her head, *please don't let any more tragedy land on the doorstep of the Battersea Tavern.*

26

Mrs Gates had tied several bedsheets and blankets together and secured a cloth bag at the end. Standing at the open window, the woman lowered the bag down to a couple of men in a boat below.

Rachel watched on. There were a few boats in the street, passing food and water up to stranded residents. Some had ropes and buckets, others, like Mrs Gates, had thought of creative ways to reach the supplies. The scenes unfolding before Rachel's eyes reminded her of the Blitz spirit: communities working together and helping each other in times of adversity.

Mrs Gates gathered up the sheets, pulling the cloth bag through the window. 'Thank you!' she called.

The man below shouted back. 'The lighthouse has gone. It went slowly into the sea, still upright. Quite a sight it was.'

'Didn't it topple over or crumble?'

'No, it stayed tall as it disappeared. I'll be back later, Mrs Gates.'

'I say, Mr Bagshot, is there any way of getting word to London?'

'To London? Why?'

'I have a guest here, a young woman. Her family will be worried.'

Mr Bagshot threw his arms in the air. 'I couldn't say, Mrs Gates. It's mayhem out here. I don't think the telephone lines are working but I'll do my best. Have you got a number I can call?'

Rachel looked around, frantically searching for a pencil and paper. Then hurrying to her bedroom, she grabbed a lipstick from her bag and jotted down the number of the brewery on a handkerchief. Rushing back to the window, she handed it to Mrs Gates.

'This is the number to call,' the woman said, dropping the handkerchief down. Thankfully, there was little more than a breeze and Mr Bagshot grabbed it with ease.

'If you can get through, tell them that Mrs Russel is safe.'

Rachel tugged Mrs Gates's sleeve. 'No, not Mrs Russel. Miss Robb. Rachel Robb.'

'Rachel Robb,' the woman called down. Then turning to Rachel, she asked, 'And you lied to me because …?'

'Sorry. I will be Mrs Russel soon. But I'm not married yet.'

Mrs Gates didn't look annoyed. 'Worse things happen at sea,' she said. And unfortunately, on the night of 31 January and 1 February, they had. Many fishermen and the crews of various sea vessels had perished. Rachel and Mrs Gates didn't yet know the extent of the damage caused or how many souls had been lost, but a neighbour had a wind-up wireless, and he'd said there had been casualties. Fields had flooded and cattle had been killed in Scotland and all the way down the coast. The North Sea storm surge had been a tragedy in the Netherlands too.

Rachel wanted to go home. She yearned to be in the Battersea Tavern with her children. Or sitting beside Roy's hospital bed and holding his hand. It wasn't looking hopeful, but she prayed that Mr Bagshot could at least get word to Winnie, though it was unlikely on a Sunday.

27

On Monday morning, Winnie stood behind the bar, hoping that the day would be busy. She couldn't bear to sit upstairs fretting about Rachel.

'You don't have to do a shift today, Winnie,' Carmen said, gently. 'I'm more than capable of managing by myself.'

'I know you are, love, but I thought being down here would take my mind off things.'

'I wish there was something more that we could do.'

'Me an' all,' Winnie sighed. 'Thanks for ringing round the hospitals. At least we know that Rachel hasn't been injured.'

'And as far as we know she's not been reported dead either. She's probably just stranded and desperate to get home.'

'Hilda's in the same frame of mind as me, keeping busy. She's gone to visit Roy at the hospital. He's worried sick too. I'm glad that Hilda has finally come round and changed her mind about Roy.'

'Isn't he being discharged this week?' Carmen asked.

'Yes, tomorrow, but he ain't got anywhere to go.'

'I'm surprised you haven't offered him a place to stay here,' Carmen guffawed.

'I would, but we're packed to the rafters. Where would we put him?'

Maureen came in, lugging bags of fruit and vegetables. 'I thought I'd do a bit of shopping whilst I was up the Northcote Road. The fruit and veg is always cheaper off the market stalls.'

'Hello, love. Did you see Mr Charring?' Winnie asked.

'Yes, and you'll be pleased to know that he's accepted the apology from Grace and won't be pressing charges.'

'Oh, that *is* a relief. Mind you, it's cost me an arm and a leg. I don't believe that half of the stock he charged me for was really damaged. I bet if I went up the market, I'd see him selling the stuff he claimed was smashed.'

'And his wrist isn't broken either,' Maureen added. Placing the bags on the floor, she glanced briefly at her engagement ring.

'Poor you,' Winnie huffed. 'We've not properly celebrated your engagement. This dreadful business with Rachel has cast a dark shadow over everything.'

'I'm not bothered,' Maureen replied, coyly. 'Do you think it's too soon? I mean, I haven't been courting Vic for long.'

It was Carmen who answered. 'No, Maureen. If you were a naïve young girl and Vic was your first love, then I'd be telling you to tread carefully. You're wise enough to know what you're doing. And Vic is a really nice bloke. You'll have a happy life with him, better than me and Winnie had with our husbands.'

'I must admit, I'm floating on cloud nine. I had no idea that true love could feel like this. Gawd, listen to me. Sorry, I'm jabbering on, and Rachel is missing. I can't wait to show her my ring. Have we heard anything from her yet?'

'No,' Winnie sighed. 'I'm thinking of asking Terry to drive me to Margate and I'll look for her meself.'

'In Terry's van?' Carmen asked, doubtingly. 'That clapped out piece of junk would be lucky to make it up Lavender Hill, let alone all the way to Margate.'

'I could ask Flo and Bill; I know he'd say yes, but I don't like to take liberties, especially as it would mean that Bill would have to miss a day's trading on his dress stall.'

'What if you get all the way there and Rachel is already on her way home? And Gawd knows what state the roads are in. They might not even be passable. Even if you do make it to Margate, it would be like looking for a needle in a haystack.'

Winnie shrugged. 'I suppose you're right. But this has made me think. I'm going to see about getting a telephone installed.'

'Ooh,' Carmen cooed, 'aren't we getting fancy in our old age,' she teased.

Winnie tried to smile, but it wasn't easy. She saw the pub door open, and was desperate to see Rachel come flouncing in. Her heart sank when it was Mr Ainsworth instead, one of her regular customers. As Carmen served the quiet gentleman, Winnie kept her eyes focused on the door.

Maureen picked up the shopping bags. 'I'll take this lot upstairs and then I've got some sewing to be getting on with. If you hear anything, you'll let me know, won't you?'

'Yes, love, of course I will.'

The door opened again, and this time Winnie's heart leaped. Charlie the drayman rushed in.

Turning to Maureen, Winnie instructed, 'Hang on, love. Charlie's just come in.' Then facing the man, she blurted, 'Have you heard from Rachel?'

Charlie smiled. 'Yeah, Winnie, and she's fine.'

'Thank the Lord!' Winnie cried, exhaling the tension from her body. Fighting back tears of relief, she asked, 'What did she say?'

'I dunno, Winnie. A bloke rang and left the message that Rachel is all right and will be home soon.'

'That's good enough. We can all rest easy now. Thanks, Charlie, thanks so much. Can I get you a drink? On the house, of course.'

'Go on then, I'll have a quick half,' he answered, his eyes on Carmen.

Winnie couldn't wipe the smile from her face as she poured Charlie's drink. The middle-aged man didn't have a neck and had arms the size of large boulders, probably from hauling barrels around. A stout fella with receding, greying hair, Winnie had known Charlie for years. And she suspected that he was sweet on Carmen, though Carmen had made it clear that the feeling wasn't reciprocated.

Placing a glass on the counter in front of him, Winnie bellowed, 'Did you hear that, everyone? Rachel will be home soon!'

There were only a few customers in the pub, and along with Maureen and Carmen, a rapturous cheer erupted.

'Hilda will be pleased,' Winnie said to Maureen. 'And when Rachel gets home, we'll have a bloody big party for your engagement.'

28

By Monday morning, Mrs Gates's house was less than ankle deep in water. But as the sea had retreated, it had left a trail of sludge behind. Rachel pushed hard on the broom, swishing the mud and water towards the front door, where Mrs Gates swept it outside.

'So much has been ruined. I don't think I'll ever get straight,' the woman grumbled.

It was all right for Rachel. She'd be back in London soon, and poor Mrs Gates would be left alone to deal with the aftermath of the storm surge. Rachel's heart went out to her.

'How are you faring, ladies?' a policeman in a long, dark coat asked as he passed the house.

Mrs Gates leaned on her broom and wiped her forearm across her brow. 'I was just saying about how much has been ruined. I had tins of food in the cupboard under the stairs and the labels have washed off so I've no idea what's inside them now.'

'The same happened at the pub. The cellar flooded and all the labels came off the bottles.'

'Mr Bagshot said that the pier is damaged. I've not ventured outside yet. Is it bad?'

The policeman nodded. 'Yes, there's terrible damage to the jetty, Westbrook Pavilion and Marine Sun Deck. You wouldn't recognise the seafront now.'

Rachel paddled barefoot along the passageway. 'I need to get back to London. Are there any trains running yet?'

'I couldn't say, but I know a lot of the track has buckled at Whitstable. However, there are several army trucks leaving for Aldershot in less than an hour. You might be able to cadge a lift with them and then catch a train from there.'

'Thank you.'

The policeman went on his way and Mrs Gates turned to Rachel. 'You'd best get packing. I'll walk you to the trucks.'

'I feel awful leaving you with all this mess.'

'It's not your responsibility. You need to be back in London with your children.'

'You're right,' Rachel agreed, and dashed up the stairs. She couldn't wait to get home!

Holding her packed bag and waiting outside in wet shoes for Mrs Gates, Rachel glanced up and down the devastated street. Some residents had left their homes. Rescuers had rowed along the street and placed ladders to the upper floor windows, taking the evacuees to nearby centres in churches and schools. Those who'd stayed had shared news of what they'd heard, calling from one window to another. Mrs Gates had told Rachel that a submarine had sunk in Sheerness harbour and a frigate was laid on its side in the dock. But Rachel had been most shocked to hear that the tidal surge had reached as far as Maidstone in Kent and even London!

'Come on, then,' Mrs Gates said as she came through

the front door. 'I shall miss you, Rachel. It's been a pleasure having you as my guest and I owe my life to you.'

'Thank you,' Rachel replied, her mind on home. Hopefully, she'd reach Battersea in time for evening dinner.

Grace ambled along Battersea High Street and towards Battersea Station. Trains hadn't stopped at the station since 1940 when incendiary bombs had hit the line. Standing on the corner of Gwynn Road, she peered up at the burned out remains of the platform buildings set high on the embankment near the railway tracks. Bored and cold, she pondered the idea of climbing the stairs to explore the wrecks.

'You'll be too young to remember the trains stopping here.'

Grace hadn't noticed the man who'd sidled beside her. She glanced up at him before looking back at the buildings. The tall man had kind, blue eyes under his curly ginger hair and she reckoned he was probably in his forties.

'Do you want to take a closer look?' the man asked. 'I've been up there loads of times. I can show you, if you like?'

Grace shrugged.

'Me name's Spencer. I used to be a train driver and I stopped my train at this station many times.'

'Don't you drive trains now?'

'No, not since I lost the sight in one of my eyes. What's your name?'

'Grace.'

'Shouldn't you be at school?'

Grace shrugged again.

'Exploring disused train stations is much more fun than school, wouldn't you say?' Spencer said, chuckling as he gently nudged Grace in the ribs.

She smiled. 'Yeah, I suppose so.'

'These walls and empty windows are all that's left of the street-level buildings. But up there on the embankment there's much more to see than what you can view from down here. Come on, let me show you something special,' he urged.

'All right,' Grace agreed, and followed him.

Spencer looked over his shoulder. 'Hurry up,' he insisted, 'We don't want to get caught,' he added, picking up his pace.

Grace sped up too.

'Look, over here,' Spencer said, beckoning Grace towards him.

Grace stood beside him and looked to where Spencer was pointing. She couldn't see anything interesting, just some charred wood. Suddenly, Spencer moved to stand in front of her and roughly grabbed her arms.

'What are you doing?' Grace snapped. 'Get off me!'

'Give us a kiss,' he husked.

As his drooling mouth came towards her, Grace turned her face, feeling disgusted as the man's tongue slobbered up her cheek. 'Stop it!' she demanded, trying to wriggle free of his strong grasp.

Spencer pushed his body against hers with such force that she almost toppled backwards.

'Let me go!' she cried.

He began to writhe his hips against her. 'Do you like that?' he asked, breathing heavily and holding her close.

Grace, her heart thumping with fear, stood rigid. Her mind raced.

She felt Spencer shove his hand up her skirt and he tried to part her legs.

'NO!' she screamed; her cry stifled by the power of Spencer's mouth over hers.

With one arm now free, she pushed hard against his broad chest, trying to shove him away.

Spencer stepped back. 'You're a fighter,' he leered. 'I like a fighter.'

He came towards her again and Grace, holding her breath, lifted her knee hard into the man's groin. She'd seen Rachel do the same to Alan in the Battersea Tavern on Christmas Day. Spencer yowled in pain and bent over, holding between his legs.

Grace felt rooted to the spot, petrified as she stared at the man. He lifted his head and she saw a look of dark rage in his eyes.

Run, she told herself in her head. *Run ... Run.*

Grace's feet pounded hard on the pavement as she pelted along Battersea High Street. She hadn't meant to land herself in trouble again, yet here she was, legging it from a deranged man. Running until she was out of breath and felt a sharp pain in her side, Grace didn't look behind her until she'd reached the busy York Road and the corner of Winders Road. Gasping for breath, she burst into tears. She couldn't tell anyone what had happened. No one would believe her – and she'd be in trouble for skipping school again.

Feeling sick and shaking with fear, she had to get home before Spencer found her! *Home,* she thought. The Battersea Tavern was home and Grace knew she'd be safe there.

29

Later that night, Winnie stood behind the bar and saw Hilda eyeing the bottles of alcohol. No one could blame the woman for wanting a drink – after all, her daughter was missing in a major catastrophe. 'Don't even think about it,' Winnie quietly warned.

'It's hard, Win. I need to be here in case Rachel comes home, but the temptation to drink is killing me.'

'Go upstairs, Hilda. There's no booze in my flat.'

'I will, thanks, Win.'

Carmen came downstairs, looking perturbed. 'Have you seen my cream cardigan?' she asked.

Winnie shook her head. 'No, love, and my blue jumper is missing too.'

'And I can't find my knitted green dress,' Maureen added.

Winnie placed her hands on her hips. 'You don't think Grace has been pinching things again, do you?'

'I haven't noticed her hiding anything in our room,' Maureen said. 'But there's something not right with her today. I can tell she's been crying; her eyes are all puffy, and she seems more withdrawn than normal.'

'Hmm,' Winnie sighed, 'I thought the same. She came home from school early, said she felt sick. I think something must have happened to upset her but getting her to speak is like getting blood from a stone.'

'Oh, thank goodness!' Carmen suddenly exclaimed. 'She's home!'

Winnie looked towards the pub door to see Rachel tramping through it. She threw her hands over her mouth, holding in a sob of emotional relief. Then, rushing from behind the bar, Winnie pulled Rachel into a warm embrace. 'We've been worried sick about you,' she whispered in her ear. 'I'm so glad you're home.'

Releasing her, Winnie turned to Maureen. 'Quick, pop upstairs and let Hilda know.'

Rachel had tears in her eyes. 'I'm knackered, Winnie. I reckon I could sleep on my feet.'

'You do look tired, love. Let me take your bag for you. Do you want to go straight up?'

'Yes. And I'm dying for a cuppa.'

Carmen beamed. 'Welcome home. Get some rest and you can tell us all about it in the morning over breakfast.'

Winnie led the way up the stairs, to be greeted by Hilda darting towards her.

'Is it true? Is my girl home?' Hilda asked, excitedly. Winnie stepped to one side and Hilda's eyes fell on Rachel. 'Oh, sweetheart, you're back!' she gushed.

'Hello, Mum,' Rachel smiled.

'She's worn out,' Winnie said. 'Get the kettle on, the girl needs a cuppa.'

In the kitchen, Rachel asked, 'How are Martha and Benny?'

'They're fine, love, right as rain.'

'Have I missed much?'

'Only Maureen and Vic getting engaged,' Hilda smiled.

'That's smashing news! Has anyone been to see Roy?'

Hilda placed a cup of tea on the table in front of Rachel. 'Yes, sweetheart, I was at the hospital today. He's been worried about you and will be so relieved to know that you're home. He's being discharged tomorrow.'

'Where's he going to go? Margate is out of the question.'

'I said he could kip on my sofa,' Hilda replied, 'But he doesn't want to stay in Battersea. I don't think he knows what to do. None of us could think straight, we've all been so concerned about you.'

'I'm sorry, really sorry.'

'Don't worry about apologies, love,' Winnie said, pulling out a chair at the table beside Rachel. 'We're just pleased you're home in one piece.'

30

It was Friday afternoon. Rachel had been frantically searching for a house to call home, and finally, after staying in lodgings all week, she'd found a semi-detached property on a nice street in Carshalton, Surrey. The house came with decent quality furniture, had a back garden and the rent was afford-able. Best of all, it wasn't close to the sea!

That same day, Roy was thrilled to tell her that he'd secured a new job in an accountant's office which was only half an hour away from their new home.

'We'd better go and fetch the kids. Martha is going to love her new bedroom, and Benny will be pleased to have a room of his own.'

'I've got another surprise for you,' Roy grinned. 'Come with me.'

Rachel wondered why Roy was leading her to the front door, and when he pulled it open, she saw a green Ford Anglia car parked outside.

'It's ours,' Roy beamed with pride.

'Can we afford it?' Rachel asked, worriedly.

'I got a good deal on it from an old boy who lives at the

end of the street, and don't tell your mum that I told you, but she chipped in some cash towards it too.'

'Oh, Roy, it's smashing! But I hope we're not living beyond our means. Look at us, a nice, suburban semi and a car. I never dreamed of anything like this.'

'You deserve it, Rachel, and my new job pays well too.'

'I grew up in a large family and we were ever so poor,' Rachel reflected, 'But look at me now, I feel like a princess!'

Roy held the car key aloft. 'Well, my princess, your carriage awaits. Let's go and pick up Martha and Benny from Battersea. They'll be back from school by the time we get there.'

Winnie wasn't convinced that Grace was unwell, but the girl had insisted she was too poorly to go to school. She'd been ill all week, *apparently*.

Standing with Winnie behind the bar, Carmen whispered, 'I reckon Grace is swinging the lead.'

'I thought the same,' Winnie said. 'But she's adamant that her tummy hurts. Maybe I should take her to the doctor, what do you think?'

'I think you'll be wasting the doctor's time. It can't be hurting her that much; she's managing to eat.'

'I don't know what it is, Carmen. She doesn't seem to want to leave her room. I want her to feel settled, so I'm reluctant to push her out the door. If she's happy in her room, then I'll leave her be – for a while.'

Winnie served a few customers and then asked Carmen if she wanted a cuppa. Just as Carmen was about to answer, Winnie saw Mr Giggs walk in. She'd never spoken to him but she knew who he was. 'Oh no,' she moaned, under her breath. 'It's the wag officer.'

'He'll be wanting a doctor's note for Grace,' Carmen remarked.

Winnie approached the man, irked at his presence in her pub. Everyone knew he was a jobsworth, and he was known to be bully with the kids he caught wagging school. He seemed to enjoy dragging the truants by the ear back to school and openly encouraged a severe caning for their misbehaviour.

'Good afternoon, what can I get you?' she asked, the short, bespeckled man.

'I'm looking for Mrs Berry,' he answered, sternly.

'You've found her,' Winnie replied, equally as stern. She didn't like Mr Giggs and thought he was a little upstart of a man.

'I'm Mr Giggs, the School Board Officer.'

'I know who you are.'

'I'm here regarding Grace Lockwood. She's been absent from—'

'Let me stop you there, Mr Giggs. Yes, I'm fully aware that Grace has been absent from school this week, but the girl is unwell. I did send a message to the school; perhaps you should check your records.'

'I have, Mrs Berry, thoroughly. And the records show that Grace has been absent for most of January.'

'Eh? That can't be right. I know she skipped school a few times, but I had firm words with the girl, and she assured me that she's been attending every day.'

'This is a matter of grave concern,' the man said, looking down his upturned nose through his round-rimmed glasses.

'I've seen Grace wandering the streets on several occasions and, though I've failed to catch her, I shouted to her that I'd have her one of these days and that there would be consequences.'

'Well, thank you for bringing the matter to my attention. Now, would you like a drink whilst you're here?'

Mr Giggs wrinkled his nose. 'This isn't the end of the matter, Mrs Berry. Unless Grace has a letter from the doctor excusing her attendance, then I shall expect to see her at school on Monday morning. There appears to be a lack of discipline here, but you can be assured that Grace will be reprimanded at school. I shall personally see to it that the girl is adequately punished.'

'Do what?' Winnie spat.

'I believe I made myself clear, Mrs Berry.'

Winnie rolled up her sleeves as anger surged through her. 'Yes, you did, and now let me make myself clear, Mr Giggs: no one, and I mean no one, is going to give Grace the cane.'

'The rules dictate that—'

'No cane,' Winnie butted in. 'I couldn't give two hoots about your rules. Grace has been through enough. She doesn't need to be punished, and if she did, it would be down to me.'

'This is most irregular. Grace *will* receive the appropriate punishment which she rightly deserves.'

'I'm warning you. If I find out that you or anyone else has laid a finger on Grace, I swear, I'll have your guts for garters. I mean it. I'll come for you, and you'll be bloody sorry!'

'Language, Mrs Berry. May I remind you that—'

'How dare you pull me up on my language!' Winnie yelled. 'Get out. Go on, bugger orf! And don't show your face in here again!'

Mr Giggs sniffed, picked up his briefcase, pulled his camel-coloured raincoat around him and marched out indignantly.

'Bleedin' cheek,' Winnie fumed.

'You told him. I don't think he'll be back,' Carmen chuckled.

'I should hope not. But did you hear what he said about Grace skipping school for most of January? I can't have it, Carmen. I shall have to have words with the girl again.'

The back door opened and Benny came running in with Martha in his wake. The lad looked very pleased with himself, and Winnie noticed he was carrying a jam jar.

'What have you got there?' Winnie called along the passageway.

'A goldfish.'

'A goldfish? Where did you get it from?'

'I, erm, I need to put him in a bowl of water, Gran,' Benny answered nervously, edging for the stairs.

'Hold your horses, young man. Where did you get the goldfish from?'

Martha smirked. 'From the rag-and-bone man,' she answered. 'I warned him not to.'

Benny threw Martha a foul look, hissing, '*Shut up.*'

Winnie stomped towards Benny, frowning at the boy. 'You must have given the rag-and-bone man quite a few woollies to have got a goldfish from him. Is that what you did, Benny?'

Benny slowly nodded his head.

'Did you give him my blue jumper?'

'I-I never see you wearing it. I didn't think you'd mind.'

'And Carmen's cream cardigan?'

'It had a hole in the cuff,' he cried.

'That makes no odds, Benny! You took things that don't belong to you. You had no right!'

'I-I – I'm sorry. But I really wanted Freddie.'

'*Freddie?*'

'Yeah, Freddie the fish. Look at him, Gran, ain't he handsome!'

'Yes, Benny, Freddie is very nice, but you can't take other people's belongings simply because you want something. We'll have to take the fish back to the rag-and-bone man and get our things back.'

'Please, Gran, please don't take Freddie back! I love him, Gran, please let me keep him.'

Winnie sucked in a long breath of air. She didn't want to break Benny's heart and it was clear that the boy was smitten with his pet fish. 'For Gawd's sake, Benny. Go and put Freddie in a bowl of water,' she snapped, annoyed with herself for not being firmer. But when Benny smiled happily at her, Winnie's heart melted and she was glad that she'd allowed the boy to keep his fish.

Roy pulled up against the kerb outside the Battersea Tavern. 'I'll wait here for you,' he said to Rachel.

'I might be a while. Are you sure you won't come in?' she asked.

'I'd rather not and take as long as you need. I'm happy here with the newspaper. Give my best regards to everyone.'

Rachel understood why Roy would want to keep a low profile. She strode into the pub, desperate to share all her exciting news and to see her children.

'Hello, Carmen. Where is everyone?'

'Winnie's gone upstairs to see to the kids and Maureen

has gone to meet Vic from work in Croydon. How are you and have you found a house yet?'

'Oh, Carmen, I'm over the moon! I got the keys this morning for a lovely semi, Roy has a new job and we've bought a car!'

'Blimey, that's bloody brilliant! I suppose you're here to pick up the kids, then?'

'Yes. Are they all right?'

'Benny's in trouble for swapping some of our woollies for a goldfish with the rag-and-bone man, but apart from that, they're fine.'

'He did what?' Rachel asked, stunned.

Carmen chortled. 'I shouldn't laugh, but it *is* funny. Winnie's let him keep the fish and he's even named it. There was a lad down the road who did the same thing a few months back. He pinched his dad's overcoat, but the lad only got a balloon from the rag-and-bone man. I remember seeing his mother chasing the cart up the street, screeching at the man to give her back her husband's coat.'

'I'm so sorry, Carmen, I can't believe that Benny took your woollies.'

'Don't worry. He'll be pleased to see you.'

Rachel walked upstairs and found Martha, Benny and Winnie cooing over a large, glass jug.

'Mum!' Martha bellowed as she ran towards Rachel and threw her arms around her. 'Benny's got a goldfish.'

'Yes, I've heard.'

'He's called Freddie,' Benny smiled, looking very pleased with himself. 'Come and see him.'

Rachel peered into the jug. 'Hello, Freddie,' she said. 'We shall have to get you a proper bowl for our new house.'

'You've found a house?' Winnie asked.

'Yes, and it's more than I could have hoped for. I can't wait for you to see it.'

'Are we moving in today?' Martha asked.

'Yes, darling, we are. Roy is outside in our new car, and he's going to drive us home.'

'We've got a car?' Benny asked, wide-eyed.

Rachel nodded, whispering to Winnie, 'Mum helped pay towards it.'

'Freddie can come too, can't he?' Benny checked.

'Yes, but we shall be having words about how you came to own Freddie,' Rachel warned.

Benny lowered his eyes.

'Are you leaving right away?' Winnie asked.

'Yes, just as soon as I've packed the last of the kids' things,' Rachel replied. She saw Winnie's face drop and knew that the woman would be sad to say goodbye. 'Have you seen my mum? I should let her know too.'

'I think she's at home, love.'

'I'll call in on my way back to Carshalton. Right, I'd better get a move on. I don't want to leave Roy waiting for too long.'

As Rachel packed the last of their things, her excitement about embarking on her new life with Roy was marred only by the fact of leaving the Battersea Tavern. She'd miss Winnie, the woman was like a mother to her. *I'll see her soon,* she thought, holding back tears as doubts crept in. *Christ, I hope I'm doing the right thing for me and the kids!*

31

On Monday morning, Winnie sniffed as she stood at the kitchen sink, filling the kettle and battling to stop her tears from falling.

'Are you all right?' Maureen asked.

'Yes, take no notice of me, I'm just being daft,' Winnie replied, dabbing her eyes with a handkerchief.

'What on earth's the matter?'

'I'm just missing Rachel and the kids. It's so quiet here without them. There's normally mayhem in the mornings with Martha and Benny getting ready for school. And it won't be the same without Rachel outside on her stall.'

'I know, but you'll get used to it. I wonder how Terry will get on. He won't be accustomed to standing outside all day in this cold weather.'

'Terry's a strong fella. Granted, he's more used to the warmth of the bakery, but he's been to war. I'm sure he'll cope with a bit of good ol' Blighty winter weather.'

'Vic said he'd forgotten how cold London can be.'

'And talking of Vic, it's about time we arranged your engagement party.'

'If it's all the same to you, Winnie, I'd rather wait until my divorce comes through. It don't seem right to be celebrating my engagement when I'm still married to Brancher.'

'Whatever you like, love. We can wait until you're ready.'

Carmen came in and poured herself a cup of tea. She sat at the table, and Winnie noticed the woman's leg jigging up and down.

'Is something bothering you, love?' Winnie asked.

Carmen closed her eyes and drew in a long breath.

'What? What is it?' Winnie pushed.

'I've had a letter from my Cheryl. I don't know how to tell you this, Winnie ...'

'Just come straight out with it.'

'Cheryl needs me to stay with her. Edith's still in the hospital and it's not likely that she'll come out. Cheryl can't cope with the kids. She's asked me to help.'

'You must, Carmen. We'll manage without you for a while.'

Carmen looked anxious. 'No, Winnie, you don't understand – Cheryl's asked me to move in with them. Permanently.'

'Oh,' Winnie mumbled.

'I don't want to, not really. But what choice do I have? I mean, I could say no to Cheryl, you chose to have five kids, you made your bed, you lie in it. But at the end of the day, they're my grandchildren.'

Winnie nodded as her mind searched for the right words. She wanted to sound gracious, but she feared that Cheryl was using Carmen. After all, the young woman had never wanted much to do with Carmen, yet now she was asking her to move in. And apart from anything else, Winnie didn't know how she'd cope with running the pub without her best friend.

Carmen continued, 'I've not had a good relationship with my daughter so this could be an opportunity to build some bridges. I'd love to be close to Cheryl like you were with Jan, and closer to my grandchildren. I feel I know Martha and Benny better than I do me own kin.'

Winnie gulped, feeling selfish. 'Of course you should be with your daughter and grandchildren, especially if you're needed.'

'But what about this place?' Carmen asked.

'Don't you worry about that. I'll be fine. This pub is in my blood. I've been running it for donkey's years. I'm not saying that it's going to be easy without you, love, but I'll manage. Anyway, I've still got Maureen here and Grace will have to pull her weight more.'

Maureen looked panicked but nodded. 'I'll do whatever I can to help.'

'See,' Winnie said, 'we'll manage. When are you leaving?'

Carmen sighed. 'She's asked me to come as soon as possible. They've made a room for me in the attic, which she swears blind is spacious and nicely done. I've got to be honest; I don't know why she can't cope with the five kids by herself, but she says she struggles, especially without Edith's help.'

'Five kids are a lot for anyone to deal with.'

'Come off it, Winnie. All right, I only had two babies myself, but there's loads of families round here with a dozen kids and more.'

'I know, but your youngest grandson must command a lot of attention. It can't be easy caring for a child with his needs.'

'No, it's not. It's not easy at all. The poor love struggles since the measles left him almost blind. Blimey, listen to me, I can sound hard sometimes.'

'You've got a heart of gold, Carmen.'

'I think, deep down, I don't really want to go. But I know I must.'

Winnie didn't want Carmen to go either, but she wouldn't make it any more difficult for her dear friend. 'Oh well,' she smiled, 'at least I'll have my bedroom back to meself!'

Grace got to the end of the street before turning on her heel and fleeing back to the safety of the Battersea Tavern. Running through the back door, she fled up the stairs, and into what had been Rachel's bedroom. Shutting the door, she threw herself onto her bed and grabbed a pillow, holding it close to her chest as her heart thudded with fear.

The door opened and Winnie stood in the frame with her hands on her hips. 'What are you doing back here, Grace?' the woman asked, frowning.

Grace gawped back at Winnie, too afraid to admit the truth.

'I can't have you off school again, Grace. I've already had the wag man round here.'

Grace could feel tears pricking her eyes.

'What's the matter? Are you worried that you'll be in trouble at school?'

No, that was the least of her worries. School didn't bother her. But Grace was terrified of bumping into Spencer again.

'Come on, I'm not having you too scared to go into school. I'll come with you and I'll have a word with your headmaster. You don't need to worry.'

'I feel sick,' Grace groaned.

'No, you don't. You're going to school, and that's final.'

'Please, Winnie, I really don't feel well,' she fibbed, desperate to stay indoors.

'You're coming with me, no arguments.'

Left with no other option, Grace reluctantly followed Winnie down the stairs and outside, her pulse racing and her stomach knotted. As Winnie marched her towards the school, Grace's eyes flicked all around, looking out for the disgusting man who'd accosted her at the disused railway station. She'd never forget the vile feeling of his tongue on her face, or the fear as he'd rubbed his groin against her. But mostly, she couldn't shake the evil way in which he'd glared at her when she'd kneed him between the legs. Grace believed that if she ever saw Spencer again, he'd likely kill her!

'I think I'm going to throw up,' she lied.

'There's no need to worry about getting the cane. I'll make sure it doesn't happen.'

Grace gave up the fight, she wasn't going to get out of going to school today. It was fine with Winnie by her side, but what about after school? Winnie wouldn't be at the gates to meet her and walk her home. *I'll run,* she thought, *I'll run home after school, and tomorrow I'll sneak a knife out with me.*

32

It had been a week since Rachel, Martha and Benny had moved out of the Battersea Tavern to their new home in Carshalton and four days since Carmen had left to live with her daughter in Balham. Yet Winnie still hadn't got used to cooking for just herself, Maureen and Grace. 'Oh well,' she sighed, rolling her eyes at the mountain of mashed potatoes left in the saucepan, 'we'll have bubble and squeak tomorrow.'

'Are you sure you wouldn't like me to cook the dinners, Winnie?' Maureen offered.

'No, love, thank you. I enjoy it. But you're more than welcome to take on my share of the laundry duties.'

'Consider it done.'

'And Grace,' Winnie added, 'I shall need you to come to the market with me tomorrow morning.'

Grace pulled a face.

'Your boat race will stay like that if the wind changes,' Winnie warned. 'Rachel and the kids are coming for Sunday lunch, so I want a hand with the shopping. And you can do the washing-up this evening an' all. It'll be busy tonight downstairs; it always is on Fridays. Are you all right mucking in, Maureen?'

'Yes, no problem. Vic said he'll sit at the end of the bar and help out too if needed.'

'I suppose you'll be staying in again all evening?' Winnie asked Grace.

The girl nodded.

'Haven't you got any friends, love?'

Grace shrugged.

'What about Pauline Middleton at the end of the street? She's in your class at school, ain't she?'

Grace pretended to gag. 'Pauline is dirty,' she stated. 'My gran used to tell me to stay away from her.'

Winnie was taken aback. As far as she knew, Pauline came from a nice family, albeit a family without two ha'pennies to rub together. Pauline's clothes were second-hand, but the girl always looked smart enough, and many households in Battersea lived in poverty. Though Winnie knew that there was no need for the Middletons to be hard up – their lack of money was due to Pauline's father being a gambler. Grace couldn't know about Mr Middleton's gambling habits, and she was surprised at the girl's comment. 'Pauline's a nice girl,' Winnie said, defensively.

'The last time the nit nurse came to school, Pauline and her brother had them and fleas as well.'

'Loads of kids get nits, that doesn't make them dirty, love.'

'That's not what my gran said.'

'Well, I wouldn't want to say your gran was wrong, but her ideas were different from mine. Maybe you should give Pauline a chance, eh? Wouldn't it be nice to have a friend who lives just a few doors up? Perhaps you'd like to invite her for dinner one evening?'

Unfortunately, Grace didn't look enthused with the notion of Pauline coming for dinner.

'This is your home, Grace. If you want to invite friends round, you're more than welcome to.'

'Thanks,' Grace replied with no enthusiasm.

'So, how about I ask Pauline's mum if Pauline would like to come for dinner tomorrow?'

Again, Grace shrugged. 'If you like,' she answered, flatly.

Winnie wondered why the girl didn't seem to have any friends. She hadn't made any effort to be pals with Martha either. Yet Grace was nice enough. Perhaps she'd spent a while caring for her gran and had lost touch with her friends. It couldn't have been easy for the girl. While all her mates were out playing, she'd been stuck indoors looking after Bertha. And Bertha might have been poorly for a long time before she'd passed away. Winnie didn't like to ask. *Least said, soonest mended,* had always been her mantra.

Later that evening, Maureen dashed up and down, serving customers and cleaning glasses. She'd never felt comfortable behind the bar and much preferred cleaning, but the pub was so busy she hardly had time to worry about her lack of confidence.

'Could you bring up a crate of tonic water?' she asked Vic.

'I'll get them,' Stephen offered, hopping off a bar stool.

Winnie bustled over. 'It's nice having two fellas offering to help,' she smiled.

Maureen bristled with pride. Vic and her brother were good men and she loved them dearly.

Winnie leaned over the bar towards Vic. 'I promise not to keep Maureen busy for too long. I'm looking for someone to help me out, and as soon as I've found the right person, you can have Maureen all to yourself.'

'Don't worry, Mrs Berry. I'm happy to sit here and look at her,' Vic replied with a wink.

Maureen could feel herself blushing.

Winnie gazed at Maureen with affection, saying to Vic, 'I don't know what I'd do without her, she's been a godsend. You've got yourself a smashing woman.'

Now Vic was looking at her too, and Maureen felt her cheeks getting redder and redder.

'I'm a lucky fella,' he smiled.

Terry breezed in, and Maureen noticed that he looked troubled.

'What's got your goat?' Winnie asked.

'I don't want to be the bearer of bad news, but I've just bumped into Hilda. I'm sure I could smell drink on her.'

Maureen's heart plummeted. She'd feared that Hilda's willpower would crack in Rachel's absence and she could see that Winnie was distraught.

'Thanks for letting me know,' Winnie sighed. 'I was hoping that she wouldn't go back to her old ways. Once Hilda starts drinking, it's a slippery slope to hell – for all of us.'

33

The next day, early on Saturday morning, Winnie hammered on Hilda's front door. When there was no answer, she assumed that Hilda was sleeping off a hangover. Huffing, she marched away. But she intended having very strong words with the woman. And she hoped that Hilda would at least be sober enough to join them for Rachel's visit tomorrow.

Back on her street, she was about to knock on Mrs Middleton's door, but paused when she heard a child whining on the other side, and Mr Middleton shouting.

'Shut that sprog up, woman!' the man yelled.

Mrs Middleton shouted back, 'All right, Bob, I'm doing me best, but I've got me hands full down 'ere. Why don't you get up and help me, you lazy git!'

'Watch your bleedin' mouth or I'll come down there and give you what for!'

'Yeah, you do that, and I'll give you as good as I get!'

Winnie gulped. She didn't think it was a good time to disturb the household. As she went to sneak away, the door flew open.

'Yes, can I help you?' Mrs Middleton asked.

Winnie smiled at the woman. Mrs Middleton had given birth to a boy five months ago, yet she looked as thin as a rake. And it appeared that she'd slept in her dishevelled clothes.

'Well?' Mrs Middleton snapped.

'I was wondering if Pauline would like to join us for dinner this evening?' Winnie asked.

'Why?'

'I thought Pauline would be nice company for Grace.'

The sound of a baby bawling came from the back kitchen of the house.

'I've got to go,' Mrs Middleton said, and went to close the door.

'Can I expect to see Pauline later?' Winnie asked, quickly.

'Yeah, whatever.'

The door closed, and Winnie shook her head. *Rude,* she thought, though she understood the pressure Mrs Middleton must be under. With three kids to feed and a newborn to boot, the woman needed her husband to be a good provider, which everyone knew he wasn't.

Returning home, Winnie stood outside the Battersea Tavern and took a moment to admire her pub. She was grateful that it had survived the war relatively unscathed. The place was more than just her business. It was her home too, and though Rachel and the kids had moved on, and Carmen had left as well, the walls still held a lot of love within them.

'Hello, Mrs Berry.'

Winnie turned to see Judith Kirby standing beside her. Judith's dad had died in a prisoner-of-war camp and her mother had been left blind when a bomb had flattened their home. Fortunately, Judith, who'd been thirteen years old at the time, had been evacuated during Operation Pied Piper.

Winnie smiled warmly at Judith. She'd blossomed into a beautiful young woman, with shining, auburn hair neatly clipped back and tumbling down her back. Her hazel eyes were framed by long, dark lashes. With full lips and a creamy complexion, Judith really was a stunner.

'How are you, love?' Winnie asked. 'And how's your mum faring?'

'We're both fine, thank you, Mrs Berry. I was on my way to see you.'

'Oh, yeah, why's that?'

'I, erm, I heard that you're looking for someone to work in the pub.'

'That's right, love, I am.'

'Well, I've never worked behind a bar, but I pick things up ever so quickly. I'm honest and I'm hard-working, and I can give you good references from my boss at Arding and Hobbs.'

She knew that Judith had worked in the cosmetic department of Arding and Hobbs since leaving school and wondered why she'd want to give up a glamorous position for the Battersea Tavern. 'You want to work here?' Winnie asked, bemused.

'Yes, Mrs Berry, I'd love to work here!'

'What's wrong with the job you have?'

'It's long hours away from my mum.'

'It's long hours here too. You'd be working day and evening shifts.'

'I know, but the evening shifts would be perfect. I could give mum her supper and then she'd settle down for the night. And the day shifts are only a few hours at lunchtime.'

Winnie could tell that Judith had given the position a lot of thought. 'You'd better come inside for a chat,' she smiled. But already, Winnie knew that she was going to offer Judith the job.

34

The next day, early on Saturday evening, Maureen finished icing a cake as Winnie prepared the dinner. She was making a special effort as Pauline was joining them, though Grace still wasn't showing any interest.

Hearing a knock on the back door, Winnie called out to Grace. 'Can you get that, love, it'll probably be Pauline.'

Minutes later, Grace ambled into the kitchen leaving Pauline standing in the doorway and looking uncomfortable.

'Hello, love,' Winnie greeted. 'You're looking very smart. You didn't have to make a special effort for us.'

'Thanks,' Pauline answered, timidly, as she smoothed down her faded, flower-patterned skirt. Winnie thought the skirt had been made from a pair of curtains, and she noticed that Pauline's blouse was very worn around the cuffs and grey around the neckline. The girl's shoes looked scuffed and appeared to be tight on her feet. Winnie felt sorry for Pauline. Her family were clearly struggling to make ends meet. It was no surprise as she knew that Pauline's father often had a flutter on the horses and that's where most of his wages went.

'Sit down, love, don't be shy with us. How's your mum?'

'She's fine, thanks, Mrs Berry.'

'I hope you're hungry cos I always cook enough to feed an army.'

Pauline nodded eagerly as she sat at the table, and Winnie noticed how skinny the girl was. She thought a hearty meal would do Pauline good.

Maureen helped to dish up the dinner. Winnie eyed Grace, hoping that she would make an effort and talk to Pauline, but so far, Grace hadn't attempted to make any conversation with her schoolmate. So Winnie broke the silence again. 'Do you like minced meat and potatoes?' she asked.

'I do, Mrs Berry, thank you.'

'Good. And Maureen has made a nice cake for afters. Get stuck in. There's plenty more where that came from.'

As they ate, Winnie glanced at Grace and nodded her head towards Pauline.

'What?' Grace mouthed, silently.

'Speak to her,' Winnie mouthed back.

Grace sighed, and Winnie glared angrily at her.

Finally, Grace spoke. 'Mr Sweetman clipped Peggy Blake around the ear yesterday. Did you see it in the assembly hall?'

'No,' Pauline answered. 'What had Peggy done?'

'She was chewing gum.'

'Peggy's always chewing gum. She thinks it makes her look good.'

'I know,' Grace smiled, 'but she's dumb. Do you like Peggy?'

'No, not much. Do you?' Pauline asked.

'No, she's a show-off.'

Maureen looked from one girl to the other. 'Haven't you two got anything nice to say?' she asked.

Grace smiled at Pauline mischievously, who returned the smile.

At last, Winnie thought, a breakthrough. The rest of the dinner went well with Grace and Pauline chatting freely.

'That was lovely, Mrs Berry, thank you very much,' Pauline gushed.

'You're welcome, love. There's loads left so I'll put it in a bowl and you can take it home with you. I'm sure your mum will appreciate a day off from cooking tomorrow.'

Pauline smiled awkwardly. Then she said to Grace, 'I'm going to the park tomorrow to meet a mate. Do you want to come too?'

Winnie wondered why Grace suddenly looked alarmed. 'Go on, Grace, that sounds like fun,' she encouraged.

'I, erm, I suppose so,' Grace answered.

Scraping her seat back, Pauline said, 'I'll meet you outside at midday.' Then as she left the kitchen, she turned to Winnie. 'Thank you again for dinner, Mrs Berry. That was the best meal I've had in ages.'

Winnie believed it probably was, and she pondered if the girl was so skinny because she often had to go without food. Another thought struck her, 'You're a bit smaller than Grace. I've got some clothes that my granddaughter left behind when she moved out last week. Would you like to take a look at them, see if any of them fit you?'

'Yes, I would, thank you!'

'Wait there, I won't be a minute,' Winnie smiled. She hurried to her bedroom and quickly pulled off the labels on the brand-new outfits she'd bought for Martha. *It's not like Martha needs any more new clothes, and Pauline's have seen better days,* Winnie reasoned as she took the bundle into the kitchen.

Pauline's eyes were on stalks as she held the skirts, blouses and jumpers in front of her, gawping at the outfits admiringly. 'These look new. Are you sure I can have them?'

'Yes, love. Martha outgrew them, and they're too small for Grace,' Winnie fibbed.

'Thanks, Mrs Berry, thanks ever so much!'

'You're welcome, love. Enjoy your day at the park tomorrow and give my regards to your mum.'

35

Grace didn't sleep well that night. Every time she closed her eyes, images of Spencer came into her mind. The hateful look in his eyes haunted her dreams.

In the morning, she mooched into the kitchen to find Maureen preparing vegetables for Sunday lunch and Rachel's visit.

'Good morning,' Maureen chirped. 'You won't be here for dinner today, will you?'

Grace yawned. 'I dunno,' she answered.

'Aren't you meeting Pauline later?'

'I don't feel like it.'

Winnie came in. 'What don't you feel like?' she asked.

'Meeting Pauline,' Grace replied.

'Why not?'

'Dunno.'

'Pauline was kind enough to invite you out to meet her friend, and you agreed. It would be rude to let her down.'

Grace yawned again. She liked Pauline more than she'd thought she would, but the idea of going outside unnerved her.

'You *will* meet Pauline, no excuses,' Winnie said, firmly.

Grace nodded. She still had a small knife in her coat pocket. If she was to bump into Spencer, at least she had a chance of defending herself. It offered her a little reassurance.

'Good,' Winnie said. 'Now, have some breakfast and then I want you to bring some coal in before you get ready to go out.'

Since Rachel and Carmen had moved out, Winnie had given Grace more chores to do. She didn't mind, especially as Winnie rewarded her with pocket money. She supposed today would be a good day to spend some of her money at the funfair in Battersea Park. Though as Grace had seen Pauline out the door yesterday, her new friend had admitted in a whisper that she never paid to enter the fair. Apparently, there was an easy way to bunk in through the small zoo. Grace grinned. Perhaps today wouldn't be so bad after all.

A few hours later, Winnie answered the knock on the back door expecting to see Rachel, Martha and Benny standing there. Instead, she was greeted by Pauline's mother holding a bundle of clothing which she promptly lobbed at Winnie.

'What do you think you're doing?' Winnie yelled, looking at the clothes scattered on the floor around her. She immediately recognised them as the items she'd given to Pauline.

'I don't need your charity,' the woman screeched. 'And you can take your minced meat and potatoes too,' she yelled, pulling a wrapped bowl from a cloth bag over her shoulder.

Winnie stared agape at the scruffy woman. Her apron was stained and ragged, her hair unkempt under a faded scarf, and her boots looked like something from the Victorian days. But she was clearly a proud woman and Winnie felt awful for offending her. 'I'm sorry,' she said, 'I was only trying to help.'

'I didn't ask for your help, did I?'

'No, you didn't, and I should have checked with you before I sent Pauline home with the clothes.'

'Yeah, you should have. And I would have told you the same as I'm telling you now – you can stick your good Samaritan malarky up your backside!'

Winnie could feel her blood boiling. 'There's no need to be discourteous! I was only trying to do you a good turn. I shan't bother in future.'

'Why would you want to do me a good turn? Feel sorry for us, do ya? Or does it make you look good, eh? I bet you love boasting about it in your pub. *I gave the poor family down the end of the street my scraps from last night's dinner. Oh, that family down the road, I had to pass on my granddaughter's hand-me-downs because their daughter ain't got no decent clobber to wear.* I know your sort. You reckon you're a cut above the rest of us. Well, you ain't. You might have a few bob in your pocket, but your granddaughter is a bastard. Me and mine are skint, but we've got morals. You lot, well, this place is a disgrace!'

Winnie stepped forward and pulled her arm back before swinging it forward and slapping Mrs Middleton across the face. She whacked her so hard that her fingers tingled, and her palm stung.

Mrs Middleton yelped and held her hand to her reddening cheek. 'Truth hurts, don't it,' she hissed.

'You don't deserve anyone's goodwill,' Winnie said, her chin jutting forward. 'Go and rot in your own muck, cos believe you me, woman, you stink.'

With that, Winnie went to slam the door in the woman's

face, but Mrs Middleton stuck her old-fashioned and worn boot in the way.

'I'll have the coppers on to you for assaulting me,' Mrs Middleton threatened.

'Go on then, see if I care. And if you ever insult my family again, I'll give you a lot more than a slap round the face. Now, move your foot out of my door.'

'You ain't heard the last of this,' Mrs Middleton sniped as she pulled her foot away.

Winnie smiled wryly to herself and instead of slamming the door shut, she pulled it wide open. 'I feel sorry for you, I do. And I felt sorry for Pauline too because the girl looked like a vagrant. Before you throw threats around and bad-mouth my family, you need to look at your own. I mean, it ain't no secret that you can't feed your kids because your husband spends his wages on the horses. Don't look so surprised. I've chucked him out of here on more than one occasion when he's been trying to raise a bet. So, if you want to compare family morals, let's start with him, shall we?'

'Mind your own!' the woman snapped, before marching away.

'Yeah, and you mind yours an' all!' Winnie shouted after her.

The bleedin' cheek! she thought, making her way back up the stairs to the kitchen. Yet what Mrs Middleton had said about Martha being a bastard had cut deep with Winnie. It was true, her granddaughter was born out of wedlock. But Winnie hadn't realised that people still spoke about Martha in that way, not after all these years. *I miss 'em, but maybe they are better off in Carshalton after all,* she mused, smiling again at the thought of seeing them at any minute soon.

Neither Grace nor Pauline minded that Pauline's friend hadn't tuned up. The girls were getting on like a house on fire and shared the same sense of humour.

Pauline linked her arm through Grace's. 'I wish we could get some candyfloss,' she said, longingly.

'We can,' Grace beamed, and fished in her coat pocket for her pocket money. 'Look,' she said, holding the coins in the palm of her hand.

'Where did you get that?' Pauline asked, sounding astonished.

'It's my pocket money. Don't you get any?'

'No,' Pauline replied, sadly. 'My mum and dad can't afford to give me anything like that. You're really lucky.'

'Here,' Grace said, handing Pauline half the coins. 'We can share.'

'Cor, thanks, Grace!'

The girls giggled as they stuffed candyfloss into their mouths and laughed loudly when a gust of wind whipped the pink, sugary sweet into Pauline's hair.

'It's stuck,' Pauline moaned. 'Help me get it out.'

'Hold still,' Grace said, facing Pauline as she tried to separate the girl's strands of hair.

'Hurry up, I want a ride on the helter-skelter.'

'I'm going as fast as—' Grace froze mid-sentence as she saw a horrific sight over Pauline's shoulder. The man she'd met at Battersea Station, the same man who'd given her nightmares, he was walking towards her with a menacing look on his face.

'What's wrong?' Pauline asked.

Grace stared at Spencer, fear surging through her trembling

body. Her legs seemed unable to move and her mouth wouldn't work either.

Pauline grabbed her wrist. 'Grace! Grace ... what's wrong with you?'

Spencer was closer now, and there was no doubt in Grace's mind that he'd seen her and was coming for her. 'Run!' she whispered, 'Run!' she urged again, louder.

'Why?' Pauline asked.

Grace heard her friend's question, but she'd already taken off, heading towards the exit of the funfair.

'Grace Wait for me!' Pauline called.

Glancing back, she saw that Pauline was running too but lagging. Grace stopped for a moment, scanning the crowd, searching for Spencer. There was no sight of him, but Grace knew he was there somewhere, lurking, waiting, ready to pounce. 'Hurry up!' she screamed at Pauline, tears rolling down her cheeks.

'Why are we running?' Pauline asked, breathless.

'Come on,' Grace insisted, and grabbed her friend's hand, pulling her through the exit and across the park.

'Grace! Stop ... stop ...!'

Grace kept running, her heart racing.

'STOP!' Pauline screamed.

Coming to a halt, Grace gripped the handle of the knife in her pocket as she looked around for any sign of Spencer. Thankfully, she couldn't see him. 'I want to go home,' she whimpered.

'Please tell me what's wrong,' Pauline asked, still trying to catch her breath.

'There was a man – he – he wants to kill me.'

'What?' Pauline spat.

'It's true, I swear it is. Look …' Grace pulled the knife from her pocket and discreetly showed it to Pauline. 'I even take it to school with me.'

'Who is he? Why does he want to kill you?'

'He … he tried to do stuff to me, so I kicked him in the privates and hurt him.'

'Sounds like the dirty git deserved it!'

'You should have seen the way he looked at me, Pauline. I know he wants to get me.'

Pauline placed her arm over Grace's shoulder. 'It's all right. There's two of us. If he comes for you, we can fight him together.'

'You won't tell no one, will you? Please, Pauline, you mustn't say anything.'

'I won't, I promise. Come on, let's go home.'

All the way across the park, and up to the back door of the Battersea Tavern, Grace was tense and kept her eyes peeled. She had an unsettling feeling that Spencer was watching her. As she said goodbye to Pauline and stepped over the threshold of home, Grace feared that the evil man now knew where she lived.

36

Late on Monday morning, Winnie banged on Hilda's ground-floor window. 'I know you're in there,' she called. 'Open the door!'

She waited a few minutes, and when Hilda didn't respond, she knocked on the window again. 'Hilda, you can't hide from me forever!'

'Go away,' Hilda called.

'No, I won't. Open the bleedin' door or I'll make a right scene out here.'

At last, Hilda came to the front door of the shared house. When Winnie set eyes on her, it became apparent that what she'd heard from various sources was true. Hilda had hit the bottle and, judging by the state of her, she'd hit it hard.

'I knew it,' Winnie said, trying not to sound judgemental. 'You've been drinking.'

'So what if I have? It's none of your business.'

'We share a granddaughter and a grandson. You're my friend. That's two very good reasons that make it my business. Let me in, we need to talk.'

'No,' Hilda said. 'I've got a splitting headache and I'm not in the mood for a lecture.'

'What are you in the mood for? Another whisky?'

'Sod off, Winnie.'

'What would Rachel say if she saw you now, eh? She was here yesterday, having lunch with me, and she was asking where you were. Don't worry, I lied for you, but I won't cover for you again.'

'What does it matter.'

Winnie sighed. 'Just because the girl ain't living in Battersea anymore, it doesn't mean she won't hear about you drinking, Hilda. Don't be so bloody selfish. She's finally got herself and the kids settled. She's happy. Do you really want to spoil her happiness?'

Hilda went to close the door, but Winnie pushed it open. 'Please, Hilda, think about Rachel and the kids. They deserve better than this.'

Hilda glared angrily. 'I knew you'd use *my* girl against me,' she spat, bitterly. 'Do you think I'm proud of meself? I don't enjoy feeling like this, Winnie. I've tried, really tried, but what's the point? I'll be lucky to see Rachel more than once a month. And what else have I got? I live in a shithole, no fella, a poxy job, me looks have gone and – and I ain't well. So you can take your *holier than thou* attitude and tootle back off to your precious castle.'

Winnie frowned. 'What do mean, *you ain't well*? You're feeling ill because you've drowned your sorrows, and you won't get no sympathy from me for that!'

'Yes, Winnie, that's what it must be,' Hilda shouted. 'I'm ill because I got drunk last night. *Of course* that's why. What else could it be.'

'All right, Hilda, stop with the brashness. If there's something else wrong, what is it?'

Hilda hung her head.

'Tell me,' Winnie demanded.

'Nothing. There's nothing wrong with me that an aspirin, a fag and a cup of coffee won't put right.'

'You're lying, Hilda. I've known you long enough to tell when you're trying to hoodwink me.'

'All right!' Hilda growled and pulled the door open. 'You'd better come in.'

Winnie wrinkled her nose at the stench in Hilda's room. She tried to ignore the mess. Empty beer bottles were scattered around the floor and the ashtray was overflowing. It was clear to see that Hilda had spent more than just a night or two on the booze. 'So, are you going to tell me what's really going on with you?'

Hilda sat at a small table in the window and lit a cigarette. 'If you must know, I've been having some women's problems.'

'Ain't you been through the change yet?'

'No, I don't think so. I was getting the sweats, but I've still been having my monthlies.'

Winnie lowered herself to sit on the edge of Hilda's unmade bed. 'What problems have you been having?' she asked.

'Bleeding, lots of it, and pain too. I didn't want to see the doctor, it's embarrassing. But it got really bad and I thought I can't afford to lose all this blood. So, I went, and he sent me to a specialist at the hospital.'

'Oh, Hilda, why didn't you say anything? I would have come with you.'

'I know, but it's not the sort of thing you talk about, is it?'

'What did the specialist say?'

'He said I need an hysterical thingy.'

'Eh?' Winnie asked, confused.

'You know, that operation when they take your lady bits out.'

'You mean a hysterectomy?'

'Yeah, yeah, that's it. They're gonna cut my stomach open and remove my womb.'

Winnie saw that Hilda was shaking. She pushed herself up and rushed over to the woman. Standing behind Hilda's chair, Winnie leaned down and wrapped her arms around her. 'You'll be fine! I know you're scared, but it's quite a common operation these days. When are you going in for it?'

Hilda stubbed out her half-smoked cigarette and placed her hand over Winnie's. Gazing out of the window, she answered, 'I don't know. I was supposed to go in two weeks ago, but what with Rachel moving and Roy coming out of hospital, there was just so much going on.'

Winnie drew in a long breath and stood straight. 'You're telling me you missed your appointment?'

Hilda nodded.

'Right, get yourself washed and dressed. We're going up the hospital to reschedule.'

'Now? Don't be daft.'

'I'm not. They don't perform these operations unless they feel they're necessary. If you're bleeding heavily, then there's clearly something wrong. The sooner you're on that operating bed, the better.'

Hilda rushed to a sink in the corner of the room. 'I'm going to be sick,' she said through her teeth.

Winnie turned her head as Hilda heaved into the basin. Then the woman splashed cold water on her face and drank from her cupped hand. 'I'm so scared, Winnie,' she sobbed, holding on to the edge of the sink.

'I know you are, love. But I'll be with you, every step of the way.'

'Can we keep this between ourselves?' Hilda asked.

'Well, Rachel will need to know.'

'No, Winnie, please. I don't want her worrying needlessly.'

'Oh, love, you have to tell her.'

'No, I don't, and I don't want you telling her either.'

Winnie's stomach flipped. She'd been in this situation once before when Jan had been dying. Jan had begged Winnie to keep it from Terry who was fighting overseas during the war. Winnie hadn't agreed with Jan's decision. Nonetheless, she hadn't told Terry until after Jan's death. Writing the letter to inform Terry that his wife had died had been one of the hardest things that Winnie had ever had to do. And now she felt that Hilda was putting her in a similar position. But it was Hilda's choice, so Winnie would have to abide by her friend's wishes.

Maureen wasn't enjoying working behind the bar. She appreciated that Winnie had been desperately looking for someone suitable to take on the job, and thankfully, a young woman called Judith was due to start next week after she'd worked her notice at Arding and Hobbs.

Terry came in from outside, blowing into his cupped hands. 'Any chance of a hot drink?' he asked.

Maureen looked around the pub. There were only three customers, including Mr Ainsworth, and each one of the men could nurse half a pint for a good thirty minutes. 'All right,' she said to Terry, 'I'm not exactly rushed off my feet. Keep an eye on the bar.'

Minutes later, she carried two cups of hot tea from the back kitchen.

'Thanks, Maureen. I needed this,' Terry smiled.

'It's not as easy as it looks,' Maureen said.

'What's not?'

'Working outside on the shellfish stall in all weathers.'

'You can say that again,' Terry guffawed. 'Rachel must be as tough as old boots. But I've gotta say, Maureen, I'm bloody loving it. It's great being me own boss.'

'I reckon it's nice for Winnie to know that you're just outside. We don't get many lairy customers in here, but it's still reassuring having a fella on call.'

'Where is Winnie?' Terry asked.

'She's popped round to see Hilda. We've not seen her all week and Winnie is worried that she's back on the booze.'

'I hope not, Maureen, but I reckon she is. None of us can handle Hilda when she's had a skinful. You've never seen her drunk, have you?'

'No, thank Gawd, but I've heard how bad she can be. I hope Winnie can talk some sense into her.'

'Me too. I'd best take this cuppa outside. I don't want to be losing business. Cheers, Maureen.'

Maureen wiped down the bar, tidied around the till, and dusted some bottles, all the while daydreaming about Vic. She was looking forward to seeing the house that he'd found near Clapham South. Vic had said it was perfect, but he wanted Maureen's approval before putting down a deposit.

The door opened and a gruff-looking man swaggered in. With his flat, crooked nose and cauliflower ears, Maureen could tell that the tall, broad-shouldered fella had been in a fight or two during his lifetime. The man's hair was cropped short and he had a threatening manner about him which made Maureen feel uneasy.

She smiled nervously at him, asking, 'What would you like?'

His voice was low and deep, almost a growl. 'You must be Maureen,' he snarled.

Maureen could feel her pulse quicken. 'Yes,' she mumbled.

The man leaned forward over the bar. His face was so close to Maureen's that she could smell his foul breath. Stepping back, she muttered, 'What do you want?'

He sneered, revealing his tobacco-stained teeth. 'I'm a friend of Brancher's. He asked me to give you a message.'

Maureen felt faint. The room began to spin. She grabbed hold of the bar to steady herself, worried that her legs were going to buckle beneath her. Rendered speechless, she gawped at the intimidating man.

He took a monkey nut out of his pocket and placed it on the bar. Then thumping his fist down hard on the nut, the shell smashed. 'That's the message.'

'I-I don't understand,' Maureen stuttered.

'Imagine that monkey nut is your fancy man's head,' he smirked. 'Victor, ain't it? Now do you understand?'

Maureen, wide-eyed, slowly nodded.

'I'll be seeing you – and so will Brancher when he gets out next week.'

The man swaggered out, leaving Maureen terrified and in tears. When she saw the door open again, she almost screamed. It was such a relief to see Winnie coming through it.

'Good Lord, what's happened?' Winnie asked, rushing behind the bar to Maureen's side.

'Brancher! He – he – oh, Winnie…' she sobbed, bile burning the back of her throat.

'It's all right, love, take a few deep breaths.'

Maureen drew in a juddering breath. 'A man came in with a message from Brancher,' she managed to get out before sobbing again.

Winnie glanced around her pub. 'Sorry, I'm closing. Drink up,' she ordered.

The customers grumbled.

'Come on, let's be having you. Drink up, I ain't got all day.'

As the customers finished supping their drinks and left one by one, Winnie bolted the doors behind them. Then turning to Maureen, she said, 'Pull yourself together, there's a good girl.'

Maureen tried to compose herself, but a painful lump of fear and grief constricted her throat.

'Stop it, Maureen, you're gonna make yourself ill. Breathe… that's it… breathe…'

Winnie put a glass of brandy in her hand. 'Get that down your neck,' she said. 'It'll help to settle your nerves.'

Terry's voice could be heard from outside as he knocked on the door. 'Winnie? Winnie, is everything all right in there?'

Winnie hurried to the door and pulled it open. 'We're all right, thanks, Terry. I just need some time with Maureen.'

Maureen gulped down the drink and eventually calmed.

'Right, tell me what happened,' Winnie demanded.

'A rough-looking bloke came in and smashed a monkey nut on the bar. He said it was a message from Brancher and the nut was Vic's head.'

246

Winnie shook her head. 'Take no notice, love. Brancher can't hurt you or Vic from behind bars.'

'He said – he said that I'll be seeing Brancher when he gets out next week.'

'Is he due out next week?' Winnie asked.

'I don't know, but what if he is? Oh, Winnie, I'm so scared!'

'Don't start bawling again, that ain't gonna help.'

'What do I do?'

'Nothing, yet. Let me make a telephone call. Thank Gawd I got one installed. I'll speak to Tommy before we do anything rash.'

Maureen nodded, her mind racing. Brancher would have received the divorce papers. Perhaps this was all just an empty threat to scare her. But what if it was more than that? Brancher was capable of hurting Vic. Her husband had it within him to cause Vic serious, life-threatening injuries, or even death.

The phone trilled. Maureen jumped. Her nerves were a jangled mess. She looked at Winnie as the woman returned to the bar. Searching her face, Maureen's heart sunk.

'That was Tommy calling me back.' Winnie said, gravely. 'It's true. He has just confirmed that Brancher is being released next week.'

Maureen felt her legs give way, and she crumpled to the floor. 'He's ruining *everything*,' she cried. 'He'll kill Vic and one day, he'll kill me too.'

37

'Have you still got that knife in your pocket?' Pauline asked Grace as they made their way home from school on Monday afternoon.

'Yeah,' Grace replied, solemnly.

'Well, I think you should tell Mrs Berry what happened.'

'No, I can't tell anyone, and you promised that you wouldn't either!'

'I haven't. I won't tell a soul.'

They walked on for a few minutes in silence, and then Pauline asked, 'Would you use it, the knife, if you had to?'

'If I ever see that man again, I'd happily cut his eyes out,' Grace boasted, full of bravado.

'Eww, I don't think I could do anything like that.'

'I could – to him. I'd stab him in his heart.'

'You'd get in big trouble,' Pauline warned. 'They might even hang you like they did Derek Bentley.'

'Don't care,' Grace lied. In truth, when she'd seen Spencer at the fair, having the knife in her pocket hadn't made her feel any braver or safer. She'd replayed the scene in her head, over and over. Not once had she considered confronting the man. Instead, she'd run away, frightened.

As they rounded the corner, Grace saw Pauline's mum standing on the doorstep outside their house with her arms folded across her chest and a scowl on her face.

'What did I tell you about hanging around with her?' the woman spat, eyeing Grace up and down contemptuously. Then pulling Pauline towards the front door and cuffing her around the back of her head, she yelled, 'You're to have nothing to do with her or anyone else from that pub. Get indoors.'

'Ouch, Mum,' Pauline moaned.

Mrs Middleton shoved Pauline through the front door and then turned to Grace, barking, 'You stay away from my girl.'

Grace was flummoxed. She couldn't understand Mrs Middleton's outburst, or why the woman didn't want her and Pauline to be friends. She hoped Winnie would be able to shed some light on it.

Grace found Maureen in the kitchen. The woman looked ghostly white and Grace noticed her red, swollen eyes. It was clear to see that she'd been crying.

'Where's Winnie?' Grace asked.

'She's had to go out with Hilda. She said you're to stay in this evening and you're not to answer the door to anyone.'

'Why? What's going on?'

'Nothing,' Maureen sniffed, averting her eyes.

Terry stood in the kitchen doorway. 'Did you tell Grace that she's to stay indoors?' he asked Maureen.

'Yeah, she knows,' Maureen nodded.

'Why?' Grace asked.

'Never you mind,' Terry answered.

Maureen sniffed again. 'Thanks, Terry. It's good to know you're just downstairs.'

'I ain't going nowhere and no one will get past me. Try not to worry, Maureen.'

Fear snaked through Grace's veins. 'Please tell me what's going on?' she pressed.

'Just do as you're told,' Terry said, before walking away.

Grace pulled out a seat at the table. 'I'm scared,' she admitted to Maureen.

'It's all right, Grace. You have nothing to be scared about.'

'So why are you upset and why is Terry *guarding* downstairs?'

Tears began to well in Maureen's eyes. 'Honestly, Grace, it's got nothing to do with you. I'm sorry you're worried, but I promise that nothing bad is going to happen to you.'

Grace sensed the tense atmosphere. No matter what assurances Maureen had given her, it was obvious that something was very wrong. Feeling unsettled, she retreated to her bedroom. *What a strange day,* she thought. First Mrs Middleton acting peculiar, and now this. She didn't like it. Reaching into her coat pocket, Grace pulled out the knife and slipped it under her pillow. *I hope I won't need it tonight,* she thought, *but it's better to be safe rather than sorry.*

Winnie trudged back from the hospital, worn out with worry. The doctor had kept Hilda in, and she was scheduled for a hysterectomy the next morning. The woman had been in a terrible state, verging on hysterical. Winnie had been relieved when a doctor had pushed a needle into Hilda's arm and whatever he'd injected her with had almost immediately calmed her. She'd felt awful leaving Hilda in the hospital, but at least the woman was heavily sedated and didn't seem to be aware of where she was. Winnie had promised to return tomorrow and she'd sworn to Hilda that she'd be there when the operation was over.

Winnie tried to push aside her worries about Hilda and focus instead on the hostile situation at home. Poor Maureen was dreadfully upset. She wished she could give Maureen some of whatever the doctor had administered to Hilda! Thank goodness for Terry. If he hadn't offered to stay with Maureen, Winnie wouldn't have been able to drag Hilda to the hospital.

'It's only me,' she called, as she came through the back door.

Terry appeared from the pub and stood in the passageway. 'How's Hilda?' he asked.

'Scared, but she'll be all right. I wish she'd let me tell Rachel. Has anything happened here?'

'No, Winnie, it's all been quiet. Listen, if you want to open the pub, I'd be happy to work behind the bar.'

'I'll think about it. And thanks ever so much for being here.'

'You don't need to thank me. I reckon it would be best if I moved in for a while. I can kip in the kids' old room.'

Winnie had been thinking the same. 'I was going to ask you to stay, but you've beat me to it.'

'I telephoned Stephen's work. He'll be round later.'

'Thanks, Terry, you're a good man,' Winnie smiled. Then lowering her voice, she asked, 'How's Maureen been?'

'Quiet. And Grace is asking questions.'

Winnie sighed, her mind turning. 'I suppose I should give

the girl an explanation, but I don't want her to feel scared in her own home.'

'It's up to you, but I think she should be told what's going on.'

'Yeah, you're probably right. I'll have a cuppa and then get the dinner on. It's smashing having you here, love.'

Upstairs, Winnie slipped into Grace's bedroom and sat on the edge of her bed. Grace had climbed under the covers and was reading a book.

'I don't want you to worry,' Winnie began, 'but I believe you're old enough to hear the truth.'

Grace listened intently as Winnie explained the situation with Maureen and Brancher, and how Maureen had been threatened.

'So, love, we all need to be extra vigilant for a while. But like I said, there's no need for alarm. Terry is here and Stephen will be round later. But I'd prefer it if you stayed indoors for a while.'

Grace readily nodded, and then asked, 'Why won't Mrs Middleton allow Pauline to be my friend?'

'Huh, won't she, indeed? I should have expected as much from her. Don't worry about it, love. You ain't done nothing wrong. But you must respect Mrs Middleton's wishes.'

'It's not fair! Pauline is my best friend.'

'You've only known her two minutes,' Winnie guffawed. 'Anyway, you're too good for the likes of that family. You'll make new friends soon enough.'

Grace pouted sadly, and Winnie felt a surge of anger towards Mrs Middleton. She'd liked to have slapped the woman's face again and tell her how petty she was being. But now wasn't the time to be concerning herself with Mrs Middleton.

Winnie had far more important matters to be dealing with. Maureen was in imminent danger. Hilda was undergoing surgery. Her pub was closed. *God give me strength,* she thought, exhausted.

38

The following morning Winnie had warned Grace that she wasn't to speak to any strangers and must go straight to school. But Grace defied Winnie. She wanted to see her friend and waited around the corner from Pauline's house.

Pauline came running over. 'I hoped you'd be here,' she said, beaming.

'Why doesn't your mum like me?' Grace asked.

The smile quickly diminished from Pauline's face as she answered, 'I dunno. She gave me a right hiding last night.'

'Why?'

'Cos I told her I hated her. She took all those lovely clothes back to Mrs Berry. It ain't fair. They were the nicest clothes I'd ever had.'

'I can sneak them back to you, if you like?' Grace offered.

'Thanks, but it ain't worth it. I'd never be allowed to wear them, and I'd get another good hiding if Mum found out.'

'It doesn't matter what your mum thinks. We're still best mates.'

'Yeah,' Pauline agreed, 'We'll just have to keep it a secret from her.'

The girls slowly made their way to school.

'We're gonna be late,' Pauline said.

'We could skip school today,' Grace suggested.

'Oh, I dunno about that. What if Charley Wag catches us?'

Grace grimaced. 'Huh, he couldn't catch a snail on a slow boat to China! Anyway, I've seen him loads of times and he never bothers chasing me. He came into the pub a little while ago and told Winnie about me skipping school. I don't know what she said to him, but I didn't get into trouble.'

'You were lucky. My mum would do her nut if she found out that I'd wagged school. We should go in. Anyway, it's too flippin' cold to hang about on the streets.'

'All right, but let's get some sweets first,' Grace said, grinning when she added, 'I'll race you to the shop!'

Running and laughing, larking about, Grace and Pauline tumbled through the shop doorway together. As Grace straightened herself, she stifled a scream when she looked up and her eyes met Spencer's. The man was standing in front of the counter, glaring at her.

The shopkeeper spoke. 'Oi, you two, I won't have any mucking about in here,' he warned the girls.

Spencer stepped towards Grace. She wanted to scream. She told herself to run. Instead, she stood mute, holding her breath as she stared up at him.

'Come on, Grace,' Pauline urged, pulling on Grace's coat sleeve. 'Shall we get a bag of black jacks?'

Still rooted to the spot with fear, Grace's eyes followed Spencer as he walked past her. Frozen with fear, she heard the bell above the door ring as he left the shop.

Finally letting out her breath, Grace tried not to cry.

'What's the matter?' Pauline asked.

'That was him,' she whispered. 'That was *that* man.'

'Are you sure? He didn't seem to know you.'

'I'm telling you, Pauline, that was him all right. I'll never forget those eyes. You should have seen the way he looked at me when we came in. Oh, Gawd, what if he's waiting outside for me?'

'Stay here,' Pauline ordered. 'I'll check.'

'I'm coming with you,' Grace replied hastily and followed her friend outside.

Grace spotted Spencer pacing up the street. 'There he is,' she said, pointing. 'He's heading towards where we live.'

'Let's watch him and see where he goes,' Pauline urged, and began walking in the same direction.

'No, please, Pauline. Leave it. We should go to school.'

'Look, he's gone in that café.'

Grace's heart was still thudding hard and fast, and though she had tried to be brave, she couldn't stop herself from crying.

'Oh, bugger, there's me mum,' Pauline grumbled. 'I'm in trouble now.'

Mrs Middleton had come out of the greengrocer's shop and was marching towards them, pushing a dilapidated pram with a squeaky wheel.

'What have I told you about staying away from her,' she said scornfully. 'And you should be in school by now!'

'Mum, there's a bad man in that café. He wants to kill Grace!'

Mrs Middleton threw a glance towards Grace, and when she saw her distress, the woman's face softened. 'Is this true, Grace?' she asked.

Grace nodded.

'What makes you think that a man wants to kill you?'

'He – he d-did things to me.'

'What things? What things did he do to you, Grace?'

Grace blurted out the whole story, retelling every detail of the ghastly event. Sobbing, she tried to catch her breath. 'Am I in trouble?' she asked.

'No, but that bastard is!' Mrs Middleton seethed. 'Pauline, watch your brother – and stay put, the pair of you.'

Grace watched as Mrs Middleton steamed towards the café.

'What do you think my mum is going to do?' Pauline uttered.

'I don't know.'

Minutes later, Mrs Middleton came back out and looked up and down the street before walking back towards the girls.

'There's never a flippin' copper when you want one,' she moaned.

'What happened, Mum?'

'I confronted *Spencer,* though it ain't his real name. He scarpered, legged it out the back. But the fella who owns the café knows him. Don't worry, his card is marked now. He won't be interfering with any more girls.'

'Are the police gonna get him?' Pauline asked.

'Maybe. But if the coppers don't take him away, then your father and his mates will see to it. Come on, let's get you two home.'

Mrs Middleton told Pauline to take her baby brother indoors and then she walked Grace to the Battersea Tavern. 'Go inside and tell Mrs Berry that I'd like a word,' she instructed.

When Grace found Winnie and informed her that Mrs Middleton was waiting downstairs, she saw a thunderous look on the woman's face. Winnie stamped down the stairs, and Grace stayed at the top, discreetly listening.

'You've got some nerve gracing my doorstep again,' Winnie seethed.

'I ain't here for a row. It's about your Grace.'

'What about her?'

'A few weeks back a dirty pervert attacked her. She's all right but it scared the life out of her. She was on her way to school this morning with my Pauline and they saw the bloke. Grace is terrified, so I brought her home.'

'She was *attacked*?' Winnie repeated.

'Yeah, and I know who did it. I'm telling you, Mrs Berry, I ain't having blokes like that walking the streets of Battersea. I mean, I've got the safety of me own kids to think about. My Bob will see to it. That filthy bloke won't be bothering Grace again.'

39

'I've tucked Grace into bed with a cup of hot milk and a few of my *good* biscuits,' Winnie said to Maureen across the kitchen table. 'That was quite an ordeal for her this morning.'

'It explains why she's not wanted to go out much. Poor Grace. I can't believe she's been carrying a knife around with her. She must have been scared half to death.'

'I think she feels better now that it's all out in the open. She didn't tell me because she thought she'd be in trouble for skipping school. I told her I already knew about that, thanks to the School Board Officer. But she said she was worried that she'd get told off for kicking the man between his legs. I said to her that she did the right thing, and I made her promise that she'd never keep a secret like that from me again.'

''Ere, what did Mrs Middleton mean about her Bob sorting it?' Maureen whispered.

'Use your imagination,' Winnie replied, tapping the end of her nose. 'I hope Bob cuts that bloke's nuts off.'

'Do you know him, Winnie?'

'Dick Lamb – that's what he's called. No, I don't think I

do. But Piano Pete will, he knows everyone. Are you sure you're gonna be all right here with Grace? Only I really want to get to the hospital to see Hilda.'

'Yes, Winnie, we'll be fine, and Terry is here an' all. Go, and give Hilda my love.'

When Winnie arrived at the hospital, she went straight to the ward to find that Hilda's bed was empty. Winnie could have kicked herself for not being there earlier. She'd wanted to see Hilda and offer her some reassurance before she was taken to the operating theatre. She knew Hilda would have worked herself into a panic so Winnie hoped the doctor had sedated her again.

A nurse pulled the covers back on Hilda's bed and straightened the pillow. She looked briefly at Winnie, saying, 'They took your friend down about an hour ago. She won't be back on the ward until late this afternoon.'

'Thanks,' Winnie replied.

There didn't seem much point in hanging around, so Winnie decided to return to the Battersea Tavern. And then she thought about making her way to Carshalton. It would take some time, but Roy could drive her back to Battersea in time to be at the hospital for when Hilda would be back on the ward. Rachel had a right to know that her mother was having major surgery. Winnie didn't feel comfortable with keeping it from her. And she knew that once Rachel found out, she'd be furious that she wasn't informed earlier. *Sod it,* she thought, *I'm going to tell Rachel, regardless of what Hilda wants!*

Rachel glanced proudly around her kitchen. Everything was gleaming and she'd even managed to lift an unsightly stain off the linoleum. She thought she might miss working on her shellfish stall, earning her own money and being a modern woman, but Rachel adored her new home and was enjoying being a good housewife. Though she knew the feeling wouldn't last and boredom would set in. But for now, Rachel felt fulfilled in making a happy home for her family.

She went to make herself a well-deserved cup of coffee but as she filled the kettle, Rachel had to look twice at the familiar figure climbing out of a taxicab outside. *It's Winnie,* she realised, wondering what the reason for the visit was, especially all the way from Battersea. Rushing to the front door, she pulled it open and saw that Winnie's expression was severe.

'Is something wrong?' Rachel blurted.

'Let's go inside, love.'

She led Winnie through to the kitchen, anxious to know why the woman was there.

Winnie's eyes roamed around as she unbuttoned her dark, green coat. 'I know you said you had a nice place, but I wasn't expecting anything as fancy as this.'

'What's wrong, Winnie? You haven't come all this way just to look at my new house.'

'No, love, I haven't, but there's no need to worry. It's your mum: she's all right, but she's in the hospital having an operation.'

'What for?' Rachel asked, instantly fearing the worst.

'Women's things. Like I said, nothing to worry about and the operation she's having is quite routine these days.'

'What operation?'

'A hysterectomy.'

'Flippin' 'ell, Winnie, that's major surgery! Is my mum going to be all right?'

'Yes, love, of course she is. Your mum is being operated on as we speak. She'll be back on the ward later today.'

'I have to be there!' Rachel exclaimed, her mind spinning.

'Of course, but don't be surprised if she seems annoyed to see you. The thing is, I wasn't supposed to tell you. She didn't want you worrying.'

'Trust her! Well, thanks for letting me know.' Her head still in a spin, she thought aloud. 'I need to call Roy. He'll have to drive us to Battersea and get back here for the kids. Oh, good grief, I can't believe my mum is under the surgeon's knife!' Feeling herself shaking, she added, 'Make yourself a cuppa, Win, I'm popping three doors up. They've got a telephone connected and said I can use it in emergencies.'

Rachel had her slippers on and dashed from the kitchen and into the passageway, frantically searching for her shoes. As she ran back into the kitchen, Winnie placed a staying hand on her arm.

'Calm down, love. Your mum will be fine, and we've got plenty of time to get to the hospital.'

Tears pricked Rachel's eyes. 'It's just such a shock.'

'Hilda won't want to see you with mascara running down your face. Take a deep breath and pull yourself together.'

Rachel breathed in deeply and slowly exhaled. 'One thing at a time,' she said, trying to muster a smile. 'You're right, I need to be strong for my mum. And whether she likes it or not, I'll be bringing her home here to recuperate.'

Winnie and Rachel had spoken to the Staff Nurse and were now making their way down the ward.

'Oh, bless, her, she looks a sorry sight,' Winnie said quietly, as they approached Hilda's bed.

'She looks old, Winnie, and so small,' Rachel whispered.

'Don't worry, love, your mum will soon bounce back, but I expect she'll be a bit groggy and away with the fairies for a while.'

Rachel gently held her mum's hand and leaned closer. 'It's me, Mum. I'm here.'

'Eh?' Hilda mumbled, her eyelids slowly lifting.

'Winnie's here too. Don't try and talk, Mum, just rest. We'll still be here when you wake up.'

Rachel looked across the bed at Winnie with tearful eyes.

'I told you not to expect much,' Winnie whispered. 'She'll come round in her own good time.'

'Do you think she's in pain?'

'I should imagine that she's a bit sore and uncomfortable, but the doctor would have given her something for the pain.'

Hilda groaned.

'It's all right, Mum, try and relax,' Rachel soothed.

Hilda's eyes opened again, and Winnie could see the confusion in them.

'Wh-where am I?' she asked, trying to focus.

'You're in the hospital, Mum. You've had surgery this morning. But it went well, and you'll be all right.'

'Oh ... yeah ... hospital ... N-need a drink.'

Rachel poured a glass of water from a jug on the bed stand and held it to her mother's lips.

'No, not water,' Hilda grumbled, turning her face away in disgust. 'A drink. Proper drink.'

Rachel's eyes shot to Winnie. The girl looked horrified.

'It'll be the medication talking,' Winnie assured.

Peering back at her mum, Rachel asked, 'How are you feeling?'

'Sick.'

'All right, rest for now. The nurse said she'll be here to see you soon.'

Winnie hid her fears, but it worried her that the first thing that Hilda wanted after a serious operation was a drink.

'I didn't die, then?' Hilda croaked.

'No, Mum, you're still alive, thank goodness.'

'What are you doing here?'

'Don't be annoyed with Winnie, but she told me what was happening. I can't believe that you didn't want me to know. Honestly, Mum, as soon as you're well enough, me and you will be having words!'

Hilda's head rolled over to face Winnie. 'You promised,' she said, accusingly, her voice weak.

'I know, but Rachel had a right to know.'

Turning back to Rachel, Hilda half-smiled. 'I'm glad you're here but bugger off.'

'No, Mum, I'm not going anywhere.'

'Please. I want to go back to sleep. I really am pleased to see you, but I need to rest.'

'All right, but I'll be back first thing in the morning.'

'Me too,' Winnie added.

'Thanks,' Hilda said quietly, her eyes closing again.

'Do you think she's asleep?' Rachel asked in a whisper.

'Yeah, I reckon so. Come on, leave her be. She'll be as right as rain in the morning.'

Winnie wasn't sure that any of them were going to get much rest that night. Having a threat from Brancher hanging over Maureen and Vic wasn't conducive with peaceful sleep. At least Terry was staying with them, and Winnie felt better knowing there was a man at home.

As they made their way out of the hospital, Winnie nudged Rachel. 'There's Piano Pete,' she said, nodding her head towards the area where the ambulances pulled up. 'I wonder what he's doing here. We'd better go and see if he's all right.'

'Pete,' Winnie called.

When he turned and saw her, the man scooted towards them.

'You've heard then?' Pete asked.

'Heard what?'

'About Dick Lamb. I thought that's why you were here.'

'No, we've just been visiting Hilda. Before you ask, she's fine. Women's problems. I certainly wouldn't be here wasting my time on the likes of Dick Lamb!'

'Who's Dick Lamb?' Rachel asked.

'You mean who *was* Dick Lamb,' Pete scoffed.

Winnie looked at Pete with curiosity. 'Is he dead?'

'As good as. If he ain't dead now, he will be soon,' Pete answered. 'He's just been brought in and he's in a bad way. I heard they had to peel him off the ground out of a puddle of his own blood. The doctors shouldn't be treating him. They should let the dirty bastard die.'

Winnie's mind raced.

She heard Rachel's voice. 'Will someone please tell me who Dick Lamb is.'

'Yeah, yeah, love, I'll explain on the way home,' she muttered.

Pete took the roll-up out of his mouth and threw it on the ground. 'I'm going to see me sister to get an update. I'll let you know what I find out, Winnie.'

'Thanks, Pete,' Winnie said, her mind still turning.

It was obvious what had happened. Mrs Middleton had

265

said that her husband, Bob, and his mates would see to Dick Lamb. She hadn't realised that they would go so far with such a brutal attack. The man deserved it, she reasoned, yet something didn't sit comfortably with her. Justice had been served, but there'd been no trial by a jury. No judge had passed a sentence. Instead, a gang of vigilantes had taken the life of a man, albeit an alleged depraved one. He'd been found guilty on the word of a troubled young girl and Winnie hoped that Grace hadn't fabricated the story of 'Spencer' attacking her at Battersea Station. She prayed an innocent man hadn't been wrongfully killed. Though she believed everything that Grace had told her, there was no denying that the girl's behaviour was odd at times to say the least. She prayed Grace hadn't made up the story as a desperate cry for attention.

40

Sitting in the kitchen the next morning, Maureen smiled across the table at Rachel. 'It's nice having you back here. It feels normal.'

Rachel brushed crumbs off her lap from the toast she'd been eating. 'I've not been away for long and I can't believe how much has happened!'

Maureen lowered her voice. 'I feel awful that Winnie isn't opening the pub.'

'I don't think she's closed it because of Brancher. You know Winnie, she wouldn't allow someone like him to stop her from opening up shop.'

'Are you sure?'

'Yes, positive. I think she just needs an extra pair of hands. She can't be in two places at once, and I know she wants to be at the hospital with my mum. When Judith starts here next week, everything will go back to how it should be. You'll see.'

'I'm dreading next week,' Maureen admitted. 'Brancher gets released.'

'Have you thought about talking to the police?'

'There's no point; they won't be interested because Brancher hasn't done anything wrong yet.'

'He might be all talk, Maureen, and making threats just to scare you. I can't see him risking the possibility of going back to prison.'

'He would. You don't know Brancher like I do. He doesn't make idle threats. Vic has said that he won't allow Brancher to bully us. He remembers Brancher from school and reckons he ain't scared of him. But I think he is and won't admit it.'

'What are you going to do?'

Maureen sighed deeply. 'I dunno. I feel like I'm a sitting duck. I can't sleep, I can't eat. It's making me ill.'

'You can come and stay with me?' Rachel offered.

'Thanks, but you'll have your mum. You won't have room for me an' all.'

'We'd make room. You're always welcome.'

'It's kind of you to offer, Rachel, but I don't want to bring trouble to your door. Brancher might find me and I wouldn't want him making a scene in front of Martha and Benny. Don't worry, I'll deal with whatever happens.'

Winnie came in and threw a newspaper onto the table. 'Have you seen this?' she asked. 'It's in the papers. Dick Lamb, murdered. Police are looking for three men, but none of the descriptions fit Bob Middleton.'

'That's a good thing, isn't it?' Maureen asked.

'Yeah, I suppose so. Maybe someone else got to Dick before Bob and his mates.'

Rachel sat rod straight. 'I don't care who did it, I'm just glad that someone got rid of him. It could have been my Martha he attacked, and I'm not sure that she would have been brave enough to fight him off like Grace did. It makes my blood run cold when I think what could have happened to my girl. I'm glad the man is dead.'

Winnie lowered her voice. 'But what if Grace was lying about what happened?'

'I don't think she was, Winnie,' Maureen said, adamantly.

'I hope not, and I don't think she was either. But she's still grieving and, let's face it, she's been quite a handful. We've had the stealing, her smashing a window and then the incident at Northcote Road market. I'm sure she was telling the truth, but I can't help worrying. Anyway, are you ready, Rachel? Your mum will be expecting us this morning.'

Maureen waved Rachel and Winnie off. She'd have liked to visit Hilda too, but she'd agreed to get the groceries in. Winnie had said that it would do her good to go out and wagged her finger, saying, *you can't hide up here forever.* Maureen knew that Winnie meant well, but she had no idea of how afraid Maureen was to step outside the front door. She empathised with Grace and understood the girl's fear. At least Grace didn't have cause to be afraid anymore, not now that her attacker had been murdered. Maureen felt awful for thinking it, but she wished that Brancher was dead too.

It took her a while to pluck up the courage to venture outside, and when she did, she loitered in front of Terry's shellfish stall.

''Ere,' Terry said, handing her some coins. 'Can you get me some baccy while you're out?'

'Sure. I'll see you later,' Maureen answered. She glanced around, nervously, reluctant to leave the security of Terry's protective eye. Then, sucking in a deep breath, she held her head high and braced herself. *Come on, you can do it,* she encouraged. *Brancher can't hurt you, he's still locked up.*

Maureen's heart hammered as she walked quickly along the street. She reasoned that the sooner she got to the shops, the sooner she'd be home.

Coming to the corner, her body jolted when she set eyes on the man who'd come into the pub and threatened her. He was leaning against a lamp post, leering at her with an ominous smirk. She stood, hardly daring to move as she watched him take a cigarette from his mouth and blow the smoke out of the side of his wicked grin.

Please don't come to me, she begged in her mind, too terrified to turn and flee. But he did. Pacing towards her with a confident swagger, the man was soon towering over Maureen.

'I'm watching you,' he snarled. 'And your husband ain't none too happy about you still seeing another bloke. Get rid of him, or Brancher will do it for you. And don't think you'll get off scot-free either.'

Maureen couldn't speak. She couldn't scream or even cry. The world was swimming around her. She swayed, stumbling sideways. And then everything turned dark.

41

Winnie was pleased to see Hilda sitting up in bed, though the woman looked haggard and was in quite a bit of discomfort.

'There's no need for you to stay in Battersea,' Hilda said to Rachel. 'I'm going to be in here for several days so there's nothing you can do. Honestly, darling, I'd feel much better if you buggered off back to Carshalton. You should be with Roy and your kids.'

'No, Mum, I want to be here.'

'Please, sweetheart, go home. You can bring Martha and Benny to see me on Saturday. I'd like that.'

'Are you sure?'

'Yes.'

'Your mum's right,' Winnie agreed. 'You should go home. I'll be here to keep her company. She'll be all right.'

Rachel took a moment and then nodded. 'Fine, but when you get out of here, you're coming to stay with me.'

'I bloody well ain't!' Hilda argued.

'Yes, you are, Mum. I can take care of you.'

'I don't need taking care of, thank you very much. And I ain't being a burden on you.'

'You won't be a burden, Mum.'

'No, I'll be going home to me own bed, and that's final. Anyway, the district nurse will come out to see me every day.'

Winnie chuckled. 'I can see where you get your stubbornness from, Rachel. Don't bother trying to change your mum's mind, she won't budge.'

Rachel rolled her eyes. 'I know she won't.'

Winnie had hoped that Hilda would stay with Rachel but wasn't surprised that she'd refused. Though Hilda's motives bothered Winnie. She suspected the woman was declining the invitation so that she could secretly drink instead.

Rachel rose to her feet. 'Visiting time is nearly over. Is there anything you'd like me to bring you on Saturday?'

'No, thanks, just you and the kids. Winnie can fetch my make-up.'

'Your make-up – are you trying to impress the doctor?' Winnie asked.

'No, but I don't want to scare Martha and Benny. I must look a dreadful sight. My lips are cracked and I'm sure I'm as white as these bed sheets.'

Winnie smiled affectionately. 'I have seen you looking better, Hilda, but considering you had a big operation yesterday, you can be forgiven for not looking your best. I'll see you tomorrow, love.'

Half an hour later, as Winnie and Rachel walked up the street towards the Battersea Tavern, Winnie noticed that Terry's stall was closed.

'That won't be good for business,' Rachel remarked.

Winnie frowned, sensing that something was wrong. Hurrying to the back door, she rushed in, calling, 'Maureen? Terry? Is everything all right?'

Terry's voice came from upstairs. He leaned over the bannisters and called down, 'Up here, Winnie. Maureen fainted.'

Winnie darted up the stairs with Rachel in her wake and found Maureen sitting at the kitchen table with a glass of water in front of her. She looked even paler than Hilda and Winnie could see that her hands were trembling.

'She's all right,' Terry assured. 'But she had a scare. That bloke was in the street and threatened her again.'

'What did he say?' Winnie asked, pulling off her coat.

Maureen swallowed hard. 'He said I had to get rid of Vic or Brancher would. And he implied that Brancher is going to hurt me an' all,' she cried.

'This ain't on. Brancher shouldn't be able to intimidate you from behind bars. I'm calling Tommy. There must be something the police can do.'

Terry scratched his head. 'Tommy is retired from the police, Win, he won't be able to do anything.'

'He can have a word with his old colleagues at the police station. Brancher can't be allowed to get away with this. I mean, look at the state of poor Maureen. We can't sit back and do nothing!'

Terry shrugged. 'It's worth a try, I suppose.'

'I–I'm not sure,' Maureen stuttered. 'What if we involve the police and it makes Brancher worse?'

'Someone has got to do something. Let me speak to Tommy and see what he says. Then we can take it from there.'

Winnie threw her coat over the banisters as she trudged downstairs to the telephone. Her feet ached, her neck was stiff and her whole body felt weary. She couldn't remember the last time she'd been this tired ... maybe during the Blitz when bombs had been landing on London almost every night and day. Granted, life wasn't as bad as it had been back then, but these were challenging times, and she wished Carmen was by her side to lighten the load. Winnie felt she had the weight of the world on her shoulders and hoped she'd be strong enough to carry it.

Pauline looped her arm through Grace's on their way home from school. 'My mum still don't want us to be friends,' she said. 'But who cares? Me and you will be best friends forever. It just means I can't invite you into my house.'

Grace smiled warmly at Pauline. She wasn't bothered about being invited into her friend's house. If anything, it was a relief that she didn't have to make excuses to avoid going inside the place. Pauline had talked about the rats and the bugs and how she could hear them scuttling around at night. Grace shuddered at the thought of it and wondered if Pauline's house was dirty. She'd heard about the slums in Battersea being infested with bugs. The Victorian terraced houses were mostly occupied with multiple families, had no running water and many had to share outside toilets. Grace knew she was fortunate to live in the Battersea Tavern with the modern comforts it offered, though she recalled when there had been a rat in the cellar once. Maureen had screamed and Carmen had chased it out with a broom. After that, Winnie had laid poison. Grace hadn't seen the rat and hoped she'd never meet one. She felt sorry for Pauline having to live with the vermin.

'Shall we go to the Saturday morning pictures at the Granada?' Pauline asked. 'We could try and bunk in.'

'We don't need to bunk in. I can pay for us, it's only

274

sixpence each. My gran used to drop me there and then go and get her shopping. I haven't been for ages. I'd love to.'

'I'll ask my mum for the money to get in, but she'll probably say she's skint. She's always skint cos me dad wastes his wages betting on the horses. I've heard them rowing about it. Mum goes mad at him and then he shuts her up with a backhander across her face. It's the same old story every week. 'Cept last night, they were talking about Dick Lamb.'

Grace stiffened. The mention of that man always made her tense. Winnie had explained that she'd get no more trouble from the man as he'd passed away. She hadn't told Grace how Dick had died, but Grace thought it was her fault because she'd wished the man dead. 'What were they saying about him?' she asked.

'They were talking about his murder, and Dad said he'd had nothing to do with it, but he would have killed him if he'd got to him first.'

'He was *murdered*?' Grace spluttered.

'Yeah, didn't you know? He was jumped on by three men. They battered him to death.'

'Blimey, I had no idea.'

'Yep, he's in a coffin and he'll be going straight to hell. I heard my mum saying that if my dad didn't beat Dick up and someone else did, then it meant that Dick must have attacked another girl.'

'I hope she's all right. I hope she got away from him like I did.'

'Yeah, me too. You ain't got to worry about him no more.'

'And it's not because of me that he's dead. That's a relief!'

'Forget about him. Shall we go up the Junction?'

'I can't. Winnie said I have to come straight home after school.'

'Go on,' Pauline urged, 'Just for a while.'

'All right, but not for too long,' Grace agreed.

Clapham Junction was unusually quiet. Grace assumed it was because of the bitterly cold weather.

'In here,' Pauline said, pulling Grace through the doors of Arding and Hobbs department store.

The grand building had been Grace's gran's favourite shop and every year Bertha had brought Grace to see Father Christmas. The fragrant aroma of the store from the perfume counter, its elegant décor, the echoing sounds – Grace's mind was flooded with fond memories of her gran.

'Up here,' Pauline said, heading towards the children's clothing department. 'The ladies' clothes are too big for me,' she said.

Browsing through a rail of expensive skirts, Pauline took one down and held it against her. 'What do you think?' she asked Grace.

'It's nice.'

'Yeah, I think so too.' Looking around, she grinned at Grace. 'Shush,' she whispered, as she stuffed the skirt inside her coat.

Grace stared at her friend, wide-eyed. 'What are you doing?' she hissed.

'I want something nice to wear to go to the pictures. Come on, I don't think anyone is watching.'

'No, Pauline, put it back. We'll get into trouble.'

'Only if we get caught,' Pauline giggled. 'Come on.'

Pauline hurried towards the sweeping staircase, leaving Grace with no choice but to follow her friend. She'd thought

Pauline was a bit of a goody-two-shoes and was shocked by her actions. *Oh Gawd, please don't get caught,* she thought, looking over her shoulder as they darted down the stairs.

The main doors were in sight. Grace's pulse was racing.

'Oi! You two!'

Grace glanced behind and saw a suited man chasing them. 'Quick,' she said to Pauline, 'Run!'

A stern, matronly woman stepped in front of Pauline with her arms spread to each side. 'Not so fast. I believe you have something that belongs to the store.'

'No, I don't. I wouldn't want anything from this stinking shop,' Pauline spat.

Grace felt a wave of heat rise inside and could feel herself getting redder and redder as a small crowd gathered to watch the commotion.

The suited man grabbed Pauline's arm. 'You're coming with me to the manager's office.'

'Get off me!' Pauline yelled, trying to yank her arm free of his grip.

'And you,' the man said, taking hold of Grace's arm too.

'I haven't done anything,' Grace protested.

'We will let the police see about that,' the stout woman said, looking pleased with herself.

The man was almost dragging Grace and Pauline through the store with the woman leading the way.

Grace wanted to cry. She was so embarrassed and she knew that she was going to be in deep trouble with Winnie! This might be the last straw and Grace feared she'd end up in the orphanage.

42

'I'm bored,' Grace moaned, slumping at the kitchen table.

'Tough,' Winnie replied. 'You should have thought about that before you had the police at my door again last week!'

'But it wasn't my fault! I told Pauline not to pinch the skirt. I ain't a thief.'

'Well, the evidence suggests otherwise.'

Grace hung her head and Winnie could see the girl was ashamed. *And so she should be,* Winnie thought. After all, it wasn't the first time Grace had been caught stealing.

'Go to your room. You're not allowed out until I say so. I've got enough on my plate without listening to your cheek an' all!'

Grace scraped her chair back, looking sulky. 'But I've not been out for nearly a week.'

'Any more backchat from you and you'll not see the light of day until next bloody Christmas!'

Grace skulked off. Winnie was irked with herself. She'd already given Grace a telling-off when the coppers had brought her home. Yet she still found herself talking harshly to the girl. She wanted to have more patience with Grace, but with Hilda due out of the hospital, Maureen reverting into her shell and afraid of her own shadow, and the pub open and busy again, it felt like one thing on top of another.

Maureen came into the kitchen, her face grim, and Winnie remembered that today was the day when Brancher was being released from prison.

'I know you're worried about today, love, but when I telephoned Tommy, he said he'd have a chat with his old colleagues and ask them to keep a close eye on things here.'

'It's Stephen I'm worried about. He said he's going to meet Brancher at the prison gates and have words with him.'

'Stephen can hold his own, love. A word in Brancher's ear from your big brother might be enough to warn him off. Bullies don't like confrontation from anyone bigger than them.'

'I hope you're right, Winnie.'

'I am. Right, I'm off to pick up Hilda from the hospital. I'll be back as soon as I can and in time for Judith to open the pub. Terry is giving me a lift there and I'll get a taxicab back.'

'How is Judith getting on? Is she learning the ropes?'

'Don't get me started on that girl! She looks smashing behind the bar and I'm sure my customers are glad to have someone pretty to look at, but she's like a fart in a colander. I couldn't leave her alone to work, not yet. I'm hoping she improves. Time will tell.'

A while later, Terry dropped Winnie off at the hospital. Hilda was sitting on her bed, dressed and ready to go.

'I can't get out of here soon enough,' she smiled, as Winnie walked beside her through the ward. 'There's nothing like your own bed, and a decent cuppa.'

'I took the liberty of tidying up your place, so it's nice and clean for you to come home to. Fresh sheets on your bed an' all.'

'Oh, Winnie, thank you. You didn't have to do that. It was a bit of a mess, sorry.'

'Well, as you refuse to go to Rachel's, I couldn't have you coming home to a mess, could I? I've also stocked your larder a bit. Now, you heard what the doctor said, no overdoing it. And I'll be in every day to check on you.'

'Thanks, Winnie. I don't know what I'd do without you.'

'You're one of my best friends, Hilda. We're family.'

After settling Hilda back at home and leaving her with a pot of tea and a fishpaste sandwich, Winnie hurried back to the Battersea Tavern.

Judith was waiting outside, and so was Piano Pete.

'It's not often that you're late opening,' he said.

'I shan't be making a habit of it,' Winnie replied.

As Winnie poured Pete half a pint, a few more customers strolled in, including Mr Ainsworth who sat at the end of the bar where Len had always plonked himself. Winnie could see that Judith was trying her best, but the young woman managed to cock-up two drinks orders and short-changed Mr Ainsworth too.

'I don't know if I'm cut out for bar work,' she said apologetically.

Winnie tried to boost her confidence. 'It can't be that much different from selling cosmetics. You'll get the hang of it. Did you use to know your customers favourite brands of make-up and what colour lipsticks they liked?'

'Yes. I had my regulars, and I always knew what they wanted.'

'It's the same here. You'll get to know who drinks what. And you'll become familiar with the bar and where everything is. The trick is to keep calm and smile. Always look as though you're in control and know what you're doing. Don't let the blokes intimidate you. Remember, when you're behind the bar, you're the boss.'

'Thanks, Mrs Berry. That helps.'

Winnie smiled. She needed Judith to be good at her job and didn't have the time to watch over her.

SMASH.

It was the third glass that Judith had broken in two days.

'Sorry,' the girl cringed.

'Don't worry. Get the dustpan and brush and sweep it up,' Winnie ordered, though she couldn't help tutting to herself.

The rest of the shift passed smoothly and by the end of it, Judith was laughing and joking with a few of the regulars.

'I reckon you're getting the hang of it now,' Winnie praised.

'I hope so, Mrs Berry. I don't want to let you down.'

'I know, love. Keep going the way you are, and you'll be fine.'

'Thank you. I think seeing Mr Ainsworth sat at the end of the bar put me off my stroke. But that pep talk you gave me really helped.'

'Why would Mr Ainsworth make you feel uncomfortable?' Winnie asked, curious. After all, the smart-looking man never said much.

'I don't like to gossip, Mrs Berry, but haven't you heard about him?'

'No, heard what?'

'Well, my mum's friend, Tabby, used to be his cleaner. It was a few years back, before the war and before Mr Ainsworth's mother lost the use of her legs. But Tabby packed in the cleaning job because she couldn't stand it. She reckoned that Mr Ainsworth's mother was a vile woman. She used to beat him with her walking stick and threatened to hit Tabby an' all. That weren't why Tabby left though. She left because of Mr Ainsworth. She reckoned he was evil.'

'Mr Ainsworth *evil*? I don't think so. He's harmless, I'm sure of it. What on earth made her think that he was evil?'

'Tabby said that she was never allowed in Mr Ainsworth's room, the door was always locked. Course, Tabby was curious. So, one day, when Mr Ainsworth was out, she sneaked a peek inside. What she saw terrified her!'

'What? What did she see?'

'His room was dark, the walls black. But there were paintings of his mother hanging everywhere – and every painting had been mutilated, the canvas sliced right across her neck. It scared the life out of Tabby. Weird, eh.'

Winnie gulped. 'That *is* a bit peculiar, but it sounds to me like the man held a lot of resentment towards his mother, and rightly so by all accounts. I'd heard she was quite domineering.'

'Oh, she ruled over him. She wouldn't even allow him to work and demanded he stay at home to care for her. His whole life has been spent doing his mother's bidding and for no thanks. No wonder he wanted her dead.'

'Judith! You can't say that!'

'It's true, Mrs Berry. Why else would he have sliced her throat on every painting? And when his mother died, everyone reckoned he had something to do with it.'

'Right, that's enough of that sort of talk. We should feel sorry for the fella. It sounds like his life has been grim enough. The last thing Mr Ainsworth needs is gossip and rumours flying around about him. Go on, get yourself home. I'll see you tonight.'

Winnie was looking forward to locking the door behind Judith. She wanted nothing more than to sit down for half an hour and put her feet up with a cup of tea and enjoy the wireless for company. 'Cor, to say I'm knackered would be an understatement,' she said as she saw Judith out. As the girl left and Winnie went to close the door, Terry pushed his way in.

'Manners, Terry! Don't mind me,' Winnie scolded.

'Win – there's been trouble. I've just seen Stephen. He's got a fat lip and two black eyes.'

Winnie felt sick. She didn't need to ask who had walloped the man.

'Brancher had a mate with him outside the prison and when Stephen confronted him, they both had a go. His mate held Stephen's arms behind his back as Brancher punched him. I swear, Win, if I get my hands on Brancher, I'll knock him from here to kingdom come.'

'This is all we need. I don't know what made me think that Stephen would have some joy talking any sense into Brancher. The man is out of control.'

'Stephen said he knows that Brancher will come for his sister. Brancher's words, *I'm going to make my wife sorry for what she's done. And Victor's a dead man walking.* Stephen reckons Maureen should go into hiding. He's going to Croydon to meet Vic from work and then he's coming back here with him to get Maureen.'

Winnie felt a cold chill run down her back and the hairs on the back of her neck stood on end. 'Christ, what do we do in the meantime?'

'Get Maureen out of here and to somewhere safe,' Terry suggested.

'What, run away from him? That ain't how I do things.'

'I know, Winnie, but you've got Grace and your pub to think about.'

'Even so, I don't believe that running away is the answer. I ain't scared of Brancher.'

'It's not you he's after. He's gunning for Maureen. We need to warn her.'

Winnie drew in a long breath. 'All right, she's upstairs. I'll talk to her. And listen to me, Terry, I mean this – you're not to confront Brancher, do you understand?'

'I won't have him hurting any of you.'

'I know, and I appreciate you being here. But remember that you've got a bullet in your back. I'd hate anything to happen to you. Please, Terry, if we get any trouble here from Brancher, you're to stay out of it as best you can.'

Terry nodded, but Winnie knew that the man would put himself in danger to protect her. He was like a son to her. As she climbed the stairs, thoughts of David drifted through her mind. There'd been many times when she'd wished that David had been more like Terry. Her son's death would always hurt, but she refused to show her pain. She couldn't bear the thought of losing Terry too.

Maureen was in the kitchen, pacing back and forth.

'I'm a nervous wreck,' she said. 'Stephen should be back by now. What if something awful has happened to him.'

'Sit down, love, we need to talk,' Winnie said, calmly.

'What is it?' Maureen asked, alarmed. 'Is Stephen hurt? Is he dead? Oh, Winnie, this is all my fault!'

Winnie grabbed Maureen squarely by the shoulders and

looked into her eyes. 'Breathe in deeply then out slowly. You must calm down, Maureen. That's it … breathe … breathe … Now sit down.'

Winnie pulled out a seat opposite. 'Stephen has seen Brancher. Your brother tried to talk to him but got a smack in the mouth for his efforts. Stephen is fine, just a bit bruised, and he doesn't want you running round there or worrying about him. He's going to Croydon to meet Vic and then they'll both come back here. Now, we can either wait here for them, or get you round to Hilda's. Brancher won't think to look for you at Hilda's, so you'll be safe there.'

Maureen covered her face with her hands. 'But if I'm at Hilda's, how will Vic and Stephen find me?'

'I'll stay here. Brancher ain't got any beef with me. It's you and Vic he wants to hurt. Go and pack a bag, as quick as you can. Me and Terry will walk you round to Hilda's.'

'It ain't fair, Winnie! I love Vic, I love him so much. I didn't know what love was until I met him. And now Brancher is going to destroy everything.'

'Listen to me, Maureen, and listen hard. We won't let that man destroy anything. Now scoot, get a move on. We don't have the luxury of time on our side.'

Maureen rushed off, leaving Winnie feeling sick in the pit of her stomach. She hoped they wouldn't bump into Brancher and his mate. And she hoped she could get Maureen out of here and to Hilda's before Brancher came looking for her.

Maureen's eyes darted around as she marched between Winnie and Terry. Hilda didn't live far away from the Battersea Tavern, but the short walk to her house felt like a hundred miles to

Maureen. She couldn't wait to get inside and out of harm's way.

Hilda looked surprised to see them on her doorstep and even more surprised when she saw Terry carrying Maureen's bag stuffed with clothes.

'Sorry, Hilda, but we need to hide Maureen here for a while.'

Hilda stepped to one side to allow them in. 'I assume Brancher is on the rampage?' she asked.

'Yes. Stephen and Vic will collect Maureen later. Is that all right?'

'Of course it is. Maureen, you can stay for as long as you need to.'

In Hilda's one room, Maureen couldn't be sure, but she thought she saw the woman kick a bottle of whisky under the bed. A layer of cigarette smoke hung in the air and Maureen saw an empty glass on the table. She suspected that Hilda was drinking again, though Winnie hadn't seemed to notice.

Maureen took her bag from Terry and stood awkwardly in the middle of the room.

Winnie looked through the net curtains, glancing up and down the street. 'I'm pretty sure that he didn't see us coming here, but it's probably best to draw your curtains. Terry, do you mind staying here until Vic and Stephen arrive?'

'That's fine by me, but I don't like the idea of you being alone in the pub.'

'I won't be alone. Grace is there now, and later, Judith will be working, and I'll have a pub full of me regulars. Tommy said the police will be keeping a close eye on the pub too. I'll be all right. I think you're needed here more.'

Maureen was relieved and grateful to know that Terry would be staying with them.

Hilda lit a cigarette. 'Put the kettle on, Maureen, you know where the kitchen is.'

'I won't stay,' Winnie said. 'I don't like leaving Grace alone. Thanks for this, Hilda. Maureen, I'll see you soon, love. Try not to worry, this will all be over soon.'

Over, Maureen thought. How was it ever going to be over? Either her husband was going to kill her and Vic, or they'd have to start a new life somewhere where Brancher would never find them. Vic had talked about America and getting his old job back. He'd said they could move to the States and have a comfortable life, but Maureen had instantly dismissed the idea. Now though, with the reality of Brancher vying for their blood, she thought fleeing to America with Vic might be their best option.

43

Winnie had warned Grace to stay in her bedroom and told the girl the reason why. Thankfully, Grace didn't appear to be unnerved by the threat of Brancher, but Winnie was. She was more than unnerved, though she put on a brave face. Standing behind her bar with her palms flat on the counter, her stomach flipped each time the door opened. Yet she kept a brave smile on her face.

'What should I do if Brancher comes in?' Judith asked.

'Just stay back and leave him to me,' Winnie answered, her eyes fixed on the door.

A fella at the end of the bar tapped a coin on the counter. 'Any chance of a drink?' he called. 'This was a pub the last time I checked.'

Judith sauntered towards him. 'And it still is,' she said, 'The beer pumps give it away.'

'I could take me money elsewhere,' the old boy smiled.

'Yeah, you could, but you won't.'

'What makes you so sure?'

'Where else would you find a pub in Battersea with a girl working behind the bar who's as pretty as me?'

'I'd find one with less lip,' the man chortled.

'Leave off, Mr Palmer, you'll never desert the Battersea Tavern. Now, what can I get you? Your usual?'

Winnie was pleased to hear that Judith had found her feet and was giving the customers as good as she got. But listening to the girl bantering with the old men didn't distract Winnie from her fears. The door opened again and Winnie tensed. She was pleased to see Terry come in.

'They've gone,' he whispered

'Where?'

'Vic said he'd find a hotel near Croydon and Stephen's gone with them. I don't know if Maureen was serious, but I heard her telling Hilda that she might move to America. Vic can have his old job back and she reckons he could get Stephen a job there too.'

'You're kidding? Maureen, move to America? Never. I'll believe it when I see it. The woman wouldn't even get in a rowing boat on the lake at Battersea Park, let alone a boat halfway round the world.'

'I'm only telling you what I heard. Let's face it, Winnie, if you had Brancher breathing down your neck, you'd be on the first boat out of here too, wouldn't you?'

'I don't know, Terry. There must be another way. Mind you, Maureen would probably have a smashing life in America. At least they ain't still living on rations like us poor buggers.'

Winnie noticed Terry's eyes following Judith. 'She's pretty, but a bit young for you.'

Looking sad, Terry sighed, 'I couldn't, Winnie. There'll never be another woman in my life. No one could ever replace Jan.'

Winnie's wounded heart felt as though the plaster had

been ripped off. 'Jan was such a special lady. She brought us so much joy. Do you ever feel her around us, Terry?'

'Yeah, Win, I do. All the time.'

'Me an' all, love. I know she's here.'

Judith's voice carried over from the end of the bar. 'Knock, knock,' she said.

'Who's there?' several men asked in unison.

'Cows go.'

'Cows go who?' the men said.

'No, cows go moo,' Judith laughed.

Winnie looked across the bar to Terry. 'That girl is going to be an asset to my pub,' she smiled. 'As long as she doesn't break any more glasses.'

Terry sat in the pub all evening.

At ten o'clock, Winnie said to him, 'I'm glad it's closing time and Brancher hasn't shown up.'

'I think you spoke too soon.'

Winnie looked past Terry, her heart sinking at the sight of Brancher and his mate striding towards the bar.

Terry jumped off the bar stall and stood glaring at Brancher.

'Evening, Mrs Berry,' Brancher sneered, looking Terry up and down.

'You ain't welcome in my pub,' Winnie said, and folded her arms across her chest.

'I wouldn't drink in 'ere if you paid me. But I know my wife is living here, and I reckon she'll be pleased as punch to see me.'

'You're wasting your time, Brancher. Maureen ain't here and even if she was, you'd be the last man on earth that she'd want to see.'

'Now, now, Mrs Berry. There's no need to be rude. Maureen is still my wife which means I've got rights. So, where is she?'

'Do you think I'd tell *you*? She's not here and you won't find her. Clear off or I'll call the police.'

'And tell them what? That I smashed a glass? Oops,' Brancher said, and knocked a glass off the counter.

'I mean it, Brancher. Get out!'

'Not until I know where Maureen is,' Brancher hissed.

Terry stepped in front of him. 'You heard, Mrs Berry. Get out.'

To Winnie's horror, she saw Brancher push Terry.

'Come on then, big man, let's see what you've got,' Brancher coaxed.

Winnie saw Terry's fists clench at his side. 'No, Terry, don't,' she shouted. 'He ain't worth it!'

Brancher turned to her, snarling. 'Where's my wife?' he ground out.

Winnie leaned forward over the bar. 'I. Ain't. Telling. You,' she stated, slowly and firmly.

Brancher spat on the floor. 'Bitch!' he snapped.

Winnie braced herself, half expecting him to leap over the bar and grab her by the throat, but instead, he sauntered towards the door, and even had the audacity to wave. Then turning, he growled, 'You'll pay for this,' and blew her a kiss.

'Jesus Christ,' she exhaled, her heart racing. 'Lock the doors, Terry. Quickly.'

'Do you think he'll be back?'

'Yeah, I'm sure of it. We ain't seen the last of Brancher Fanning.'

44

Grace was still awake hours after Winnie and Terry had gone to bed. Earlier that day, in school, Grace had said to Pauline that because they weren't allowed out, they should skip a day off school and have some fun. Pauline had said yes and suggested that Grace should pinch a bottle of booze. Neither of them had ever drunk alcohol, and they'd agreed it might be a laugh.

Grace pushed open her bedroom door, her ears pricked, listening intently. She could hear Winnie snoring. Good, the woman was sound asleep. Creeping past Terry's closed bedroom door Grace felt sure that he'd be sleeping too.

She snuck down the stairs and into the pub. It looked different in the dark, the street lamps outside shining through the windows and casting strange shadows on the walls. Grace slipped behind the bar. Her eyes searched the bottles. Gin, vodka, rum, whisky... There were so many, and she didn't know which one to take.

As she tried to decide, a sudden loud, shattering noise pierced the silence and made her jump out of her skin. Stifling a scream, and spinning around, she looked through the smashed window and saw the dark figure of a man running away. And then, to her horror, she noticed that on the floor among the shards of glass, blue and orange flames leaping into the air and spreading over the floorboards.

'F-f – FIRE!' she screamed.

Grace stared, terrified, as the flames grew higher, licking the ceiling and setting the curtains alight. She could feel the searing heat of the fire prickling her skin, and thick, black smoke began to choke her. Dropping to her knees, she crawled from behind the bar and tried to find her way to the stairs. But the smoke stung her eyes and made it impossible to see where she was going. Feeling her way along a skirting board, desperate to escape the roaring blaze, Grace found herself in the small back kitchen. She slammed the door closed and sucked in some cleaner air. But her heart hammered when she noticed that smoke was beginning to seep under the door. Grace remembered the smog, and how Winnie had used wet towels around the windows. Thinking quickly, she soaked a couple of tea towels in water before pushing them to the bottom of the door.

'HELP!' she cried at the top of her voice. 'FIRE! WINNIE! TERRY! WAKE UP! FIRE!'

Grace didn't think that they would hear her upstairs and through closed doors. And the roaring sound of the fire would have drowned out her cries. But she had to keep trying. She couldn't give up. Grace didn't want to burn to death or suffocate, and she feared that Winnie and Terry would die in their beds. 'FIRE! FIRE!' she screeched, again and again until her throat felt red raw. 'WINNIE! WAKE UP! WINNIE!'

The door flew open and smoke wafted in. Grace covered her mouth and squinted her eyes.

'This way,' Winnie called. 'Hurry!'

Reaching through the darkness, Grace found Winnie's hand and grasped it tightly. The woman was coughing and spluttering as she pulled Grace through the dense smoke and out of the back door. At last, she gasped for breath.

'Are you all right?' Winnie asked.

Tears streamed down Grace's soot-covered face. She nodded as she gawped at Winnie. The woman's hair looked singed and her cheek, the side of her neck and down one arm were covered with red, swollen blisters. 'You're hurt, Winnie,' Grace sobbed.

'It's fine. Come on, we need to find Terry.'

'Oh, God, Winnie, he's not in there, is he?'

'No, love, he got out,' Winnie winced, clearly in pain. 'He'll be round the front somewhere.'

Terry came running around the corner. 'Thank Gawd, you found her!' he said, and dropped to his knees, coughing. 'Is she all right?' he gasped.

'Yes,' Winnie answered. 'Grace is fine. Are *you*?'

'Yeah, I'll survive. But you're burned. You need an ambulance.'

'Don't worry about that now. We need to call the fire brigade. My pub, Terry – my pub is burning down!' Winnie cried.

'The fire brigade are already here. Come on,'

Rushing around to the front of the building, Grace was shocked to see flames coming out of the downstairs windows. She could hear bottles exploding as the fire crackled and fought for life against the water from the firemen's hoses. Several neighbours had poured out onto the street and stood watching the Battersea Tavern burning.

'Save my pub,' Winnie whimpered. 'Please, save my pub!'

Mrs Middleton placed a blanket over Winnie's shoulders. 'You're injured, Mrs Berry. There's an ambulance here for you.'

'No, I can't leave my pub,' Winnie protested.

'Go, Winnie. I'll stay here,' Terry coughed. 'Take Grace with you.'

Two ambulancemen eased Winnie into the back of their ambulance and helped Grace in too. As the doors closed, Grace reached for Winnie's hand.

'My pub!' the woman howled, 'Everything we own – it's gone. It's all gone up in flames!'

45

The next day, against the advice of the fire brigade, Winnie stepped into the burned ruins of the Battersea Tavern. The fire had destroyed the bar and the tables and chairs. The windows were boarded over and the mirror on the back wall had been shattered. She peered around at the charred remains of her pub, fighting back tears. But at least the fire hadn't reached upstairs, though the fire brigade had warned her that she would find a lot of smoke damage.

Grace called from outside the back door: 'Can I come in now?'

'Yes, I think it's safe enough.'

'Flippin' 'ell,' Grace gulped, gazing at the blackened ceiling and soaked embers all around.

'There's nothing left,' Winnie sniffed.

'At least we're all alive.'

'Yes, that's a blessing,' Winnie sighed.

Something had been playing on her mind. And now, amidst the destruction, Winnie asked, 'What were you doing in the back kitchen, Grace? Why wasn't you in your bedroom? Had you tried to escape?'

Grace hung her head which further heightened Winnie's suspicions.

'Please, Grace, we've been through enough. No lies. Just tell me what happened. You can tell me the truth, I'm too tired to be angry. Did you start the fire?'

'No, Winnie, no, I swear, I didn't!'

'So, what was you doing downstairs?' Winnie asked, distrustfully. She didn't want to believe that Grace was responsible for causing the fire, but it seemed a plausible explanation.

Grace's bottom lip began to quiver and Winnie assumed the girl was feeling guilty.

'I was going to pinch a bottle of booze for me and Pauline,' Grace cried. 'I'm sorry, Winnie, I know it was wrong. But before I had a chance to take one, I heard the window smash and saw a bloke outside. He ran off and then I saw the flames. I think he'd thrown something through the window that started the fire.'

Winnie's eyes widened. 'Did you recognise the man?'

'No.'

'Can you describe him?'

'No, it was too dark.'

'We need to tell the police about this.' Winnie seethed. She knew who'd set her pub alight. Brancher. He'd thrown a petrol bomb through the window and destroyed everything that Winnie had worked so hard for. He'd taken away her livelihood and he'd left her with a burned-out shell and a broken heart. One way or another, Winnie would see to it that Brancher paid for what he'd done.

★

An hour later, in a state of shocked numbness, Winnie had seen enough of the damage caused by the fire. Upstairs stank of smoke and black soot covered everything. It would take weeks to get the flat clean and all their clothes and bedding would need washing. The community were kind, a stream of concerned neighbours popping in with bowls of stew, clean clothes, blankets, cups of tea and comforting words. Winnie was grateful, but their generosity couldn't bring back the Battersea Tavern.

The police had called in too, and Grace had told them what she'd seen the night before. Though with a lack of a description of the man outside, they'd said there was little they could do apart from check to see if anyone in the street had noticed anything. But considering the time of the arson attack, they doubted that there'd be witnesses.

'We'd better check on Hilda and let her know what's happened,' Winnie said to Grace. 'Come on, love, we'll worry about cleaning this place later. I haven't got the energy to face it now.'

As Winnie and Grace opened the back door, Piano Pete was about to knock.

'I'm so sorry, Winnie. What can I do to help?' the man asked.

'Thanks, love, but there's nothing you can do unless you know anything about who started the fire?' Winnie asked, hopefully.

'There's rumours that Brancher did it, but it's only gossip, Winnie. You'll be all right, won't you? I mean, you're insured, ain't you? The insurance will pay out to cover the costs of repairs.'

Winnie was so tired she hadn't thought about repairs and insurance. A spark of hope ignited inside and she smiled. 'Pete, you're a bloody genius!'

Tramping back up the stairs, Winnie rifled through a drawer in her bedroom where she kept her important paper-work. Birth certificates, death certificates, the deeds to the Battersea Tavern, and sitting on top of it all, the insurance policy. Grabbing the document, she sat on the edge of her bed, her eyes scanning through the complicated wording, searching for fire-related damage. Her heart soared as she tried to comprehend the terms and conditions, but the way she understood it, the insurance company would send an assessor who would calculate the cost of damage and repair.

Holding the document to her chest, Winnie closed her eyes and leaned her head back, a smile on her face. It would take some time, but one day soon, the Battersea Tavern would be open for business again.

Terry tapped on the bedroom door. 'You all right, Winnie?'

'Yes, love, I'm better than all right.'

'You look sore,' he said, pointing at the bandages on her arms and plasters on her neck.

'It smarts a bit, but the burns aren't deep. Where have you been?'

'Down the café for some breakfast.'

'Well, Terry, I've got some smashing news,' Winnie grinned. 'Look at this,' she said, shoving the document into his hands. 'It's the insurance policy for the pub. It covers fire. I should get a good enough pay out to have the place made shipshape again.'

Terry sat beside Winnie on the bed, frowning as he studied the papers.

Winnie pointed to the paragraphs about fire damage. 'Look, it says so right there.'

Terry turned his face to look at her, his expression grave. 'Have you renewed this? Have you got another policy?'

'Eh? What do you mean?'

'Winnie, I'm sorry, but this insurance expired a month ago.'

Winnie snatched the document from Terry's hands. 'What?' she spluttered, 'Let me see.'

Reading the date three times, she stared blankly ahead as her heart plummeted and her stomach twisted. She remembered the letters she'd received from the insurance company. The ones she'd put to one side and had every intention of dealing with. But somehow, with everything that had happened lately, she'd forgotten to address renewing the policy. Any hope or dream of reopening the Battersea Tavern faded as silent tears rolled down Winnie's face.

Grace offered to stay with Terry and start on the cleaning upstairs. Several neighbours mucked in too, and Winnie's dear friend, Flo, oversaw the clean-up operation. Winnie left them to it and traipsed around to see Hilda.

When she knocked on the door and there was no answer, she assumed that Hilda was sleeping as the woman was still recovering from the major surgery. She tapped on the window too, but Hilda still didn't answer. Fear crept in. Had Brancher got to Hilda too? Banging loudly on the window again, Winnie tried to peer through a clink in the drawn curtains, but she couldn't see anything.

'Hilda? Hilda?' she called.

She hammered on the door. Nothing.

Convinced that some terrible fate had met the woman, Winnie hurried back to the Battersea Tavern.

'Terry, I can't raise Hilda. I'm worried that she's dead or Brancher has got to her.'

They rushed back to Hilda's. Winnie stood anxiously as Terry banged on the front door and then on the window.

'She's in there, I know she is. What should we do?' Winnie asked.

'I can kick the door in, or we can call the police.'

'There's no time to call the police. Do it, Terry. Kick the door in. She could be lying in there, desperate for help.'

Terry pulled back his booted foot and kicked at the door three times before the wood splintered and gave way. He went in first, with Winnie right behind him. Turning the handle of the door to Hilda's room, it wasn't locked. He pushed it open just a crack. Winnie dreaded what they might find on the other side.

'Do you want to wait here, Winnie?'

'No, go on,' Winnie urged.

When Terry pushed the door open wider, an awful stench wafted out. Winnie recognised the smell. Stale tobacco, booze and vomit.

Inside, the only light came through the small clink in the curtains, but in the darkness, Winnie saw Hilda on the floor beside the bed. Terry pulled open the curtains as Winnie rushed to her friend.

'Hilda! Hilda, it's me, Winnie. Wake up, love.'

Hilda's eyes opened, and as she smacked her lips together,

she gazed blearily at Winnie. That's when Winnie realised that the woman was drunk. Glancing around, she saw the empty whisky bottle and the half-drunk glass on the table.

'You stupid, stupid cow!' Winnie barked. 'I've a good mind to leave you to wallow in the booze. Me pub's gone, Hilda, I can't be dealing with you an' all!'

'Bugger off,' Hilda said, and dribbled.

'Yeah, I think I will. You're a bloody waste of space, Hilda.' Then looking at Terry, she said, 'Come on. Sod her and sod her bleedin' drinking.'

'You can't leave her like that,' Terry said, quietly.

'I bloody well can, and I will!'

Winnie stamped out of the door. 'Can you fix this?' she asked Terry, nodding to the broken frame.

'Yeah, Win, I'll sort it.'

Winnie marched back to the Battersea Tavern, angry with Hilda and upset. She needed her friend, but Hilda had let her down. A cascade of worrying thoughts bombarded Winnie's brain. The telephone wasn't working, so how would Maureen let them know where she was? And Rachel, should Winnie protect her from her mother's drinking? She needed to tell them about the fire. And Carmen too. Of everyone, Winnie missed Carmen the most. Her mind raced. What if Brancher came back to finish her off? Grace could have been killed. They could all have burned to death!

'Argh!' Winnie cried, grabbing hold of a garden wall to steady herself and clutching her fist to her chest as a sharp pain stabbed at her heart. 'Oh, Christ,' she groaned, struggling to catch her breath. The pain went across her shoulders and down her arms. It felt as though a clamp was around her chest, slowly tightening and squeezing the life out of her. *I'm not ready to meet you yet,* she said in her head to God. *Don't take me. Don't you dare bloody take me!*

46

Grace dipped a sponge into a bucket of soapy water and scrubbed the bannisters upstairs. Several people were in the flat, washing, scrubbing and airing the place, trying to get it nice for Winnie again.

Glancing through the bannisters, she saw Mrs Middleton coming up the stairs, a baby on her hip and Pauline behind. Grace wanted to run into Pauline's arms, but she didn't in case Mrs Middleton scolded her.

Mrs Middleton spoke to Flo who was in charge. Flo normally worked on a stall in the market, selling dresses alongside her husband, Bill, but today, like many, she'd abandoned her work to muck in at the Battersea Tavern.

'I told Pauline she can have the day off school. We're all knackered. I don't think anyone on the street got much sleep last night what with all the goings on. As you can see, I've got me hands full, but Pauline can help where it's needed.'

Flo wiped her hands down the front of her apron. 'Thanks, Mrs Middleton. There's so much to do.'

Mrs Middleton looked from Grace to Pauline. 'Stay out of trouble, the pair of you.'

'Don't worry,' Flo smiled, 'I'll be keeping them too busy to get into any mischief.'

'Pauline can help me,' Grace quickly suggested.

'Get on with it then,' Mrs Middleton urged, nudging her daughter.

Once Mrs Middleton was out of sight, Grace threw her arms around Pauline. 'I'm glad you're here,' she said.

'How are you? It must have been an awful fright!'

'I thought I was going to die! I've never been so scared. Winnie saved my life!'

'How? What happened?'

'I'd sneaked downstairs to pinch us a bottle of something, and that's when the fire started. It took a hold really quickly, and before I knew it, the pub was filled with smoke. I couldn't see where I was going and ended up trapped in the back kitchen. That's where Winnie found me and dragged me outside. Terry had gone round the front of the building to try to get to me, but the flames fought him back. If Winnie hadn't of risked her life to save mine, I'd be cinders now.'

'Blimey, Grace!'

'And Winnie got burned. She's all right, but she got hurt saving me. Can you believe that? Can you believe she did that for me?'

'Mrs Berry is so brave! She must think a lot of you to have done that.'

Grace nodded. 'I thought the same. I didn't think she cared about me, but she does. She cares a lot! And do you know what? I don't think she's ever gonna take me to the children's home.'

'Mrs Berry wouldn't do that! Did you think she would?'

'Yeah, Pauline, I did. Especially after I told her that I was going to pinch a bottle of booze. But from now on I'm gonna pull me socks up and behave meself.'

Flo came past, carrying a bundle of bedclothes. 'I can hear a lot of chatter here, but I can't see much work getting done.'

'Sorry,' Grace said, and soaked her sponge. She thought the woman looked harsh with her hair pulled into a tight bun, but Grace knew that Flo was a good friend to Winnie. Many people had turned up to help, which made Grace realise that Winnie was very well regarded in the neighbourhood. And she could understand why people thought highly of her. *I'm lucky to have Winnie to take care of me,* she thought. And she vowed to herself that from now on, she wouldn't cause the woman any more trouble and she'd show Winnie a lot more appreciation.

As the girls washed the soot from the bannisters, Piano Pete bounded up the stairs, calling for Terry.

Terry emerged from the kitchen, asking, 'What?'

'Terry,' Pete said, panting, 'you've gotta come quick, mate. It's Winnie. She's in the hospital.'

'Why? What's happened?'

'I dunno, mate, I think she's had an heart attack.'

Grace dropped the sponge. *Nooo!* she screamed in her head. *Winnie can't die!*

47

Roy was worried about Rachel. He'd seen the stress on her face when he'd dropped her at the hospital to visit Winnie. And on top of Winnie's heart attack, the Battersea Tavern had burned down, and Rachel had found her mother in a drunken stupor.

Roy's knuckles turned white as he clutched the steering wheel. He had to be strong for Rachel. He couldn't go back to his old ways of dealing with things and risk losing her. But he yearned to feel the comfort of a silky dress against his skin. He wanted to slick a red colour on his lips and tell Lillian how he felt. He knew his sister couldn't hear him but talking to her helped him to unload his feelings.

Battling the urge to don a frock, he reminded himself, *you're a man.* Then his father's words rang in his head, *big boys don't cry. You're soft, a queer, you've let me down.* He remembered the look of disgust in his dad's eyes when his brother had announced his dirty secret in the Battersea Tavern for all to hear. And he recalled the excruciating pain he'd felt when his brother and his father had almost battered him to death. Yet through it all, Rachel had stuck by him. She'd given up her life, her friends, her family and her business to move away from Battersea with him. He owed it to her to keep to his word. No matter how difficult life might get or what challenges they might have to overcome, Roy vowed that he'd always love Rachel in the way she deserved. And that meant no more dressing in women's clothes and talking to Lillian. Deep down, though, Roy knew that his strength would eventually fail. His other persona was a part of him, something he doubted he'd be able to deny himself. But if he gave in to his urges, he knew he'd have to keep it a secret from Rachel.

Rachel was too familiar with the hospital. First Roy, then her mum and now she was sitting beside Winnie. She looked across the bed to Carmen, saying, 'Maureen should be here too.'

'I know. I should imagine she's at Southampton docks, waiting to board the ship that will take her off to America.'

'I never thought she'd go. Did you?'

Carmen shook her head. 'No, not Maureen. She must think a lot of Vic. I hope they have a happy life together.'

Terry joined in the conversation. 'She'll be all right. She's got her brother with her – Stephen will keep an eye on her. And Charlie the drayman said that when she telephoned the brewery, she said to let us all know that she'd write as soon as she arrives.'

Rachel glanced at Grace. The girl had been exceptionally quiet. 'Are you worrying about Winnie?' she asked.

Grace nodded, tears welling in her eyes.

'She'll be fine. Winnie is as tough as old boots. Trust me, she'll be bossing us all around soon and smiling.'

'I miss her smile,' Carmen lamented. 'Come rain or shine, Winnie always had a smile on her face.'

'Yeah, she did,' Terry agreed. 'She was always a jolly soul.'

Rachel sniffed. 'Battersea won't be the same without the Battersea Tavern and Winnie behind the bar to greet everyone.'

'You can say that again,' Carmen said. 'That pub and Winnie are going to be sorely missed.'

'I ain't dead yet,' Winnie croaked. 'So stop talking about me like I'm a goner.'

Rachel leaped to her feet and leaned over the bed. 'Winnie, you're awake!'

'I've been awake for bleedin' ages, listening to you lot harping on about me and the pub. Cor, you're a morbid bunch.'

Rachel turned to Grace, grinning. 'See, I told you she'd be fine.'

'That's right, I am. Though I must admit, I did think for a moment that I was off to meet him upstairs. But me old ticker is still beating nice and strong.'

'Maybe so, but you've got to slow down, Winnie,' Carmen cautioned. 'You were lucky this time but take this heart attack as a warning.'

'Yeah, yeah, yeah, stop nagging,' Winnie smiled. 'Has anyone seen the doctor? Have they said when I'm being discharged?'

'See what I mean?' Carmen said. 'Slow down!'

Rachel shook her head. 'You're going to be in here for a few days yet.'

'I can't! There's too much to do,' Winnie protested.

'Everything's in hand,' Terry assured. 'You're not to worry about a thing.'

Winnie looked at Rachel. "'Ere, love, you couldn't get me a fresh jug of water, could you?' she asked.

Rachel passed the jug to Grace, asking the girl, 'Do you mind filling it up?'

Grace readily took it.

'Rachel, would you go and fetch the nurse for me please?'

'Why?'

'I'd like a quick word with her.'

'If you're going to badger the nurse about when you'll be discharged, then no, I won't fetch her.'

Winnie huffed. 'Can you see if there's any tea available? I bet you're all parched.'

'Are you trying to get rid of me?' Rachel asked. 'Do this, do that ... if you're wondering do I know about my mum, then the answer is yes. Roy drove me round there to bring her here, but she couldn't stand up straight.'

'Oh, Gawd, I'm so sorry, love. I've been reluctant to tell you, but she's been like it for a while.'

'I tried telling her about the fire and about you being in here, but she was incoherent. I suppose I'll have to drag her home with me. She can't be trusted to be left alone to look after herself.'

Out of the corner of her eye, Winnie saw a chap walking through the ward with a big bunch of colourful flowers in his hand, obscuring his face. But there was something about the way he walked that reminded her of someone. 'I don't believe it,' Winnie muttered. 'It's Tommy Bradbury!'

'Hello, Winnie,' he beamed.

'What on earth are you doing here?' Winnie asked. Though they spoke regularly on the telephone, she hadn't seen Tommy in years, not since he'd moved out of London. The man hadn't changed much. His hair was a little thinner, but his skin had a healthy glow and his face had filled out a bit.

'I had a call from the police station about the fire. Cor blimey, Winnie, what have you been up to?'

'She's been working too hard and worrying about everyone else too much,' Carmen explained.

'Huh, nothing new there then,' Tommy chuckled.

'Give Tommy your seat, Rachel,' Winnie ordered. 'The man has had a long journey.'

Grace had returned with the jug of water, and Rachel smiled at her, saying, 'Winnie's bossing us around again. I told you it wouldn't be long before she'd be back to herself.'

As Rachel rose to her feet, Tommy shook his head. 'No, young lady, you keep your seat.' Then gazing warmly at Winnie, he said, 'I've got some good news that might make you feel better.'

'Oh yeah, go on then, I could do with some good news.'

Tommy looked around from one person to another, and then announced, 'Brancher Fanning is going to be charged with arson and attempted murder.'

'*What*? Have your lot caught him?'

'No, not yet, but they will. And when they do, there's enough evidence to send him back to prison for a long, long time.'

Grace spoke quietly. 'But I thought I was the only witness – and I didn't see him properly.'

'The police went door to door making enquiries. It turns out that Mrs Middleton saw Brancher walk past her window. She was wide awake seeing to the baby, and when she saw Brancher, she guessed he was up to no good at that time of the night. So, she stepped outside and that's when she saw

311

him light a rag that was stuffed into a bottle and then she said he threw it through the pub window. The woman is willing to stand up in court and testify to what she saw.'

'Well, I never!' Winnie exclaimed.

Rachel thought it was odd that Mrs Middleton hadn't mentioned what she'd seen to anyone else.

'And, to support Mrs Middleton's account, the milkman said he saw Brancher running away from your street. I doubt there's a judge in Britain who won't put Brancher back where he belongs.'

'Then Maureen can come home,' Rachel mused.

'Not so fast,' Carmen said, 'They've got to catch Brancher first.'

'That *is* good news, but it won't bring back my pub,' Winnie sighed.

Rachel knew how much the loss of the Battersea Tavern had hurt Winnie. She wished there was something they could do, but no one had the money it would take to rebuild the pub. She'd considered a local whip-round, but she'd quickly dismissed that idea. Rachel doubted that they'd raise enough and, in any case, she knew that Winnie wouldn't want charity.

'It's getting dark outside,' Carmen commented. 'I should be getting off.'

'Yes, me too,' Rachel said. 'Roy is meeting me outside and then I suppose I'd better think about dragging my mum home with me.'

'She'll kick and scream,' Winnie warned. 'Don't let her upset you, love. You know how nasty she can be when she's drunk.'

'Drink makes her say wicked things, but I won't take any notice. I'd like to know where she's been getting the booze from. Someone must have brought it to her. Mum's not been in a fit state to go out and get it for herself.' Rachel suspected it was the fella who lived upstairs. And he'd probably charged her mother well over the odds for it. 'I'll see you on Saturday, Winnie.'

'I'll be out of here by then!'

'I wouldn't count on that. Just make sure you do as the doctors tell you,' Rachel smiled as she walked away.

Meandering through the hospital, Rachel's thoughts went back to her mother. She was dreading Roy seeing how awful her mum could be. She silently prayed that her mother wouldn't mention anything about Roy wearing women's clothes. She knew that Roy would die of embarrassment. It was all behind them now. Roy had promised that he wouldn't do it again and, as far as Rachel knew, he'd kept to his word. *Please don't drag it up again, Mum,* Rachel thought. No one liked her mum when she was drunk, least of all Rachel. Still, it wouldn't take long to get her sober. And if Rachel had to guard her mum for every minute of every day, she would. Anything to keep her mum from drinking again.

Winnie was tired, and though she was grateful for everyone visiting her, she felt relieved when they bade her goodbye. Then, as they went to meander away, Winnie spotted Maureen rushing along the ward towards her bed.

'Maureen!' Carmen exclaimed. 'What are you doing here? We assumed you'd be at Southampton docks and on a boat by now.'

'I was supposed to be, but I couldn't leave without seeing Winnie.'

'I'm all right, love,' Winnie smiled warmly. 'You really shouldn't have risked coming back to Battersea.'

'I know, but I couldn't leave knowing that you were in the hospital. I can't stop though – Vic is waiting outside in a taxicab. But I had to see you for meself. Oh, Win, it's awful seeing you in that bed.'

'I told you, I'm fine, love. Have you heard? The police are looking for Brancher. He's going down for setting my pub alight.'

Maureen's eyes stretched wide. 'Really? Does that mean me and Vic are safe?'

'Not yet,' Tommy answered. 'We've not caught him, but we will.'

'I-I don't have to go to America...' Maureen mumbled, her eyes glazing.

'I'm not so sure,' Winnie said, frowning, 'there's no guarantee that the police will catch Brancher any time soon and you can't hide away in that hotel in Croydon forever. Anyway, ain't you excited about starting a new life in America? It's a smashing opportunity.'

Maureen looked nervous, and Winnie noticed that she was wringing her hands.

'I'm terrified, Winnie. I'd much rather stay here.'

Carmen shook her head. 'Don't you dare think about backing out now,' she warned. 'You've seen what Brancher is capable of. I can't say I'm happy about you leaving, but I'd rather that than standing at your graveside. That man shouldn't be underestimated and he's crafty. He could slip under the Old Bill's noses and get to you and Vic. You *must* make your safety a priority, Maureen.'

'Carmen's right, love,' Winnie added. 'He could have killed

me, Grace and Terry. Please, as much as it hurts to say it, please leave.'

Tears welled in Maureen's eyes as she slowly nodded her head.

'Don't start crying,' Winnie warned. 'You'll start me off an' all,' she smiled.

'Oh, Win, I'm going to miss you so much. I'm gonna miss all of you,' Maureen cried, her voice cracking.

'And we'll all miss you too,' Winnie sniffed. 'You're a changed woman, Maureen. You're strong now, and very capable. I'm so proud of you and I know Len and Renee would be proud of you too. Your grandparents would have wanted you to be happy. Don't let them down, love. Be happy and be bold. Have a good life with Vic. It's clear for all to see that you were made for each other.'

Maureen reached into her small clasp bag and pulled out a handkerchief. 'I do love him, and I want to spend the rest of my life with him, but you make leaving for America sound so final, like I'm never going to see any of you again. I–I don't think I can say goodbye forever,' she sobbed.

'Now, now, now, that's enough of that,' Carmen chided. 'We'll always be here, Maureen. You can visit us whenever you like and who knows, maybe one day, we'll all get on a boat and come and see *you*. No one's dead, so pack it in with the tears. Come here, give us a cuddle.'

As Carmen embraced Maureen, Winnie fought to stop herself from bawling her eyes out. 'Oi, don't forget me,' she said, holding her arms out.

Maureen squeezed Winnie, whispering in her ear, 'I love you, Winnie, and I'll never forget everything that you did for me.'

'I love you too, but get orf, you're squashing me,' she chortled.

Winnie's laugh masked her sorrow. Her pub was gone, and her family were falling apart. Hilda had hit the bottle, Carmen had moved to Balham, Rachel and the children to Carshalton, and now Maureen was going to be on the other side of the world. Sadness engulfed her heart and for a moment, Winnie felt as though she wanted to give up on life. But then her eyes met with Grace's. The girl gazed back lovingly. *You're still needed,* Winnie reminded herself. *That young girl needs you and you're all Grace has got.* She had to get well again and give Grace a secure home. Her family were separated, but they were connected by love, and Winnie knew that was worth its weight in gold.

48

Four days later Grace stood proudly at the top of the stairs, eager to greet Winnie. She couldn't wait to show her how hard everyone had worked to make their home gleaming. There was still a whiff of smoke in the air because the fire had tainted everything. But their clothes, the curtains, the bedding and even a couple of rugs had been freshly laundered. There wasn't a trace of soot anywhere in the flat and the windows were spotless.

Terry had gone to collect her and, standing at the bottom of the stairs, he announced, 'Here she is.'

Grace smiled widely. Winnie looked pleased to be home, though she took a moment to look towards her blackened pub.

Trudging up the stairs, she returned Grace's smile. 'Hello, love.'

'I'm so glad you're home,' Grace squealed, and threw her arms around the woman.

'What a smashing greeting,' Winnie said happily.

'Come and see what we've done. Everyone helped, even

Pauline's mum volunteered Pauline to clean. Cor, Winnie, Flo is even bossier than you!'

'Ha, yes, she is, which is why I left her in charge. My, my, the place looks wonderful.'

'I've got the kettle on, and I made sure we've got your good biscuits in.'

'I'm not supposed to have any biscuits, but a couple won't hurt. The doctor said I need to lose a few pounds, the cheeky bugger,' Winnie guffawed.

Pulling out a seat at the table for Winnie, Grace nodded to a small vase on the table. 'I got some flowers an' all,' she said, proudly.

'Thanks, love, that was thoughtful. And listen, I'm sorry that I asked you if you'd started the fire.'

Grace shrugged. 'It doesn't matter. I'm sorry that I've been so much bother. I won't be anymore, Winnie, I promise.'

'I always knew you were a good girl really,' Winnie winked. 'Now, has that kettle boiled yet? I'm gasping.'

As Grace poured the tea and plated some biscuits, she offered, 'I can cook the dinner this evening.'

Terry pulled a grimacing face.

'I think I can manage,' Winnie replied.

'I'll help then.'

'Listen, love, I appreciate you making such an effort, but I'm fine. There's no need to worry.'

'I know you're all right — I just want to show you how grateful I am. I mean, you could have slung me in the orphanage, but you didn't. And you saved my life!'

'I've said it before and I'll say it again — we're family, Grace. We look out for each other, and no matter what happens, you ain't going nowhere. You're stuck with me now, whether you like it or not.'

Grace smiled. She liked it. She liked being stuck with Winnie very much.

When someone knocked on the back door, Terry said, 'I'll get it,' before sloping out of the kitchen.

He returned two minutes later with Pauline and Mrs Middleton.

'It's good to see you home, Mrs Berry.'

'Thank you. And I'm grateful for you sending Pauline to help with the clean-up.'

'It's like the days of the Blitz. We all look out for each other and help where we can.'

'I hear you've spoken to the police about what you saw on the night of the fire. I can't tell you how much that means to me.'

Mrs Middleton's back stiffened. 'He did it, didn't he? Brancher Fanning.'

'Yes, I'm sure it was him.'

'Then he'll get what's coming to him. To think what could have happened. I mean, he could have killed Grace! I can't stand men like that. And you're sure it was him?'

'Yes, I believe so. But you saw him, didn't you?'

'Not me,' Mrs Middleton smiled wryly. 'The baby sleeps right through the night. Always has.'

'But—'

'But the police don't know I've got a good sleeper, do they?'

Grace's eyes widened and Winnie was agape. Mrs Middleton had lied to the police!

'I, erm, I don't know what to say,' Winnie mumbled. 'The

milkman, Mr Mockford … did he see Brancher running away from here?'

'You must be kidding! Old Milky Mockford is lucky to get his bottles to your doorstep before lunchtime. He don't get out of bed till most of us have had our second cuppa of the day. No, Milky was out for the count. But he's good mates with my Bob.'

'Blimey, Mrs Middleton, I'm rarely at a loss for words. All I can say is thank you very much.'

'No need for thanks. Like I said, I can't stand blokes like Brancher Fanning. He had no regards for young Grace's life. Gawd, I hope they catch him soon.' Then turning to the girls, she added, 'And not a peep out of you two about what you just heard, all right?'

'I don't know what you mean, Mum. I never heard a thing,' Pauline said and nudged Grace.

'Me neither,' she said. 'I didn't hear nothing.'

'Good girls.'

Winnie cleared her throat. 'Grace, love, why don't you take Pauline to your room?'

Grace nodded eagerly. 'Come on,' she said to her friend. 'I've got some nail colours that Rachel gave me. We can paint each other's nails.'

Grace was nervous of Mrs Middleton, though she didn't know why, and she was keen to get out of her sight. 'I can't believe your mum lied to the police,' she whispered.

'I'd be too scared to. I don't think my mum is scared of anything or anyone, not even me dad.'

'But you said your dad hits your mum.'

'Yeah, he does, and nine times out of ten she hits him back, and a lot flippin' harder than he hits her.'

The girls fell about giggling. It felt good to laugh, especially as there hadn't been much to laugh about lately. Though things were better now because Winnie was home, and that meant the world to Grace.

'There's tea in the pot and biscuits here that need eating,' Winnie smiled at Mrs Middleton.

'Thanks. I don't mind if I do.'

Terry grabbed a biscuit. 'I'll leave you to it. I'm going to see about getting my stall ready to open for tomorrow.'

'I wouldn't count on much business, love, not with the pub being closed.'

'I think you'd be surprised, Winnie. Folk like to come and gawp.'

Winnie rolled her eyes. 'See you later, love.'

'He's a good bloke,' Mrs Middleton said.

'Terry, yeah, he's like a son to me.'

'It's a shame there ain't more men in the world like him. Still, at least we'll all be seeing the back of Brancher Fanning.'

'Have you had any problems with him?' Winnie asked.

'I've never liked the bloke. I had a run-in with him once years ago when he was only a lad. Horrible, mouthy sod he was, even back then.'

'Well, I really can't thank you enough for what you've done.'

'I've already said there's no need for thanks.'

'Do you mind me asking why you've lied to the police for me?'

'For you?' Mrs Middleton spluttered. 'Don't flatter yourself, Mrs Berry. I'll do anything to help anyone, me, but telling fibs to the Old Bill is a different kettle of fish.'

Winnie was confused. 'Why did you do it then?'

'I told you; I can't stand blokes like him.'

'So, you're saying that you told the police a load of lies simply because you don't like Brancher Fanning?'

Mrs Middleton shifted uncomfortably on her seat. 'Yeah, something like that,' she replied.

'I think there's more to it.'

'There is, but it's none of your business.'

'Brancher Fanning could have killed me. It *is* my business, Mrs Middleton.'

The woman drummed her bitten-down fingernails on the table and Winnie could see she was agitated.

'All right, if you must know, I've had to put up with a lot of crap in my life. Men have shit on me from great bleedin' heights. So when I hear of a bloke hurting a young girl, it really gets my goat. And if I can do something to stop that bloke from ever hurting a girl again, then flippin' 'eck, as God is my witness, I will. I'd do whatever it takes.'

Winnie saw pain in Mrs Middleton's eyes. 'I'm sorry, I shouldn't have pushed you.'

Mrs Middleton's chin jutted forward. 'I'm not ashamed of what happened to me. I was, for a bloody long time, I was ashamed and disgusted with meself. But now I've got kids of me own, I can see that it wasn't my fault that my dad and my uncle took advantage of me. I was just a child, see. I was too young to understand. I knew it hurt and I wanted it to stop. But I was powerless. Well, I ain't so powerless now, am I? Dick Lamb, Brancher Fanning... there's others an' all. I pity any bloke who harms girls and crosses my path.'

Now it made sense to Winnie. She could understand Mrs Middleton's drive to protect girls, and her passion for self-delivered justice. 'No, Mrs Middleton, you ain't powerless now. You're a strong woman, and I admire you.'

'Steady on, Mrs Berry. Anyone would think that we're friends,' she smiled.

'Well, it's about time you called me Winnie. Another cuppa?'

49

One month later

Winnie stood in the street, her neck craned back, gazing at her pub. The windows were still boarded over, and weeds were poking through the cracks in the pavement. She tutted. 'We can't have this,' she said, bending down and yanking a green shoot from the ground.

Spring was in the air. The bitterly cold winter weather was behind them. Winnie thought that everything looked better in the sunshine, but nothing apart from a huge wedge of money could improve the appearance of the Battersea Tavern. The place looked desolate, especially since Terry had thrown in the towel and given up the shellfish stall. With the pub closed, Terry's business wasn't making enough income. Fortunately, he'd quickly found work as a train driver. Winnie was pleased that his job was sedentary which meant there was less risk of the bullet near his spine moving, but she missed him. With Brancher arrested and locked up on remand, Terry had moved back to his own place.

'Rover! Rover! Come back here, Rover!'

Winnie looked up the street to see a small black dog running towards her and Mr Ainsworth giving chase. The man was still shouting his dog's name as it ran up to Winnie and jumped up, it's tail wagging.

'Hello, Rover,' she smiled, tickling the dog behind the ears.

'Thank you,' the man panted. 'He slipped his collar and lead.'

'You're a naughty boy, Rover,' Winnie chuckled.

Mr Ainsworth put Rover's collar back around his neck and ruffled the top of the dog's head. 'Are you a dog person?' he asked. 'I only ask because Rover seems to like you.'

Winnie was taken aback. Though Mr Ainsworth had been a regular in her pub, always sitting where Len had once sat, the man had hardly spoken more than a few words to her in the past. 'I used to have a dog,' Winnie replied. 'Well, my granddaughter did, and she used to live here with me. She named her pup Cake, but Cake sadly passed away two years ago. He was run over.'

'I'm sorry,' the smartly dressed man said with genuine empathy in his pale blue eyes. 'I'm just returning Rover to his owner. My late Mother's friend has been in hospital and asked me to care for her dog. Never again!' Mr Ainsworth smiled. 'So, you're still living here, you say? Despite the pub in ruins?'

'Yes, upstairs. Fortunately, my flat was saved when my pub went up in flames.'

'It's good to see you, Mrs Berry. Sorry, I've frequented your former establishment many times, but I don't believe I've ever introduced myself properly to you. I'm Walter Ainsworth, and can I say what a great pleasure it is to see you again?'

'Likewise,' Winnie answered, politely. She thought Mr Ainsworth spoke much nicer than most folk in Battersea. She wouldn't have called him posh, but he pronounced his words well. She recalled the conversation she'd had with Judith about Mr Ainsworth. Surely talk of him murdering his mother was nothing more than hearsay? He didn't seem to have it in him to be a killer. And anyway, from what she'd heard about how his mother had treated him, maybe Mr Ainsworth had good cause for wishing the woman's demise. Winnie had never cared for gossip. In her experience, stories that were spread through the labyrinth of Battersea streets were normally blown out of all proportion.

'Do you have any plans to reopen the pub?'

'I'd love to, but sadly the Battersea Tavern will remain closed for the foreseeable.'

'That is a great shame, Mrs Berry.'

'Yes, it is. But there's no coffers in the pot to start rebuilding works.'

'Hmm, insurance companies are notorious for delaying claims. They will use every trick in the book to avoid paying out.'

Winnie nodded, too embarrassed to admit that she'd allowed her insurance policy to expire.

'I say, Mrs Berry, have you considered partnering with an investor?'

'No,' Winnie answered, thinking the well-spoken man was being a bit too nosey.

'Is it something you would consider?'

'I'm sorry, Mr Ainsworth, I don't mean to sound rude, but it really isn't any of your business.'

'I beg your pardon,' he said, doffing his fedora hat to reveal his dark-grey hair. 'I should have made myself clearer. In a nutshell, Mrs Berry, I would be interested in investing in the Battersea Tavern.'

Winnie eyed the man up and down. Walter Ainsworth was only slightly taller than her. Smartly dressed, with highly polished shoes, he looked out of place on her street. Winnie wondered why a man of his calibre would want to invest in her business. 'I don't think so, Mr Ainsworth, but thank you for your interest. Good day, to you.'

'Please, Mrs Berry, if I could take a few minutes of your time, I'd like to explain my thoughts about the Battersea Tavern. You see, I believe we could form a mutually beneficial partnership.'

Winnie rolled her eyes. Knights in shining armour don't just suddenly appear on the street and rescue you. That only happens in fairy tales, not in real life. 'Go on then, let's hear it,' she said, sceptically.

'Perhaps we could go inside and talk?' he suggested.

'No, anything you have to say, you can say it to me here.'

'As you wish. Simply put, I will provide the money to repair the pub in exchange for 50 per cent of the business.'

She didn't need to think about it. 'No, thank you. I'm not looking for a business partner.'

'Please, Mrs Berry, consider my offer. You don't need to answer in haste.'

'I've thought about it, and the answer is still no.'

'So be it, but if you reconsider your decision, may I leave you with my telephone number?'

Winnie's mind was made up, but she accepted Mr Ainsworth's contact details out of courtesy.

Making her way indoors, she stuffed the piece of paper with Walter Ainsworth's telephone number into her cardigan pocket. *Blinkin' lunatic,* Winnie thought, shaking her head.

★

Later that day, Grace arrived home from school to find Winnie in the kitchen baking a cake.

'Hello, love. My cakes never turn out as good as Maureen's. There's a letter from her on the table. It sounds like she's enjoying America. She talks about how big everything is. Have a read, it's ever so interesting.'

Picking up the envelope, Grace asked, 'Why are you baking a cake?' She knew that Winnie only made cakes when they were expecting visitors.

'Didn't I tell you, love? Rachel is dropping Hilda off soon.'

'Oh. Is Hilda moving in here?' Grace hoped not. She liked it being just her and Winnie and they were becoming close.

'No, Hilda will be going home. But they're stopping here first for dinner. Carmen is coming too and she's going to stay the night. I can't wait to see her. Go and have a wash and then you can give me a hand with the dinner.'

Half an hour later, the kitchen was full of steam and the aroma of a freshly baked sponge.

'That'll be them,' Winnie said when there was a knock on the back door. 'Can you let them in, love. Rachel must have forgotten to bring her keys.'

Grace skipped down the stairs and opened the back door to Hilda and Rachel. She thought Hilda looked a lot better than the last time she'd seen her.

'I swear you've grown a foot,' Hilda smiled.

'Good job I've brought a couple of new skirts for you,' Rachel said, patting a bag over her arm. 'And don't tell Winnie, but I've got a lipstick in here for you too.'

As Grace went to close the door, Carmen came around the corner.

'Hello, Grace. I hear you've been a great comfort to Winnie

328

and a very good girl. This is for you,' she whispered, and placed a coin into Grace's hand. 'Good behaviour deserves to be rewarded, but there's no need to tell Winnie.'

Grace grinned, brimming with pride. It warmed her to know that Winnie had been speaking well of her.

Upstairs, Maureen's letter was being passed around the table, everyone chatting and commenting with lots of laughter.

'I miss this,' Winnie smiled.

'Well, I won't be far away, so you'll be seeing more of me,' Hilda said.

'Have you been lonely?' Rachel asked.

'A bit. But I've got Grace here to keep me company.'

'Excuse me,' Rachel said, rising to her feet. 'I'm busting for the bathroom.'

When Rachel was out of sight, Hilda whispered, 'Cor, I'm glad to be going home.'

'Haven't you enjoyed being at Rachel's?' Carmen asked.

'Don't get me wrong, I'm grateful that she took me in and looked after me, but she's so house-proud, it drives me batty. I felt like if I stood still for too long, she'd be sweeping me up or dusting me down. Honestly, you dare not forget to use a coaster, or the look she throws! I was worried if I dropped a crumb.'

'That doesn't sound like Rachel,' Winnie frowned.

'I think she's bored,' Hilda said. 'Housework, housework and more housework.'

'Are you talking about me?' Rachel asked, coming back into the kitchen.

'I was just saying what a good housewife you are,' Hilda answered quickly.

'Are you bored with it?' Winnie asked.

'No. I enjoy being at home. You must be bored though, Winnie. The pub being closed must be a shock to your system.'

'Not 'alf. I can't lie, I miss it. 'Ere, you'll never guess what happened today ... I was outside, and that fella who used to sit in Len's place, Mr Ainsworth, he started talking to me. He said he wanted to buy into the pub.'

'What do you mean?' Carmen asked.

'He said he'd give me the money to do the repairs and be a 50 per cent partner.'

'Wow!' Rachel gasped.

'Blimey, Win, did you bite his hand off?' Hilda asked.

Winnie shook her head. 'No, of course not.'

Hilda looked surprised. 'Why not? It sounds like the answer to your problems.'

'I don't want a business partner.'

Carmen shook her head. 'Surely having a business partner is better than having nothing? Because let's face it, Winnie, *nothing* is what you have now.'

'Carmen's right,' Hilda nodded. 'The money to mend the pub ain't gonna come out of thin air.'

'He's probably a lunatic,' Winnie dismissed with a wave of her hand.

'What makes you think that?' Rachel asked.

'I don't know. It just seemed an odd conversation to have.'

Carmen spoke again. 'Or maybe he could see a good business opportunity. Did you tell him an outright *no*?'

'Yes, but he gave me his telephone number in case I change my mind. Do you all think I should have considered his offer?'

Winnie's eyes roamed around the table as everyone nodded.

Even Grace. She wanted Winnie to be happy, and though the woman plastered on a smile, Grace knew she was miserable underneath her cheerful front. And since the pub had closed, Grace's pocket money had halved.

'I'll think about it,' Winnie said. 'There's nothing I'd like more than to open up the Battersea Tavern again. But I'm not sure about Mr Ainsworth. You know me, I'm not one for gossip but I've heard some unsettling things about the man.'

'Like what?' Hilda asked.

'That he killed his mother,' Winnie admitted.

Carmen shook her head, her lips set in a thin line. 'Half the people round here ain't got nothing better to do than spread vicious rumours. Do you really think he'd be walking the streets if he had murdered his mother?'

'No, I doubt it very much. From what I've heard, he cared for his mother his whole life, sacrificing everything to meet her demands. I don't believe for one second that he finished her off. If anything, I reckon he's a very sad and lonely man.'

Hilda shrugged. 'Maybe he's offered to go into business with you for those exact reasons, eh? Perhaps he wants to be a part of something and craves some company.'

Winnie rolled her eyes. 'Are you looking for the good in people, Hilda?'

'I'm just saying that we've all been judged on gossip about us. Perhaps you should give the fella a chance. It could be good for both of you.'

'Maybe,' Winnie mused. 'I must admit, with you all approving, the thought of accepting Mr Ainsworth's offer is rapidly becoming more appealing.'

50

Two weeks later, work had started in the Battersea Tavern and Winnie was there, watching over the workmen and barking her orders.

'I really think the counter would be better placed over here,' Walter Ainsworth argued.

'No, it's going where it's always been,' Winnie insisted. She'd hoped that Mr Ainsworth would have been more of a sleeping partner, but that wasn't proving to be the case. The man had an opinion on everything, and his opinions always differed from Winnie's. Most of their conversations rapidly turned into a heated debate.

'I understand that you would like the *new* Battersea Tavern to be a replica of the old, but now is the perfect opportunity to ring in the changes.'

Winnie clenched her jaw. 'There's no need for changes. *My* business was successful. With respect, Mr Ainsworth, I've been in this game a lot bloody longer than you!'

Winnie saw the man cringe. He always did when she used bad language.

'May I remind you, Mrs Berry, it is *my* money that is

funding the project and I have a contract clearly stating that I am a 50 per cent partner in the Battersea Tavern. Therefore, I am entitled have a say in the refurbishment of the pub and its day-to-day running.'

'I don't need reminding. The day I signed that bleedin' contract is fast becoming a day I regret!'

Winnie stamped away upstairs. She had to get away from Mr Ainsworth before she blew her top and said something she'd regret. Sitting at the kitchen table, she drew in a calming breath. But when Mr Ainsworth tapped on the kitchen door, Winnie's temper erupted. 'How dare you come upstairs un-invited!' she yelled. 'You're a partner in the pub but this flat is *my* home and *my* domain. You've no right to wander up here when you feel like it!'

'I came to tell you that there is a representative from the brewery downstairs who'd like to speak to you about restock-ing. I did try to call up the stairs, but I assumed you couldn't hear me over the noise of the workmen.'

Winnie gulped. 'I'll be right down,' she mumbled.

As Winnie spoke to the brewery man, she could see that Mr Ainsworth was in discussions with the site foreman.

'I think that's all for now,' she told the brewery man, usher-ing him towards the door. 'Thanks for coming by.' Then bustling over to Mr Ainsworth, she asked, 'What are you talking about?'

'Nothing for you to concern yourself with, Mrs Berry,' he replied.

Winnie glared at the foreman. 'Were you, or were you not discussing the works being carried out here?'

'Yes, Mrs Berry, we were,' he replied, looking uncomfortable.

'Please let your men know that there are to be no, and I

mean *no* changes made from the original plans without my say-so.'

The foreman looked at Mr Ainsworth for clarification.

Mr Ainsworth offered a smarmy smile. 'There really isn't any need for you to be involved in the small details, Mrs Berry. Remember, your health is important. We don't want you overdoing it now, do we?'

'Don't patronise me, Mr Ainsworth,' Winnie seethed. 'I mean what I say. Stick to the plans, or else!'

Winnie marched away, her arms swinging and her feet thumping heavily on the floorboards. The refurbishment of the Battersea Tavern wouldn't give her another heart attack, but she thought that being stuck with Walter Ainsworth as a business partner was enough to put her in an early grave.

Winnie thought about popping in to see Hilda, but Hilda had just started a new job cleaning at the hospital with Piano Pete's sister. She would have liked to have talked to Carmen, but she knew that Carmen had taken her grandchild to see a specialist about his eyesight. The blindness had progressed, causing the child a great deal of distress. And Rachel had said that she was taking Martha and Benny shopping for new shoes after school, so she wouldn't be home either. Winnie was desperate to hear a friendly voice.

Slipping into a telephone box, she rang Tommy.

'Hello,' a woman answered on the other end of the line.

Winnie, feeling flustered, replied, 'Oh, erm, sorry, I think I might have the wrong number. I wanted to speak to Tommy. Tommy Bradbury.'

'Just a minute, my husband is in the greenhouse. I'll fetch him. Who can I say is calling, please?'

Winnie's mind whirred.

'Hello?' the woman said. 'Are you still there?'

'Er, yes. Sorry. It's Winnie. Winnie Berry.'

A few moments later, Tommy's voice crackled down the line. 'Winnie, hello, what a smashing surprise. I wasn't expecting to hear from you today.'

'I ... I, erm, I ... Tommy, are you married?'

'Oh ...' There was a long pause, then he continued, 'Yes, Winnie, I am.'

'When did that happen?'

'Last year.'

'*What*? Why didn't you tell me?'

'I don't know. I didn't want to upset you.'

'Oh, Tommy, you silly old bugger. I'm happy for you.'

'Are you? Aw, that's good, Winnie. Irene is a smashing woman. You'd like her.'

'Well, the Battersea Tavern will be having a grand reopening soon and I'll be throwing a big party to celebrate. I hope you and Irene will be there.'

'We wouldn't miss it for the world, Winnie.'

Minutes later Winnie wandered up the street, dumbfounded. Tommy, married? Well, that had been a shock! Years ago, Winnie had declined Tommy's hand in marriage and there was a small part of her that regretted that decision. She'd missed out on a life of companionship with a good man, instead choosing the Battersea Tavern and the warmth of her *family* around her. But she could never have known then that the Battersea Tavern would burn down, and Carmen, Rachel and Maureen would be living elsewhere. Still, she had Grace, and she'd grown very fond of the girl.

'Cooee!'

Winnie looked sideways to see Mrs Mary Middleton standing on the doorstep of her scruffy house. 'Hello, love,' Winnie said, forcing a smile.

'The kettle's just boiled,' Mary stated. 'If you don't mind three-time used tea leaves?'

'Just as long as it's wet and warm. I could do with a cuppa.'

Winnie had been in Mary's kitchen a few times now. The place was damp. Big, black mould patches covered one wall and had crept across the ceiling. The linoleum was worn and through to the floorboards in some patches. But Mary kept the place as clean as she could, though it wasn't unusual to see silverfish crawling along the skirting boards, and Winnie had spotted mouse droppings behind the door, none of which was Mary's fault due to lack of hygiene.

'How's the work coming on in the pub?' Mary asked as she placed a weak cup of tea on the table in front of Winnie.

'It's getting there. I'm hoping to be open in two weeks. You'll come to the opening party, won't you?'

'Just try and stop me,' Mary grinned. 'Who's doing the cleaning now that Maureen has gone?'

'Me, I suppose, and Grace can help.'

'Will you be looking for someone to take it on?'

'Probably. Why? Do you want the job?'

'Yes, I'd love it!'

'Then it's yours. I hope you don't think I'm talking out of turn, but can I suggest that you keep your wages away from Bob.'

'Don't worry, I will. My old man won't be getting his hands on *any* of my money. He'd only waste it on the horses. Thanks, Winnie – or shall I call you Mrs Berry as you're going to be my boss now?'

'Don't be daft, Mary, Winnie will do.'

'You look worn out. You ain't doing too much, are you? You know you're supposed to be slowing down and resting well. None of us want to see you back in hospital.'

'I'm fine. I'm just fed up to the back teeth with Mr bloody Ainsworth. He's really getting on my nerves.'

'Oh dear. You're stuck with him now, though.'

'Don't I know it!'

'What do you know about him?' Mary asked.

'Not a lot, only idle gossip, none of which I'm going to repeat because I don't believe it. To be honest, I try not to speak to him unless I really have to. He's a bleedin' pain in my backside. Why do you ask?'

'I don't know, he seems a bit sinister, don't you think?'

Winnie shrugged. She hadn't seen Walter Ainsworth as sinister, but Mary's words got Winnie's mind turning. She knew very little about the man, except what she'd heard from Judith. She didn't even know where he lived. 'I wonder where he got his money from?' she mused. The hairs on the back of her neck stood on end as she considered the ridiculous notion that he might have killed his mother. 'And now you mention it, you're right, Mary, there *is* something peculiar about the man. I hope I haven't made a terrible mistake!'

51

Winnie stood in the middle of her pub and glanced around, smiling. It had been a tough few weeks but finally the Battersea Tavern was opening its doors for business again. Winnie couldn't have been happier, except for Mr Ainsworth who was proving to be a thorn in her side. The man had a habit of creeping up on her. It seemed that every time she looked over her shoulder, he'd be there, watching her every move. And it had become apparent that he didn't like being told what to do. The man's pronunciation was perfect, but Winnie found his carefully chosen words were always demeaning. In some ways, he reminded her of her husband. Brian had possessed the same knack of being able to make her feel small and insignificant, always undermining her confidence and putting her down. But at least she wasn't afraid of getting a punch off Mr Ainsworth as she had been with Brian. Though the thought that he might have murdered his mother was never far from her mind.

Carmen stood by Winnie's side. 'You must be feeling on top of the world,' she said. 'The pub looks wonderful, Winnie, well done.'

'Thanks, love. I wish it was me and you behind the bar like the old days.'

'Me an' all, Winnie. I miss this place, but I'm needed in Balham more than ever now. I've grown a lot closer with Cheryl, which is nice. In fact, she told me the other day that I'm her best friend. I never thought I'd hear those words from my daughter. It means the world to me.'

'I'm pleased for you, Carmen. I know it's what you've wanted for a long time.'

'Hey, I tell you what, Winnie, I'm looking forward to meeting Tommy's new wife.'

'She's hardly new, they've been married for over a year. Fancy him not telling me.'

'Well, if you ask me, married or not, he's still holding a torch for you. I saw the way he looked at you in the hospital.'

'If you say so. And Charlie the drayman is still sweet on *you*. He always asks after you.'

'He's got no chance. I'll never have another man in my bed.'

'Me neither,' Winnie said, though she'd never felt lonelier...

Hilda came in through the back door. 'Hello, ladies. I've just popped in to see if there's anything I can do to help?'

'No, thanks, love. It's all under control. I'll be opening the doors soon and Piano Pete will be here to play us some tunes and get the party going. I borrowed a piano from Mr and Mrs Coe around the corner. It wouldn't be a party in the Battersea Tavern without a good ol' knees up around the piano. I must admit, though, I feel a bit nervous.'

'That's not nerves, Win, it's excitement,' Hilda smiled. 'Have a smashing night. I shall look forward to hearing all about it tomorrow. Sorry I can't stay.'

'It's fine, Hilda, you're better off out of temptations way. And by the way, the curtains you made look lovely, thanks, love.'

Winnie went behind the bar to do a final check that everything was where it should be. 'For Gawd's sake,' she grumbled, putting the bottles back in the order she liked them. Mr Ainsworth had moved them into alphabetical order again.

She could feel someone watching her and turned to see him standing on the other side of the bar, his eyes boring into her.

'May I make myself of use tonight?' he asked.

'Yeah, stay out of my way!' Winnie snapped.

His eyes narrowed, and he muttered, 'Wench,' under his breath.

Winnie chose to ignore him. She wouldn't allow Mr Ainsworth to ruin her reopening of the Battersea Tavern. Tonight was going to be the biggest party that she'd thrown in years.

Someone knocked on the back door, and Carmen went to answer it, returning with Judith.

Winnie was pleased to see that the girl had made an extra special effort. 'You'll knock 'em dead tonight, love,' she smiled.

'Thanks, Mrs Berry. There's already quite a crowd outside.'

'They'll be here for the free grub,' Winnie chuckled.

'Don't undermine yourself,' Carmen said. 'I don't think you realise how much you and this pub have been missed.'

'Pack it in, Carmen, I'm already an emotional wreck. You'll have me in tears. Right then, are we all ready?'

'Where's Piano Pete?' Carmen asked.

'He's outside,' Judith answered. 'I saw him waiting to come in with the others.'

'Let's get the doors open, then,' Winnie beamed.

Standing behind her bar, she stood, smiling, waiting to greet her regulars back. Twenty or more people flooded through the doors, all eyes glancing around at the newly refurbished pub. More people arrived, quickly filling the Battersea Tavern, and Winnie, Carmen and Judith were rushed off their feet. Pete looked to be in his element on the piano. Rachel arrived and so did Mary Middleton. Minutes later, Tommy came in with Irene.

The mad rush for drinks eventually slowed down. Winnie was pleased for the lull. She wanted to welcome her customers and thank them for their support. Reaching for the bell, she rang it several times until silence fell across the pub. Taking a deep breath, she was about to bellow a jolly welcome, but Mr Ainsworth stepped in front of her.

'Welcome to the Battersea Tavern,' he shouted. 'I'm sure you will all agree that my pub is looking at its very best, the best it's ever looked. I've invested much of my money and my time to ensure that each and every one of you enjoy yourselves. Please, drink and be merry!'

'Oi, that should have been Winnie's speech,' Carmen barked.

'Yeah, that's right,' Rachel said. 'And the Battersea Tavern isn't *your* pub. It's Winnie's!'

'Quieten down, ladies. It's no secret that the Battersea Tavern wouldn't be open if it wasn't for my investment.'

'Don't you tell me to quieten down!' Carmen snapped.

Winnie interrupted. 'It's all right, Carmen, Rachel. Thanks.

Let's just get on with the party, eh?' Then raising her voice, she yelled, 'Drinks all round, on the house!'

Mr Ainsworth glared at Winnie, scathingly. 'The drinks you're giving away will be coming out of your profits, not mine!'

'Oh, shut up!' she hissed. 'And if you're going to be like that, then you can pay for your own drinks an' all.'

The doors opened again, and Winnie was overjoyed to see the firemen who'd saved her home from burning to the ground. She'd made a point of inviting them, but she hadn't thought that they'd come.

'My heroes,' she beamed. 'What can I get you – on me, of course.'

Tommy pushed his way through the crowd. 'Hello, mate,' he grinned, shaking a fireman's hands.

'Tommy, me old mucker, how are you? And how's married life?'

'All good, Arnie, I can't complain. You know Mrs Berry, do you?'

Arnie looked across the bar at Winnie. Their eyes met and Winnie's heart stopped.

'I haven't had the pleasure of formally meeting Mrs Berry yet. I was here with my men on the night of the fire, but we didn't get a chance to speak.'

'Winnie, this is Arnie Potter. He's the boss of this lot,' Tommy said, indicating the firemen. 'Arnie and me have been mates since the beginning of time. He was best man at my wedding to Irene.'

'How do you do, Mrs Berry?' Arnie asked, his grey eyes holding her gaze.

'Call me Winnie,' she said, feeling stupidly giddy. Arnie had a smouldering look that made her pulse quicken. His white hair contrasted with his swarthy skin, and the way he looked at her made Winnie hope that he didn't have a woman at home.

'May I buy you a drink?' he asked.

'Thanks, but I'm a bit busy at the moment,' she replied, unable to take her eyes off him. 'But what can I get you?' she asked.

'I'd like … a promise of a drink with you later, when you have some time,' he said, his voice low.

Winnie wanted to believe he was flirting with her, but thought he was just having a joke. 'We'll see, but as you can see for yourself, I'm very much in demand tonight,' she replied, playfully.

'I'll have a whisky with a splash of water whilst I wait for you to join me.'

The evening flew by and Winnie enjoyed catching up with her regulars. She managed to spend some time with Tommy and Irene and found that she liked the woman. But she couldn't take her eyes off Arnie, and every time she looked in his direction, he was gazing back at her.

'I'm not sure about that Ainsworth bloke,' Tommy whispered.

'Mary's not keen either,' Winnie admitted.

'You know me, Winnie, I trust my instincts,' he said, and tapped his nose, 'and they've never let me down, and I'm telling you, there's something not right about him. Watch yourself, and if you get any problems, be sure to call me.'

'I will, thanks, Tommy.'

Irene leaned towards Winnie. 'I think you've got an admirer,' she whispered, nodding towards Arnie.

'Is he married?' Winnie asked.

'No. His wife passed away about ten years ago. I met him when he came to our wedding. What a dish, eh? I said to my Tommy, *where have you been hiding him?* If I'd met Arnie before Tommy, I might have been Mrs Potter instead of Mrs Bradbury.'

Winnie knew that Irene was only kidding. If she'd believed that Irene had been serious, Winnie would have jumped to Tommy's defence. 'I'm sure Arnie's only larking about with me,' Winnie said.

'I don't think so, Winnie. He can't keep his eyes off you, and I've noticed you looking at him too. Go and talk to him.'

'No, no I couldn't. I wouldn't know what to say.'

'Go on. Put the poor chap out of his misery,' Irene smiled. 'Just be yourself and I'm sure you'll find the words.'

Winnie's stomach fluttered with butterflies as she ambled down the bar towards Arnie. She hadn't felt like this in years and was surprised at herself. Any notions of love or fanciful thoughts of men had been a long way from Winnie's mind. Yet here she was, feeling like a woman half her age. 'Are you enjoying yourself?' she asked Arnie, smiling, her heart pounding.

'I am, but I'd enjoy myself a lot more if you joined me for a drink.'

Winnie could feel Arnie eyeing her and felt self-conscious as, with trembling hands, she poured herself a small sherry.

'Who's the bloke at the end of the bar giving me the evil eye?' Arnie asked.

'That's Walter Ainsworth, my business partner. We don't get on. He's got no right to be looking at you like that and I'm not having it. Excuse me, I'm going to have words with him.'

344

As Winnie went to walk away, Arnie reached across the bar and grabbed her hand. 'Leave it,' he said. 'I'll deal with him in my own good time. But I can see you're used to fighting your own battles.'

'I am, and I'm good at it too,' Winnie smiled.

'I like a strong woman,' Arnie said. 'I bet you don't get much bother in here.'

'Hmm, I've had my moments. But all in all, my customers know how to behave themselves. I've trained them well.'

'My lot can get a bit boisterous at times,' he grinned, glancing at the fire crew. 'Maybe you could give me some tips on how to keep them in line.'

Winnie chuckled. She liked Arnie and was beginning to relax in his company. She thought the man was ever so good-looking, though his weathered face made him look older than his years.

'You're busy tonight, but can I see you again?' Arnie asked.

'You're always welcome in the Battersea Tavern.'

'Can you be pulled away from your pub? Maybe dinner one evening?'

The attraction she felt towards Arnie was strong, and she wanted to accept his invitation, but something held her back. 'I'm not sure,' she answered. Her heart was screaming at her to accept his invitation, but Winnie's head warned her to proceed with caution. It had been a tough few months, and on top of all that had happened lately, Grace had only just settled down. Winnie didn't want to upset the apple cart and she wasn't sure that she had the energy for romance.

'We don't have to be formal, Winnie. Just fish and chips, a bottle of ginger beer, maybe a stroll by the Thames. The nights are long at this time of year. Long and lonely. I'd appreciate your company.'

'Well,' Winnie smiled, 'when you put it like that, how can I say no?'

Arnie had hit a raw nerve – *long and lonely nights.* As much as Winnie thought the world of Grace, she missed Carmen, Rachel and Maureen. *But,* Winnie told herself, *I shall have to make sure my feelings for Arnie don't run away with themselves. Proceed with caution!*

52

A week later, sitting in Notarianni's ice cream parlour, Grace sucked on her straw and swallowed the last of her milkshake. 'That was delicious,' she said, licking her lips, 'Thank you.'

Pauline looked pleased with herself. 'It's nice that I can treat you for a change. I've been getting pocket money since my mum has been cleaning the pub. Mind you, I have to work for it.'

'Me too, and now that there's only me and Winnie, I have to do a lot more chores. I don't mind, though, and Winnie is very generous. Anyway, it's my home so I'm happy to help with anything that needs doing.' Grace finally felt settled, and she thought the world of Winnie. She missed her grandmother and Winnie could never replace her, but she felt loved, cared for and wanted. And she'd always be grateful to Winnie for saving her from the fire.

'I used to think she was a stuck-up cow, but she's not. Mrs Berry is really nice.'

'What made you think she was stuck up?' Grace asked.

'My mum said she was stuck-up, but they're friends now.

Mum reckons that Mrs Berry likes Mr Potter a lot. What do you think of him?'

Grace smiled. It tickled her how Pauline always referred to Winnie as Mrs Berry, and now to Arnie as Mr Potter. Pauline's mum was a bit rough around the edges, but she'd raised Pauline to have good manners.

'Well?' Pauline asked.

'Oh, he seems all right. I like him. He makes Winnie smile and it's lovely to see her happy. Talking of which, we should get home, it's getting late, and Arnie is taking Winnie out again tonight.'

She'd enjoyed spending time with Pauline, feeling carefree, and generally behaving childishly. Grace had spent the last couple of years of her life worrying about her gran's health, and then, after Bertha's death, she'd felt scared and alone. Now, thanks to Winnie, she had a home and instead of being responsible for someone, Grace was the one being cared for. She could be a thirteen-year-old girl, slurping milkshakes and giggling at silly things. As Winnie had told her, *you've got the rest of your life to be a grown up. Go out with Pauline and enjoy yourself.*

After saying farewell to her friend, Grace slipped through the back door. As she went to go upstairs, she glanced through to the pub. Arnie was standing at the bar and gave her a friendly wave. She waved back as Mr Ainsworth snaked up to Arnie and spoke to him. Grace didn't like Mr Ainsworth, especially his attitude towards Winnie. The man sloped away and Arnie waved at Grace again, though the twinkle had left his eye and his shoulders had slumped. Turning, he mooched out of the pub.

Grace ran to the door that led through to the bar. 'Judith!' she hissed. 'Judith …'

'Wotcha Grace, are you all right?' Judith asked.

'Yeah, but I'm not supposed to be down here,' Grace whispered. 'What did Mr Ainsworth say to Arnie?'

Judith looked to each side before whispering back, 'He said that Mrs Berry wasn't available this evening because she's gone out for dinner with Mr Pane. Do you know who Mr Pane is?'

'No, I've never heard of him,' Grace replied, surprised.

Going up the stairs, she wondered why Winnie would go to dinner with another man when she'd already made plans with Arnie. Grace was shocked with Winnie, especially as she knew that the woman had been looking forward to seeing Arnie tonight.

As she reached the top of the stairs, a cheerful humming tune reached her ears, and Grace realised it was Winnie. *What's going on?* she wondered.

She tapped on Winnie's bedroom door.

'Come in, love,' Winnie called.

Grace pushed the door open and saw Winnie checking her reflection in the mirror.

'I've had my hair done and I've bought meself a new dress. What do you think?' she asked Grace, doing a small twirl.

'You look beautiful, Winnie, but I thought you was out to dinner with Mr Pane?'

'Who the bleedin' 'eck is Mr Pane? I'm going out with Arnie tonight. Remember, I told you this morning.'

'Yeah, I know, but Arnie's just left because Mr Ainsworth told him you're out with Mr Pane.'

'Do what? Why would he do that? Are you sure?'

'Yes. Go and ask Judith if you don't believe me.'

'What on earth is that 'orrible bloody man playing at!' Winnie seethed, shaking her head. 'I'll swing for him one of these days, I swear I will!'

Fury was written all over Winnie's face as she stormed past Grace and thumped down the stairs. Grace followed but stayed in the passageway.

'Where is he?' Winnie snapped at Judith.

'Mr Ainsworth has gone home.'

'Lucky for him, or I'd have skinned him alive. I gather you heard him tell Arnie that I was out with Mr Pane?'

'Yes, I did. I thought it was odd, because I was pretty sure that you were upstairs. I'm sorry, Mrs Berry.'

'Don't apologise, love, it wasn't your fault. But wait till I get my hands on Mr Ainsworth!'

Oh dear, thought Grace, *there's going to be trouble!*

Winnie knocked on Arnie's door, still simmering but trying to keep her temper at bay.

'Winnie!' Arnie exclaimed. 'I thought you were otherwise engaged this evening.'

'I don't know what game Mr Ainsworth is playing and I've no idea who Mr Pane is – and I'm flippin' starving, so I hope dinner is still on offer.'

Arnie's face broke into a broad smile. 'Come in,' he offered. 'And you can share my piece of toast.'

'Is that the best you can do?' she grinned. 'I was hoping for at least a pickled onion with half a cheese sarnie.'

Making herself comfortable on Arnie's sofa, she accepted the glass of beer he handed her. As the hours ticked by, Winnie laughed until her face ached, and her ribs hurt. 'You're such good company,' she said. 'But it's nearly midnight and I really must be going.'

'I'll walk you home,' Arnie offered as he helped Winnie into her coat.

Walking arm in arm, Winnie contemplated, 'What would the neighbours think, eh? Me sneaking out of your house in the dead of night. There'll be gossip tomorrow.'

'They'll be saying what a lucky fella I am to have the wonderful company of a good woman. Half of them have been trying to marry me off for the past few years.'

'Have you ever come close to marrying again?' Winnie pried.

'No – well, not until I met you.'

Winnie playfully punched Arnie's arm. 'Don't talk daft,' she said. 'We've only known each other a week.'

'Yes, but when you know, you know. And at my age, Winnie, I haven't got time to hold back. Don't panic, I'm not going to get down on a bended knee with an engagement ring, but I want you to know that I'm serious about you.'

Winnie didn't say anything, but she felt the same. Though it was far too soon to be thinking about marriage: Arnie would have to prove himself first. She'd need to know that she could trust him. Her husband, Brian, he had been a charmer and full of promises when they'd first met, yet once his ring was on her finger, he'd shown his true colours. Winnie had spent years under his thumb, jumping to do his bidding and often getting a clout. Then she'd fallen for Carmen's husband, Harry. Another man with the gift of the gab who'd turned out to be a let-down. Winnie's guard was up. She wouldn't give her heart to a man again, only to end up having it trampled on.

53

The next day, Winnie pulled Judith to one side. 'Listen, love. I shall be having strong words with Mr Ainsworth today so I'm going to apologise in advance.'

'What are you apologising for?'

'For the mess! I swear, I'm going to spill the man's blood all over this floor.'

Judith's eyes widened and she looked horrified.

'I'm only kidding,' Winnie smiled. 'But you might hear some bad language. I'm absolutely fuming.'

'I can't say I blame you, Mrs Berry.'

'What do you think about him?' Winnie asked.

'It's not my place to say, Mrs Berry. He's my boss.'

'Whatever you say will stay between us, I promise. And Mr Ainsworth might think he's the boss, but believe you me, he isn't!'

Judith looked down at the floor and said clearly, 'I hate him.'

'That's a strong word to use, though I can't disagree with you. But why do you hate him?'

'When he can be bothered to talk to me, it's the way he

speaks. I can't put my finger on it, but the things he says makes me feel small.'

Winnie nodded. She understood what Judith meant. Mr Ainsworth had a superior attitude and it was clear that he had no respect for women. 'You've turned out to be a good barmaid, Judith, and I wouldn't want to lose you. If you're ever thinking of handing in your notice because of Mr Ainsworth, promise that you'll talk to me first. I won't have you leaving because of that awful man.'

'Thanks, Mrs Berry. I promise.'

Mary came up from the cellar carrying a mop and bucket. 'Did I hear you talking about Mr Ainsworth?' she asked.

Winnie nodded. 'Yes. You'll never guess what he did last night – when Arnie came to pick me up, Mr Ainsworth told him that I was out with another man!'

Mary looked astounded. 'He never did!'

'Yes, it's true. Can you believe the audacity of the man?'

'Yeah, Winnie, I can. I've always said that there's something not right about him. Do you know what he said to me the other day? Bear in mind that he never lowers himself enough to speak to the likes of the cleaner, but he had the nerve to tell me that I couldn't bring my baby to work.'

'Did he, indeed? I hope you told him where to get off!'

'I did, Winnie, you know me. I ain't shy and I don't mince my words. I told him that you and me had agreed that I could bring the baby in as long as the pub is closed. And if he don't like it, then he can shove his hands down the privy and do the cleaning himself. He threatened to sack me and get another cleaner. I told him I don't take my orders from him and the only person who could sack me was you. I could tell that he didn't like that!'

Winnie rolled her eyes. 'I bet he didn't. But it's true and that goes for you an' all, Judith. Mr Ainsworth can't sack you. So don't let him pick on you or make you feel uncomfortable.'

'I won't! Right, that's me done for the day. I'll see you tomorrow, Winnie.'

'Hang on, love. Have you got time for a cuppa?' Winnie asked, wanting to pick Mary's brain.

'Yeah, go on then. He's still sleeping,' Mary answered, nodding her head towards the pram in the corner.

In the back kitchen, Winnie was keen to get Mary's opinion. 'Why do you think that Mr Ainsworth told Arnie that I was out with another man?'

Mary pulled out a seat. 'My first thought was that he wants you for himself. But I don't think it is that. I'm not convinced that he likes women.'

'What, you think he likes the fellas?'

'No, I don't mean in that way. I mean, he has a contempt for women. The way he speaks to women, even the way he looks at them, especially you.'

'Funnily enough, I thought the same,' Winnie agreed. 'But if he doesn't like women, least of all me, then why go into business with me?'

'Gawd knows. Maybe he thought he could lord it over you, but he's come unstuck because you're not a pushover.'

'Hmm,' Winnie said, deep in thought. 'Perhaps he's punishing me for not being a pushover. Maybe that's why he lied to Arnie. But whatever his reasons, I'm not having it. Mr Ainsworth is going to get a piece of my mind!'

★

Walter Ainsworth arrived at the Battersea Tavern seconds before opening time. 'You're going to be late,' he barked at Judith. 'Every minute that the doors are closed results in lost business. Your pay will be deducted to reflect the drop in revenue.'

Winnie was standing in the door that led down to the cellar and she could hear every word. Stepping out, with her hands on her hips, she bellowed, 'Judith will receive full pay plus a bonus for her hard work. She's not late opening up, and never is.'

Mr Ainsworth pulled a pocket watch from his waistcoat and looked at the time. 'The doors should have been opened two minutes ago.'

'And they would have been if you hadn't distracted Judith. I know how to run my pub, Mr Ainsworth, so you don't need to be here every bloody minute of every bloody day checking on us.'

Mr Ainsworth ran a finger around the neck of his white, starched collar. Then, pushing his nose in the air, he announced, 'I'd like to see the accounts.'

'I'll bring you the books,' Winnie replied, faking a smile.

Passing Judith, she winked at the girl. Then hurrying upstairs, Winnie collected the books, came back down, and found Mr Ainsworth sitting at a table. Slamming the books down heavily, she leaned towards the man. 'You've every right to run your eyes over the accounts, but I'm warning you, *Walter,* if you *ever* interfere in my life again, I'll make sure you regret it.'

'I beg your pardon?' the man said, trying to look dumbfounded.

'Don't pretend you don't know what I'm talking about. I

can't begin to fathom why you would lie to Mr Potter about my whereabouts last night, and did you really believe that I'm so flippin' stupid that I wouldn't find out? I ain't no one's fool, *Walter,* so don't cross me again. Is that clear?'

Mr Ainsworth rose to his feet, seemingly unfazed. He sighed heavily. 'Women and drama. The two go hand in hand,' he said, shaking his head. 'You will address me as *Mr Ainsworth.* We are not and never will be friends, Mrs Berry. On that note, I'll add that I'm not concerned about your love life, but I am concerned about the accounts. I hope your records are accurate, but I expect you will require a lesson in bookkeeping. Now, if you'll excuse me whilst I peruse the books?'

Winnie frowned. She'd been dismissed by the man, and he hadn't offered an explanation, an apology or a defence for his actions last night. Still, she'd made her point, though she felt Mr Ainsworth hadn't taken her seriously. Time would tell and she'd meant what she'd said – if the man poked his beak into her life again, she'd make sure he lived to regret it.

54

Two days passed without incident in the Battersea Tavern. Winnie ignored Mr Ainsworth, and though he was always there, always hovering and casting his beady eyes over her, he pretty much ignored her too. Yet even when he was talking to the customers, he kept his eyes on her.

Sitting in the back kitchen with Mary before the pub opened had fast become a routine.

'Did you enjoy yourself with Arnie last night?' Mary probed, eyeing Winnie over the rim of her cup of tea and grinning.

'Yeah, I did. He gets on well with Grace, which is nice to see. And would you believe, he insisted on washing up after dinner. He said it was the least he could do after I'd cooked it.'

'Blimey! I don't think my old man even knows where the sink is,' Mary laughed. 'You've got yourself a good man there.'

'I reckon I have. It's funny though, cos I never thought I'd be courting a fella at my time of life. You don't think I'm being a fool, do you?'

'No, Winnie, not at all. Fate brought the pair of you

357

together for a reason. And age makes no difference. Look at me, lumbered with a baby. I thought my *getting in the family way* days were over. What's meant to be will be.'

'I don't know if I believe in fate, but I know that we've both been lonely. It's been nice having a bit of company, and Arnie's got a wicked sense of humour. I haven't laughed so much in ages.'

'Good. You deserve to have a good laugh after putting up with Ainsworth all day!'

'Oh, I ain't told you the latest, have I?'

'No, go on,' Mary urged.

'He told Piano Pete that his services were no longer required – and you know that second-hand piano I saw? Well, Ainsworth reckons we won't be purchasing it for the pub. The cheeky sod! Pete has been my potman here on and off for as long as I can remember. And a party in the Battersea Tavern wouldn't be a party without Pete on the piano.'

'Did you say something to Ainsworth?' Mary asked.

'Of course I bleedin' did! Needless to say that once I'd put me foot down and told Ainsworth how things are going to be, Pete is back collecting glasses when needed and the piano is being delivered this afternoon.'

'Good for you. That Ainsworth oversteps the mark.'

'He does, Mary, but I won't stand for it. Honestly, I don't know what I'd do without Piano Pete. He keeps an eye on the bar now and then, he helps change barrels, collects the glasses, entertains us all, and I don't have to pay him. He's happy to help for a few beers in exchange. And best of all, I trust him.'

'He's a good 'un, and he always knows what's going on in

Battersea because he goes from pub to pub, doing the same as he does here.'

'I know, bless him.'

Winnie heard a knock on the pub front door.

'I'll get it,' Judith called from the bar.

Winnie looked back at Mary, smiling as she said, 'Talk of the devil, I wouldn't be surprised if that's Pete.'

Moments later, he was stood in the kitchen doorway.

'Told you,' Winnie winked to Mary, then looking at Pete, she added, 'We were just talking about you.'

'Win, you've gotta come quick. Something's wrong with Hilda.'

Winnie sighed, her heart plummeting. 'Has she been drinking again?'

'I don't know. Me sister said Hilda ain't been at work for a few days, so I went round to her place, but she's not answering the door. I know she's in there cos I could see her in bed through the window.'

'Pissed or hungover, no doubt,' Winnie scowled. Then with a huff, she pushed herself to her feet. 'I suppose I'd better check on her. But if she's been drinking again, I swear I'll wash me hands of her this time.'

Mary stood too. 'If she wouldn't answer the door to Pete, then how are you going to get in?'

'I've got a key. I made her give me one after Terry had to kick her door in.'

'I'll come with you,' Mary offered.

'Thanks, love. But I should warn you, when Hilda's drunk, she's not easy to deal with.'

The women marched to Hilda's with Mary pushing the pram and Piano Pete in tow.

'I'll have a look at that perambulator for you later,' Pete offered, 'See if I can't stop that wheel from squeaking.'

Reaching Hilda's, Winnie let herself in through the front door and paused outside Hilda's room. Turning to Mary, she warned, 'If Hilda's as bad as I think she is, this ain't going to be a pretty sight.'

'It's all right. I've handled my old man enough times when he's been three sheets to the wind. I'll do what I can to help.'

Winnie pushed the door open, surprised to see the room in good order and clean. Hilda was in the bed and Winnie rushed over as the woman groaned and writhed in obvious pain.

'Hilda! Hilda, love, it's me, Winnie. What's wrong?'

Hilda was clutching her stomach. Her skin was mottled, and her hair was wet with sweat. 'I don't feel well,' she moaned. 'Is Martha still under the bed?'

'Eh? Martha isn't here, love. You don't look too clever. What is it, your belly?'

Hilda nodded. 'My stitches … not been right for weeks. Ice cream making me cold.'

Winnie glanced at Mary, worried. 'She's confused. I'd be surprised if there's anything wrong with her stitches. She had that operation nearly three months ago. But something ain't right.'

'It hurts!' Hilda groaned. 'Can't play hide and seek.'

'Let me take a look at your belly,' Winnie said, and eased back the bedclothes.

Winnie tried not to gasp. Hilda's clothes and the sheet beneath her were wet through with sweat, yet Hilda was shivering. And as Winnie lifted Hilda's nightdress, she wrinkled her nose at a putrid smell that emanated from Hilda's scar.

Winnie's eyes widened. Hilda's lower stomach was swollen, and the skin around her scar had turned black. Puss oozed through several holes where the stitches had been.

Winnie spoke softly, 'You've got an infection, Hilda. Why didn't you go to the doctor?'

'Rachel is fixing the car. Princess Elizabeth taught my girl to be a mechanic.'

Winnie glanced over her shoulder to Mary. 'Can you run back to the pub and call an ambulance, please? She's delirious and running a fever. I think she's got blood poisoning. Hurry, love, as quick as you can.'

Mary nodded, her eyes wide. 'Come with me,' she told Pete who was lingering at the door.

Winnie rushed to the sink and fetched a cool, damp cloth which she placed on Hilda's forehead. But Hilda began shaking her head from side to side as she struggled for breath.

'It's all right,' Winnie soothed. 'Calm down, love. Take a deep breath.'

Hilda faced Winnie and stared into her eyes. Winnie could see that the woman was frightened, terrified, and she reached for Hilda's hand. 'It's all right, love, the ambulance will be here soon.'

Suddenly and unexpectedly, Hilda's body went rigid, and her eyes rolled to the back of her head. She pulled in a strained, gurgled breath. Then her head fell to one side and her hand went limp.

This couldn't be happening! 'HILDA!' Winnie screamed. 'Hilda, wake up,' she insisted, shaking the woman. 'Hilda … Hilda, please don't die! Come on love, wake up …'

Hilda didn't respond and Winnie could see that her friend's

chest was still. 'Don't do this, Hilda! Please, please, Hilda, don't leave.'

But Winnie knew it was hopeless. Holding Hilda's hand to her face, she kissed the woman's fingers, her tears dripping on to Hilda's skin. 'Oh, Hilda,' Winnie cried. 'You were loved, so very much-loved, my dear, dear friend ... Give my love to Jan when you see her.'

55

'I can't believe she's dead,' Winnie cried into Carmen's arms. 'She died before the ambulance arrived ... Why on earth didn't she go to the doctor earlier?'

'I should have been here,' Carmen sobbed.

Winnie eased away from Carmen and pulled a hand-kerchief from the sleeve of her cardigan. 'There was nothing you could have done, love. She must have been poorly for a while, but she never mentioned anything to anyone.'

'Hilda liked to be independent,' Carmen sniffed. 'Bloody hell, Winnie, the woman was younger than me. She shouldn't be dead. It ain't right.'

'I know. Life ain't fair. Look at my Jan, the cancer killing her before she even turned thirty.'

'He takes the good ones young, though I always thought Hilda would outlive us all. After all, I hate to say it, but she'd pickled her body. I imagined she would have been well preserved.'

Winnie tried to smile. 'Me an' all, love, I thought the same. I assumed Hilda would live long after me. It's such a shock. Hilda had her demons to deal with, but she had a heart of gold. Oh, Carmen, I'm going to miss her. But we must pull ourselves together. Rachel will be here soon and the girl is going to need our support.'

Rachel sat in the passenger seat beside Roy. She stared ahead in silence, numb. Winnie had telephoned Roy at work and broken the tragic news. When Roy had told Rachel, there'd been no tears. Shock, disbelief, guilt, yes, but she hadn't cried and it still didn't seem real.

Roy pulled up outside the Battersea Tavern and Rachel said nothing, just climbed out of the car.

'Do you want me to come in with you?' Roy asked.

Rachel shook her head. She knew Roy would never feel comfortable in Battersea. Standing on the pavement and leaning into the car, she told him, 'Go home. Be there for the kids – but don't say anything about my mum. Pick me up this evening and I'll tell them later.'

She closed the car door and watched Roy drive away. Turning to face the Battersea Tavern, Rachel wasn't surprised to see it was open. She couldn't face the condolences of the customers, so walked around to the back door. After letting herself in, she climbed the stairs and heard Winnie and Carmen talking.

'I suppose we need to think about the funeral,' Winnie said, sadly. 'It goes without saying that we'll have some drinks and food downstairs.'

'And there's Hilda's belongings to sort through. Do you think Rachel will be up to facing that? If not, I can do it by myself.'

Rachel hadn't considered the funeral or sorting her mum's things. It still hadn't sunk in that her mum was dead.

Winnie turned and saw her standing in the kitchen doorway. She rushed towards her, pulling her into a tight embrace.

'Oh, love, I'm so sorry!' Winnie cried as she held Rachel.

'It was so unexpected,' Carmen said, dashing away a tear.

Rachel pulled away. 'What happened? How did my mum die?' she asked, her tone matter-of-fact.

'Sit down, love, there's tea in the pot,' Winnie encouraged.

Rachel walked across the kitchen in a mechanical fashion. Sitting at the familiar table, she glanced at where her mum had often sat. Never again would she see her mum pour hot tea from her teacup into the saucer and slurp the liquid.

Winnie sat beside her, her voice soft as she explained, 'Your mum had an infection in the scar from her operation. She must have had the infection for some time and it spread and went into her blood.'

'Did she suffer? Did she know she was going to die?'

'I'm not going to lie, love. Yes, she did suffer, but not for long. When I found her, she was in a bit of pain but to be honest, she wasn't thinking straight. She talked about you fixing the car, playing hide and seek and Martha being under the bed. I don't think she had any idea that she was going to die.'

'I should never have let her come home. If she'd stayed with me, she'd be alive now.'

'You weren't to know, love, none of us were.'

Carmen walked around the table and stood behind Rachel, placing her hands on Rachel's shoulders. 'And at least your mum wasn't alone. Winnie was there to hold her hand.'

Rachel felt a thick ball of grief tightening her throat. She tried to swallow it down. 'I-I can't breathe,' she gasped. Panic swamped her as she struggled for air. Her chest hurt and her heart raced. With wide eyes, she looked from Winnie to Carmen. 'Can't breathe,' she said, 'Can't … breathe …'

Winnie grabbed her hands and looked into her eyes, speaking calmly, 'It's all right, love, you can breathe. I promise you, you can breathe. Take a deep breath in through your nose …'

Rachel shook her head. 'Can't …'

'Yes, love, yes you can. Look at me … that's it, slowly through your nose. Keep your eyes on me … through your nose and then out through your mouth … go on, that's right …'

Staring into Winnie's eyes, Rachel managed to get the air into her lungs and as her pulse slowed, the ball of grief in her throat gave way and tears flooded her eyes. 'My mum! I want my mum,' she wept. 'Oh, Christ, I want my mum so much but she's never coming back, is she?'

Rachel drew in a juddering breath and Carmen and Winnie wrapped their arms around her.

'No, love,' Winnie sobbed. 'She's never coming back. She'll be with my Jan now and they'll both be watching over us.'

56

The skies were dark, and it rained heavily on the day of Hilda's funeral. In the Battersea Tavern, the mood was subdued as mourners shook off water from their umbrellas and hats.

Rachel sat at a table with Martha and Benny, Winnie, Arnie and Grace, all dressed in their smartest black attire.

Piano Pete wandered over with half a pint in his hand and a roll-up stuck on his bottom lip. 'It was a smashing service,' he said. 'You did your mum proud.'

'Thanks, Pete,' Rachel replied with a weak smile, 'It was a good turnout.'

Winnie thought Rachel had done well to get through the service without breaking down in tears. She'd carried herself with dignity, even managing to say a few, poignant words about Hilda. Her strength had surprised Winnie. 'He's right. Your mum would have been very proud of you today,' she whispered in Rachel's ear.

A loud clap of thunder roared above, rattling the windows.

'That's my mum,' Rachel sniffed. 'She's telling us that this isn't what she wants. We shouldn't be sitting around, miserable. Mum would want us to celebrate her life.'

'You're right,' Winnie agreed. 'Your mum loved music and singing. Do you remember that Christmas when she blew all our socks off with her rendition of that Judy Garland song?'

'Yes, I do. My mum had the voice of an angel.'

'Hilda liked a drink, often to her detriment, but she'd want us to raise a glass to her and remember the good times. Pete, get on the piano.' Then, calling across the pub, Winnie told Carmen, 'Drinks all round, on the house, for Hilda.'

Carmen had offered to work behind the bar with Judith, and the women had arranged a decent buffet too. She poured the drinks and then rang the bell.

Rachel rose to her feet with her glass aloft. 'To my mum,' she said, 'Down the hatch!'

'To Hilda!' the pub echoed.

Pete played one of Hilda's favourite tunes and soon Hilda's loved ones and friends were all exchanging funny and warm memories of the woman.

Flo came to the table. 'My Bill always had a soft spot for your mum,' she told Rachel. 'And when she'd had a drink, he was good with her. But her drinking problems aside, there were many layers to Hilda. Your mum was a very talented seamstress and dressmaker. She did an awful lot for charity, and she was so brave during the war with her fire-watching duties. I couldn't have stood on roofs watching for incendiary bombs like your mum did.'

'Yeah, I'd forgotten about that,' Rachel said. 'She was very brave.'

'Hilda was a godsend when Jan first came to us. It was your mum who got Jan making dresses and selling them to Flo and Bill for their market stall,' Winnie added.

'This is better,' Rachel smiled with unshed tears in her eyes. 'This is what my mum would have wanted.'

Winnie thought so too, though judging by the disapproving look on Mr Ainsworth's sour face, she didn't think he agreed. Winnie watched as he pushed past the customers and approached Pete on the piano. She couldn't hear what the man was saying to Pete, but she saw Pete frown, and then stick his two fingers up in Mr Ainsworth's face.

Winnie hurried over. 'What's the problem?' she asked.

'Him,' Pete griped as he played the piano. 'He's telling me to pack it in with the music.'

Winnie glowered at Mr Ainsworth.

'This is disrespectful and nor is it appropriate,' the man stated.

'Get out,' Winnie hissed. 'This is a private function and you ain't invited.'

'I do not need an invitation into *my* pub, Mrs Berry.'

'Get out, or I'll throw you out,' Winnie warned. 'And don't think I won't. I've slung out bigger men than you, Ainsworth, so sling your bleedin' hook.'

Arnie came to stand beside Winnie. 'I suggest you leave. It won't be Winnie chucking you through that door, it'll be me, and your feet won't touch the ground until you land somewhere on the other side of the Thames.'

Mr Ainsworth, appearing flustered, mumbled as he walked away. 'I'll be talking to my solicitor about this!'

'Yeah, you do that!' Winnie shouted after him. 'And when you're there, ask him about ending this bloody, rotten partnership!'

Arnie placed his arm over Winnie's shoulder and gave her a gentle squeeze as Rachel came over.

'He makes my blood boil. I wish I'd never signed a flippin' contract with him. Of all the days to make a fuss, he had to choose today.'

'Don't worry, Winnie. You said my mum is watching over us. Well, she'd be enjoying that scene.'

'Yeah,' Winnie said. 'Your mum would have been egging me on to throw Ainsworth out. Gawd, I'm gonna miss my dear friend.'

57

Three months later

The beginning of May brought the sunnier and warmer weather with it. Winnie had been looking forward to the summer and with Queen Elizabeth's coronation only a month away, she was busy preparing for a big Battersea Tavern party. All of Britain and the Commonwealth would be celebrating the crowning of the young Queen in Westminster Abbey. To mark the occasion, Winnie had finally invested in a television which she would set up in the pub for the special day. It was the first time that a royal coronation could be viewed by the public, and Winnie didn't want to miss it. She was sure that the wise investment would bring in the customers too. Mr Ainsworth, on the other hand, disagreed and believed that the purchase of the television was a waste of money. *Tough,* she'd told him. *We're buying one, so like it or lump it.* But when he'd further protested, she'd bought the box with her own money and had it upstairs in her front room.

Grace came bouldering through the kitchen door. She dropped her school bag onto the floor, made her way to the biscuit tin and helped herself to three of Winnie's *good* biscuits.

'So that's where my biscuits have been disappearing too,' Winnie chuckled.

'I'm doing you a favour, Winnie. When you had that heart attack, the doctor said you need to lose a few pounds.'

'You cheeky mare! Do you want to come shopping with me? I want to nip up the Junction and get Rachel and Roy's wedding present.'

'Haven't you got them one yet?'

'No, they said they didn't want a fuss, but I hummed and hawed and decided we should mark the occasion.'

'But they're getting married tomorrow!'

'I know. So, shake a leg – are you coming with me or not?' Winnie asked as she grabbed her handbag.

'Yeah, I'm coming. I couldn't leave you to choose a gift for them. You'd probably buy them a saucepan set or something boring like that.'

'That's exactly what I was going to get them. Have you got a better suggestion then, madam?'

Grace grinned. 'I know *exactly* what to get them,' she said.

Two hours later, and Winnie had to admit that she was pleased with Grace's suggestion. Back from Clapham Junction and sitting at the kitchen table, she admired the chrome-plated toaster. It was top of the range and a brand-new model out that year. Winnie had thought that a toaster was a waste of time. What was the point when most ovens had a grill. But after seeing a demonstration, she'd been astonished at how quickly the machine had toasted the bread, and on both sides at the same time! *All these modern conveniences,* Winnie thought with a shake of her head. *Housewives today don't know how lucky they are!*

Popping downstairs to the pub, she found Judith chatting with Terry.

'Hello, love, it's nice to see you,' she smiled. 'How are you?'

'Can't complain, Winnie. I popped in to see if you and Grace want a lift to Rachel's wedding tomorrow?'

'Aw, thanks, love, that's good of you, but Arnie is taking us. You're more than welcome to come too. I should imagine that Arnie's car is more comfortable than your van and more reliable an' all. In fact, I can't believe your old van's still running.'

'You've got a good point there, Winnie. If you're sure it'll be all right with Arnie?'

'Yes, love, it won't be a problem.'

'Are we all coming back here after for a bit of a do?'

Winnie rolled her eyes. 'No, more's the pity. Rachel insisted on no fuss. Just a simple registry office ceremony and then back to hers for tea and sandwiches. And there's only going to be us and Carmen there.'

'Fair enough. I'll see you tomorrow then, Win.'

'Yes, love, see you.'

'Did you find a nice gift for the happy couple?' Judith asked.

'Yes, a toaster. It's ever so posh. It was Grace's idea.'

'Fancy!'

'You'll be all right here by yourself tomorrow, won't you?' Winnie asked.

'Yes, but I won't be by myself,' Judith answered, flicking her eyes to Mr Ainsworth.

Winnie tutted. 'I'd hoped that the novelty of being in the pub every day would have worn off by now, but he sticks around like a bad smell in the drains. Right, it's quiet this evening. I'm going to put me feet up for an hour or two. I'll be down at closing.'

Upstairs, Winnie turned on the wireless and sank into the sofa. She closed her eyes and soon drifted into a light sleep. Images of Hilda floated through her mind, and then she saw Jan, dressed in a white, floaty gown, a bright light gleaming behind her. When a picture of David came to mind, Winnie woke with a jolt.

'Who's there?' she called.

'It's only me,' a friendly, familiar voice replied.

'Tommy?' Winnie asked, disbelievingly, heaving her body off the sofa.

Tommy was standing in the passageway.

'What are you doing here?' she asked.

'Judith said to come up. Sorry, Winnie, I didn't mean to disturb you.'

'Don't be daft. Go and sit down, I'll bring us a cuppa.'

'No, it's fine, thanks, I can't stop. I'm staying at my daughter's for a couple of nights. We've only just arrived and Irene is there waiting for me. We'll be around for a few days, so I'll catch up with you properly, but I had to pop in to tell you something. I got my old mates at the police station to do a bit of digging. It turns out that Walter Ainsworth lived with his mother and when she died he inherited her house and some money, which is where the cash came from to do up this place. From what I'm told, it seems that Mr Ainsworth was under his mother's thumb and was badly treated. The woman was a tyrant.'

'I knew he'd lived with his mother, and I'd heard that she was quite overbearing. Judith told me she used to beat him with her walking stick. I suppose that explains his dislike for women.'

'That's not all, Winnie. Mrs Ainsworth's death was suspicious. She couldn't walk and was confined to her bed, but she died following a fall down the stairs. The police looked into it and couldn't find any evidence to charge Ainsworth, but my mate at the station is convinced the man pushed her down the stairs.'

'Really?'

'Yes, so watch yourself. Like I said, I can't stop now, but I'll call back in tomorrow.'

Winnie nodded, trying to smile. 'Rachel's getting married tomorrow.'

'Ah, smashing. Pass on my congratulations. I'll see you the day after then.'

'Yeah, and thanks for the information, Tommy.'

Sitting back on the sofa, Winnie mulled over what Tommy had said. She'd thought the gossip about Walter Ainsworth killing his mother had been nonsense, but now she was contemplating that it could be true! Could her business partner really be a murderer? Capable of killing his mother? If so, then the man was worse than a monster, and he was alone in the pub with Judith!

Winnie rushed down the stairs.

'I thought you were putting your feet up?' Judith asked.

'I was, but I got bored,' Winnie fibbed, glancing at Mr Ainsworth with suspicion. 'I've been thinking… It's too much to expect you to run this place by yourself tomorrow so I'm going to ask Mary to stay on until I get back from Carshalton.'

Judith looked confused. 'But I've done it loads of times before.'

'I know, and you're very capable. I'd just feel more relaxed if I knew that you had Mary to back you up if any problems were to arise.'

Judith shrugged. 'If you say so, Mrs Berry.'

Winnie couldn't tell young Judith what Tommy had said about Mr Ainsworth, but she'd be having words with Mary in the morning. And in the meantime, Winnie decided to play the man at his own game. She hopped onto a stool at the end of the bar and watched him. *See how he likes having someone staring at him all the time,* she thought. Though a cold shiver ran down her back. Could she be antagonising a killer? Winnie didn't care, and Mr Ainsworth didn't scare her. But the man was sly, and that unnerved her more than she cared to admit.

58

Winnie held a handkerchief to her nose and dabbed her eyes as Rachel and Roy exchanged their vows. Then, rushing out of the registry office, she stood poised, ready to throw confetti over the newlyweds.

'Rachel looks beautiful,' Grace said. 'I love her outfit.'

'She does look a treat,' Winnie agreed, proudly. The woman was like a daughter to Winnie, even more so now that Hilda had passed away.

'Here they come!' Grace said excitedly, stretching her neck.

'Congratulations,' they yelled, throwing the paper petals over the couple.

Roy stood tall. 'Ladies and gentlemen,' he said, 'I'd like to introduce my wife, Mrs Rachel Russel.'

'It's about time,' Carmen said. Holding her Kodak Brownie camera to face the happy couple, she called, 'Smile.'

'Kids, come and have your photograph taken with me,' Rachel beckoned.

Grace looked at Winnie. 'It's a shame the photograph won't show the pretty pink colour of Rachel's dress and hat.'

'Or the lovely colours of the flowers in her posy,' Winnie added. 'But we'll always have the memories in our heads.'

Rachel waved Winnie towards her. 'You too, Winnie – I want a photograph with you.'

Winnie tried to hold her belly in as Carmen aimed the camera at them.

'I wish my mum was here,' Rachel said, sadly.

'I'm sure she is, love. Your mum wouldn't have missed this day for the world.'

As Winnie smiled for the camera, she spotted a small, red and black butterfly fluttering towards Rachel. The butterfly flew around her head and then landed on a pink rose in Rachel's posy. 'Goodness,' Winnie beamed, tears filling her eyes, 'Jan is here too.'

'Do you really think so, Winnie?'

'Yes, love, I *know* so. Jan *always* lets me know when she's around. If you watch carefully, and listen, I'm sure you'll feel your mum here too.'

Carmen handed the camera to Roy. 'Take a photo of us ladies,' she instructed.

Standing on the step beside Rachel, she said quietly, 'If your mum was here, she'd be saying, *I'm glad to see it's you who's wearing a wedding outfit and not Roy!*'

Rachel and Winnie burst out laughing.

'That's going to make a smashing photograph,' Roy beamed. 'What are you all laughing about?'

'Nothing,' Carmen answered. 'We were just talking about Hilda.'

'Roy is going to drive me to Battersea tomorrow. I want to put my wedding flowers on my mum's grave.'

'That's a lovely idea,' Winnie said, and watched as the butterfly fluttered away. *See you again soon, Jan,* she said in her mind. *And send Hilda my love.*

During the journey home from the registry office, Rachel slipped her jacket and hat off, and left her flowers under the car seat.

'What are you doing?' Martha asked from the back seat.

'I don't want it to look like I've just got married,' Rachel replied. 'Please don't blurt anything to the neighbours. As far as they're concerned, me and Roy have been married for years.'

'That's silly,' Martha said.

'I know, but it's not respectable to live with a man unless you're married.'

'But, Mum, how do you know if you want to marry a man if you haven't lived with him first?'

'Good question... Roy, what do you think?'

'I don't think, not unless I have to.'

Rachel looked over her shoulder to her daughter. 'If you love a man, I mean really, really love a man, then it must be right to marry him.'

'How will I know if I love a man?'

Rachel reached for Roy's hand. 'You'll know, sweetheart. I can't explain how you'll know, you just will.'

Benny spoke up. 'I'm never getting married.'

'Why not?' Rachel asked.

'Girls are 'orrible.'

'You think that now, but I'm sure when you're older, you'll come to like girls.'

'I won't. Girls are bossy and they play silly games with dolls.'

'I don't play with dolls, not anymore,' Martha pointed out.

'No, but you're bossy!' Benny said.

'And you're stupid,' Martha jibed, sticking out her tongue.

'All right, that's enough,' Rachel barked. 'Today is going to be a nice day. No arguing and I don't want any sauce from either of you.'

'Yes, Mum,' Martha and Benny replied together.

Martha sat forward on her seat. 'Roy, now that you've married my mum, can me and Benny call you Dad?'

Rachel's head snapped round to look at Roy. She was pleased to see him glowing with happiness.

'Yes, Martha, I'd like that very much,' he answered.

Rachel had never felt so content. She missed her mum, especially today, but marrying Roy and becoming an official family had been the best day of her life.

In Rachel's bright and airy kitchen, Winnie and Carmen were making the tea and plating the sandwiches that Rachel had prepared that morning.

Carmen gave Winnie a gentle nudge. 'Will it be you and Arnie tying the knot next?'

'Oh, I don't know about that. He mentioned marriage when we first met, but it's a big step.'

'Would you marry him if he asked you?'

Winnie had mulled over that question many times in her head and always came to the same conclusion. 'I honestly don't know. I think a lot of him, and we're spending a great deal of time together, but, you know, the *other* thing? I'm not sure how I feel about it.'

'I see,' Carmen said, raising her eyebrows. 'You do like him in that way, don't you?'

'Yes, but look at me, Carmen. I haven't got your figure. When I take my girdle off, my belly hangs down.'

'Oh, Winnie, if that's all you're concerned about then you've no need to worry. Arnie loves you, it's clear for anyone to see, and he'll love your belly too! All right, you're not the same shape as you were thirty years ago, but you're still an attractive woman. And let's face it, as attractive as Arnie is, the man looks a good ten years older than his age.'

'You think I'm worrying needlessly?'

'Yes, Winnie, I do. I can't believe you'd even consider turning down a marriage proposal from Arnie simply because you think you're fat!'

Winnie chortled. 'When you put it like that, I suppose it does sound a bit silly.'

In the front room, Roy was sitting on the arm of the sofa with his arm draped across Rachel.

'You make a handsome couple,' Winnie gushed.

'Have you heard from Maureen?' Rachel asked.

'Yes, love, and she was very disappointed that she couldn't be here today. She sounded a bit unhappy in one of her letters, but the last one was much more upbeat. She's joined a club, the Crumpets. Maureen said it's all British women, mostly war brides, who've moved from Blighty to America.'

'That's nice for her. *The Crumpets,* how funny! She'll feel more at home with some British friends. It *is* a pity Maureen isn't here,' Rachel said, suddenly looking coy, 'because me and Roy, well, while we're all together, there's something that we want to tell you ...'

'Don't keep us in suspense, then,' Carmen called out.

Rachel gazed lovingly at her husband and then addressed the room. 'Me and Roy, we're, erm, we're having a baby,' she grinned.

Terry rushed towards Roy, grabbing his hand and shaking it vigorously. 'Congratulations, mate,' he enthused. 'That's terrific news.'

Winnie stood with her jaw hanging wide.

'Did you hear me, Win?' Rachel asked.

Winnie nodded, finally finding her voice as she fought back her emotions. 'Yeah, I heard you, all right... Blimey, I can't believe it. I'm over the moon for you both, truly I am. When is the baby due?'

'In about seven months,' Rachel answered, placing her hand on her still flat stomach. 'I hope with my mum not being here, then you'll be happy to be a grandma to this baby?'

Tears fell from Winnie's eyes. 'I'd be honoured,' she sniffed. 'Oh, Gawd, look what you've gone and done to me now. I'm blubbering again.'

Arnie placed his arm around her waist. 'Congratulations, Grandma,' he said softly, and pecked her cheek with a gentle kiss.

Roy rose to his feet. 'We've decided that if the baby is a girl, we're going to name her Hilda.'

'Gawd, no, please don't do that,' Carmen protested. 'Hilda didn't like her name. She wouldn't want her granddaughter named after her.'

'Really?' Rachel asked.

'Yes, really. Hilda told me she couldn't stand her name and if she could have chosen one for herself, she would have picked Madeleine, after Edith Madeleine Carroll, the film star.'

Rachel and Roy exchanged a glance. 'Then Madeleine it is,' he announced.

Carmen clapped her hands. 'Your mum would approve.'

A few hours later, Rachel was in the kitchen with Winnie, admiring her new toaster.

'I'm glad you like it. Grace chose it.'

'How has she been lately?' Rachel asked, quietly.

'As good as gold. I can't fault the girl. In fact, I've grown very fond of her and can't imagine life without her now.'

'That's nice, she's a good kid and is obviously fond of you too.'

'Do you think so?' Winnie asked, hopefully.

'It's clear to see, Winnie.'

The notion of Grace being fond of her gave Winnie a warm feeling inside.

'Sorry to interrupt,' Arnie said, coming into the kitchen, 'but it's getting late. We should think about leaving soon.'

'Yes, of course,' Winnie said, and yawned. It had been a wonderful but long day, and she was feeling tired. Though the thought of returning to the Battersea Tavern made her stomach knot. Winnie had managed to push aside her concerns about Walter Ainsworth but the prospect of seeing him again brought her worries back to the forefront of her mind.

'Are you all right?' Rachel asked.

'Yes, love,' Winnie fibbed. She didn't want to ruin Rachel's day. 'I'll see you very soon.'

Grace and Terry were quiet on the way home. Winnie glanced at the back seat and saw they were both dozing.

Arnie reached for her hand. 'It's been a good day,' he said, 'Thank you for inviting me.'

'It was good, wasn't it? It's just a bloody pity that it's been spoiled by the idea of seeing Ainsworth.'

'Does he upset you that much?' Arnie asked, scowling.

Winnie checked over her shoulder again and was sure that Grace was sleeping. 'Tommy came to see me yesterday. He told me things about Ainsworth that have given me cause for concern.'

'Like what?'

'I'll tell you later,' Winnie whispered. Then pointing behind her, she added, 'Little pigs have big ears.'

At least Winnie knew that Mary would be in the pub. The woman had been horrified by what Winnie had told her about Ainsworth and had vowed to keep a close eye on Judith. In return, Winnie had said she'd pay Pauline to look after her baby brother. Knowing that Mary was in the Battersea Tavern brought Winnie some peace of mind. But she still dreaded going home.

59

The next day, Winnie sat with Arnie and Tommy, huddled in the kitchen upstairs. The door was closed, and they talked with hushed voices.

'Are you sure it's true, Tommy, and not just hearsay?' Arnie asked.

'I'm afraid everything I've told you about Walter Ainsworth is true. I popped up to Clapham Police Station and spoke to the desk sergeant there. The sergeant there is an old mate of mine and he did me a favour, and pulled out Ainsworth's file. I read it for meself, it was all there in black and white. Even the coroner suspected foul play.'

Winnie shook her head. 'I can't believe that he murdered his own mother!'

'Well,' Tommy said, 'we can't say for certain that he did. Ainsworth was taken in for questioning on several occasions but he stuck to his story every time, didn't deviate from it once. He insisted his mother's fall was an unfortunate accident, but it's difficult to explain how a woman with no mobility managed to get her chair to the top of the stairs and fall down them. According to Ainsworth, his mother was always making attempts to break free from the constraints of her bedroom. He claims he helped her into the chair so that she could sit in front of the window, then he went downstairs to make lunch. That's when he heard a crash and his mother scream. He said he found her and the chair at the bottom of the stairs.'

'It makes no sense,' Arnie said. 'If she couldn't walk, how did she get the chair from her bedroom to the top of the stairs?'

'Ainsworth got a doctor to say that he'd prescribed strong painkillers for his mother and it was suggested that with the painkillers, Mrs Ainsworth was able to use the chair to lean on and shuffle to the stairs.'

Winnie didn't believe Ainsworth's account. 'No. Painkillers or no painkillers, if the woman couldn't walk, then there's only one way she got to the stairs – Ainsworth. And then he pushed her in the chair down the stairs. That's what happened.'

'I'm with you, Winnie. He had a lot to gain from his mother's death. Not to mention being free of her. The police spoke to the neighbours who said that Mrs Ainsworth would screech at her son – they could hear her through the walls – and she was always criticising him and ordering him about. One neighbour even said she didn't blame him for killing the old witch!'

'I feel so stupid,' Winnie lamented. 'I'd heard talk of Ainsworth killing his mother, but I chose to ignore it. I wanted to believe he was a lonely, sad man, who'd been stuck in a rotten and depressing life with his wicked mother. What a fool I've been!'

Arnie rose to his feet and went to the window. Then he

turned back to the table and asked Tommy, 'Do you think Winnie is at risk with Ainsworth?'

'Yes, Arnie, I do. Who knows what the man is capable of?'

'Right, in that case, there's only one thing for it. I'll move in here with you, Winnie, so that I can protect you.'

Winnie rolled her eyes. 'Don't be daft, Arnie. I appreciate your sentiment, but what would people say, eh? And not only that, but you can't be here with me every minute of every day. You've got a job to go to. No, you moving in isn't the answer.'

'So, what is?'

'You need to get out of the partnership,' Tommy said.

'It's not as easy as that,' Winnie sighed. 'The only way to get out of it would be to buy him out, and I can't afford to do that. If I had that sort of money to hand, then I'd never have gone into business with him in the first place!'

'There must be something you can do, Tommy?' Arnie pleaded.

'Like what?'

'Get him arrested for something! Can't you fit him up with something?'

'That would be against the law,' Tommy replied.

'And so is murdering your mother,' Winnie hissed.

The telephone rang. 'Excuse me,' she said.

Closing the kitchen door behind her, she dashed down the stairs and picked up the telephone receiver.

'Slow down, Rachel,' she coaxed. Winnie could hear Rachel sobbing, and she couldn't understand a word that the girl was saying. 'What did you say?'

'I'm losing the baby!' Rachel wailed.

'All right, love, stay put. I'm coming straight over.'

Winnie rushed back into the kitchen, breathless after running up the stairs. 'Sorry,' she said, 'but that was Rachel on the telephone. She thinks she's losing the baby. Do you mind driving me over there?'

Arnie jumped to his feet. 'Come on,' he said, heading towards the door. 'Sorry, Tommy, I'll speak to you soon, mate.'

Winnie's heart raced as Arnie drove at speed out of London. 'I still think it would be best if I moved in,' Arnie said.

'I'm sorry, love, but I can't think about that at the moment. Sod Ainsworth. I'm worried sick about Rachel and the baby.'

'I know. I hope she's all right. Your family could do without any more bad luck.'

'Cor, you can say that again. This past six months have been one thing on top of another. Nothing good has happened.'

Arnie offered a small smile. 'You met me,' he said, cheekily.

Winnie smiled too. 'Yes, I did, but apart from meeting you, it's been a rubbish time lately.'

Pulling up outside Rachel's house, Winnie hurried to the front door as Arnie called, 'I'll wait here.'

She expected Roy to be home, but his car wasn't parked in the street.

Rachel pulled open the door, looking sheepish. 'I'm sorry, Winnie, I didn't mean for you to come all the way over here.'

'Are you all right?'

'Yes, I'm fine. Come in.'

In the front room, Winnie sat on the sofa as Rachel explained. 'I had a bit of blood, only a small amount, and I assumed I was losing the baby. But after I telephoned you, I called the midwife at the hospital. She said it was normal, and if it's just a small amount, then there's nothing to worry about. I just have to take it easy.'

Winnie sighed. 'For Christ's sake, Rachel, you nearly gave me another bleedin' heart attack!'

'I'm really sorry. I did try to call you back, but you'd already left.'

'It's fine, I'm just relieved to know that little Madeleine is all right.'

'It might not be a girl,' Rachel grinned.

'I've got a feeling it is.'

'I was thinking of asking Leena to lay the tarot cards and see what they say.'

'Don't waste your money. You'll find out for yourself in seven months.'

'Ha, that's what Roy said too. Thanks for coming here so quickly, Winnie, and I'm sorry to have wasted your time.'

'I'm happy to come any time I'm needed. You only have to call.' Then Winnie chuckled. 'Talking about calling, how many times a day do you telephone Roy at work?'

'Once or twice,' Rachel answered, blushing.

'Yeah, and the rest. I bet he regrets having the telephone installed.'

Rachel cringed. 'I can't help myself, Winnie. I get bored, and then I think, I know, I'll call Roy. But he did say that he'll get in trouble at work if I keep calling.'

Winnie tutted. 'It costs money an' all. You should be saving your pennies. Babies don't come cheap, you know. Anyway, if you're sure you're all right, then we need to get back. I don't want to leave Judith alone to open the pub.'

'I thought you said she's great at her job?' Rachel questioned.

'She is, but I don't trust Walter Ainsworth. It's a long story, I'll call you this evening and tell you all about it. And in the meantime, if you're worried about that baby, make sure you call me!'

Back in the car, Winnie pondered on the idea of Arnie moving in. She had room upstairs; they could have separate bedrooms. But she didn't relish the idea of being the focus of local gossip again. And it could be uncomfortable bumping into him in the middle of the night if she got up to use the toilet.

Her mind turned with all the reasons for why Arnie moving in wasn't a good idea. *I like me own space too much and I'm too set in my ways,* she concluded, which didn't bode well for ever marrying the man!

60

The following day, Judith came in early to help Winnie sort through the bunting, ready to decorate the pub in June for the Queen's coronation.

In the cellar, rifling through the boxes, Winnie held up some Union Jack flags on a string. 'This has all seen better days,' she moaned, shoving it back into the box with a huff. 'Mind you, it's not seen the light of day since we won the war. Cor, what a party that was!'

'My mum still talks about it. She was here when you had the Victory in Europe party.'

'She was, and if my memory serves me right, your mum had to be carried home,' Winnie chuckled. 'She's blind as a bat, but she was blind drunk that night!'

'*Carried home*? She never told me that!'

Mary's voice from upstairs reached Winnie's ears.

'How bloody well dare you!' the woman screeched.

'For Gawd's sake, what now?' Winnie mumbled as she made her way to the stairs.

In the pub, Mary was standing with one hand on her hip,

the other hand shaking a finger at Mr Ainsworth. 'What proof have you got? Go on, tell me. Prove it!'

'Prove what?' Winnie asked.

Mary turned to face Winnie, looking furious. 'He's just accused me of stealing!' she shouted. 'You know me, Winnie, I'd *never* pinch anything from you.'

'No, I know you wouldn't.'

Mr Ainsworth stepped forward. 'You've mislaid your trust, Mrs Berry. The woman is a thief and I caught her red-handed.'

'Is that right? So, what exactly did you catch Mary stealing?'

'She had her hands in the cash register and appeared most perturbed when I caught her. The look of guilt was written all over her face.'

Winnie found Mr Ainsworth's accusations difficult to believe.

'I was nowhere near the blinkin' till,' Mary protested. 'He's lying!'

Mr Ainsworth rubbed his clean-shaven chin. 'If that is the case, then you'll have nothing to hide. You won't object to being searched.'

'I bleedin' well will! You ain't touching me, you filthy git!'

'I've no desire to lay my hands on you, Mrs Middleton, but Mrs Berry can check your pockets.'

'Go on then,' Mary said, throwing her arms in the air. 'Search me, Winnie, but you won't find nothing cos I ain't a bloody thief!'

Winnie shook her head. 'I don't need to search Mrs Middleton.'

'I must insist that you do, Mrs Berry. The woman is relying on your friendship, but she is a thief and a liar.'

'Do it, Winnie. Just flippin' search me,' Mary urged.

Winnie blew out a long breath of air. She had no desire to search her friend. Shoving her hand into the pocket of Mary's dress, all Winnie found was a packet of five cigarettes and a box of matches. The other pocket was empty.

'See,' Mary spat, glowering at Mr Ainsworth.

'Her apron,' he said. 'Check the pocket of her apron.'

Winnie, standing in front of Mary, mouthed a silent apology. Then reaching into Mary's apron, she felt something papery. Pulling it out, Winnie peered, stunned, at a ten-shilling note.

'That's not mine!' Mary blurted. 'I swear, Winnie, I didn't know that money was in my pocket. I didn't put it there. It ain't mine.'

'Quite right, Mrs Middleton,' Mr Ainsworth said smugly. 'The money is *not* yours. It belongs to the Battersea Tavern and was taken unlawfully from the cash register. As I said, you have been caught red-handed.'

'Winnie, he's lying. I swear I didn't take it. Please, Winnie, you do believe me, don't you?'

'Actually, Mr Ainsworth, I placed the cash in Mrs Middleton's pocket earlier today and I forget to mention it because we were so busy sorting coronation things. In fact, the money is for new bunting. Mrs Middleton kindly offered to shop for some for me.'

Mr Ainsworth's face flushed red. 'That's not true!' he bellowed.

'So, you're calling me a liar too?' Winnie challenged.

'No ... erm ... I meant that I'm sure you must be mistaken. I saw the woman steal the money!'

'No, Mr Ainsworth, I think it's *you* who is mistaken. And I believe you owe Mrs Middleton an apology.'

The man grimaced at Winnie, grunted and walked away.

'Did you really put that money in my pocket?' Mary whispered.

'No, *he* did.'

'Why? Why would he do that?'

'To get rid of you, I suppose. You're a strong woman and you're not afraid of him. Maybe you remind him of his mother,' Winnie smirked.

'Christ, it's creepy.'

'Yes, Mary it is. And me and you need to be careful. We must watch each other's backs.'

Grace arrived home from school to find a note pushed under the back door. Opening up the folded piece of paper, she read the scribbled words.

Winnie Berry, you're a dirty whore!

Arnold Potter is engaged to me. Keep your hands off my man or I'll do a better job of burning down your pub, and I'll make sure you're in it!

Grace gaped at the note, her hands trembling. She still had nightmares of being burned alive. The thought of the Battersea Tavern going up in flames again terrified her.

Running up the stairs, she fled into her room and shoved the note under her pillow. Then, sitting beside her bed, she hugged her knees to her chest and tried to dismiss the memories of that dreadful night. She could almost taste the acrid smoke in her mouth and remembered how her eyes had stung and she'd been blinded, almost choking. The heat from the fire had been overwhelming and if Winnie hadn't of found her sheltering in the downstairs kitchen, Grace had no doubt that she'd be dead now.

There was a tap on the bedroom door, and Winnie pushed it open. 'I thought I heard you come home ... Hey, what's wrong?'

Grace looked up at Winnie with tears streaking down her face. 'I-I'm scared,' she cried.

'What of, love?'

'Fire.'

'I'm not surprised. We had a nasty encounter, but we all got out alive. What's brought this on, eh?'

Grace shrugged. She didn't want to show Winnie the note and upset her.

Winnie sat on the edge of the bed and placed a comforting hand on Grace's shoulder. 'The chances of a fire ever happening here again are slim to none. And we've got Arnie now, he's the boss of the firemen. Who better to save us from a burning building, eh? I know what happened was bloody scary, but it won't happen again, Grace.'

'You don't know that!'

'Yes, love, I do. Brancher is locked up behind bars. He won't be coming out until he's an old man. He started the fire, but he can't get to us ever again.'

'What if someone else wants to hurt you?' Grace asked.

'Like who? I haven't got any enemies that I know of.'

Grace chewed on her thumbnail, questions bombarding her brain. 'Do you think that Arnie could have another girlfriend?'

'No,' Winnie guffawed. 'When would he get the chance to see another woman? He's either at work or he's round here most of the time. What made you ask me that? It's a funny question to ask.'

Grace pushed herself to her feet. Winnie was right, it really did seem unlikely that Arnie could be engaged to another woman. She hoped not, because she liked Arnie, and he made Winnie happy. Reaching under her pillow, she handed Winnie the note. 'It was under the back door when I got home.'

Winnie's eyes stretched wide as she read the words. Her lips pursed, and she folded the note in half and put it into the pocket of her cardigan. 'You're not to take any notice of this. It's not true, and no one, and I mean no one, is going to set light to my pub.'

'Who do you think sent it?'

'I don't know, love. Someone with a very twisted mind. You're not to worry about it. Leave it with me, I'll get to the bottom of it. Are you all right now?'

'Yeah, I think so. It just scared me.'

'I expect it did. But it's all lies. You're safe here, Grace, and I'll *always* protect you. You know that, don't you?'

Grace threw her arms around Winnie and hugged her.

Winnie cuddled her back. 'You're my family, Grace, and family care for each other.'

'Thank you,' Grace smiled, enjoying the warmth of Winnie's embrace. Though Bertha had loved her, Grace had never known the love of a mother and she imagined that this is what it felt like. If she could have chosen anyone to be her mum, Grace would have chosen Winnie Berry.

Later that evening, Winnie sat beside Arnie on her sofa and waited for his reaction to the note.

'If it wasn't so threatening towards you, I'd laugh. But this isn't a laughing matter, Winnie. You know there's no truth in it, don't you?'

'Of course. I didn't believe a word of it, not for a second. But it frightened the life out of Grace.'

'I'll speak to her and give her some reassurance. You've no idea who sent it?'

'I've got my suspicions – Ainsworth.'

'Would he stoop this low?' Arnie asked, doubtfully.

'This is nothing compared to killing his mother.'

'True. But what is he hoping to achieve with this?'

Winnie sighed. 'Do you remember when we first met and he tried to cause problems between us. He told you I was out with another man. This stinks of him. I'm sure he's behind it, and I think I know why. This morning, he planted some money on Mary and accused her of stealing it. I stepped in and said that I'd put the money in Mary's pocket. He knew I hadn't, but he couldn't admit that he'd put it there, could he? This note is him attempting to get his own back on me.'

Winnie saw Arnie's jaw clench with anger. 'I can't have this, Winnie. I know you said you can fight your own battles, but you don't have to do it alone anymore. Let me help you.'

'Thanks, Arnie, but what can you do? If you say anything to him about the note, he'll only deny it.'

'Who said anything about speaking to him?'

'Please don't go downstairs with your fists flying. Ainsworth is a cunning sod, he'll get you arrested.'

'I want to punch his bloody lights out,' Arnie seethed.

'I know how you feel. I've wanted to do the same for ages. But it's not the answer and it won't achieve anything. You need to calm down and think about it clearly.'

Arnie rose to his feet. 'You're right,' he said, drawing in a long breath. 'I'll go and have a word with Grace and let her know that there's nothing to worry about.'

'Thanks, love, and don't mention that we think the note came from Ainsworth. He's here almost every hour that the pub is open and I don't want Grace feeling afraid of him.'

'You and Grace shouldn't have to live like this. I'm going to get this sorted, Winnie. One way or another, Ainsworth won't be in your life for much longer.'

61

Tuesday, 2 June 1953

Winnie woke up and pulled back her bedroom curtains. Glancing out of the window she noted the dark clouds hanging low in the sky, but no amount of rain would dampen today's celebrations. Today was the coronation of the twenty-seven-year-old mother of two, Queen Elizabeth the Second. The streets outside were silent. No shops or businesses were opening because a national bank holiday had been decreed and most of the country would be watching the grand royal event on television.

Winnie quickly washed and dressed. 'You'll have to make your own breakfast this morning,' she told Grace. 'But I want you downstairs as soon as possible. There's so much to do – we're going to be packed to the rafters today.'

Grace yawned. 'There's not much to do, Winnie, everything is ready. We did most of it last night.'

'I know, but I want everything to run perfectly today.'

Downstairs, Terry had arranged the seats in the pub so that they all faced the television set which he'd carried down with Pete's help from Winnie's front room and Judith and Mary had been in charge of the decorations. Winnie glanced around, pleased with what she saw. Red, white and blue bunting swooped from corner to corner. There were small flags on sticks on the tables and the buffet table was covered with a Union Jack paper cloth.

There was a tap on the back door, and Winnie checked the time. *That'll be Mary,* she thought.

'You and Judith have done a smashing job,' she trilled. 'Thanks, love, my pub looks very fitting for a royal do.'

'I'm no royalist, me, but you can't help getting caught up in the excitement of it all,' Mary said, pulling off her coat. 'Right,' she added with a clap of her hands, 'what do you want me to do first?'

'Nothing. As Grace rightly pointed out earlier, it's all done. I want you to sit back and enjoy yourself.'

'I can help you bring the food out,' Mary offered.

'No, Grace and Carmen will be doing that. Me and Judith will be behind the bar. Terry and Piano Pete will collect glasses and Rachel and Martha are on the tea urn. I tell you what, though, Mary, it's days like today that I really miss Hilda. She would have loved to have seen the coronation on the television. I can picture her, sat up the front with a cup of tea, waving a flag, mesmerised by the whole thing.'

'I know you miss her, Winnie. And I expect you're missing Maureen too?'

'Yes, but it's funny to think that Maureen will be watching the same thing as us, all those miles away and halfway around the world. I don't know how the television people do it, it's a flippin' marvel.'

'I can tell you this for nothing – I won't be sitting up the front near the television. Me and the baby will be right at the back, away from any radiation damage.'

Winnie had to bite her tongue and stop herself from laughing. *Radiation damage,* she thought, chuckling in her head.

Judith arrived, and Carmen shortly after. Roy dropped off Rachel and Martha and Benny, and Terry turned up next with Piano Pete. It was half an hour before the doors were due to open, but already the atmosphere was jolly, until Mr Ainsworth walked in.

'Even he won't spoil my day today,' Winnie whispered to Mary.

'Have you got the prize ready for the best fancy dress?' Rachel asked. 'Martha and Benny have gone upstairs to get changed into their costumes. They can't wait for you to see them.'

'Yes, of course I've got a prize ready. There's a coronation mug that I've filled with sweets and two tickets to the picture house. I've put a ten-shilling note in an' all.'

'That's very generous,' Mary said, raising her eyebrows. 'My Pauline wanted to come as a mermaid, but I put me foot down and told her no. I said to her, it's all right for the little ones to wear a shell bra, they're flat chested, but you're sprouting – it wouldn't be decent. So she's bringing the baby and is coming as Minnie Mouse.'

'Oh, I can't wait to see her,' Winnie smiled. 'Grace didn't want to do fancy dress. She's wearing a red, white and blue dress that I bought from Flo.'

Mr Ainsworth sidled over. Looking down his nose, he said to Winnie, 'I assume you had the foresight to test that the television set is working?'

Winnie glared at the man. 'I'm not stupid,' she snapped.

'Good, good,' he said. 'And may I say, Mrs Berry, you have

organised a splendid display and I'm sure that today will proceed swimmingly.' Smiling, he turned on the tip of his toe and walked away.

'Blimey,' Mary drew out, 'what's got into him?'

'I don't know if I like seeing him so happy. It makes me nervous,' Winnie chortled. 'But like I said, he won't spoil today, so let's get the doors open, eh?'

Terry switched on the television as customers streamed in, all eager to see the historic event.

Mary's neighbour bustled in with her husband and three children. Her eldest was dressed as a cowboy, and her two daughters as hula girls. ''Ere, Mrs Berry, you're the only person on the street with a television set so I reckon you're gonna be full in here today. You might have to open the windows to let people outside see the Queen.'

All the seats were soon taken and the children sat at the front on the floor. Grainy black-and-white images flickered on the small screen. A hush fell over the pub as the pictures of the royal procession were aired. There were a few 'oohs' and 'aahs', and then they got the first glimpse of Queen Elizabeth riding in a carriage.

'Look at that, it's golden!' Pauline announced.

'How do you know that?' Mary called from the back. 'It's a black-and-white picture.'

Pauline's head flicked round. 'Everyone knows it's a golden coach, Mum.'

Winnie could feel the emotion in the pub. A tingling, buzzing, patriotic atmosphere that made her proud to be British. 'No one can do pomp and ceremony like us Brits,' she whispered to Arnie who had turned up late.

As hour after hour passed, rain poured on London.

'It's a bit boring,' Mary moaned. 'You can't see much except for hats. None of the cars have got the roofs down cos of the weather.'

'Shush!' someone from the front hissed. 'They're going into Westminster Abbey now.'

When the Queen emerged from the golden carriage, astonished whispers filled the air of the Battersea Tavern.

'She looks beautiful,' Grace gasped.

'Look how small her waist is,' someone said.

'Her dress ... it's stunning!'

In the abbey, when the crown was placed on the royal head, Martha chirped, 'I look just like her now!'

Winnie smiled at her granddaughter who was dressed as Queen Elizabeth and Benny as the Queen's husband, Philip. There were so many imaginative and wonderful costumes, Winnie knew she was going to have a difficult decision on picking the best one.

'Have you seen Ainsworth?' Arnie whispered in her ear.

As Richard Dimbleby's clipped English accent came through the television commentating on the ceremony, Winnie looked towards the end of the bar and saw Mr Ainsworth had tears rolling down his cheeks. He didn't seem to be ashamed of his display of emotion, and she noticed that he had a large glass of port in his hand. It was the first time that she'd seen the man drink.

'He's enjoying himself,' she said, astonished.

The ceremony came to an end and the guests inside the abbey began to leave. Everyone was thrilled to see the rather robust Queen Sālote of Tonga sitting in an open carriage, despite the rain, and waving emphatically at the crowds that lined the streets. Opposite her, the Sultan of Kelantan appeared miserable in contrast.

'Oh, I love her!' Carmen grinned. 'Look at her, she's really enjoying herself and she's got the crowds cheering.'

Most of the children were becoming restless, so Winnie thought now would be a good time to have them parade around the pub, showing off their fancy dress costumes. She hadn't accounted for Flo's husband, Bill, turning up as Old Mother Riley. Wearing a long dress, a shawl over his shoulders and a grey wig, his antics had everyone roaring with laughter.

'That's enough now, Bill,' Flo admonished. 'Put that stupid rolling pin away!'

Winnie couldn't choose a best costume, so she asked her customers to cheer for their favourite. She was pleased when Mrs Coe's son won it for his Royal Guardsman outfit including a big, furry hat that kept slipping over his eyes.

'There's ten shillings in that mug,' Winnie said quietly to Mrs Coe. 'You might want to slip it in your purse,' she suggested, knowing that the woman was living on the breadline.

Cakes and sandwiches were enjoyed and then everyone gathered around the television set again to see the newly crowned Queen on the balcony of Buckingham Palace.

'Where's Ainsworth?' Winnie asked Judith.

'I don't know. I haven't seen him for a while.'

Rachel dashed towards the bar. 'Winnie, we're running out of milk for the tea.'

'I've got more upstairs – I'll be back in a tick.'

Winnie trudged to the stairs, and found Mr Ainsworth sitting on them, blowing his nose into a crisp, white handkerchief, his eyes red-rimmed and glistening with tears.

'Are you all right there?' she asked.

Mr Ainsworth leaped to his feet. 'Excuse me,' he said, 'it's been quite a day.'

'It has. And you'll be pleased to know that we've turned a good profit.'

'You find me irritable, and I suspect you think I'm only concerned with the money that the Battersea Tavern makes.'

Winnie was taken aback by Mr Ainsworth's forthrightness. But she'd never been one to shy away from a directness. 'I've made no secret of the fact that I don't like you, and you've made it clear that you only care about the profits.'

Mr Ainsworth burped, rather loudly, 'Pardon me,' he said.

Winnie got a whiff of the alcohol on his breath. She realised that he was swaying too.

'You have no notion of what the Battersea Tavern means to me,' he said, his words slightly slurring. 'This place is all I have. If I didn't have the Battersea Tavern, my existence would be a lonely one. I don't come here every day to assert my authority, Mrs Berry. I come for the companionship and the conversation with our customers.'

Winnie rolled her eyes. She was used to having to listen to drunken, rambling men.

'It's true,' Mr Ainsworth insisted. 'I can see that you don't believe me, but the first day that I ever walked into this pub was a turning point in my life. Up until then, I wouldn't see anyone apart from my mother for days, sometimes weeks at a time. This pub has been my saving grace so it felt only right that I should invest in rebuilding it.'

'If you say so,' Winnie said, edging past the man.

As she walked up the stairs, Mr Ainsworth continued talking.

'After my mother's tragic death, there was nothing left

for me. I'd spent so many years caring for her that I soon discovered that I had no life of my own. I wanted to die, Mrs Berry, and I had planned to kill myself. But then I met you outside, and a light switched on inside me, which chased away the darkness. Thank you, Mrs Berry. Thank you for saving my life.'

Winnie was at the top of the stairs. She turned around and looked down at Mr Ainsworth. Though she detested the man, she had an idea of how soul-destroying loneliness could feel, and she couldn't help feeling sorry for him. 'Have a cup of coffee and sober up,' she said. 'And maybe tomorrow, me and you can start again on fresh footings.'

62

A few days later, Winnie was sitting at the kitchen table reading another letter from Maureen. She smiled, pleased to know that Maureen was happy and would be married soon, though her letter was filled with words about how much she missed Battersea. And Stephen had a girlfriend – apparently the American ladies were quite taken with her brother's English accent.

Mary tapped at the kitchen door.

'Come in, love,' Winnie said. 'Pour yourself a cuppa.'

'Ooh, I'd love one. I've just fed the baby and he'll sleep now for a while, so I've left him downstairs in his pram.'

'I'm surprised at how quiet he was during the coronation. He slept most of the way through it.'

'That'll be the drop of brandy I put in his bottle. He had a terrible cough, but a bit of brandy cleared it up. My mum always swore it was the best remedy for coughs and sleep,' Mary said.

'Have you noticed a change in Ainsworth?' Winnie asked.

'Funny you should ask … That's what I popped up to tell

you. You'll never believe this. He gave me a teddy for the baby!'

'You're pulling my leg!'

'No, Winnie, straight up. I didn't know what to say.'

'Well, I'll be buggered.'

'And yesterday he gave Judith a pair of opal studs that he said belonged to his mother.'

Winnie shook her head. 'I want to believe he's seen the errors of his ways and that he's genuine, but I don't trust him, Mary.'

'Do you reckon this *nice* Mr Ainsworth is all an act?'

'I don't know. But in my experience, a leopard don't change its spots. I had years of my husband and my son telling me how sorry they were for their rotten behaviour and promising to change. They would, for a short while, but they always ended up reverting back to their 'orrible selves. I wouldn't be surprised if Ainsworth keeps this act up for a week or two.'

'You're so cynical, Winnie,' Mary smiled, 'And that's one of the things I like about you. But why would he put on this act?'

'Gawd knows. I shudder to think what goes on in his mind. Keep your guard up, love.'

'I will, thanks. How's Arnie?'

'He's another one who's got me wondering what's going on,' Winnie replied.

'What do you mean?'

'I don't know, I can't put my finger on it. He's been a bit cagey lately. Secretive. And he seems distant. I'm sure he's up to something, but I've no idea what.'

'You don't need to worry about Arnie. He's a good bloke.'

408

'I know, but if *we* think he's a good bloke, then so will other women.'

'Oh, Winnie, you don't suspect him of seeing another woman, do you?'

'I hope not, Mary. I don't want to lose Arnie. It would break my heart.'

That evening, once Martha and Benny were in their beds, Rachel sat beside Roy on the sofa.

'I wish I could knit,' Rachel mused. 'If I could knit, I'd make the baby lots of matinee jackets and little booties. My mum would have had her needles out by now and knitted loads of pink dresses for Madeleine.'

Roy folded his newspaper in half and placed it beside him. Placing his hand on Rachel's leg, he joked, 'And knowing your mum's wicked sense of humour, she probably would have knitted me a dress too.'

Rachel's head shot round to look at Roy. He'd never mentioned about the dressing in women's clothes. 'Would you have worn it?' she asked, her voice serious.

'No, darling. I shouldn't think it would have been flattering.'

Rachel punched his arm, playfully. 'You silly bugger,' she smiled.

'I promised you that I'd never do it again, and I haven't.'

'Thank you. I've not wanted to ask, but I have wondered,' Rachel admitted.

'Let's leave the past where it is.'

Rachel nodded. She could tell that Roy was beginning to feel uncomfortable with the conversation. She wanted to believe he'd stuck to his promise, but Rachel suspected that he'd been dressing up again. She was sure her lipstick had worn down rather quickly, and she'd found a pair of her earrings in the bathroom that should have been in her jewellery box.

'You know, you can talk to me about anything,' she assured Roy.

'I know.'

'You don't have to bottle up your feelings. You can share them with me.'

Roy sucked in a deep breath, saying dismissively, 'I'm not wearing dresses and talking to Lillian, so can we drop the subject.'

Rachel thought it was probably best to ignore her suspicions. After all, they had a baby on the way. 'Ooh!' she said, her eyes widening.

'What? What's wrong?' Roy asked with urgency.

'Nothing – it's the baby She just kicked me!'

Roy leaned forward. 'May I?' he asked, his hands poised to place them on Rachel's stomach.

'Yes, here,' she answered, directing his hand.

They waited a moment, and then Rachel felt it again.

'Oh my goodness,' Roy exclaimed, 'Are you sure we've got a girl in there? That was one helluva kick. I reckon we've got a little footballer.'

'I'm convinced it's a girl. I hope so because we can't call a boy Madeleine.'

The baby kicked again. 'Hello in there, baby Russel. It's me and your daddy out here.'

Roy lowered his head, closer to Rachel's stomach. 'We can't wait to meet you,' he swooned.

Rachel smiled affectionately at her husband. 'I love you, Roy.'

'I love you too,' he said. 'And I think you deserve a cup of tea and a slice of cake.'

'I'll put the kettle on,' Rachel said, pushing herself up from the sofa.

'No, you stay where you are. You're doing all the hard work by growing our baby.'

Rachel gazed at her husband adoringly. She couldn't remember a time in her life when she'd ever been so happy. The only blot on her landscape was the ache in her heart for her mum – and the niggling fear that Roy was hiding his secret again.

It was a quiet night in the pub, so Winnie left Judith to see to the customers and went upstairs and joined Grace on the sofa.

'I knew this thing would waste my time,' she chuckled to Grace. 'There's a hundred and one things I could be doing instead of sitting on my backside and watching the television.'

'That serial *Stand by to Shoot* is just about to start.'

'You won't be watching it, young lady. It's time you were in bed.'

'Oh, go on. We can watch it together,' Grace pleaded.

'No, it's late and you've got school tomorrow. Off you go. Sweet dreams.'

Grace skulked out, and Winnie heard footsteps coming up the stairs. She hoped it was Arnie and wondered where he'd been all evening.

'Hello, Win,' he said, awkwardly, then kissing her cheek, he sat down beside her.

Winnie would have liked to ask him about his whereabouts and who he'd been seeing, but she didn't want him to lie to her and neither did she want to hear the truth.

'You all right?' he asked.

She nodded, her lips pursed.

'Sorry I'm late,' he said.

Unable to contain herself, she blurted, 'Where have you been?'

'I've been working late.'

Winnie didn't believe him. 'Are you sure about that?'

Arnie frowned, saying, 'I've been busy.'

'Hmm, I bet you have!'

'What's that supposed to mean?' he asked.

'Busy with another woman?' Winnie accused.

To Winnie's dismay, Arnie threw his head back and roared with laughter.

'What's so bloody funny?'

'Oh, Win, you couldn't be further off the mark if you tried! No, I haven't been busy with another woman. You don't really believe that, do you?'

'I don't know, Arnie. You've seemed distracted lately and I've not seen much of you.'

'Sorry. You're right, I *have* been distracted. I've, erm, I've sold my house, so I've been busy packing and sorting things.'

'What?' Winnie spat. 'You've sold your house? When? Why? And why didn't you tell me?'

The colour drained from Arnie's face. 'I want to marry you, Winnie, and look after you. That means getting rid of Ainsworth. I've sold my house so that you can buy him out and dissolve the partnership.'

Winnie's eyes blinked hard and fast as she tried to digest Arnie's words. 'You've sold your house? But what if I say no to marrying you? Where will you live?'

'Are you going to say no?' he asked, looking gobsmacked.

'You'll have to ask me to marry you before I give you my answer,' she smiled.

Arnie lowered himself onto one knee. His hand shook as he ran his hand through his hair. 'Winnie, will you marry me?'

Winnie gazed into his eyes.

'Well, will you?' Arnie pressed.

'Yes,' she answered, surprising herself. Winnie hadn't thought that she wanted to share her bed or her home with Arnie but fearing that she may have lost him to another woman had made her realise how much she loved him.

Arnie eased himself to his feet and pulled Winnie into his arms. 'I'll take you shopping tomorrow for an engagement ring,' he said, 'And then we can make it official.'

Still in a state of shock, she mumbled, 'If you've sold your house to buy Ainsworth out, will that make you my business partner?'

Arnie sat on the sofa, and gently pulled Winnie down to sit beside him. 'I'm due to retire from the fire brigade in three months. It's not something I've been looking forward to because I didn't know what I'd do with my time. So yes, if you're agreeable, I'd be a partner in the Battersea Tavern, but I'm under no illusion who the boss will be,' he smiled.

'Living *and* working together – sounds perfect!'

'I've also taken the liberty of speaking to a solicitor. He's getting the paperwork drawn up for Ainsworth to sign.'

'Blimey, you *have* been busy. I don't know what I'm looking forward to most, shopping for an engagement ring or telling Ainsworth that he can clear off!'

63

When Winnie woke up the next morning she thought she'd had the most wonderful dream, but then she realised that it hadn't been a dream, it had really happened. 'I'm getting married!' she said, throwing off the bed covers with vigour.

It felt like ages until Grace eventually came through to the kitchen and Winnie couldn't wait to share her news. 'I've got something to tell you,' she grinned. 'Come and sit down,' she added, patting the table.

Grace rubbed the sleep out of her eyes.

'You're the first person to know – Arnie has asked me to marry him and I've said yes!'

In that moment, Grace's sleepy face came alight. 'That's wonderful, Winnie. Can I be a bridesmaid?'

Winnie chuckled. 'We won't be having a big church wedding, love. But you're happy about Arnie coming to live here with us?'

'Yeah, *really* happy.'

'Good. He's taking me shopping later to buy a ring. Will you come with us and help me choose it?'

Grace jumped up and hugged Winnie. 'I'd love to, thank you. Can I tell Pauline?'

'Yes, love, of course you can. I'm looking forward to telling Mary too.'

'When are you getting married?'

'I'm not sure, we haven't set a date yet, but it'll be very soon.'

'Another party in the Battersea Tavern,' Grace smiled.

Later that morning, Winnie broke her news to Mary.

'Congratulations, I'm so pleased for you,' Mary trilled.

'Thanks, love. I can't wait to get rid of Ainsworth too. Arnie has sold his house and is going to buy him out.'

'Well, that's even better news,' Mary laughed.

The baby coughed in his pram.

'He's still not right, that cough is back and he's running a temperature. I'm going to whizz round my work today, get it done as quickly as I can and then take him to see the doctor.'

Winnie glanced around the pub. 'Leave it, love, you'll get your full pay, but get the little 'un to the doctor.'

'No, Winnie, it's fine. I'd rather do me job properly.'

'All right, but just empty the ashtrays and give the tables a wipe. Don't worry about anything else. Judith is off today an' all, she's gone down with a chesty cough too. No arguments, Mary, just ashtrays and tables. I need to do a stock check, so I'll be in the cellar if you need me. I reckon my customers drank the place almost dry on Coronation Day.'

Winnie stood in the cellar with a pad and pencil, counting bottles and tutting to herself. She missed Carmen. The woman was far better at organising and ordering stock than Winnie was and Carmen had kept the cellar in better order than it was now. She glanced around, remembering the many nights they'd sheltered there from the bombs. It seemed impossible to contemplate sleeping down here now, but they had, night after night, fretting as explosions had thundered around them. Somehow, apart from a few scratches, the Battersea Tavern had survived the war.

'See you tomorrow, Winnie!' Mary yelled down the stairs, snapping Winnie from her memories.

Back to counting and it soon became apparent to Winnie that she urgently needed to place an order. Heading for the stairs, she glanced up, startled when she saw a figure looming.

'Oh!' she gasped. 'Mr Ainsworth, you made me jump.'

As Winnie began to climb the stairs, Mr Ainsworth pulled the door closed behind him.

Winnie stopped and looked up at the man. His eyes were icy cold, and his top lip curled and twitched on one side.

'What are you doing?' she asked, fear making her skin crawl.

'I heard you talking with Mrs Middleton,' he replied.

Winnie gulped.

'Have you considered that I might not be willing to sell my half of this business?'

Winnie shook her head.

'I've told you how much it means to me. And I've made an effort to be more pleasant to our employees. Why, Mrs Berry, why would you want to take this away from me?'

Winnie's heart hammered. She tried to pacify the man, saying gently. 'You must see that I'd rather have my husband as my business partner. It's nothing personal, Mr Ainsworth.'

'I don't believe you and your reasons for wishing to dissolve our partnership are inconsequential. I won't sell.'

'Please, Mr Ainsworth, let's not be hasty or unreasonable. You'll be offered a fair price, better than fair, in fact. We need to sit down and discuss it properly.'

'No, Mrs Berry, we don't. I'm tempted to ask you nicely, to request that you please, please don't take this pub, my life, everything away from me. But I've no need to beg or plead. The simple fact is that my share in this establishment is not for sale. However, there's something that I've been giving a great deal of thought to – what would happen to your share of the business if you were to meet an unfortunate end?'

'Eh?' Winnie muttered, alarmed.

'Perhaps you didn't read the finer details of our contract. I have a copy here,' he said, holding a bundle of papers towards her. 'I've underlined the relevant lines.'

'What are you on about?' Winnie asked, her mouth dry and her legs feeling wobbly with fear.

'It clearly states here that in the event of your untimely death, your shares would revert to me. And likewise, although I don't assume that I will be dropping dead any time soon. Look, you can see it for yourself.' Mr Ainsworth was still holding the papers towards her.

Winnie was scared. She knew there was no one to hear her scream.

'Come, take a look,' Mr Ainsworth urged.

'No. Do you think I'm stupid enough to walk up these stairs for you to push me down them like you did your own mother?'

Mr Ainsworth's expression was surprisingly blank. He stood for a moment, staring coldly down at Winnie. And then he turned, switching off the light switch at the top of the stairs before walking out and slamming the door closed.

Winnie heard him turn the key in the lock. She'd been left in pitch-blackness. Dropping her pad and pencil, she felt for the cold brick wall beside her. Feeling her way, she carefully stepped down the couple of stairs she'd climbed and, with her pulse racing and with trembling hands, she edged along the wall towards the back of the cellar. She was still reeling from blurting out the accusation of him pushing his mother down the stairs. She could have kicked herself. What a stupid thing to have said when she was in such a vulnerable position!

'Shit!' she hissed, tripping over a crate. Winnie tumbled forwards, bashing her knee and scraping her hands as she landed on the floor. Her leg throbbed as she scrambled back to her feet, peering around and trying to adjust her eyes to the darkness. But she couldn't see anything, not even shadows. Only a tiny glimmer of light came through the smallest of holes in the trapdoors that the draymen used to unload barrels of beer. If she could reach up, maybe she could force them open. But the doors were out of her range and she'd need to stand on something. But what? Crates? Where were they? How could she pile them up in the dark? The trapdoor escape felt impossible in the blackness. And with Ainsworth lurking and waiting somewhere at the top of the stairs, Winnie couldn't flee that way either.

'Help!' she called, her voice echoing, knowing it would be fruitless – no one would hear her cries. *I've got to get out of here,* she thought, panicking. What if Grace came home from school early and Ainsworth hurt her? Mustering all her courage, Winnie pulled a bottle of something from one of the crates and smashed it against the wall. Holding the neck of the bottle with the jagged glass edge in front of her, she fumbled her way through the cellar and back to the stairs.

Slowly creeping up the stairs, Winnie held her breath, listening for sounds of Ainsworth. She reached the top, switched the light on and then rattled the door, shouting, 'Let me out of here!'

Footsteps approached. Winnie's heart thudded and she worried she might have another heart attack. Poised with the broken bottle, ready to launch at Ainsworth if he attacked her, she waited for the door to open.

Winnie couldn't have been more relieved to see Judith standing there.

'Mrs Berry! How did you manage to lock yourself in the cellar?' the girl asked.

'I didn't. Ainsworth locked me in. Where is he?'

'I don't know. The bottle ... are you all right?'

'Yes. What are you doing here? I thought you were poorly.'

'I was, but I feel better. What's going on, Mrs Berry?' she asked, looking concerned.

'Nothing. Take no notice of this broken bottle. I, erm, I tripped over in the cellar and broke it. Would you mind taking the dustpan and brush down to clear up the broken glass?'

'No problem,' Judith answered, though she was peering doubtfully at Winnie. 'Why did Mr Ainsworth lock you in the cellar?'

'Oh, I don't suppose he meant to,' Winnie said, forcing a smile. 'He probably didn't realise that I was down there. It's an easy mistake to make. Have you seen him?'

'Only when he let me in. He said he had business to attend to and would be back later.'

Winnie breathed a sigh of relief. At least the man wasn't in the building – for now.

Winnie was still gripping the broken bottle when the pub door opened and Mr Ainsworth breezed in.

'Oh, Mrs Berry, I'm so relieved to see that Judith has unlocked the cellar door. I must have had a lapse in concentration and absent-mindedly turned off the light and locked the door. As soon as I realised what I'd done, I rushed back here. Please accept my sincere apologies.'

Winnie stared at the man, wishing she could thrust the broken bottle into his self-righteous face. 'That was no accident!' she hissed. 'You *deliberately* locked me down there.'

'You're very much mistaken, Mrs Berry. I do hope you can forgive me.'

'*Forgive you,*' Winnie parroted. 'You threatened to kill me!' she spat, quietly, hoping that Judith couldn't hear.

Mr Ainsworth threw Winnie an incredulous look. 'I refute that accusation, Mrs Berry. I made no such threats and you suggesting that I did is a slur on my character.'

'With me, now,' Winnie ordered, marching towards the back kitchen.

Clutching the broken bottle, her arm at her side, she stood beside the sink and eyed a small knife on the draining board.

Mr Ainsworth sat at the table. 'I think we should clear the air, Mrs Berry, wouldn't you agree?'

'Yes, I bloody well would!'

'I hope we can put this morning's unfortunate incident behind us. I believe that a harmonious partnership between us would be better for business.'

Winnie couldn't believe the audacity of the man. 'See, that's the thing, Ainsworth. I don't want to be in business with you, and nothing is going to change my mind.'

Mr Ainsworth smiled, wryly. 'I don't think you understand, Mrs Berry. You don't have a choice ... Unless you're offering to sell me your share?'

'Never!' Winnie barked. 'The Battersea Tavern is *my* pub and always will be.'

'I agree with you somewhat. You are, most definitely, the face of the Battersea Tavern, and I'm under no illusion of the importance of your role in this business. But let's not overlook my substantial investment – and I will not relinquish my share, Mrs Berry. No offer, no matter how generous, will tempt me. It appears we are at a stalemate.'

'Stalemate, my arse!' Winnie retorted. 'What will it take to get rid of you?'

Mr Ainsworth looked at his lap and flicked a small piece of fluff off his brown trousers. Then looking back at Winnie, his voice dripping with sincerity, he said, 'I'm here to stay, Mrs Berry. The port I drank on Coronation Day loosened my tongue, and I expressed my feelings to you in an overly emotional fashion. However, my words were spoken with truth. This pub, the people in it, the business, it's all I have. I refuse to return to the empty life I led. So, you'll understand my refusal to sell.'

Before Winnie could respond, Mr Ainsworth scraped his seat back and walked away.

Winnie finally relaxed and breathed a sigh of relief. She began to question the events in the cellar. Had Mr Ainsworth made a genuine mistake? Had she overreacted? After all, she couldn't recall the man making an actual threat. But the insinuation had been there. Winnie had *felt* threatened, and she didn't feel safe with Ainsworth in the pub, although there was a small part of Winnie's heart that felt sorry for the man. *Don't be daft,* she told herself, *and remember – he may have murdered his mother!*

64

Grace rushed home from school, eager to shop for Winnie's engagement ring.

'We'll have to be quick,' Winnie said, running a brush through her hair. 'Arnie's only got an hour off work. We're meeting him at the jewellery shop.'

Grace had been giving Winnie's engagement ring a lot of thought. 'I reckon you should choose a big, green emerald, a square one, with diamonds all around it.'

'I don't think so, love. I wouldn't want anything show-offy. One neat, small diamond will suffice. Something understated.'

'Why? You're getting married and it's a big thing, Winnie. Don't you want to shout it from the rooftops?'

'No, love, not at my age,' Winnie chuckled.

Grace had to walk at quite a pace to keep up with Winnie. The woman marched rather than walked and she didn't stop for traffic either.

'Winnie!' Grace exclaimed, when the woman stepped into the road.

A car hooted its horn and screeched to a halt.

'Didn't you see that car coming?' Grace asked.

'Yes, but it's got brakes. It can stop.'

'Cars can't stop on the spot, Winnie.'

'I've been crossing roads for nigh on fifty years, love. I don't need lessons on it.'

Grace rolled her eyes, copying one of Winnie's most used facial expressions.

'There he is,' Winnie said, pointing towards Arnie. 'Do you think he looks worried? I hope he ain't having second thoughts!'

'He probably is worried,' Grace giggled. 'He'll be worried that you're going to choose an expensive ring.'

'Good afternoon, ladies,' Arnie greeted. He smiled at Grace, 'I hope you're here to stop Winnie from spending all my money.'

In the shop, Winnie tried on several rings. Most wouldn't fit and the shop assistant talked about resizing.

'I've got fingers like fat sausages,' Winnie laughed.

'That one, Winnie, try that one on,' Grace suggested, pointing through the glass counter at a simple ring with three diamonds in a line. The larger diamond in the middle sparkled brilliantly in the light.

'Oh yes,' Winnie said, holding the ring and admiring it. 'That's the one.'

Grace smiled proudly.

Outside, Winnie sighed. 'It's a pity I've got to wait for the ring to be made to fit me.'

'Are we going to have a party in the pub to celebrate your engagement?' Grace asked, enthusiastically.

'I suppose so. What do you think, Arnie?'

'I think my men would be disappointed if we didn't.' Then turning to Grace, he said, 'This is for you, Grace,' and handed her a small box which had the name of the jewellery shop embossed on the top.

'What is it?' she asked.

'Open it and see.'

Grace lifted the lid and saw a fine, gold chain and a locket engraved with delicate flowers. 'It's beautiful,' she gasped.

'I thought you might like to put a picture of your gran inside the locket,' Arnie suggested.

Tears welled in Grace's eyes. 'I would, thank you. And I'd like to put a picture of you and Winnie in it too. All my special people ...'

Arnie gave Winnie a quick kiss on her cheek before returning to work, and Grace and Winnie headed back home.

When they arrived, Winnie went up the stairs first, but stopped halfway. 'Wait here,' she whispered to Grace. 'I think I heard someone.'

Grace grabbed Winnie's hand. 'Don't go up by yourself,' she pleaded.

'It'll be all right,' Winnie assured, pulling her hand away. 'Shush.'

'No, Winnie, please ...'

But Winnie was already climbing the rest of the stairs.

Grace clutched the gold locket hanging on the chain around her neck, her pulse racing. Winnie reached the top of the stairs and turned to look at Grace.

'Stay there,' she mouthed.

As Winnie tiptoed towards the kitchen, Grace waited, her blood rushing loudly between her ears. Then she heard Winnie's voice boom.

'Maureen! What are you doing here?'

Grace ran up the stairs and burst into the kitchen.

'Surprise!' Maureen grinned.

'I can't believe it,' Winnie said, her voice cracking with emotion. 'Grace, pinch me. Am I seeing things? Lord above, I can't believe it!'

'It's good to be home,' Maureen said, her arms outstretched.

'Oh, love, I can't tell you what a joy it is to see you,' Winnie gushed, holding Maureen tightly. 'How long are you back for?'

Maureen pulled away. 'Forever, Winnie. America was nice, but it wasn't for me. Stephen has stayed on – he loves it there – but me and Vic have moved into a house nearby. I missed it here, and I missed the Battersea pong.'

'You're as mad as a blinkin' hatter, but I'm over the moon! Do Rachel and Carmen know you're back?'

'Not yet. I was hoping you'd all come for lunch on Sunday?'

'I'm sure everyone will be thrilled to see you, but you should all come here. I've got some news to share.'

'Winnie's getting married,' Grace piped up.

'Blimey! When did that happen?' Maureen asked.

'Last night. Arnie asked me to marry him, and I said yes. In fact, we've just got back from shopping for a ring.'

'I can't wait to meet Arnie.'

'He's the best,' Grace enthused. She thought the world of Arnie, and often fantasised about him being her dad. Only yesterday, two girls in her class were talking about a small fire in one of the factories on York Road and Grace had proudly boasted how her *dad* had helped to extinguish the flames. The girls had been impressed. Her dad, Arnie, the brave fireman and hero …

65

On Sunday, Grace walked into the kitchen to find Winnie looking pink, hot and flustered as she prepared lunch.

'Can I help?' Grace offered.

'No thanks, love, it's all under control.'

Grace didn't think it was, but Winnie was used to cooking for lots of people. She knew that today meant a great deal to her, especially as Maureen was home.

In a cloud of steam, draining a large pan of potatoes, Winnie asked, 'Can you pop downstairs to Judith and see if she needs me? I hope she's not too busy down there.'

Grace skipped happily down the stairs and along the passageway. She was just about to call to Judith when she heard Tommy Bradbury's voice in the back kitchen. Tommy's manner was usually friendly, but there was something in the man's tone that made Grace stop and listen. Hiding next to the door, out of sight, her ears pricked.

Tommy's voice was low and serious. 'You obviously haven't grasped what I'm telling you, Ainsworth.'

'I understand fully, but as I've already told Mrs Berry, I'm not prepared to sell.'

'Then let me put it another way: sell up or you'll be going to the gallows. At best, you'll be spending the rest of your miserable years behind bars. It's as simple as that.'

Mr Ainsworth sniggered. 'The police failed to find any evidence to prosecute me. The case is closed, Mr Bradbury.'

'You threw your poor, defenceless mother down the stairs, killing her outright, and I can prove it.'

'Ridiculous! All you have, Mr Bradbury, are idle threats. There's no proof of any wrongdoing on my part.'

Grace had to stifle a gasp, horrified. Mr Ainsworth, a murderer!

'See, the thing is, Ainsworth, Mrs Berry is a very good friend of mine and I don't like the idea of a sly, callous bastard like you being around her. I wasn't going to show my hand because I hoped you'd do the decent thing and willingly sell your share of the Battersea Tavern. So here it is: at the time of your mother's death your cleaner, Mrs Stokes claimed that she wasn't in the house. Mrs Stokes is now willing to testify that she *was* in the house, and she witnessed you dragging your mother to the stairs and pushing her down. She will state that she feared you and feared for her life, so she readily took the money you offered in exchange for her silence and promptly left your employment. Mrs Stokes is a good woman and she could no longer live with herself, so has now come forward to tell the truth. Sell up, Ainsworth, or Mrs Stokes will tell a judge everything she knows.'

There was a long silence. Grace could hear her heart thumping loudly.

Mr Ainsworth then spoke clearly: 'Mrs Stokes is a liar. She wasn't in the house, and I never bribed her.'

'It'll be your word against Mrs Stokes, and there's already

suspicion around your mother's death. You can keep the Battersea Tavern and have your day in court, but it's a big risk to take.'

Another silence and then Mr Ainsworth spat, 'You must have paid Mrs Stokes to make such ludicrous claims!'

'You're not a well-liked man, Ainsworth. It didn't take too much persuasion or much of my retirement fund to convince Mrs Stokes to speak against you. We both know that Mrs Stokes wasn't in the house at the time of your mother's death – even you wouldn't be so stupid to kill the woman with the cleaner present. But Mrs Stokes has always believed that you murdered your mother, and she reckons your mother knew that you were going to do it. Guilty or not, Ainsworth, you're going down for it – unless you sell.'

Grace heard a chair scrape back and ran for the stairs, not wanting to be caught eavesdropping. Fleeing into her bedroom, she sat on her bed, her pulse racing and head spinning. Could it be true? Had she been under the same roof as a cold-bloodied killer all this time? And was Tommy, a retired copper, really willing to lie to get rid of Mr Ainsworth? It was all so shocking!

She stiffened when she heard a knock on her door.

'Hello, Grace,' Tommy said, popping his head around. 'Can I come in?'

Grace nodded.

'I think you heard my conversation with Mr Ainsworth, didn't you?'

Again, Grace nodded.

'It's all right, pet, there's nothing to be scared of. Mr Ainsworth will be gone soon and you'll never see him again. But what you heard; do you think you can keep it to yourself? I know it's a big secret, but Arnie is a good man and he wouldn't like it if he knew what I'd done. And you're old enough to understand that I could get in a lot of trouble with the law if anyone ever finds out.'

'Did he really kill his mum?' Grace asked.

'I don't know. Maybe. But I shall sleep a lot sounder knowing that he's not around you and Winnie any longer.'

Grace wanted to throw her arms around Tommy, but she didn't know the kind man well enough. 'Thank you! Thank you, Tommy. I promise I'll never tell a soul, not even Pauline,' she said, and she meant it. Tommy's secret would be safe with her forever.

Winnie's eyes passed over each of her guests around the table. Carmen looked tired, worn out, yet contented. The woman had been up half the night with her grandson, calming the lad following a spate of nightmares. Rachel was glowing – pregnancy suited her – and Roy, as always, was doting on his wife. Winnie smiled inwardly. Rachel was spoiled rotten. Roy treated her like a princess, and Rachel lapped it up. Martha, Benny and Grace were growing fast and in a couple of years, they'd be leaving school and would be young adults. She wondered what career Grace wanted for herself. The girl had mentioned how she'd like to be the landlady of the Battersea Tavern. Winnie would like that too. But not yet. There were plenty of years left in her, and she wasn't ready to hand over the reins … Maureen looked relaxed and comfortable, a far cry from the tense, petrified woman who'd fled Battersea. Vic held Maureen's hand under the table. Winnie didn't think it would be long before Maureen would be in the family way like Rachel. She hoped that Maureen could have children, because Winnie knew that Maureen would be a wonderful mother. Only Terry appeared a little lost. Winnie wished he'd meet a good woman, but the man still hadn't moved on from losing Jan. Hopefully, though, time would heal Terry's shattered heart one day. Mary was looking back at Winnie with fondness. Her baby was quiet and her daughter, Pauline, was chatting with Grace. Winnie had noticed that Mary was wearing a new dress and the old-fashioned Victorian scruffy boots had been replaced with a pair of fashionable shoes, even with a bit of a heel. *Good,* she thought, *the woman is spending some of her earnings on herself for a change.* She glanced at Tommy, who was sharing a joke with Irene. *They make a lovely couple,* Winnie mused, *and Tommy and Irene are a good example of how you're never too old to find love, just like Arnie and me.*

She met Arnie's loving gaze. 'What are you thinking?' he asked.

Taking a seat beside him, she whispered, 'Nothing much, I'm missing Hilda.'

Arnie squeezed her hand. 'I've got some news to share too,' he said. 'Do you mind?'

'Fill your boots, love,' Winnie smiled.

Arnie rose to his feet and tapped the side of his teacup with a spoon. It fell quiet around the table.

Clearing his throat, he glanced around. All eyes were on him. 'I know Winnie is overjoyed to have you all here today and thank you for your best wishes on our engagement. I promise to look after Winnie and Grace,' he said, looking sideways at the girl and giving her a wink. 'But there's something I'd like to share with you all, especially with my future wife.' Reaching under his seat, he picked up a cardboard file and pulled out some papers. 'This,' he said, passing the papers to Winnie, 'this is the official documentation dissolving your partnership with Walter Ainsworth, signed by the man and sale agreed.'

'What?' Winnie spluttered. 'How? Ainsworth was adamant that he wouldn't sell. How did you get him to change his mind?'

Arnie shrugged. 'I'm as surprised as you. I just saw him downstairs and he couldn't wait to get his signature on the paper. I don't know why he had a change of heart, but who cares? You're now looking at your new partner in the Battersea Tavern.'

'Is this a joke?'

'No, Winnie. It is what you wanted, isn't it?' Arnie asked, apprehensively.

'Not 'alf! Oh, Arnie, I couldn't be happier! This is bloody great!'

A cheer went up around the table, applauds too.

'Perfect,' Rachel said. 'Absolutely perfect!'

'About flamin' time,' Carmen added. 'I'm glad we've all seen the back of Ainsworth. Now that's all sorted, don't you think that you two should set a date for the wedding?'

Winnie nodded, her face beaming. 'Yes, I suppose we should.'

'Tommy, will you be my best man?' Arnie asked.

'I'd be honoured, mate, truly honoured,' Tommy answered, smiling widely.

Conversation flowed over the full plates of food and laughter bounced off the walls.

Arnie leaned closer to Winnie, saying quietly, 'I've been thinking. You and Grace come as a package. Once we're married, do you think we should make it official with Grace too?'

'What do you mean?' Winnie asked.

'We should look into adopting her.'

Winnie had thought the same and had considered the idea many times. 'I don't know if they'll allow us to adopt her because of our age, but we could try. I think she'd love that.'

At the other end of the table, Winnie heard Pauline urge, 'Go on, give it to her now,' and she saw the girl gently elbow Grace.

Grace appeared bashful and hurried from the kitchen, quickly returning with a small package wrapped in brown paper.

'This is for you and Arnie,' she said, handing it to Winnie. 'A gift for your engagement.'

'Oh, love, you shouldn't have,' Winnie smiled.

She unwrapped the paper to reveal a beautiful china ornament. Two colourful butterflies, their wings spread, perched on a white rose. Blinking back tears of happiness, she beckoned Grace to her, and kissed the girl's cheek.

'Thank you, love, it's the handsomest gift I've ever had.'

'Do you like it?' Grace asked.

'I love it,' Winnie answered.

Two butterflies. Grace couldn't have known what the butterflies meant to Winnie, but Winnie knew that Jan was there and would be with them forever. And Hilda too, both of them giving Winnie their stamp of approval.

Winnie had accepted that she'd never meet the daughter she'd been forced to give up at birth. And she'd never again have that close bond that she'd shared with Jan. But she'd come to love Grace and hoped their relationship could be sealed with a piece of paper officially making her the girl's mother and Arnie her father.

Arnie whispered in Winnie's ear, 'Can I ask Grace how she feels about, you know, what we were just talking about?'

Winnie nodded and took Grace's hand in her own.

Arnie leaned forward. 'Grace, me and Winnie were wondering how you'd feel about us trying to adopt you?'

Grace's big eyes stretched even wider. 'You'd be my proper mum and dad?' she asked.

'Yes, love,' Winnie said. 'But only if it's what you want.'

'Yes! Of *course* it's what I want! Yes, and double yes!'

'I reckon that's a yes,' Arnie laughed.

Winnie's heart soared. She'd always wanted the perfect little family. There had been a time when she'd thought she'd had it all. David, the child she'd longed for, and a husband, Brian. Both had been a heart-wrenching disappointment and the pain of losing David would never leave her. But she'd been blessed with a second chance and her dreams had come true. She now had the family she'd always yearned for, and Mr and Mrs Arnold Potter were now the landlord and landlady of the Battersea Tavern public house.

Acknowledgements

Thank you to my lovely agent, Judith Murdoch.

Thank you to my brilliant Editor, Rhea Kurien, and the fab team at Orion.

Thank you to Lizzy Dingemans who kindly donated money to a cat shelter in return for me writing the line, 'Get outta my pub!'

Thank you to everyone on Facebook for your support, it means the world to me.

And if you're reading this, thank you, and I hope you enjoy the book.

Credits

Kitty Neale and Orion Fiction would like to thank everyone at Orion who worked on the publication of *An Orphan's Hope* in the UK.

Editorial
Rhea Kurien
Sanah Ahmed

Copyeditor
Jade Craddock

Proofreader
Laetitia Grant

Audio
Paul Stark
Jake Alderson

Marketing
Brittany Sankey

Contracts
Anne Goddard
Humayra Ahmed
Ellie Bowker

Design
Charlotte Abrams-Simpson
Joanna Ridley
Nick Shah

Editorial Management
Charlie Panayiotou
Jane Hughes
Bartley Shaw
Tamara Morriss

Finance
Jasdip Nandra
Sue Baker

Production
Ruth Sharvell

Operations
Jo Jacobs
Sharon Willis

Publicity
Becca Bryant

Sales
Jen Wilson
Esther Waters
Victoria Laws
Rachael Hum
Anna Egelstaff
Frances Doyle
Georgina Cutler

Discover how Winnie's story began with the heart-wrenching first book in the *Battersea Tavern* saga

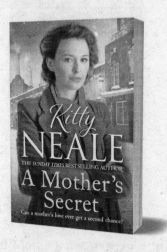

Can she put right the secrets of the past?

London, 1939. Winnie Berry has been the landlady of the Battersea Tavern for nearly twenty-five years, and the pub is like home to her – a place of tears and laughter, full of customers that feel like family. A place where she's learned to avoid the quick fists of her husband, and where she's raised her beloved son, David.

He's inherited his father's lazy streak and can't seem to hold down a job, but when war is declared Winnie is determined to keep her son safe. She's still haunted by the choice she made years ago as a desperate young woman, and she won't make the same mistake of letting her family be taken from her…

But when a young woman crosses her path, the secrets of Winnie's past threaten to turn her world upside down. There's nothing stronger than a mother's love – but can it ever have a second chance?

And follow up with the second book in the *Battersea Tavern* saga...

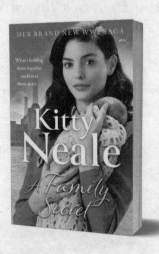

In a time of war, what's holding them together could tear them all apart...

London, 1940. Winnie Berry is at the heart of the community in her pub, the Battersea Tavern. Her door is always open to those in need of a cup of tea and sympathy.

Winnie's abusive husband has left and she finds herself foolishly falling in love with black-market trader, Have-it Harry Hampton. But Harry is married and Winnie soon finds herself tied up in his web of secrets.

Meanwhile Winnie's son is back in London – not to visit his own child, but to charm the latest barmaid at the Battersea Tavern, which will lead to devastating consequences for the family.

With bombs dropping all around them, is it too late for Winnie to uncover the secrets of those closest to her in order to protect her true family?

**And next with the third book
in the *Battersea Tavern* saga** …

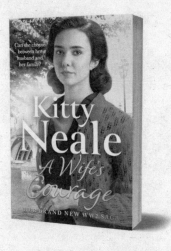

Can she choose between her husband and her family?

London, 1944. With bombs raining over London,
keeping the Battersea Tavern open is no easy feat for
owner Winnie Berry – but the community need the
warmth and familiarity of the pub more than ever.

After marriage, Maureen Fanning had moved out to
Wandsworth with her bad-tempered husband Brancher.
But when he loses both his job and their lodgings,
the only people who will take them in are her kindly
grandparents, Len and Renee. Getting a cleaning job at
the Battersea Tavern is the least she can do to pay them
back. It would all be fine … if it weren't for Brancher.

Winnie is determined to take timid Maureen under her
wing. But when tragedy strikes, it will be up to Maureen
to find the strength she didn't know she possessed …